KISSED BY AN ANGEL

Kissed
BY AN
Angel

Elizabeth Chandler

MACMILLAN

First published 1995 by SIMON PULSE, an imprint of Simon and Schuster, USA

This edition published 2009 by Macmillan Children's Books
a division of Macmillan Publishers Limited
20 New Wharf Road, London N1 9RR
Basingstoke and Oxford
Associated companies throughout the world
www.panmacmillan.com

ISBN 978-0-330-51149-0

11 13 15 17 19 18 16 14 12 10

A CIP catalogue record for this book is available from the British Library.

Typeset by Intype Libra Limited
Printed and bound in the UK by CPI Mackays, Chatham ME5 8TD

For Pat and Dennis

1

"I never knew how romantic a backseat could be," Ivy said, resting against it, smiling at Tristan. Then she looked past him at the pile of junk on the car floor. "Maybe you should pull your tie out of that old Burger King cup."

Tristan reached down and grimaced. He tossed the dripping thing into the front of the car, then sat back next to Ivy.

"Ow!" The smell of crushed flowers filled the air.

Ivy laughed out loud.

"What's so funny?" Tristan asked, pulling the smashed roses from behind him, but he was laughing, too.

"What if someone had come along and seen your father's Clergy sticker on the bumper?"

Tristan tossed the flowers into the front seat and pulled her toward him again. He traced the silk strap of her dress, then tenderly kissed her shoulder. "I'd have told them I was with an angel."

"Oh, what a line!"

"Ivy, I love you," Tristan said, his face suddenly serious.

She stared back at him, then bit her lip.

"This isn't some kind of game for me. I love you, Ivy Lyons, and one day you're going to believe me."

She put her arms around him and held him tightly. "Love *you,* Tristan Carruthers," she whispered into his neck. Ivy did believe him, and she trusted him as she trusted no one else. One day she'd have the nerve to say it, all of the words out loud. I love you, Tristan. She'd shout it out the windows. She'd string a banner straight across the school pool.

It took a few minutes to straighten themselves up and move back to the front of the car. Ivy started laughing again. Tristan smiled and watched her try to tame her gold tumbleweed of hair – a useless effort. Then he started the car, urging it over the ruts and stones and onto the narrow road.

"Last glimpse of the river," he said as the road made a sharp turn away from it.

The June sun, dropping over the west ridge

of the Connecticut countryside, shafted light on the very tops of the trees, flaking them with gold. The winding road slipped into a tunnel of maples, poplars, and oaks. Ivy felt as if she were sliding under the waves with Tristan, the setting sun glittering on top, the two of them moving together through a chasm of blue, purple, and deep green. Tristan flicked on his headlights.

"You really don't have to hurry," said Ivy. "I'm not hungry any more."

"I ruined your appetite?"

She shook her head. "I guess I'm all filled up with happiness," she said softly.

The car sped along and took a curve sharply.

"I said, we don't have to hurry."

"That's funny," Tristan murmured. "I wonder what's—" He glanced down at his feet. "This doesn't feel . . ."

"Slow down, okay? It doesn't matter if we're a little late— Oh!" Ivy pointed straight ahead. "Tristan!"

Something had plunged through the bushes and into the roadway. She hadn't seen what it was, just the flicker of motion among the deep shadows. Then the deer stopped. It turned its head, its eyes drawn to the car's bright headlights.

"Tristan!"

They were rushing toward the shining eyes.

"Tristan, don't you see it?"

Rushing still.

"Ivy, something's—'"

"A deer!" she exclaimed.

The animal's eyes blazed. Then light came from behind it, a bright burst around its dark shape. A car was coming from the opposite direction. Trees walled them in. There was no room to veer left or right.

"Stop!" she shouted.

"I'm—"

"Stop, why don't you stop?" she pleaded. Tristan, *stop?!*"

The windshield exploded.

For days after, all Ivy could remember was the waterfall of glass.

At the sound of the gun, Ivy jumped. She hated pools, especially indoor pools. Even though she and her friends were ten feet from the edge, she felt as if she were swimming. The air itself seemed dark, a dank mist, bluish green, heavy with the smell of chlorine. Everything echoed – the gun, the shouts of the crowd, the explosion of swimmers in the water. When Ivy had first entered the domed pool area, she'd gulped for breath. She wished she were outside in the bright and windy March day.

"Tell me again," she said. "Which one is he?"

Suzanne Goldstein looked at Beth Van Dyke. Beth looked back at Suzanne. They both shook their heads, sighing.

"Well, how am I supposed to be able to tell?" Ivy asked. "They're hairless, every one of them, with shaved arms, shaved legs, and shaved chests – a team of bald guys in rubber caps and goggles. They're wearing our school colors, but for all I know, they could be a shipload of aliens."

"If those are aliens," Beth said, rapidly clicking her ballpoint pen, "I'm moving to that planet."

Suzanne took the pen away from Beth and said in a husky voice, "God, I love swim meets!"

"But you don't watch the swimmers once they're in the water," Ivy observed.

"Because she's checking out the group coming up to the blocks," Beth explained.

"Tristan is the one in the center lane," said Suzanne. "The best swimmers always race in the center lanes."

"He's our flyer," Beth added. "The best at the butterfly stroke. Best in the state, in fact."

Ivy already knew that. The swim team poster was all over school: Tristan surging up out of the water, his shoulders rushing forward at you, his powerful arms pulled back like wings.

The person in charge of publicity knew what she was doing when she selected that photo. She had produced numerous copies, which was a good thing, for the taped-up posters of Tristan were continually disappearing – into girls' lockers.

Sometime during this poster craze, Beth and Suzanne had begun to think that Tristan was interested in Ivy. Two collisions in the hall in one week was all that it took to convince Beth, an imaginative writer who had read a library of Harlequin romances.

"But, Beth, I've walked into *you* plenty of times," Ivy argued with her. "You know how I am."

"We do," Suzanne said. "Head in the clouds. Three miles above earth. Angel zone. But still, I think Beth is onto something. Remember, *he* walked into *you.*"

"Maybe he's clumsy when he's outside the water. Like a frog," Ivy had suggested, knowing all the while there was nothing clumsy about Tristan Carruthers.

He had been pointed out to her in January, that first, snowy day when she had arrived at Stonehill High School. A cheerleader had been assigned as a guide to Ivy and was leading her through a crowded cafeteria.

"You're probably checking out the jocks," the cheerleader said.

Actually, Ivy was busy trying to figure out what the stringy green stuff was that her new school was serving to its students.

"At your school in Norwalk, the girls probably dream about football stars. But a lot of girls at Stonehill—"

Dream about *him*, Ivy thought as she followed the cheerleader's glance toward Tristan.

"Actually, I prefer a guy with a brain," Ivy told the fluffy redhead.

"But he's got a brain!" Suzanne had insisted when Ivy repeated this conversation to her a few minutes later.

Suzanne was the only girl Ivy already knew at Stonehill, and she had somehow found Ivy in the mob that day.

"I mean a brain that isn't waterlogged," Ivy added. "You know I've never been interested in jocks. I want someone I can talk to." Suzanne blew through her lips. "You're already communicating with the angels—"

"Don't start on that," Ivy warned her.

"Angels?" Beth asked. She had been eavesdropping from the next table. "You talk to angels?"

Suzanne rolled her eyes, annoyed by this interruption, then turned back to Ivy. "You'd think that somewhere in that wingy collection of yours, you'd have at least one angel of love."

"I do."

"What kind of things do you say to them?" Beth interjected again. She opened a notepad. Her pencil was poised as if she were going to copy what Ivy said, word for word.

Suzanne pretended Beth wasn't there. "Well, if you do have an angel of love, Ivy, she's screwing up. Somebody ought to remind her of her mission."

Ivy shrugged. Not that she wasn't interested in guys, but her days were full enough – her music, her job at the shop, keeping up her grades, and helping to take care of her eight-year-old brother, Philip. It had been a bumpy couple of months for Philip, their mother, and her. She would not have made it through without the angels.

After that day in January, Beth had sought out Ivy to question her about her belief in angels and show her some of her romantic short stories. Ivy enjoyed talking to her. Beth, who was round-faced with shoulder-length light-brown hair and clothes that ranged from crazy to dowdy, lived many incredibly romantic and passionate lives – in her mind.

Suzanne, with her magnificent long black mane of hair and dramatic eyebrows and cheekbones, also pursued and lived out many passions – in the classrooms and hallways, leaving the guys of Stonehill High emotionally exhausted. Beth and Suzanne had never really been friends before Ivy's arrival at Stonehill, but late in February they became allies in the cause of getting Ivy together with Tristan.

"I heard that he is pretty smart," Beth had said at another lunch in the cafeteria.

"A total brain," Suzanne agreed. "Top of the class."

Ivy raised an eyebrow.

"Or close enough."

"Swimming is a subtle sport," Beth continued. "It looks as if all they're doing is going back and forth, but a guy like Tristan has a plan, a complex winning strategy for each race."

"Uh-huh," Ivy said.

"All we're saying is that you should come to one swim meet," Suzanne told her.

"And sit up front," Beth suggested.

"And let me dress you that day," Suzanne added. "You know I can pick out your clothes better than you."

Ivy had shaken her head, wondering then and for days after how her friends could think a guy like Tristan would be interested in her. But when Tristan had stood up at the junior class assembly and told everyone how much the team needed them to come to the last big school meet, all the time staring right at her, it seemed she had little choice.

"If we lose this meet," Suzanne said, "it's on your head, girl."

Now, in late March, Ivy watched Tristan shake out his arms and legs. He had a perfect build for a swimmer, broad and powerful shoulders, narrow hips. The cap hid his straight brown hair, which she remembered to be shortish and thickish.

"Every inch of him hard with muscle," breathed Beth. After several clicks of her pen, which she had taken back from Suzanne, she was writing away in her notebook. "'Like glistening rock. Sinuous in the hands of the sculptor, molten in the fingers of the lover . . .'"

Ivy peered down at Beth's pad. "What is it this time," she asked, "poetry or a romance?"

"Does it make a difference?" her friend replied.

"Swimmers up!" shouted the starting official, and the competitors climbed onto their blocks.

"My, my," Suzanne murmured, "those little suits don't leave much to the imagination, do they? I wonder what Gregory would look like in one."

Ivy nudged her. "Keep your voice down. He's right over there."

"I know," Suzanne said, running her fingers through her hair.

"On your marks . . ."

Beth leaned forward for a look at Gregory Baines. "'His long, lean body, hungry and hot . . .'"

Bang!

"You always use words that begin with *h,*" Suzanne said.

Beth nodded. "When you alliterate *h,* it sounds like heavy breathing. Hungry, heated, heady—"

"Are either of you bothering to watch the race?" Ivy interrupted.

"It's four hundred meters, Ivy. All Tristan does is go back and forth, back and forth."

"I see. Whatever happened to the total brain with his complex winning strategy in the subtle sport of swimming?" Ivy asked.

Beth was writing again. "'Flying like an angel, wishing his watery wings were warm arms for Ivy.' I'm really inspired today!"

"Me too," Suzanne said, her glance traveling down the line of bodies in the ready area, then skipping over the spectators to Gregory.

Ivy followed her glance, then quickly turned her attention back to the swimmers. For the last three months Suzanne had been in hot – *heated, hungry* – pursuit of Gregory Baines. Ivy wished that Suzanne would get herself stuck on somebody else, and do it soon, real soon, before the first Saturday in April.

"Who's that little brunette?" Suzanne asked. "I hate little petite types. Gregory doesn't look right with someone petite. Little face, little hands, little dainty feet."

"Big boobs," Beth said, glancing up.

"Who is she? Ever seen her before, Ivy?"

"Suzanne, you've been in this school a lot longer than—"

"You're not even looking," Suzanne interrupted.

"Because I'm watching our hero, just like I'm supposed to be doing. What does *waller* mean? Everybody shouts 'Waller!' when Tristan does a turn."

"That's his nickname," Beth replied, "because of the way he attacks the wall. He hurls himself head first into it, so he can push off fast."

"I see," Ivy said. "Sounds like a total brain to me, hurling his head against a concrete wall. How long do these meets usually last?"

"Ivy, come on," Suzanne whined, and pulled on her arm. "Look and see if you know who the little brunette is."

"Twinkie."

"You're making that up!" Suzanne said.

"It's Twinkie Hammonds," Ivy insisted. "She's a senior in my music class."

Aware of Suzanne's continuous staring,

Twinkie turned around and gave her a nasty look. Gregory noticed the expression and glanced over his shoulder at them. Ivy saw the amusement spreading over his face.

Gregory Baines had a charming smile, dark hair, and gray eyes – very cool gray eyes, Ivy thought. He was tall, but it wasn't his height that made him stand out in a crowd. It was his self-confidence. He was like an actor, like the star of a movie, who was part of it all, yet when the show was over, held himself apart from the others, believing he was better than the rest. The Baineses were the richest people in the wealthy town of Stonehill, though Ivy knew that it wasn't Gregory's money but this coolness, this aloofness, that drove Suzanne wild. Suzanne always wanted what she couldn't have.

Ivy put her arm lightly around her friend. She pointed to a hunk of a swimmer stretching out in the ready area, hoping to distract her. Then she yelled, "Waller!" as Tristan went into his last turn. "I think I'm getting into this," she said, but it appeared Suzanne's thoughts were on Gregory now. This time, Ivy feared, Suzanne was in deep.

"He's looking at us," Suzanne said excitedly. "He's coming this way."

Ivy felt herself tensing up.

"And the Chihuahua is following him."

Why? Ivy wondered. What could Gregory have to say to her now after almost three months of ignoring her? In January she had learned quickly that Gregory would not acknowledge her presence. And as if bound by some silent agreement, neither he nor Ivy had advertised that his father was going to marry her mother. Few people knew that he and Ivy would be living in the same house come April.

"Hi, Ivy!" Twinkie was the first to speak. She squeezed herself in next to Ivy, ignoring Suzanne and barely glancing at Beth. "I was just telling Gregory how we always sit near each other in music class."

Ivy looked at the girl with surprise. She had never really noticed where Twinkie sat.

"He said he hasn't heard you play the piano. I was telling him how terrific you are."

Ivy opened her mouth but could think of nothing to say. The last time she had played an original composition for the class, Twinkie had shown her appreciation by filing her nails.

Then Ivy felt Gregory's eyes on her. When she met his look, he winked. Ivy gestured quickly toward her friends and said, "You know Suzanne Goldstein and Beth Van Dyke?"

"Not real well," he said, smiling at each in turn.

Suzanne glowed. Beth focused on him with

the interest of a researcher, her hand clicking away on the ballpoint.

"Guess what, Ivy? In April you won't be living far from my house. Not far at all," Twinkie said. "It will be a lot easier to study together then."

Easier?

"I can give you a ride to school. It will be a quicker drive to your house."

Quicker?

"Maybe we can get together more."

More?

"Well, Ivy," Suzanne exclaimed, batting her long, dark lashes, "you never told me that you and Twinkie were such good friends! Maybe we can all get together more. You'd like to go to Twinkie's house, wouldn't you, Beth?"

Gregory barely suppressed his smile.

"We could have a sleepover, Twinkie."

Twinkie didn't look enthused.

"We could talk about guys and vote on who's the hottest date around." Suzanne turned her gaze upon Gregory, sliding her eyes down and up him, taking in everything. He continued to look amused.

"We know some other girls, from Ivy's old school in Norwalk," Suzanne went on cheerily. She knew that Stonehill's high-class commuters to New York City would have nothing to do with blue-collar Norwalk. "They'd love to come. Then we can all be friends. Don't you think that would be fun?"

"Not really," Twinkie said, and turned her back on Suzanne.

"Nice talking to you, Ivy. See you soon, I hope. Come on, Greg, it's crowded over here." She tugged on his arm.

As Ivy turned back to the action in the pool Gregory caught her chin. With the tips of his fingers he tilted her face up toward him. He was smiling.

"Innocent Ivy," he said. "You look embarrassed. Why? It works both ways, you know. There are plenty of guys, guys I hardly know, who are suddenly talking like they're my best friends, who are counting on dropping by my house the first week of April. Why do you suppose that is?"

Ivy shrugged. "You're part of the in crowd, I guess."

"You really *are* innocent!" he exclaimed. She wished that he would let go of her. She glanced past him to the next set of bleachers, where his friends sat. Eric Ghent and another guy were talking to Twinkie now and laughing. The ultra-cool Will O'Leary looked back at her.

Gregory withdrew his hand. He left with just a nod at her friends, his eyes still bright with laughter. When Ivy turned back to the pool again, she saw that three rubber-capped guys in identical little swimsuits had been watching her. She had no idea which, if any, of them, was Tristan.

2

"I feel like a fool," Tristan said, peeking through the diamond-shaped window in the door between the kitchen and the dining room of the college's Alumni Club. Candelabra were being lit and crystal glasses checked. In the large kitchen where he and Gary were standing, tables were laid out with polished fruit and hors d'oeuvres. Tristan had no idea what most of the hors d'oeuvres were or if they were to be served in any special way. He hoped simply that they and the champagne glasses would stay on the up side of his tray.

Gary was struggling with his cuff links. The cummerbund of his hired tuxedo kept unwrapping itself from his waist, its Velcro failing to stick. One of his shiny black shoes, a size too small, was tied with an emergency purple sneaker lace. Gary was a real friend, Tristan thought, to agree to this scheme.

"Remember, it's good money," Tristan said aloud, "and we need it for the Midwest meet."

Gary grunted. "Well see what's left after we pay for the damages."

"All of it!" Tristan replied with confidence. How hard could it be to carry this stuff around? He and Gary were swimmers. Their natural athletic balance had given them the right to fib about their experience when they interviewed with the caterer. A piece of cake, this job.

Tristan picked up a silver tray and surveyed his reflection. "I don't just feel like a fool – I look like one."

"You *are* one," said Gary. "And I want you to know I'm not that much of a fool to believe your line about earning money for the Midwest meet."

"What do you mean?"

Gary snatched up a mop and held it so its spongy strings flopped over his head like hair. "Oh, Tristy," he said in a high-pitched voice, "what a surprise to see you at my mother's wedding!"

"Shut up, Gary."

"Oh, Tristy, put down that tray and dance

with me." Gary smiled and patted the mop's spongy head.

"Her hair doesn't look like that."

"Oh, Tristy, I just caught my mother's bouquet. Let's run away and get married."

"I don't want to marry her! I just want her to know I exist. I just want to go out with her. Once! If she doesn't like me, well . . ." Tristan shrugged as if it didn't matter, as if the worst crush he'd ever had in his life might really disappear overnight.

"Oh, Tristy—"

"I'm going to kick your—"

The kitchen door swung open. "Gentlemen," said Monsieur Pompideau, "the wedding guests have arrived and are ready to be served. Could Fortune be so smiling upon us that you two *experienced* garçons would be available to help serve them?"

"Is he being sarcastic?" Gary asked.

Tristan rolled his eyes, and they hurried to join the other waiters at their stations.

For the first ten minutes, Tristan occupied himself with watching the other workers, trying to learn his job. He knew that girls and women liked his smile, and he used it for all it was worth, especially when the caviar he was serving leaped like a fully evolved fish into an older woman's lap.

He worked his way around the large reception hall, searching for Ivy, sneaking peeks while big-bellied men unloaded his trays. Two of them went away wearing their drinks and muttering, but he barely noticed. All he could think about was Ivy. If he came face-to-face with her, what would he say? "Have some crab balls?" Or perhaps, "May I suggest *le ballée de crabbe?*"

Yeah, that would impress her.

What kind of guy had he turned into? Why should he, Tristan Carruthers, a guy hanging up in a hundred girls' lockers (maybe a slight exaggeration), need to impress her, a girl uninterested in hanging in his locker or anybody else's, for all he could tell? She walked the same halls he did, but it was as if she traveled in another world.

He'd noticed her on her first day at Stonehill. It wasn't just her different kind of beauty, that wild tangle of kinky gold hair and her sea green eyes, that made him want to look and look, and touch. It was the way she seemed free of things other people were caught up in – the way she focused on the person she was talking to, without scanning the crowd to see who else was there; the way she dressed not to look like everyone else; the way she lost herself in a song. He had stood in the doorway of the school

21

music room one day, mesmerized as she played the piano. Of course, she hadn't even noticed him.

He doubted that Ivy knew he existed. But was this catering thing really a good way to clue her in? After recovering a fat crab ball that had rolled to a stop between some pointy-toed shoes, he was starting to doubt it.

Then he saw her. She was in pink – and pink and pink: yards of pink sparkly stuff that fell off her shoulders and must have had some kind of hoop under its skirt to hold it out.

Gary passed by him then. Tristan turned a little too quickly and their elbows hit. Eight glasses shivered on their stems, spilling dark wine.

"Some dress!" Gary said with a quiet snicker.

Tristan shrugged. He knew the dress was cheesy, but he didn't care. "Eventually she'll take it off," he reasoned.

"Pretty cocky there, buddy."

"That's not what I meant! What I—"

"Pompideau," Gary warned, and the two of them quickly parted. The caterer snagged Tristan, however, and hauled him into the kitchen. When Tristan emerged again, he was carrying a low-lying spread of vegetables and a shallow bowl of dip – stuff that couldn't spill. He noticed that some of the guests seemed to recognize him now and moved quickly out of his way when he approached. Which meant he carried a full tray round and round, hardly needing to look where he was going, and had plenty of time to scope out the party.

"Hey, swimmer. Sssswimmer."

It was someone from school calling him, probably one of Gregory's friends. Tristan had never liked the guys or girls in Gregory's crowd. All of them had money and flaunted it. They did some stupid things and were always looking for a new thrill.

"Sssswimmer, are you deaf?" the guy called out. Eric Ghent, thin-faced and blond, lounged against the wall, one hand hanging on to a candle sconce.

"I'm sorry," said Tristan. "Were you talking to me?"

"I know you, Waller. I know you. Is this what you do between laps?" Eric let go of the sconce and swayed a little.

"This is what I do so I can afford to do laps," Tristan replied.

"Great. I'll buy you ssssome more laps."

"What?"

"I'll make it worth your time, Waller, to get me a drink."

Tristan looked Eric over. "I think you've already had one."

Eric held up four fingers, then dropped his hand limply.

"Four," Tristan corrected himself.

"This is a private party," Eric said. "They'll serve under age. Private party or not, they'll serve whatever to whoever old Baines wants them to ssserve. The man buys everybody, you know."

That's where Gregory learned it from, Tristan thought to himself. "Well, then," he said aloud, "the bar's over there." He tried to move on, but Eric placed himself squarely in front of Tristan. "Problem is, I've been cut off."

Tristan took a deep breath.

"I need a drink, Waller. And you need some bucks."

"I don't take tips," Tristan said.

Eric started to laugh. "Well, maybe you don't *get* them – I've been watching you bump around. But I think you'd take 'em."

"Sorry."

"We need each other," Eric said. "We've got a choice. We can help each other or hurt each other."

Tristan didn't reply.

"Know what I mean, Waller?"

"I know what you mean, but I can't help you out."

Eric took a step toward him. Tristan took a step back. Eric stepped closer again.

Tristan tensed. Gregory's friend was a lightweight in Tristan's book, the same height but nowhere near as broad as Tristan. Still, the guy was drunk and had nothing to lose – such as a large tray loaded with vegetables.

No problem, thought Tristan. A quick sidestep would send Eric plunging to his knees, then flat on his face.

But Tristan hadn't counted on the bridal party passing through at that moment. Catching sight of them out of the corner of his eye, he suddenly had to shift direction. He slammed into the lurching Eric. Celery and cauliflower, mushrooms and pepper curls, broccoli and snow peas were launched toward a chandelier, then rained down upon the party.

And then she looked at him. Ivy, sparkling Ivy. For a moment their eyes met, hers round as the cherry tomatoes that rolled onto her mother's train.

Tristan was sure that she finally knew he existed.

And he was just as sure that she'd never go out with him. Never.

"Maybe you were right, Ivy," Suzanne whispered as they looked down at the splatter of raw vegetables. " On land, Tristan's a klutz."

What is he doing here? Ivy wondered. Why didn't he stay in his pool, where he belongs? She knew her friends would be convinced he was following her around, and it embarrassed her.

Beth picked her way toward them, spearing a tomato with her high heel. "Perhaps this is how he earns money," she said, reading Ivy's troubled face.

Suzanne shook her head. "Throwing broccoli at the bride?"

"That cute redheaded swimmer is here, too," Beth went on. Her messy hair was piled up on her head that night, making her look even more like a sweet-faced owl.

"Neither of them knows what he's doing," Suzanne observed. "They're here just for tonight." Ivy sighed.

"I guess Tristan's hard up," Beth said.

"For money or for Ivy?" Suzanne asked, and they both laughed.

"Oh, come on, Ivy," Beth said, touching her gently on the arm. "It's funny! I bet his eyes got big when he saw what you were wearing." Suzanne made her eyes gigantic and started humming the theme from *Gone with the Wind.*

Ivy grimaced. She knew she looked like Scarlett O'Hara dropped in a bucket of glitter.

But it was the gown her mother had picked out especially for her.

Suzanne kept humming.

"I bet Gregory's eyes got big when he saw what you *weren't* wearing," Ivy told her friend, hoping to shut her up. Suzanne was in a plunging black dress that left little to the imagination.

"I certainly hope so!"

"And speaking of," said Beth.

"There you are, Ivy." Gregory's voice was warm and almost intimate. Suzanne swung toward him. He offered Ivy his arm. "We're expected at the top table."

With her hand resting lightly on his arm, Ivy fell into step beside him, wishing Suzanne could go in her place. Her mother looked up as the two of them approached, beaming at Ivy in her flouncy gown.

"Thank you," Ivy said as Gregory held out her chair for her.

He smiled at her — that secret kind of smile she had first seen at the swim meet. He leaned down, his lips close to her bare neck. "My pleasure, ma'am."

Ivy's skin prickled a little. He's playing, she told herself. Just play along. Since the swim meet, he had been teasing her and trying to be friendly, and she knew she should give him credit for that; but Ivy preferred the old, cold Gregory.

She had understood completely his icy response when she arrived at his school. She knew it must have been a terrible shock when he found out that Maggie was moving her brood from their apartment in Norwalk to one his father was leasing in Stonehill, and that this was in preparation for marriage.

Andrew and Maggie's affair had begun years earlier. But affairs were affairs, people said, and Andrew and her mother were such an odd romantic pair – a very wealthy and distinguished president of a college and his wife's hairdresser. Who'd have guessed that years after their fling, years after Andrew's divorce, he and Maggie would tie the knot?

It had been a shock even to Ivy. Her own father had died when she was an infant. She had grown up watching her mother run through a series of boyfriends, and thought it would always be that way.

Ivy leaned forward to look down the table at her mother. Andrew caught her eye and smiled, then nudged his new wife. Maggie beamed back at Ivy. She looked so happy.

Angel of love, Ivy prayed silently, watch over Mom. Watch over all of us. Make us a loving family, loving and strong.

"Should I tell you that your – uh – sparkles are dipping in the soup?"

Ivy sat back quickly. Gregory laughed and offered her his napkin.

"That dress can get you in a lot of trouble," he teased. "It nearly blinded Tristan Carruthers."

Ivy could feel the warmth spreading in her cheeks. She wanted to point out that it was Eric, not she—

"I feel sorry for the table he's waiting on tonight. He and that other jock," Gregory said, still grinning. "I hope it's not ours."

They both glanced around the room.

Me too, Ivy thought, me too.

Shortly after the raw vegetable shower, Tristan was told he could leave and should leave, immediately. Tired and humiliated, he would have been glad to clear out, but he was Gary's ride home. So he poked around behind the kitchen until he found a storeroom to hole up in.

It was dark and peaceful there, the shelves stacked with large boxes and cans. Tristan had just settled down comfortably on a carton when he heard rustling behind him. Mice, he thought, or rats. He really didn't care. He tried to console himself, imagining himself standing on the top winner's block, the flag of the United States rising behind him while the anthem played, Ivy watching on TV and sorry she had missed her chance to go out with him.

"I'm an idiot!" he said, dropping his head in his hands. "I could have any girl I want and—"

A hand rested lightly on his shoulder. Tristan's head shot up and he looked into the pale, triangular face of a kid. The kid, who looked about eight years old, was all dressed up, his tie knotted tightly and his dark hair plastered down. He must have been one of the wedding guests.

"What are you doing in here?" Tristan demanded.

"Would you get me some food?" the boy asked.

Tristan frowned, annoyed that he had to share his hideout, a cozy place for pining over Ivy. "Why can't you get your own food?"

"They'll see me," said the boy.

"Well, they'll see me too!"

The boy's mouth formed a thin, straight line. His jaw was set. But his eyes looked uncertain and his brow was puckered.

Tristan spoke in a gentler voice. "Looks as if you and I are up to the same thing. Hiding out."

"I'm really hungry. I didn't eat breakfast or lunch," the kid said.

Through the door, which was open a crack, Tristan could see the other waiters whisking in and out. They had just begun to serve the dinner.

"I might have something in my pocket," he told the kid, and pulled out a squashed crab ball, several shrimp, three stalks of stuffed celery, a handful of cashews, and something unidentifiable.

"Is that sushi?" asked the boy.

"Got me. All of this was on the floor and then it was in my pocket, and I don't know where this jacket has been, it was hired."

The boy nodded solemnly and studied Tristan's selection. "I like shrimp," he said at last, picking up one, spitting on it, then wiping it clean with his finger. He did this with each shrimp in turn, then the crab ball, then the celery. Tristan wondered if he'd spit on each tiny nut. He wondered how big a problem this kid was carrying around to make him not eat all day and hide in a dark storeroom.

"So," said Tristan, "I guess you don't really like weddings."

The kid glanced at him, then took a nibble out of the unrecognizable thing.

"Do you have a name, kid?"

"Yes."

"Mine's Tristan. What's yours?"

The kid set aside the unrecognizable hors d'oeuvre and began working on the nuts. "I'd like dinner," he said. "I'm real hungry."

Tristan peered through the crack. Waiters were rushing in and out of the kitchen. "Too many people around," he said.

"Are you in some kind of trouble?" the kid asked.

"Some kind. Nothing serious. How about you?"

"Not yet," said the kid

"But you will be?"

"When they find me."

Tristan nodded. "I guess you've already figured out that you can't stay here forever."

Squinting, the boy surveyed the shelves in the dim room, as if he were seriously considering its possibilities.

Tristan laid his hand gently on the boy's arm. "What's the problem, pal? Want to tell me about it?"

"I'd really like dinner," the boy said.

"All right, all right!" Tristan said irritably.

"I'd like dessert, too."

"You'll take what I can get!" snapped Tristan.

"Okay," the boy replied meekly.

Tristan sighed. "Don't mind me. I'm grouchy."

"I don't mind you," the boy assured him softly.

"Look, pal," Tristan said. "Only one waiter left, and plenty of food. You coming with me? Good! There he goes. Raiders, take your mark, get set—"

"Where's Philip?" Ivy asked.

The wedding party was halfway through their dinner when she realized that her brother wasn't in his chair. "Have you seen Philip?" she said, rising from her seat.

Gregory pulled her back down. "I wouldn't worry, Ivy. He's probably messing around somewhere."

"But he hasn't eaten all day," said Ivy.

"Then he's in the kitchen," Gregory said simply.

Gregory didn't understand. Her little brother had been threatening to run away for weeks. She had tried to explain to Philip what was happening and how nice it would be in their big house with a tennis court and a view of the river, and how great it would be to have Gregory as an older brother. He didn't buy any of it. Actually, Ivy didn't, either.

She pushed back her chair, too quickly for Gregory to stop her, and hurried off to the kitchen.

"Dig in," said Tristan. On the box between the kid and him sat a mound of food – charred filet mignon, shrimp, an assortment of vegetables, salad, and rolls with lots of whipped butter.

"This is pretty good," said the kid.

"Pretty good? This is a feast!" said Tristan. "Eat up! Well need our strength to capture dessert."

He saw a trace of a smile, then it disappeared.

"Who're you in trouble with?" the boy wanted to know.

Tristan chewed for a moment. "It's the caterer, Monsieur Pompideau. I was working for him and spilled some things. You know, I wet a few people's pants."

The boy smiled, a bigger smile this time. "Did you get Mr. Lever?"

"Should I have aimed for him?" Tristan asked.

The kid nodded, his face brightened considerably by this thought.

"Anyway, Pompideau told me to stick to things that didn't spill. Imagine that."

"You know what I'd tell *him*?" said the kid. The pucker in his brow was gone. He was gulping down food and talking with his mouth full. He looked about a hundred times better than he had fifteen minutes earlier.

"What?"

"I'd tell him: Stick it in your ear!"

"Good idea!" said Tristan. He picked up a piece of celery. "Stick it in your ear, Pompideau."

The kid laughed out loud, and Tristan wedged in the stalk.

"Stick it in your other ear, Pompideau!" the kid commanded.

Tristan snatched up another piece of celery.

"Stick it in your hair, Dippity-doo!" the boy crowed, carried away with the game.

Tristan took a handful of shredded salad and dropped it on his head. Too late he realized the greens were covered with vinaigrette.

The kid threw back his head and laughed. "Stick it in your nose, Doo-be-doo!"

Well, why not? Tristan thought. He had been eight years old once, and remembered how funny noses and boogers seemed to little boys. He found two shrimp tails and stuck them in, their pink fins flaring out of his nostrils.

The kid was falling off his box laughing. "Stick it in your teeth, Doo-be-doo!"

Two black olives worked well, each stuck on a tooth, so he had two black incisors.

"Stick it in—"

Tristan was busy adjusting his celery and shrimp tails. He hadn't noticed how the crack of light had widened. He didn't see the kid's face change. "Stick it where, Doo-be-doo?"

Then Tristan looked up.

3

Ivy froze. She was stunned by the sight of Tristan, celery stuck in his ears, salad shreds in his hair, something squishy and black on his teeth, and – hard as it was to believe that someone older than eight would do this – shrimp tails sticking out of his nose.

Tristan looked just as stunned to see her.

"Am I in trouble?" Philip asked.

"I think I am," Tristan said softly.

"You're supposed to be in the dining room, eating with us," Ivy told Philip.

"We're eating in here. We're having a feast."

She looked at the assortment of food piled on the plates between them, and one side of her mouth curled up.

"Please, Ivy, Mom said we could bring any friends we wanted to the wedding."

"And you told her you didn't have any, remember? You said you didn't have one friend in Stonehill."

"I do now."

Ivy looked at Tristan. He was careful to keep his eyes down, concentrating on the celery, shrimp, and squashed black olives, lining them up on the box in front of him. Disgusting.

"Mademoiselle!"

"It's Doo-be-doo!" cried Philip. "Close the door! Please, Ivy!"

Against her better judgment, she did, for strange as it seemed, her brother looked happier than he had in weeks. With her back to the storeroom, Ivy faced the caterer.

"Is something wrong, mademoiselle?"

"No, sir."

"Are you *très certaine?*"

"*Très,*" she replied, taking Monsieur Pompideau's arm and walking him away from the door.

"Well, you are wanted in the dining room," he said crisply. "It is time for the toast. Everyone is waiting."

Ivy hurried out. They were indeed waiting, and she couldn't avoid making an entrance. Ivy blushed as she crossed the room. Gregory pulled her toward him, laughing. Then he handed her a champagne glass.

A friend of Andrew's made the toast. It went on and on.

"Hear, hear," all the guests cried out at last.

"Hear, hear, sister!" Gregory said, and drank down the contents of the glass. He held it out to be filled again.

Ivy took a small sip from hers.

"Here, here, sister," he said again, but low and soft this time, his eyes burning with a strange light. He clinked his glass against hers and downed the champagne once more.

Then he pulled Ivy to him, so close she couldn't breathe, and kissed her hard on the mouth.

Ivy sat at her piano, staring at the same measures of music she had opened to five minutes before, one hand resting lightly on her lips. She dropped her hand down to the yellowed keys and ran her fingers over them, eliciting ripples of music, not quite in tune. Then she ran her tongue over her lips. They weren't really bruised; it was all in her mind.

Still, she was glad that she had talked her mother into letting Philip and her stay in their apartment until after the honeymoon. Six days alone with Gregory in that huge house on the ridge was more than she could face, especially with Philip acting up.

Philip, who in their crowded Norwalk apartment had rigged up old curtains around his bed because he wanted to be away from "the girls," had been begging to sleep with her for the past two weeks. The night before the wedding she had let him bring his sleeping bag into her room. She had awakened to find him and Ella the cat on top of her. After their long day at the wedding, she'd probably let him sleep in her room again that night.

He was on the floor behind her, playing with his baseball cards, arranging dream teams on the scatter rug. As usual, Ella wanted to stretch out in the middle of the baseball diamond. The pitcher rode on her black belly, up and down. Every once in a while, a soft phrase would escape Philip. "Fly ball deep to center field," he'd whisper, then Derek Jeter would make his home-run trot around the bases.

I shouldn't let him stay up this late, Ivy thought. But she herself couldn't sleep, and she was glad for his company. Besides, Philip had eaten such a conglomeration of party food, and so many sweets on top of that – thanks to Tristan – he'd probably throw up all over his sleeping bag. And clean sheets, like almost every-thing else in their apartment, were packed.

"Ivy, I decided," Philip said suddenly. "I'm not going to move."

"What?" She lifted her legs and spun around on the piano bench.

"I'm staying here. Do you and Ella want to stay with me?"

"And what about Mom?"

"She can be Gregory's mother now," Philip said.

Ivy winced, the way she did each time her mother made a fuss over Gregory. Maggie was warmhearted and affectionate – and trying hard, much too hard. She had no idea how ridiculous Gregory found her.

"Mom will always be *our* mother, and right now she needs us."

"Okay," Philip said agreeably. "You and Ella go. I'm going to ask Tristan to move in with me."

"Tristan!"

He nodded, then said softly to himself, "Walked the batter. Tying run coming up to the plate."

Apparently he had made up his eight-year-old mind and didn't figure that the matter needed to be discussed further. He played contentedly. It was the strangest thing, how he had begun to play again after his fun with Tristan.

What had Tristan said to Philip that helped him so? Perhaps nothing, Ivy thought. Perhaps instead of trying to explain their mother's marriage for the last three weeks, she should have just stuck some shrimp in her nose.

"Philip," she said sharply.

The tying run had to come home before he was willing to talk to her again. "Huh?"

"Did Tristan say anything to you about me?"

"About you?" He thought for a moment "No."

"Oh." Not that I care, she told herself.

"Do you know him?" Philip asked.

"No. No, I just thought that maybe, after I found you in the storeroom, he'd say something about me."

Philip's brow knitted. "Oh, yeah. He asked me if you like to wear pink dresses like that, and if you really believe in angels. I told him about your collection of statues."

"What did you tell him about my dress?"

"Yes."

"Yes?" she exclaimed.

"You told Mommy you thought it was pretty."

And her mother had believed her. Why shouldn't Philip?

"Did Tristan say why he was working there tonight?"

"Yup."

The inning was over. Philip was setting up a new defense.

"Well, why?" Ivy asked, exasperated.

"He has to make some money for a swim

meet. He's a swimmer, Ivy. He goes to other states and swims. He needs to fly, I can't remember where."

Ivy nodded. Of course. Tristan was just hard up, earning his way. She should stop listening to Suzanne.

Philip stood up suddenly. "Ivy, don't make me go to that big house. Don't make me go. I don't want to eat dinner with him!"

Ivy reached out for her brother. "New things always seem scary," she reassured him. "But Andrew has been nice to you, right from the start. Remember who bought you Derek Jeter's rookie card?"

"I don't want to eat dinner with Gregory."

She didn't know what to say to that.

Philip stood next to her, his fingers moving silently over the old piano's keys. When he'd been younger he used to do that and sing the tunes he was supposed to be playing.

"I need a hug," she said. "How about it?"

He gave her an unenthusiastic one.

"Let's do our new duet, okay?"

He shrugged. He'd play along with her, but the happiness that she had glimpsed in him earlier had disappeared.

They were five measures through when he slammed his hands down on the piano. He banged and banged and banged.

"I won't go! I won't go! I won't!"

Philip burst into tears, and Ivy pulled him toward her, letting him sob in her arms. When he had settled into exhausted hiccups, she said, "You're tired, Philip. You're just tired," but she knew it was more than that.

While he rested against her she played him his favorite songs, then softened the medley into lullabies. Soon he was almost asleep and much too big for her to carry into bed.

"Come on," she said, helping him up from the bench. Ella followed them into her room.

"Ivy."

"Hmmm?"

"Can I have one of your angels tonight?"

"Sure. Which one?"

"Tony."

Tony was the dark brown one, carved out of wood, Ivy's father angel. She stood Tony next to the sleeping bag and Derek Jeter. Then Philip crawled into the bag, and she zipped him in.

"Do you want to say an angel prayer?" she asked.

Together they said, "Angel of light, angel above, take care of me tonight. Take care of everyone I love."

"That's you, Ivy," Philip added, and closed his eyes.

4

Ivy felt as if she floated through most of the week that followed the wedding, with one day slipping into the next, marked only by frustrating discussions with Philip. Suzanne and Beth teased her about her absent-mindedness, but more gently than usual. Gregory passed her in the hall once or twice and made little jokes about straightening up his room before Friday. Tristan didn't cross her path that week – at least she didn't see him.

Everyone in school knew by then about her mother and Andrew's marriage. The wedding had made all the local papers as well as the *New York Times*. Ivy shouldn't have been surprised, for Andrew was often in the paper, but it was odd to see photos of her mother as well.

Friday morning finally arrived, and Ivy nosed her rusty little Dodge out of the apartment driveway, feeling suddenly homesick for every crowded, noisy, dilapidated rental place her family had ever lived in. When she returned from school that afternoon, she'd enter a different driveway, one that climbed a ridge high above the train station and river. The road to the house hugged a low stone wall and ran between patches of woods, daffodils, and laurel. Andrew's woods, daffodils, and laurel.

That afternoon Ivy picked up Philip from school. He had given up the fight and rode next to her in silence. Halfway up the ridge, Ivy heard a motorcycle on the bend above them, roaring downhill. Suddenly the cyclist and she were face-to-face. She was already as far to the right as she could get. Still he came head-on. Ivy slammed on her brakes. The cycle swerved dangerously close to them, then sped past.

Philip's head spun around, but he didn't say anything. Ivy glanced in the rearview mirror. It was probably Eric Ghent. She hoped Gregory was with him.

But Gregory was waiting for them at the house, along with Andrew and her mother, who were just back from their honeymoon. Her mother greeted them with big hugs and lipstick kisses and a cloud of some new kind of perfume. Andrew took both of Ivy's hands in his. He was wise enough to smile at but not touch Philip. Then Ivy and Philip were turned over to Gregory.

"I'm the tour guide," he said. Leaning toward Philip, he warned, "Stay close. Some of these rooms are haunted."

Philip looked around quickly, then glanced up at Ivy.

"He's just kidding."

"I'm not," said Gregory. "Some very unhappy people have lived here."

Philip glanced up at Ivy again. She shook her head.

On the outside the house was a stately white clapboard home with heavy black shutters. Wings had been added to each side of the main structure. Ivy would have liked to live in one of the smaller wings with their deep sloping roofs and dormer windows.

In the main part of the house, some of the high-ceilinged rooms seemed as large as apartments that they had once lived in. The house's wide center hall and sweeping stair separated the living room, library, and solarium from the dining room, kitchen, and family room. Beyond the family room was a gallery leading to the west wing with Andrew's office.

Since her mother and Andrew were talking

in the office, the downstairs tour stopped at the gallery, in front of three portraits: Adam Baines, the one who had invested in all the mines, looking stern in his World War I uniform; Judge Andy Baines, in his judicial robes; and Andrew, dressed in his colorful academic gown. Next to Andrew there was a blank spot on the wall.

"Makes you wonder who's going to hang there," Gregory remarked dryly. He smiled, but his gray, hooded eyes had a haunted look. For a moment Ivy felt sorry for him. As Andrew's only son, he must have felt a lot of pressure to do well.

"You will," she said softly.

Gregory looked in her eyes, then laughed. His laughter was touched with bitterness.

"Come upstairs," he said, taking her hand and leading her to the back stairway that ran up to his room. Philip tagged along silently.

Gregory's room was large and had only one thing in common with other guys' rooms – an archaeological layer of discarded underwear and socks. Beneath that, it showed money and taste: dark leather chairs and low tables, a desk and top-of-the-range computer, and an expensive mini system. Covering the walls were museum prints with striking geometric shapes. In the center of it all was a king-size bed.

"It's double-sprung. Try it," Gregory urged.

Ivy leaned down and prodded it tentatively with her hand.

He laughed at her. "What are you afraid of? Come on, Phil" – no one calls him Phil, Ivy thought – "show your sister how. Climb on top and give it a good roll around."

"I don't want to," said Philip.

"Sure you do." Gregory was smiling, but his tone of voice threatened.

"Nope," said Philip.

"It's a lot of fun." Gregory grasped Philip's shoulders and pushed him back forcefully toward the bed.

Philip resisted, then tripped and fell onto it. He sprang off just as quickly. "I hate it!" he cried. Gregory's mouth hardened into a line. Ivy then sat down on the bed. "It *is* fun," she said. She bounced slowly up and down. "Try it with me, Philip." But he had moved out into the hallway.

"Lie back on it, Ivy," Gregory urged her, his voice low and silky.

When she did, he lay down close to her.

"We really should get to our unpacking," Ivy said, sitting up quickly.

They crossed through a low-roofed passage that was just above the gallery and into the section of the main house where Philip and she had their bedrooms.

Her door was closed and when she opened it, Philip rushed through to Ella, who was stretched out luxuriously on Ivy's bed. Oh no, Ivy groaned silently as she glanced around the elaborately decorated room. She had feared the worst when her mother said she was in for a big surprise. What she saw was lots of frills, white wood hung with muslin, and a four-poster bed. "Princess furniture," she muttered aloud.

Gregory grinned.

"At least Ella looks at home. She's always thought of herself as a queen. Do you like cats, Gregory?"

"Sure," he said, sitting on the bed next to Ella. Ella promptly got up and walked to the other end of the bed.

Gregory looked annoyed.

"That's a queen for you," Ivy said lightly. "Well, thanks for the tour – I've got a lot to unpack."

But Gregory lounged back on her bed. "This was my room when I was a kid."

"Oh?"

Ivy lifted an armload of clothes from a bag and pulled open a door to what she thought was a closet. Instead she faced a set of steps.

"That was my secret stairway," Gregory said.

Ivy peered up into the darkness.

"I used to hide up in the attic when my mother and father fought. Which was every day," Gregory added. "Did you ever meet my mother? You must have; she was always getting done over."

"At the beauty shop? Yes," Ivy replied, opening the door to a closet

"Wonderful woman, isn't she?" His words were heavy with sarcasm. "Loves everyone. Never thinks of herself."

"I was young when I met her," Ivy said tactfully.

"I was young, too."

"Gregory . . . I've been wanting to say this. I know it must be hard for you, watching my mother move into your mother's room, having Philip and me take over space that was once yours. I don't blame you for—"

"For being glad that you're here?" he interrupted. "I am. I'm counting on you and Philip to keep the old man on his best behavior. He knows others are watching him and his new family. Now he's got to be the *good* and *loving* papa. Let me help you with that."

Ivy had picked up her box of angels. "No, really, Gregory, I can handle this myself."

He reached in his pocket for a penknife and slit the tape on the carton. "What's in it?"

"Ivy's angels," said Philip.

"The boy speaks!"

Philip pressed his lips together.

"Soon enough, you won't be able to shut him up," Ivy said. Then she opened the box and began to take out her carefully wrapped statues.

Tony came out first. Then an angel carved out of soft gray stone. Then her favorite, her water angel, a fragile porcelain figure painted in a swirl of blue-green.

Gregory watched as she unwrapped fifteen statues and set them on a shelf. His eyes were bright with amusement. "You don't take this stuff seriously, do you?"

"What do you mean by seriously?" she asked.

"You don't really believe in angels."

"I do," said Ivy.

He picked up the water angel and made her zoom around the room.

"Put her down!" Philip cried. "She's Ivy's favorite."

Gregory landed her facedown on a pillow.

"You're mean!"

"He's just playing, Philip," Ivy said, and calmly retrieved the angel.

Gregory lay back on the bed. "Do you pray to them?" he asked.

"Yes. To the angels, not the statues," she explained.

"And what wonderful things have these angels done for you? Have they captured Tristan's heart?"

Ivy glanced at him with surprise. "No. But then, I didn't pray for that."

Gregory laughed softly.

"Do you know Tristan?" Philip asked.

"Since first grade," Gregory replied, then lazily extended an arm toward the cat. Ella rolled away from him.

"He was the good kid on my Little League team," Gregory said, pulling himself up so he could reach Ella. She rose at the same time and walked to the other end of the bed. "He was the good kid on *every* team," Gregory said. He reached again for Ella.

The cat hissed. Ivy saw the color rising in Gregory's cheeks.

"Don't take it personally, Gregory," Ivy said. "Just let Ella be for a while. Cats often play hard to get."

"Like some girls I know," he remarked. "Come here, girl." He thrust his hand toward her. The cat raised a quick black paw, claws extended.

"Let her come to you," Ivy warned.

But Gregory took the cat by the scruff of the neck and pulled her upward.

"Don't!" Ivy cried.

He pushed his other hand up under her belly. Ella bit him hard on the wrist.

"Shoot!" He threw Ella across the room.

Philip ran for the cat. The cat ran to Ivy. She scooped her up in her arms. Ella's tail switched back and forth; she was angry rather than hurt. Gregory watched her, the color still high in his cheeks.

"Ella's a street kitten," Ivy told him, fighting to keep her own temper. "When I found her, she was a little bit of fur backed against a brick wall, holding her own against a big, torn-up tom. I tried to tell you. You can't come on to her that way. She doesn't trust people easily."

"Maybe you should teach her to," Gregory said. "*You* trust me, don't you?" He gave her one of his crooked, questioning smiles. Ivy put down Ella. The cat sat under the chair and glowered at Gregory. At the sound of footsteps in the hall, she scooted under the bed. Andrew stood in the doorway. "How's everything?" he asked.

"Fine," Ivy lied.

"It stinks," said Philip.

Andrew blinked, then nodded graciously. "Well, then," he said, "we'll have to try to make things better. Do you think we can?"

Philip just stared at him.

Andrew turned to Ivy. "Did you happen to

open that door yet?" Ivy followed his glance to Gregory's secret steps. "The light for the upstairs is on the left side," he told her.

Apparently he wanted her to investigate. Ivy opened the door and turned on the light. Philip, growing curious, slipped under her arm and scooted up the steps.

"Wow!" he shouted from above them. "Wow!"

Ivy glanced at Andrew. At the sound of Philip's excited voice, his face flushed with pleasure. Gregory stared intently out the window.

"Ivy, come see!"

Ivy hurried up the steps. She expected to see a Nintendo Wii or maybe a life-size cardboard cut-out of Derek Jeter. Instead she discovered a baby grand piano, an incredible music system and two cabinets filled with her musical scores. An album cover with Ella Fitzgerald's face was framed on the wall. The rest of her father's old jazz records were stored next to an old-school record player.

"If there is anything missing . . ." Andrew began. He was standing next to her, puffing a little from the steps, looking hopeful. Gregory had come halfway up, just far enough to see.

"Thanks!" was all Ivy could say. "Thanks!"

"This is cool, Ivy," Philip said.

"And it's for all three of us to share," she told him, glad that he was too excited to remember to sulk. Then she turned to speak to Gregory, but he had disappeared.

Dinner that night seemed to last forever. The lavishness of Andrew's gifts, the music room for Ivy and a well-stocked playroom for Philip, was both overwhelming and embarrassing. Since Philip, growing moody once more, had decided he would not speak at all at dinner – "Maybe never again," he'd told Ivy with a pout – it was up to her to express their gratitude to Andrew. But in doing so, she walked a tightrope: when Andrew asked a second time if there was anything else she and Philip wanted, she saw how Gregory's hands tensed.

In the middle of dessert, Suzanne telephoned. Ivy made the mistake of only going as far as the hall outside the dining room to speak to her. Suzanne was hoping for an invitation to the house that evening. Ivy told her the next day would be better.

"But I'm all dressed!" Suzanne complained.

"Of course you are," Ivy replied, "it's only seven-thirty."

"I meant dressed to come over."

"Gee, Suzanne," Ivy said, playing dumb, "you don't have to wear anything special to visit *me*."

"What's Gregory doing tonight?"

"I don't know. I haven't asked him,"

"Well, find out! Find out her name and where she lives," Suzanne ordered, "and what she's wearing and where they go. If we don't know her, find out what she looks like. I just know he has a date," she wailed, "he must!"

Ivy had expected this. But she was worn out by the childishness of Philip and Gregory; she didn't feel like listening to the whining of Suzanne. "I've got to go now."

"I'll die if it's Twinkie Hammonds. Do you think it's Twinkie Hammonds?"

"I don't know. Gregory hasn't told me. Listen, I've got to go."

"Ivy, wait! You haven't told me anything yet."

Ivy sighed. "I'll be taking my usual lunch break at work tomorrow. Call Beth and meet me at the mall, okay?"

"Okay, but Ivy—"

"I'd better get going now," Ivy said, "or else I'll miss my chance to hide in the trunk of Gregory's car." She hung up.

"So, how's Suzanne?" Gregory asked. He was leaning against the frame of the door that led into the dining room, his head cocked, smiling.

"Fine."

"What's she doing tonight?"

The laughter in his eyes told her that he had overheard the conversation, and that this was a tease, not sincere interest in the information.

"I didn't ask her and she hasn't told me. But if you two would like to talk it over with each other—"

He laughed, then touched Ivy on the tip of her nose. "Funny," he said. "I hope we keep you."

5

It was a relief to go to work on Saturday morning, a relief to be back in territory that Ivy knew. Greentree Mall was in the next town over but drew high-school kids from all the surrounding towns. Most of them cruised the stores and hung around the food court. 'Tis the Season, where Ivy had worked for the last year and a half, was directly across from the food court.

The shop was owned by two old sisters, whose selection of costumes, decorations, paperware, and knickknacks was as eccentric as their style of business. Lillian and Betty rarely returned merchandise, and it was as if all the seasons and holidays had run into one another in one small corner of the world. Vampire costumes hung with the Stars and Stripes; Easter chickens roosted next to miniature plastic menorahs, pine-cone turkeys, and Vulcan ears from the last Trekkie convention.

Just before one o'clock on Saturday, while waiting for Suzanne and Beth to arrive, Ivy was glancing over the day's special orders. As always, they were scrawled on Post-it notes and stuck on the wall. Ivy read one of the tags twice, then pulled it off. Couldn't be, she thought, couldn't be. Maybe there were two of them. Two guys named Tristan Carruthers?

"Lillian, what does this mean? 'For pick-up: Bl Blup Wh and 25 pnc.'?"

Lillian squinted at the paper. She had bifocals, but they usually rode her chest at the end of a necklace.

"Well, twenty-five plates, napkins, and cups, you know that. Ah yes, for Tristan Carruthers – an order for the swim team party. Blue blow-up whale. I've already got it ready. He called to check on the order this morning."

"Trist – Mr. Carruthers called?"

Now Lillian reached for her glasses. Settling them on her nose, she looked hard at Ivy. "Mr. Carruthers? He didn't call you Miss Lyons," she said.

"Why would he call me anything?" Ivy wondered aloud. "I mean, why did my name come up?"

"He asked what hours you were working. I told him you take lunch between one and one-forty-five, but otherwise you'd be here till six." She smiled at Ivy. "And I put in a few good words for you, dear."

"A few good words?"

"I told him what a lovely girl you are, and what a shame it is that someone like you couldn't find a deserving gentleman friend."

Ivy winced, but Lillian had removed her glasses again, so she didn't notice.

"He came into the shop last week to place the order," Lillian continued. "He's quite a chunk."

"Hunk, Lillian."

"Pardon me?"

"Tristan's quite a *hunk.*"

"Well, she's finally admitting it!" said Suzanne, striding into the store. Beth came in behind her. "Good work, Lillian!" The old woman winked, and Ivy stuck the Post-it back on the wall. She began to dig in her pockets for money.

"Don't expect to eat," Suzanne warned her. "This is an interrogation."

Twenty minutes later, Beth was just about finished with her burrito. Suzanne had made inroads on her teriyaki chicken. Ivy's pizza remained untouched.

"How should I know?" she was saying, waving her arms with frustration. "I didn't get into his medicine cupboard!" They had hashed and rehashed and interpreted and reinterpreted every detail that Ivy had observed about Gregory's room.

"Well, I guess you've only been there one night,' Suzanne said, "But tonight, maybe. You must find out where he's going tonight. Does he have a curfew? Does he—"

Ivy picked up an egg roll and stuffed it in Suzanne's mouth. "It's Beth's turn to talk," she said.

"Oh, that's all right," Beth said. "This is interesting."

Ivy opened Beth's folder. "Why don't you read one of your new stories," she said, "before Suzanne makes me totally crazy."

Beth glanced at Suzanne, then cheerfully pulled out a sheaf of papers. "I'm going to use this new one for drama club on Monday. I've been experimenting with *in medias res.* That means starting right in the middle of the action."

Ivy nodded to her encouragingly and took the first bite out of her pizza.

"'She clutched the gun to her breast,'" Beth read. "'Hard and blue, cold and unyielding. Photos of him. Frail and faded photos of him – of him with *her* – torn-up, tear-soaked, salt-crusted photos lay scattered by her chair. She'd wash them away with her own blood—'"

"Beth, Beth," Suzanne cut in. "This is lunch. Something a pound lighter?"

Beth agreeably shuffled through the papers and began again. "'She clutched his hand to her breast. Warm and damp, soft and supple—'"

"His hand or her breast?" Suzanne interrupted.

"Quiet," said Ivy.

"'—a hand that could hold her very soul, a hand that could lift' – a whale, a blue plastic whale, I think. What *else* could that be?" Ivy turned around quickly and looked across the mall to the shop. Betty was holding up a big piece of blue plastic and chatting away to Tristan. Lillian was standing behind Tristan at the shop entrance, beckoning furiously to her. Ivy glanced at her watch. It was 1.25, halfway through her lunch break. "She wants you," said Beth.

Ivy shook her head at Lillian, but Lillian kept waving at her.

"Go get 'im, girl," said Suzanne.

"No."

"Oh, come on, Ivy."

"You don't understand. He knows I'm on lunch break. He's avoiding me."

"Maybe," said Suzanne, "but I've never let a thing like that stop me."

Now Tristan had turned around and, noticing Lillian's imitation of a highway flagman, surveyed the crowd in the food court until his eyes came to rest on Ivy. Meanwhile, Betty had managed to hook the inflatable whale up to the store's helium canister.

"Yo!" exclaimed Beth as the whale took on a life of its own, growing like a blue thundercloud behind Tristan and Lillian. Betty disappeared on the other side of it. She must have cut it loose suddenly, for it rose to the ceiling. Tristan had to jump to nab it. Beth and Suzanne started laughing. Lillian shook her finger at Ivy, then turned to talk to Tristan.

"I wonder what she's saying to him," Beth said.

"A few good words," mumbled Ivy.

Minutes later Tristan emerged from the shop clutching the bag of party stuff, which had been tied up by the sisters with a fancy blue bow. The whale trailed above and behind him. He kept his eyes straight ahead and marched toward the mall exit. Suzanne called out to him.

Bellowed, actually. He couldn't pretend not to hear her. He looked in their direction and then, with a rather grim expression on his face, made his way toward them. Several small children followed him as if he were the Pied Piper.

"Hi," he said stiffly. "Suzanne. Beth. Ivy. Nice to see you."

"Nice to see *you!*" Suzanne said, then eyed the whale. "Who's this? He's kind of cute. Newest member of the swim team?"

Ivy noticed that Tristan's knuckles were white on the hand that held the whale's string. Muscles all the way up his arm were tense and bulging. Behind him, the kids were jumping up and down, punching at the whale.

"Actually, the newest member of my act," he said, and turned to Ivy. "You've seen part of it – the carrot-and-shrimp-tail routine I do? I don't know what it is. Eight-year-olds find me irresistible." He glanced back at the kids. "Sorry, got to go now."

"Noooo!" the kids cried. He let them take a few more bats at the whale, then left, weaving his way quickly through the Saturday shoppers.

"Well!" huffed Suzanne. "Well!" She poked Ivy with her chopstick. "You could have said something! Really, girl, I don't know *what* is wrong with you."

"What did you want me to say?"

"Anything! Something! It doesn't matter – just let him know it's all right to talk to you."

Ivy swallowed hard. She couldn't understand why Tristan did some of the things he did. He made her so self-conscious.

"You always feel self-conscious at first," Beth said, as if reading Ivy's thoughts. "But sooner or later you'll figure out how to act around each other."

Suzanne leaned forward. "Your problem is that you take it all too seriously, Ivy. Romance is a game, just a game."

Ivy sighed and glanced at her watch. "I've got ten more minutes on break. Beth, how about finishing your love story?"

Suzanne tapped Ivy's arm. "You've got two more months of school," she said. "How about starting yours?"

6

Ivy stood barefoot on the clammy floor, curling up her toes. The humidity and the pool's strong smell of chlorine invaded the locker room. Metal doors slammed and the cinder-block room echoed like a cave. Everything about the pool area gave her the creeps.

The other girls in the drama club were checking out one another's suits, rehearsing their lines, and giggling self-consciously.

Suzanne laid a hand on Ivy's shoulder. "You all right?"

"I can handle this."

"You're sure?" Suzanne didn't sound convinced.

"I know my lines," said Ivy, "and all we have to do is jump up and down on the diving board." On the *high* diving board, at the *deep* end, without falling in, Ivy thought to herself.

Suzanne persisted. "Listen, Ivy, I know you're McCardell's star, but don't you think you should mention to him that you don't know how to swim and are terrified of water?"

"I told you I can do this," Ivy said, then pushed through the swinging locker room door, her legs feeling like soft rubber beneath her.

She lined up with eleven girls and three guys along the pool's edge. Beth stood on one side of Ivy, Suzanne on the other. Ivy gazed down into the luminescent blue-green pool. It's just water, she told herself, nothing more than stuff to drink. And it's not even deep at this end.

Beth touched her on the arm. "Well, I guess Suzanne is pleased. You invited Gregory."

"Gregory? Of course I didn't!" Ivy turned swiftly to Suzanne.

Suzanne shrugged. "I wanted to give him a preview of coming attractions. There'll be lots of places to sunbathe on that ridge of yours."

"You do look great in your suit," Beth told her.

Ivy fumed. Suzanne knew how hard this was for her, without adding Gregory to the scenario. She could have restrained herself just this once.

Gregory wasn't alone in the bleachers. His friends Eric and Will were watching, as well as some other juniors and seniors who had slipped away from their projects during the activity period. All of the guys watched with intense interest as the girls in the group did their stretching exercises.

Then the class walked and trotted around the perimeter of the pool, performing their vocal drills.

"I want to hear every consonant, every *p*, *d*, and *t*," Mr. McCardell called out to them, his own voice amazingly distinct in the huge echo chamber of the pool. "Margaret, Courtney, Suzanne, this isn't a beauty pageant," he hollered. *"Just walk."*

That elicited some soft booing from the stands.

"And for heaven's sake, Sam, stop bouncing!"

The audience snickered.

When the students had finished several circuits, they gathered at the deep end of the pool, beneath the high dive.

"Eyes here," their teacher commanded. "You're not with me." Leaning close to them, he said, "This is a lesson in enunciation *and* concentration. I'll find it unforgivable if any one of you lets those groundlings distract you."

At that, nearly everyone in the class glanced toward the stands. The pool door opened, and more spectators entered, all of them guys.

"Are we ready? Are we preparing ourselves?"

For the exercise, each student had to memorize at least twenty-five lines of poetry or prose, something about love or death – "the two great themes of life and drama," Mr. McCardell had said.

Ivy had patched together two early-English love lyrics, one funny and one sad. She silently ran over their lines. She thought she knew them by heart, but when the first student climbed the thin metal ladder, every word went out of her head. Ivy's pulse began to race as if she were the one on the ladder. She took deep breaths.

"Are you okay?" Beth whispered.

"Tell him, Ivy!" Suzanne urged. "Explain to McCardell how you feel."

Ivy shook her head. "I'm fine."

The first three students delivered their lines mechanically, but all of them kept their balance, bouncing up and down on the board. Then Sam fell in. With arms wheeling like some huge, strange bird, he came crashing down into the water.

Ivy swallowed hard.

Mr. McCardell called her name.

She climbed the ladder, slowly and steadily, rung by rung, her heart pounding against her ribs. Her arms felt stronger than her shaky legs. She used them to pull herself up onto the board, then stopped. Below her the water danced, dark wavelets with fluorescent sparkles.

Ivy focused on the end of the board, as she had been taught to do on a balance beam, and took three steps. She felt the board give beneath her weight. Her stomach dropped with it, but she kept on walking.

"You may begin," said Mr. McCardell.

Ivy turned her thoughts inward for a moment, trying to find her lines, trying to remember the pictures she had imagined when she first read the poetry. She knew that if she did this simply as an exercise, she would not get through it. She had to perform, she had to lose herself to the poems' emotions.

She found the first few words of the humorous poem, and suddenly in her mind's eye saw the pictures she needed; a glittering bride, stunned guests, and a shower of rolling vegetables. Far below her, her audience laughed as she recited lines about the silliness of love. Then, continuing her jumping motion, she found the slower, sadder rhythm of the second poem:

Western wind, when will thou blow,
The small rain down can rain?
Christ, if my love were in my arms
And I in my bed again!

She jumped for two beats more, then stood still at the end of the board, catching her breath. Suddenly applause rang out. She had done it!

When the cheers died down, Mr. McCardell said, "Nice enough,' which was high praise from him.

"Thank you, sir," Ivy replied. Then she tried to turn around for the walk back.

As she started to turn she felt her knees buckle, and she quickly stiffened herself. Don't look down.

But she had to see where she was stepping. She took a deep breath and attempted to turn again.

"Ivy, is there a problem?" Mr. McCardell asked.

"She's afraid of water," Suzanne blurted. "And she can't swim."

Below Ivy the pool seemed to rock, its edges blurred. She tried to focus on the board. She couldn't. The water came rushing at her, ready to swallow her up. Then it receded, dropping away, far, far below her. Ivy swayed on her feet. One knee went down.

"Oh!" The cry echoed up from the spectators.

Her other knee went down and slipped off the board. Ivy clung with the desperation of a cat. She dangled, half on, half off the board.

"Somebody help her!" cried Suzanne.

Water angel, Ivy prayed silently. Water angel, don't let me fall. You helped me once. Please, angel . . .

Then Ivy felt movement in the board. It trembled in her arms. Her hands were damp and slippery. Just drop, she told herself. Trust your angel. Your angel won't let you drown. Water angel, she prayed a third time, but her arms wouldn't let go. The board continued to vibrate. Her hands were slipping.

"Ivy."

She turned her face at the sound of his voice, scraping her cheek on the board. Tristan had climbed the ladder and was standing at the other end. "Everything is going to be all right, Ivy."

Then he started toward her. The fiberglass plank flexed under his weight.

"Don't!" Ivy cried, clinging desperately to the board. "Don't bend it. Please! I'm afraid."

"I can help you. Trust me."

Her arms ached. Her head felt light, her skin cold and prickly. Beneath her, the water swirled dizzily.

"Listen to me, Ivy. You're not going to be able to keep holding on that way. Roll on your side a little. Roll, okay? Get your right arm free. Come on. I know you can do it."

Ivy slowly shifted her weight. For a moment she thought she was going to roll right off the board. Her freed arm waved frantically.

"You got it. You got it," he said.

He was right. She had a good hold, both hands squarely on the board.

"Now inch up. Pull yourself all the way onto the board. That's the way." His voice was steady and sure. "Which knee is your favorite knee?" he asked.

She frowned up at him.

"Are you right-kneed or left-kneed?" He was smiling at her.

"Uh, right-kneed, I guess."

"Loosen up your right hand, then. And pull your right knee up, tuck it under you." She did. A moment later both knees were under her.

"Now crawl to me."

She looked down at the rocking bowl of water.

"Come to me, Ivy."

The distance was only eight feet – it looked like eight miles. She made her way slowly along the board. Then she felt a hand gripping hard on each arm. He stood up, pulling her up with him, and quickly turned her around. Ivy went limp with relief.

"Okay, I'm right behind you now. We'll take one step at a time. I'm right here." He began to move down the ladder.

One step at a time, Ivy repeated to herself.

If only her legs would stop shaking. Then she felt his hand lightly on her ankle, guiding it down to the metal rung. At last they stood together at the bottom.

Mr. McCardell glanced away from her, obviously uncomfortable.

"Thank you," Ivy said quietly to Tristan.

Then she rushed into the locker room before Tristan or the others could see her frightened tears.

In the parking lot that afternoon, Suzanne tried to talk Ivy into coming home with her to the Goldstein house.

"Thanks, but I'm tired," Ivy said. "I think I should go . . . home." It was still strange to think of the Baines house as home.

"Well, why don't we just drive around some first?" Suzanne suggested. "I know a great cappuccino place where none of the kids go, at least none from our school. We can talk without being interrupted."

"I don't need to talk, Suzanne. I'm okay. Really. But if you want to just hang out, you can come home with me."

"I don't think that would be a good idea." Ivy cocked her head. "You would think you were the one who'd been stranded up there on the diving board."

KISSED BY AN ANGEL

"It felt like it," said Suzanne.

"If I didn't know better, I'd think you'd fallen from the ladder and hit your head on the concrete. I just invited you to Gregory's house."

Suzanne fiddled with her lipgloss, rolling it up and down, up and down in its case. "That's just it. You know how I am, Ivy – like a bloodhound on the hunt. I can't help myself. If he's there, I'll get completely distracted. And right now you need my attention."

"But I don't need anybody's attention! I had a bad time in drama club and—"

"Got rescued."

"Got rescued—"

"By Tristan."

"By Tristan, and now—"

"You'll live happily ever after," said Suzanne.

"Now I'll go home, and if you want to come with me and start baying at Gregory, fine. It will keep us all entertained."

Suzanne debated for a moment, then stretched her freshly slicked lips. "Did I get it on my teeth?"

"If you didn't talk constantly, you wouldn't have this problem," Ivy said, and pointed to a smudge of pink. "Right there."

When they arrived home, Gregory's BMW was in the driveway. "Well, we're all in luck," said Ivy.

But when they got inside the house, Ivy could hear her mother's voice, high and excited, being answered quickly each time by Gregory's. She and Suzanne exchanged glances, then followed the sound of the voices to Andrew's office.

"Is something wrong?" asked Ivy.

"That's what's wrong!" said her mother, pointing to a silk-covered chair. Its back hung in shreds.

"Ouch!" Ivy exclaimed. "What happened to it?"

"Perhaps my father was filing his nails," Gregory suggested.

"It's Andrew's favorite chair," said Maggie. Her cheeks were quite pink. Her sprayed hair was falling out of its twist in grasslike wisps. "And this fabric is not exactly cheap, Ivy."

"Well, Mother, I didn't do it!"

"Let me check your nails," said Gregory.

Suzanne laughed.

"Ella did it," Maggie said.

"Ella!" Ivy shook her head. "That's impossible! Ella's never scratched anything in her life."

"Ella doesn't like Andrew," Philip said. He had been standing quietly in the corner of the room. "She did it because she doesn't like Andrew."

Maggie whirled around. Ivy caught her

mother by the hand. "Easy," she said. Then she examined the back of the chair. Gregory watched her and examined the chair himself. It seemed to Ivy to be too finely shredded – a job too convincing for Philip to have pulled off. Ella must have been guilty.

"We're going to have to declaw her," said Maggie.

"No!"

"Ivy, there are too many valuable pieces of furniture in this house. They cannot be ruined. Ella will have to be declawed."

"I won't let you."

"She's just a cat."

"And this is just a piece of furniture," Ivy said, her voice cold and steely.

"It's that, or get rid of her."

Ivy folded her arms across her chest. She was two inches taller than her mother.

"Ivy—" She could see her mother's eyes misting over. That was what she had been like for the past few months, emotional, pleading, insisting with tears. "Ivy, this is a new life, these are new ways for all of us. You told me yourself: For all the good things that are happening, this isn't a fairy-tale ending. We all have to try to make it work."

"Where is Ella now?" Ivy asked.

"In your bedroom. I closed the hall door,

and the attic one too, so she wouldn't ruin anything else."

Ivy turned to Gregory. "Would you get Suzanne something to drink?"

"Of course," he said.

Then Ivy went up to her room. She sat for a long time, cradling Ella in her lap and gazing up at her water angel.

"What do I do now, angel?" she prayed. "What do I do now? Don't tell me to give up Ella! I can't give her up. I can't!"

In the end, she did. In the end, Ivy couldn't take the outdoors away from Ella. She couldn't leave her fierce little street cat vulnerable to anything that would take a swipe at her. Though it just about broke her heart, and Philip's too, she posted the adoption ad on the school bulletin board on Thursday afternoon.

On Thursday night she got a call. Philip was in her room doing his homework and picked up the phone. He somberly handed it over to her. "It's a man," he said. "He wants to adopt Ella."

Ivy frowned and took the receiver. "Hello?"

"Hi. How are you?" the caller asked.

"Fine," Ivy replied stiffly. Did it matter how she was? She immediately disliked this person – because he hoped to take away Ella.

"Good. Uh . . . did you find a home for your cat?"

"No," she said.

"I'd like to have her."

Ivy blinked hard. She didn't want Philip to see her cry. She should be glad and relieved that someone wanted a full-grown cat.

"Are you there?" asked the caller.

"Yes."

"I'd take good care of her, feed her and wash her."

"You don't wash cats."

"I'd learn what I have to do," he said. "I think she'd like it here. It's a comfortable place."

Ivy nodded silently.

"Hello?"

She turned her back on Philip. "Listen," she said into the phone. "Ella means a lot to me. If you don't mind, I'd like to see your home myself and talk to you in person."

"I don't mind at all!" the caller replied cheerfully. "Let me give you my address."

She copied it down. "And who is this?" she asked.

"Tristan."

7

"But you're a dog person," Gary said on Friday afternoon. "You've always been a dog person."

"I think my parents will enjoy a cat," Tristan replied. He moved quickly around the living room, clearing piles of stuff off the chairs: his mother's pediatrics journals, his father's hospital chapel schedules and stacks of photocopied prayers, his own swim schedules and old copies of *Sports Illustrated,* the previous night's tub of chicken. His parents would wonder why he had gone to all the trouble. Usually the three of them sat on the floor to read and eat.

Gary was watching him and frowning. "You think your *parents* will enjoy it? Does the cat have a disease? Does it have a religion? If your mother the doctor can't cure it and your father the minister can't pray for and counsel it—"

"All homes need a pet,' Tristan cut in.

"In homes where there's a cat, the *people* are the pets. I'm telling you, Tristan, cats have minds of their own. They're worse than girls. If you think Ivy can drive you crazy— Wait a minute . . . wait a minute . . ." Gary tapped his fingers on the table. "I remember an ad on the bulletin board."

"That's nice," Tristan said, and handed his friend his gym bag. "You said you had to get home early today."

Gary dropped his bag. He had figured out what was up. "And miss this? I was there the last time you made a fool of yourself; why shouldn't I stay for the fun this time?" He threw himself down on the rug in front of the fireplace.

"You're really enjoying my misery, aren't you?" Tristan murmured,

Gary rolled over on his back and put his hands behind his head. "Tristan, me and the guys have been watching you get all the girls for the last three years – no, for the last seven; you were hot even in fifth grade. Darn right I'm enjoying it!"

Tristan grimaced, then turned his attention to a coffee stain that seemed to have tripled in size since he'd last noticed it. He had no idea how to get something like that out of a rug.

He wondered if Ivy would find his family's old frame house small and worn and unbelievably cluttered.

"So, what's the deal?" Gary asked. "One date for taking her cat? Maybe one date for each week you keep it," he suggested.

"Her friend Suzanne said she's very attached to this cat." Tristan smiled, rather pleased with himself. "I'm offering visitation rights."

Gary snorted. "What happens when Ivy doesn't miss the old furball anymore?"

"She'll miss me," Tristan said, sounding confident.

The doorbell rang. His confidence evaporated.

"Quick, how do you pick up a cat?"

"Buy her a drink."

"I'm serious!"

"By the tail."

"You're kidding!"

"Yup. I'm kidding."

The doorbell rang again. Tristan hurried to answer it. Was it his imagination, or did Ivy blush a little when he opened the door? Her mouth was definitely rosy. Her hair shone like a halo of gold, and her green eyes made him think of warm, tropical seas.

"I've brought Ella," she said.

"Ella?"

"My cat."

Looking down, he saw all kinds of animal paraphernalia on the porch beside her.

"Oh, *Ella!* Great. Great." Why did she always reduce him to one-word sentences?

"You're still interested, aren't you?" A small line of worry creased her brow.

"Oh, he's interested all right," Gary replied, rising up behind Tristan.

Ivy stepped into the house and looked about without putting down her cat carrier.

"I'm Gary. I've seen you around a lot at school."

Ivy nodded and smiled somewhat distantly. "You were at the wedding, too."

"Right. Me and Tristan. I'm the one who made it all the way through dessert before being fired."

Ivy smiled again, a friendlier smile this time, then she got back to business.

"Ella's litter pan is outside," she said to Tristan. "And some cans of food. I also brought her basket and cushion, but she never uses them."

Tristan nodded. Ivy's hair was blowing in the draft from the door. He wanted to touch it. He wanted to brush it off her cheek and kiss her.

"How would you feel about sharing your bed?" she asked.

Tristan blinked. "Excuse me?"

"He'd love to!" Gary said.

Tristan shot him a look.

"Good," said Ivy, failing to notice Gary's wink. "Ella can be a pillow hog, but all you have to do is roll her over."

Gary laughed out loud, then he and Tristan brought in the pile of stuff.

"Are you a cat person?" Ivy asked Gary.

"No," he replied, "but maybe there's hope for me." He leaned down to peer into the carrier. "I mean, look how fast Tristan converted. Hello, Ella. We're going to have a great time playing together."

"Too bad you'll have to wait till next time," said Tristan. "Gary was just leaving," he told Ivy.

Gary straightened up with a look of mock surprise. "I'm leaving? So soon?"

"Not soon enough," Tristan said, holding open the front door.

"Okay, okay. Catch you later, Ella. Maybe we can hunt mice together."

When Gary left, the room grew suddenly quiet. Tristan couldn't think of anything to say. He had a list of questions – somewhere – behind the sofa where all the other stuff was jammed.

But Ivy didn't seem to expect conversation. She unlatched the door of the cat carrier and pulled out Ella.

The cat was funny-looking, mostly black, but with one white foot, a tip of white on her tail, and a splash of it on her face.

"Okay, baby," Ivy said, holding Ella in her arms, stroking her softly around the ears.

Ella blinked her huge green eyes at Tristan, happily soaking up Ivy's attention.

I can't believe I'm jealous of a cat, Tristan thought.

When Ivy finally set Ella on the floor, Tristan held out his hand. The cat gave him a snooty look and walked away.

"You have to let her come to you," Ivy advised him. "Ignore her, for days, for weeks, if necessary. When she gets lonely enough, she'll come around on her own."

Would Ivy ever?

Tristan picked up a yellow pad. "How about giving me feeding instructions?"

She had already typed them up for him. "And here are Ella's medical records, and here's the list of shots she gets regularly, and the vet's number."

She seemed in a rush to get it over with.

"And here are her toys." Ivy's voice faltered.

"This is hard for you, isn't it?" he said gently.

"And here's her brush; she loves to be brushed."

"But not washed," Tristan said.

Ivy bit her lip. "You don't know anything about cats, do you?"

"I'll learn, I promise. She'll be good for me, and I'll be good for her. Of course, you can visit her as much as you like, Ivy. She'll still be your cat. She'll just be my cat too. You can come see her whenever you want."

"No," Ivy said firmly. "No."

"No?" His heart stopped. He was still sitting upright holding a pile of kitty stuff, but he was sure he'd just had a cardiac arrest.

"It will only mix her up," Ivy explained. "And I don't think – I don't think I can stand to."

He longed to reach out to touch her then, to take one of her slender hands in his, but he didn't dare. Instead he pretended to study the little pink brush and waited for Ivy to regain her composure.

Ella came over to sniff her brush, then pushed her head against it. Tristan gently ran it along her flank.

"She likes it best around her head," Ivy said. She took his hand and guided it. "Under her chin. And her cheeks – that's where her scent glands are, the ones she uses for marking things. I think she likes you, Tristan."

She took her hand away. Tristan continued to brush Ella. The cat suddenly rolled over on her back.

Ivy laughed. "Well, well! You little tramp!"

With his hand Tristan rubbed her belly. The fur was luxuriously long and soft.

"I wonder why cats don't like water," he mused. "If you threw one in a pool, would it swim?"

"Don't you dare!" Ivy said. "Don't you dare do that!"

The cat leaped to its feet and scooted under a chair.

Tristan looked at Ivy with surprise. "Of course I wouldn't. I was just wondering."

She dropped her eyes. Color crept into her cheeks.

"Is that what happened to you, Ivy?"

When she didn't answer, he tried again. "What made you afraid of water?" he asked quietly. "Something from when you were a little kid?"

Ivy wouldn't look at him. "I owe you big time," she said, "for getting me down from that board."

"You don't owe me anything. I was just asking because I was trying to understand. Swimming is my life. It's hard for me to imagine what it's like not to love water."

"I don't see how you could understand," Ivy

said. "Water to you is like wind to a bird. It lets you fly. At least that's how it looks. It's hard for me to imagine how that feels."

"What made you afraid of it?" he persisted. "Who made you afraid of it?"

She thought for a moment. "I don't even remember his name. One of my mother's boyfriends. She had a lot of them and some of them were nice. But he was mean. He took us to a friend's pool. I was four, I think. I didn't know how to swim and didn't want to go in the water. I guess I got annoying after a while, hanging on to Mom."

She swallowed and glanced up at Tristan.

"And?" he said softly.

"Mom went inside for a few minutes, to help with sandwiches or something. He grabbed hold of me. I knew what he was going to do and started kicking and screaming, but Mom didn't hear me. He dragged me over to the pool's edge. 'Let's see if she'll swim!' he said, 'Let's see if the cat will swim!' He picked me up high and threw me in."

Tristan flinched, as if he were there, actually watching it.

"The water was way over my head," Ivy continued. "I floundered around, kicking and moving my arms, but I couldn't keep my face above water. I started choking on it, swallowing it. I couldn't get up for air."

Tristan stared at her, incredulous. "And this guy, did he jump in after you?"

"No." Ivy had risen to her feet and was moving around the room like a restless cat. Ella poked her head out to watch, a dust ball hanging from her whiskers.

"I'm pretty sure he was drunk," Ivy said. "Everything started getting blurry to me. Then dark. My arms and legs seemed so heavy, and my chest felt like it would burst. I prayed. For the first time in my life, I prayed to my guardian angel. Then I felt myself being lifted up, held above the water. My lungs stopped hurting, my eyes grew clear. I don't remember much about the angel, except that she was shining, and many colors, and beautiful."

Ivy glanced sideways at Tristan, then broke into a wide smile. She came back to him and sat on the floor again, facing him.

"It's okay. I don't expect you to believe me. Nobody else did. Apparently my mother had come out to see what was going on and her friend had turned around to speak to her, so no one saw how I made it back to the pool's edge. They just figured that, thrown in, a kid would learn to swim." Her face was wistful. She was somewhere else again, still remembering.

"I'd like to believe in your angel," Tristan said. Then he shrugged. "Sorry." He had heard stories like it before. His father occasionally brought such tales home from the hospital. But it was just the way the human mind worked, he thought; it was the way certain minds respond in a crisis.

"You know, when I was up there on the board on Monday," Ivy said, "I prayed to my water angel."

"But all you got was me," Tristan pointed out.

"Good enough," she replied, and laughed a little.

"Ivy—" He tried to still the tremor in his voice, not wanting her to know how much he was hoping. "I could teach you how to swim."

Her eyes opened wide.

"After school. The coach would let us in the pool."

Her hands, her eyes, everything about her was still and watching him.

"It's a great feeling, Ivy. Do you know what it's like to float on a lake, a circle of trees around you, a big blue bowl of sky above you? You're just lying on top of the water, sun sparkling at the tips of your fingers and toes. Do you know how it feels to swim in the ocean? To be swimming hard and have a wave catch you and effortlessly lift you up—"

Without realizing what he was doing, he put a hand on each arm and lifted her. Her skin was covered with goose bumps.

"Sorry," he said, letting her down quickly. "I'm sorry. I got carried away."

"It's okay," she said, but she wouldn't look at him again.

He wondered which she was more afraid of, the water or him.

Probably him, he thought, and he didn't know what to do about it "I'd make it fun, just like when I teach the kids at summer camp," Tristan said encouragingly. "Think about it, okay?"

She nodded.

Clearly he made her uncomfortable. He wished he could apologize for plowing into her in the hall, for showing up at her mother's wedding, for calling her about her cat He wanted to promise her that he wouldn't bother her anymore, hoping that would put her at ease. But she suddenly looked so confused and tired; it seemed best not to say anything else.

"I'll be real good to Ella," he told her. "If something changes and you want her back, give me a call. And if you decide that you do want to visit her, I don't have to be around. Okay?"

Ivy looked up at him wonderingly.

"So," he said, standing up. "I'm the cook Tuesdays and Fridays. I'd better start dinner."

"What are you fixing?" Ivy asked.

"Liver bits and gravy. Oh, no, sorry, that's Ella's can."

It was a weak joke, but she smiled.

"Stay and play with Ella as long as you like," he told her.

"Thank you."

Then he headed toward the kitchen to give her some time alone with the cat. But before he had gotten to the doorway he heard her say, "Good-bye, Ella." A moment later, the front door clicked shut behind her.

When Ivy emerged from the locker room, Tristan was already in the water. Coach had let her into the locked pool area. She had expected the older man to stare at her in disbelief – "You mean you don't know how to swim?" But his face, which was long and lined like a raisin, was kind and unquestioning. He greeted her, then retreated to his office.

It had taken Ivy a week to decide to do this. She had swum in her dreams, for miles some nights. When she told Tristan she wanted to learn, his eyes had lit up. Ivy was pretty sure she had successfully discouraged any romantic interest he had in her – according to Suzanne, he was dating two other girls. But she felt as if he was her friend. Getting her down from the board, taking in Ella, helping her face her greatest fear – he was there when she needed him, the way no other guy had been, the way a real friend would be.

Now she watched him doing laps. The water flowed past his muscular body; it lifted him up as he moved swiftly and powerfully through it. When he swam the butterfly, his arms pulling up out of the water like wings, he was visual music – strong, rhythmic, graceful.

Ivy watched for several minutes, then came back to the reason she was there. She walked to the pool's edge at the shallow end and stared down at it. Then she sat down and slipped in her legs. It was warm. Soothing. Still, she was cold all over. She gritted her teeth and slid off the side. The water rose to just below her shoulders. She imagined it inching up over her throat, her mouth. She closed her eyes and gripped the side of the pool, trying to stop the fear rising within her.

Water angel, she prayed, don't let go of me. I'm trusting you, angel. I'm in your hands.

Tristan stopped swimming. "You're here," he said. "You're in."

He looked so pleased that for a moment, a very brief moment, she forgot her fear.

"How are you doing?" he asked.

"Fine. You don't mind if I just stand here and shake, do you?"

"You'll warm up if you move around," he told her.

She glanced down at the water.

"Come on, let's take a walk." He took her

hand and walked her along the edge of the pool, as if they were walking the mall, though in the resistant water each step was in slow motion.

"Do you want me to tell you about Ella and the chaos she's creating at home?"

"Sure," said Ivy. "Did she find that tub of chicken wedged into your television cabinet?"

Tristan looked startled for a moment, then recovered. "Yes, right after she burrowed through all the stuff I'd crammed behind the sofa." He chattered on, telling her several Ella stories, walking her up and down the short end of the pool.

When they stopped, he said, "I think we'd better get some water on your face."

She had been dreading that.

He scooped handfuls of it up over her forehead and cheeks as if he were washing a baby.

"I do that in the shower," Ivy said tartly.

"Well, excuse me, Miss Advanced. We'll go on to the next step." He grinned at her. "Take a big breath. I want to see you looking at me under there. The chlorine will sting a little, but I want to see those big green eyes and little bubbles coming out of your nose. Suck in above the water, blow out below it. Got it? One, two, three." He pulled her down with him. Up and down they bobbed, he holding her down there a little longer each time, making faces at her.

Ivy came up to the surface, sputtering and choking.

"Now, if you can't follow a few simple directions . . ." he began.

"You're making me laugh!" said Ivy. "It's no fair when you make me laugh."

"All right. Now we get serious. Sort of."

He taught her how she would breathe when swimming, pretending the water was a pillow, turning her head to the side to breathe in. She practiced, gripping the side of the pool with her hands. Then he took her hands and pulled her through the water. She naturally started kicking her feet to keep them afloat behind her. It was tempting to pull her head up and look at him. Once Ivy did and found him smiling at her.

They worked on kicking for a while. After she practiced on the side, they played train. He had her grab his ankles, following behind him in the water, he swimming with his arms and she kicking her feet. It amazed her that he could pull her so swiftly with just the strength of his arms.

When they stopped, he asked her, "Are you getting tired? Do you want to sit up on the side for a few minutes?"

Ivy shook her head no. "If I get out, I don't know if I'll get in again."

"You've got guts," he said.

She laughed. "I'm standing in water just up to my shoulders and you call that guts?"

"Yup." He swam in a circle around her. "Ivy, everyone has something they're afraid of. You're one of the few people who face their fear. But then, I always knew you were the gutsy type. I knew from the first day, when I saw you striding across the cafeteria, that cheerleader, who was supposed to be leading you around, following."

"I was hungry," Ivy said. "And that was a bit of a performance."

"Well, you carried it off."

She smiled and he reflected her smile, his hazel eyes alight and lashes spangled with water drops.

"Okay," he said. "Want to float on your back?"

"No. But I will."

"It's easy." Tristan stretched back in the water and floated, looking entirely relaxed. "You see what I'm doing?"

Looking *awfully* good, she thought, then thanked her angels that he couldn't read minds as well as Beth.

"I keep my hips up, arch my back, then just let everything else go. You try it."

Ivy did, and sank. The old panic returned for a moment.

"You were sitting," he told her. "You let your seat drop down. Try again."

As she lay back again he slid an arm under her. "Easy now, don't fight it. Back arched. That's the way." He slipped his arm out from under her.

Ivy pulled her head up and started to sink again. She stood up angrily. Her wet hair was coming loose out of her ponytail holder and slapped against her neck.

Tristan laughed. "That's how I imagine Ella would look if she ever got wet."

"A little kid could do this," Ivy told him.

"Kids can do a lot of things," he replied, "because kids trust. The trick in swimming is not to fight the water. Go with it. Play with it. Give yourself over to it." He splashed her lightly. "How about trying again?"

She lay back. She felt his left arm under the arch in her back. With his right hand he gently eased her head back. The water lapped around her forehead and chin. Ivy closed her eyes and gave herself over to the water. She imagined being in the center of a lake, sunlight sparkling at her toes and fingertips.

When she opened her eyes, he was looking down at her. His face was like the sun, warming her, brightening the air around it. "I'm floating," she whispered.

"You're floating," he said softly, his face bending closer.

"Floating . . ." They read it off each other's lips, their faces close, so close—

"Tristan!"

Tristan straightened up and Ivy sank.

It was Coach, calling from the door of his office. "Sorry to toss you two out," he hollered, "but I got to head home in about ten minutes."

"No problem, Coach," Tristan called back.

"I'll be staying late tomorrow," the older man added, coming a few feet out of his office. "Maybe then you can pick up where you left off?"

Tristan looked at Ivy. She shrugged, then nodded, but kept her eyes down.

"Maybe," he said.

8

Ivy took a long route home that afternoon, driving a road that ran south from the center of Stonehill, following a tangle of shady streets lined with newer houses. She drove round and round, unwilling to make the final turn and head for the ridge. There was so much to think about. Why was Tristan doing this? Was he just feeling sorry for her? Did he want to be her friend? Did he want more than a friendship?

But it wasn't these questions that kept her driving. It was the luxury of remembering: how he had looked rising out of the water, a shimmer of drops spilling off him; how he had touched her, gently, so gently.

At home, she'd have to listen to her mother's story about the latest round of snobbery that

Maggie was encountering; she'd talk about the ups and downs of Philip's life as a third grader; she'd find a new way to say thanks for the things Andrew kept giving her, and walk on eggshells around Gregory. With all that going on, the moments of the afternoon would fade and be lost forever.

In her mind, Ivy saw Tristan in slow motion, swimming in a circle around her. She remembered the way his hands had felt when he helped her float, the way he had slowly tilted her head back in the water. She trembled with pleasure, and a little fear.

Angels, don't let go of me! she prayed.

This was something different from a crush. This was something that could flood out every other thought and feeling.

Maybe I should back out now, Ivy thought, before I'm in over my head. I'll call him tonight.

But then she remembered how he had pulled her through the water, his face full of light and laughter.

Ivy didn't see the car coming. Lost in thought, responding only to what was directly in front of her, she didn't see the dark car run the stop sign until the very last second. She slammed on her brakes. Both cars squealed and spun around, and for a moment were side by side, lightly touching. Then they veered away from each other. Letting her breath out slowly, Ivy sat still in the middle of the intersection.

The other driver threw open his door. A stream of four-letter words came rushing at her. Without even glancing in his direction, Ivy rolled up her window and checked her door locks. The shouting stopped suddenly. Ivy turned to look coolly at the driver.

"Gregory!"

She put her window down.

His skin was pale except for the scarlet that had crept up his cheeks. He stared at her, then glanced around the intersection, looking surprised, as if he were just now recognizing where he was and what had happened.

"Are you okay?" she asked.

"Yes . . . yes. Are you?"

"Well, I'm breathing again,"

"I'm sorry," he said. "I – I wasn't paying attention, I guess. And I didn't know it was you, Ivy." Though his anger had subsided, he still looked upset.

"That's okay," she said. "I was driving in a daze, too."

He glanced through the window at the wet towel on her front seat.

"What are you doing around here?" he wanted to know.

She wondered if he would make the connection

between the wet towel and swimming and Tristan. But she hadn't even told Beth or Suzanne what she was doing. Besides, it wouldn't matter to Gregory.

"I needed to think about something. I know it sounds crazy, with all the space we have at the house, but I, well—"

"Needed other space," he finished for her. "I know how that is. Are you heading home now?"

"Yes."

"Follow me." He gave her a brief, lopsided smile. "Behind me, you'll be safer."

"You're sure you're okay?" she asked. His eyes still looked troubled.

He nodded, then returned to his car.

When they arrived home, Andrew pulled into the driveway after them.

He greeted Ivy, then turned to Gregory. "So how is your mother?"

Gregory shrugged. "Same as always."

"I'm glad you went to visit her today."

"I gave her your good wishes and fondest regards," Gregory said, his face and voice deadpan.

Andrew nodded and stepped around a spilled box of colored chalk. He bent over to look at what had once been clean, white concrete at the edge of his garage.

"Is anything new with her? Is there anything

I should know about?" he asked. He was studying the chalk drawings done by Philip; he didn't catch the pause, didn't see the emotion on Gregory's face that passed as fast as it came. But Ivy did.

"Nothing new," he said to his father.

"Good."

Ivy waited till the door closed behind Andrew.

"Do you want to talk about it?" she asked Gregory.

He spun around, as if he had forgotten that she was there.

"Talk about what?"

Ivy hesitated, then said, "You just told your father that everything's fine with your mom. But from the look on your face, at the intersection and just now, when you were talking about her, I thought maybe . . ."

Gregory played with his keys. "You're right. Things aren't fine. There may be some trouble ahead."

"With your mother?"

"I can't talk about it. Look, I appreciate your concern, but I can handle this myself. If you really want to help me, then don't say anything to anyone, all right? Don't even mention our little run-in. Promise me." His eyes held hers.

Ivy shrugged. "Promise," she said. "But if

you change your mind, you know where to find me.

"In the middle of an intersection," he said, giving her one of his wry smiles, then went inside.

Before going in, Ivy stopped to study Philip's concrete masterpiece. She recognized the bright aqua of her water angel, and the strong brown lines of Tony. After a moment, she identified the characters from Ben 10. Philip's dragons were easy to spot; they usually looked as if they had swallowed a vat of lighter fluid, and they always fought Ben 10 and the angels. But what was that? A round head, with funny bits of hair and a green stick coming out of each ear?

The name was scrawled on the side. Tristan.

Picking up a piece of black chalk, Ivy filled in two olive teeth. Now he looked like the guy who was kind enough to cheer up an eight-year-old having a very tough day. Ivy remembered the look on Tristan's face when she had yanked open the storeroom door. She threw back her head and laughed.

Back out now? Who was she kidding?

Tristan was sure he had scared Ivy away that first day, but she came back, and from the second lesson on he was very careful. He barely touched her; he coached her like a professional; and he kept dating what's her name and that other girl. But it was getting more difficult for him each day, being alone with Ivy, standing so close to her, hoping for some sign that she wanted something other than lessons and friendship.

"I think it's time, Ella," he said to the cat after two frustrating weeks of lessons. "She's not interested, and I can't stand it anymore. I'm going to get Ivy to sign up at the Y."

Ella purred.

"Then I'm going to find myself a monastery with a swim team."

The next day he made a conscious decision not to change into his bathing suit. He pocketed a brochure for the Y, strode out of the pool office, then stopped.

Ivy wasn't there. She forgot, he thought, then he saw Ivy's towel and ponytail holder down by the deep end. "Ivy!"

He ran to the edge of the pool and saw her in the twelve-foot section, lying all the way at the bottom, motionless. "Oh, my God!"

He dove straight off the side, pulling, pulling through the water to get to her. He yanked her up to the surface and swam for the pool's edge. It was difficult; she had come to and was struggling with him. His clothes were an extra, dragging weight. He heaved Ivy up on the side of the pool and sprang up beside her.

"What in the world—?" she said. She wasn't coughing, wasn't sputtering, wasn't out of breath. She was just staring at him, at his soaked shirt, his clinging jeans, his sagging socks. Tristan stared back, then threw his waterlogged shoes as far as he could, down several rows of bleachers.

"What were you doing?" she asked.

"What were *you* doing?"

She opened her hand to show him a shiny copper penny. "Diving for this."

Anger surged through him. "The first rule of swimming, Ivy, is never, never swim alone!"

"But I had to do it, Tristan! I had to see if I could face my nightmare without you, without my – my lifeguard close by. And I could. I did," she said, a dazzling smile breaking over her face. Her hair was hanging loose around her shoulders. Her eyes were smiling into his, the color of an emerald sea in brilliant sunlight.

Then she blinked. "Is that what you were doing – being a lifeguard, being a hero?"

"No, Ivy," he said quietly, and stood up. "I was proving once again that I'm a hero to everyone but you."

"Wait a minute," she said, but he started to walk away.

"Wait a minute!" He didn't get far, not with the weight of her hanging on to one leg.

"I said wait."

He tried to pull away, but she had him firmly anchored.

"Is that what you want, for me to say you're a hero?"

He grimaced. "I guess not. I guess I thought it would get me what I want. But it didn't."

"Well, what do you want?" she asked.

Was there any point in telling her now?

"To change into dry clothes," he said. "I've got some sweats in my locker."

"Okay." She released his leg. But before he could move away, she caught his hand. She held it in both of her hands for a moment, then lightly kissed the tips of his fingers.

She peeked up at him, gave a little shrug, then let go. But now it was he who held on, twining his fingers in hers. After a moment of hesitation, she rested her head against his hand. Could she feel it – the way just her lightest touch made his pulse race? He knelt down. Taking her other hand in his, he kissed her fingertips, then he laid his cheek in her palm.

She lifted up his face.

"Ivy," he said. The word was like a kiss. "Ivy."

The word became a kiss.

9

"He beat me!" Tristan said. "Philip beat me two out of three games!"

Ivy rested her hands on the piano keys, looked over her shoulder at Tristan, and laughed. It had been a week since their first trembling kiss. Every night she had fallen asleep dreaming about that kiss, and each kiss after.

It was all so incredible to her. She was aware of the lightest touch, the softest brush against him. Every time he called her name, her answer came from somewhere deep inside her. Yet there was something so easy and natural about being with him. Sometimes it felt as if Tristan had been a part of her life for years, sprawled as he was now on the floor of her music room, playing checkers with Philip.

"I can't believe he beat me two out of three!"

"Almost three out of three," Philip crowed.

"That will teach you not to mess with Ginger," Ivy said.

Tristan frowned down at the angel statue that stood alone on the checkerboard. Philip always used her as one of his playing pieces.

The three-inch china angel had once been Ivy's, but when Philip was in kindergarten, he'd decided to pretty her up. Sparkly-pink nail polish on her dress and crusty gold glitter on her hair had given her a whole new look; and Ivy had given her to Philip.

"Ginger's very smart," he told Tristan.

Tristan glanced up doubtfully at Ivy.

"Maybe next time Philip will let you borrow her and *you* can win," Ivy said with a smile, then turned to Philip. "Isn't it getting late?"

"Why do you always say that?" her brother asked.

Tristan grinned. "Because she's trying to get rid of you. Come on. We'll read two stories, like the last time, then it's lights out."

He walked Philip down to his bedroom. Ivy stayed upstairs and began to flip through her piano books, looking for songs that Tristan might like. He was into hard rock, but she couldn't exactly play it on the piano. He knew nothing about Beethoven and Bach. Tristan's idea of classical music was the musicals from his parents' collection. She ran through several songs from *Carousel,* then put the old book aside.

All night there had been music running through her like a silver river. Now she turned out the lights and played it from memory, Beethoven's *Moonlight Sonata.*

Tristan returned in the middle of the sonata. He saw the slight hesitation in her hands and heard the pause in the music.

"Don't stop," he said softly, and came to stand behind her.

Ivy played to the end. For a few moments after the last chord, neither of them spoke, neither of them moved. There was only the still, silver moonlight on the piano keys, and the music, the way music can linger on sometimes in silence.

Then Ivy rested her back against him.

"You want to dance?" Tristan asked.

Ivy laughed, and he pulled her up and they danced a circle around the room. She laid her head on his shoulder and felt his strong arms around her. They danced slow, slower. She wished he would never let go.

"How do you do that?" he whispered. "How do you dance with me and play the piano at the same time?"

"At the same time?"

"Isn't that *you* making the music I hear?"

Ivy pulled her head up. "Tristan, that line is so . . . so . . ."

"Corny," he said. "But it got you to look up at me." Then he swiftly lowered his mouth and stole a long, soft kiss.

"Don't forget to tell Tristan to stop by the shop sometime," Lillian said "Betty and I would love to see him again. We're very fond of chunks."

"*Hunks,* Lillian," Ivy said with a grin. "Tristan is a hunk." My hunk, she thought, then picked up a box wrapped in brown paper. "Is this everything to be delivered?"

"Yes, thank you, dear. I know it's out of your way."

"Not too far," Ivy said, starting out the door.

"Five-twenty-eight Willow Street," Betty called from the back of the store.

"Five-thirty," Lillian said quietly.

Well, that narrows it down, Ivy thought, passing through the door of 'Tis the Season. She glanced at her watch. Now she wouldn't have time to spend with her friends.

Suzanne and Beth had been waiting for her at the mall's food court.

"You said you would be off twenty minutes ago," Suzanne complained.

"I know. It's been one of those days," Ivy replied. "Will you walk me to my car? I have to deliver this, then get right home."

"Did you hear that? She has to get right home," Suzanne said to Beth, "for a birthday party, that's what she *says*. She *says* it's Philip's ninth birthday."

"It's May twenty-eighth," Ivy responded. "You know it is, Suzanne."

"But for all we know," Suzanne went on to Beth, "it's a private wedding on the hill."

Ivy rolled her eyes, and Beth laughed. Suzanne still hadn't forgiven her for keeping the swimming lessons secret.

"Is Tristan coming tonight?" Beth asked as they exited the mall.

"He's one of Philip's two guests," Ivy replied, "and will be sitting next to Philip, not me, and playing all night with Philip, not me. Tristan promised. It was about the only way to keep my brother from coming with us to the prom. Hey, where did you two park?"

Suzanne couldn't remember and Beth hadn't noticed. Ivy drove them around and around the mall lot. Beth looked for the car while Suzanne advised Ivy on clothes and romance. She covered everything from telephone strategies and how not to be too available to working hard at looking casual. She had been giving volumes of advice for the last three weeks.

"Suzanne, I think you make dating too complicated," Ivy said at last. "All this plotting and planning. It seems pretty simple to me."

Incredibly simple, she thought. Whether she and Tristan were relaxing or studying together, whether they were sitting silently side by side or both trying to talk at the same time – which they did frequently – these last few weeks had been incredibly easy.

"That's because he's the one," Beth said knowingly.

There was only one thing about Ivy that Tristan couldn't understand. The angels.

"You've had a difficult life," he had said to her one night. It was the night of the prom – or rather, the morning after, but not yet dawn. They were walking barefoot in the grass, away from the house to the far edge of the ridge. In the west, a crescent moon hung like a leftover Christmas ornament. There was one star. Far below them, a train wound its silver path through the valley.

"You've been through so much, I don't blame you for believing," Tristan said.

"You don't blame me? You don't *blame* me? What do you mean by that?" But she knew what he meant. To him, an angel was just a pretty teddy bear — something for a child to cling to.

He held her tightly in his arms. "I can't believe, Ivy. I have all I need and all I want right here on earth," he said. "Right *here*. In my arms."

"Well, I don't," she replied, and even in the pale light, she could see the sting in his eyes. They started to fight then. Ivy realized for the first time that the more you love, the more you hurt. What was worse, you hurt for him as well as for yourself.

After he left, she cried all morning. Her phone calls hadn't been returned that afternoon. But he came back in the evening, with fifteen lavender roses. One for each angel, he said.

"Ivy! Ivy, did you hear anything I just said?" Suzanne asked, jolting her back to the present. "You know, I thought if we got you a boyfriend, you'd come down to earth a little. But I was wrong. Head still in the clouds! Angel zone!"

"*We* didn't get her a boyfriend," Beth said quietly but firmly. "They found each other. Here's the car, Ivy. Have a good time tonight. We'd better dash, it's going to storm."

The girls jumped out and Ivy checked her watch again. Now she was really late. She sped over the access road and down the highway.

When she crossed the river, she noticed how rapidly the dark clouds were moving.

Her delivery was to one of the newer houses south of town, the same neighborhood where she had driven after her first swimming lesson with Tristan. It seemed as if everything she did now made her think of him.

She got just as lost this time, driving around in circles, with one eye on the clouds. Thunder rumbled. The trees shivered and turned over their leaves, shining an eerie lime green against the leaden sky. The wind began to gust. Branches whipped, and blossoms and tender leaves were torn too soon from their limbs. Ivy leaned forward in her seat, intent on finding the right house before the storm broke.

Just finding the right street was difficult. She thought she was on Willow, but the sign said Fernway, with Willow running into it. She got out of her car to see if the sign could have been turned – a popular sport among kids in town. Then she heard a loud motor making the bend on the hill above her. She stepped out into the street to wave down the motorcyclist. For a moment, the Harley slowed, then the engine was gunned and the cyclist flew past her.

Well, she'd have to go with her instincts. The lawns were steep there, and Lillian had said that Mrs. Abromaitis lived on a hill, a flight of stone steps lined with flowerpots leading up to her house.

Ivy drove around the bend. She could feel the rising wind rocking her car. Overhead the pale sky was being swallowed up by inky clouds.

Ivy screeched to a halt in front of two houses and pulled the box out of the car, struggling with it against the wind. Both houses had stone steps that ran up side by side. Both had flowerpots. She chose one set of steps, and just as she cleared the first flowerpot it blew over and crashed behind her. Ivy screamed, then laughed at herself.

At the top of the steps she looked at one house, then the other, 528 and 530, hoping for some kind of clue. A car was pulled around the back of 528, hidden by bushes, so someone was probably home. Then she saw a figure in the large window of 528 – someone looking out for her, she thought, though she couldn't tell if it was a man or a woman, or if the person actually beckoned to her. All she could see was a vague shape of a person as part of the window's reflected collage of thrashing trees backlit by flashes of lightning. She started toward the house. The figure disappeared. At the same time, the front porch light went on at 530. The screen door banged back in the wind.

"Ivy? Ivy?" A woman called to her from the lit porch.

"Whew!" She made a run for it, handed off the package, and raced for her car. The skies opened, throwing down ropes of rain. Well, it wouldn't be the first time Tristan had seen her looking like a drowned rat.

Ivy, Gregory, and Andrew arrived home late, and Maggie looked miffed. Philip, of course, didn't care. He, Tristan, and his new school pal, Sammy, were playing a computer game, one of the many gifts Andrew had bought for his birthday.

Tristan grinned up at the drenched Ivy. "I'm glad I taught you to swim," he said, then got up to kiss her.

She was dripping all over the hardwood floor. "I'll soak you," she warned.

He wrapped his arms around her and pulled her close. "I'll dry," he whispered. "Besides, it's fun to gross out Philip."

"Ew," said Philip, as if on cue.

"Mush," agreed Sammy.

Ivy and Tristan held on to each other and laughed. Then Ivy ran upstairs to change her clothes and wring out her hair. She put on lipstick, no other makeup – her eyes were already bright and her cheeks full of color. She scrounged around in her jewelry box for a pair of earrings, then hurried downstairs just in time to see Philip finish opening his presents.

"She's wearing her peacock ears tonight," Philip told Tristan as Ivy sat down to dinner across from the two of them.

"Darn," said Tristan, "I forgot to put in my celery sticks."

"And your shrimp tails." Philip snickered.

Ivy wondered who was happier at that moment, Philip or her. She knew that life did not seem so good to Gregory. It had been a rough week for him; he had confided in her that he was still very worried about his mother, though he wouldn't tell her why. Lately his father and he had had little to say to each other. Maggie struggled to converse with him but usually gave up.

Ivy turned to him now. "The tickets to the Yankees game were a terrific idea. Philip was thrilled with the present."

"He had a funny way of showing it."

It was true. Philip had thanked him very politely, then leaped up with excitement when he saw the old *Sports Illustrated* spread on Derek Jeter that Tristan had dug up.

During dinner Ivy made an effort to keep Gregory in the conversation. Tristan tried to talk to him about sports and cars but received mostly one-word replies. Andrew looked irritated, though Tristan didn't seem to take offense.

Andrew's cook, Henry — who'd been let go after the wedding, but reinstated after six weeks of Maggie's cooking — had made them a delicious dinner. Maggie, however, had insisted on baking her son's birthday cake. Henry carried in the heavy, lopsided thing, his eyes averted.

Philip's face lit up. "It's Mistake Cake!"

The rich and lumpy chocolate frosting supported nine candles at various angles. Lights were quickly extinguished and everyone sang to Philip. With the last measure, the doorbell chimed. Andrew frowned and rose to answer it.

From her seat, Ivy could see into the hall. Two police officers, a man and a woman, talked with Andrew. Gregory leaned into Ivy to see what was going on.

"What do you think it's about?" Ivy whispered.

"Something at the college," he guessed.

Tristan looked across the table questioningly and Ivy shrugged her shoulders. Her mother, unaware that there might be something wrong, kept cutting the cake.

Then Andrew stepped back into the room.

"Maggie." She must have read something in

his eyes. She dropped the knife immediately and went to Andrew's side. He took her hand.

"Gregory and Ivy, would you join us in the library, please? Tristan, could you stay with the boys?" he asked.

The officers were still waiting in the hall. Andrew led the way to the library. If there were a problem at the college, we wouldn't be gathering like this, thought Ivy.

When everyone was seated, Andrew said, "There's no easy way to begin. Gregory, your mother has died."

"Oh, no," Maggie said softly.

Ivy turned quickly to Gregory. He sat stiffly, his eyes on his father, and said nothing.

"The police received an anonymous call about five-thirty P.M. that someone at her address needed help. When they arrived, they found her dead, a gunshot wound to her head."

Gregory didn't blink. Ivy reached out for his hand. It was cold as ice.

"The police have asked— They need— As a matter of normal procedure—" Andrew's voice wavered. He turned to face the police officers. "Perhaps one of you can take over from here?"

"As a matter of procedure," the woman officer said, "we need to ask a few questions. We are still searching the house for any information that might be relevant to the case, though it seems fairly conclusive that her death was a suicide."

"Oh, God!" said Maggie.

"What evidence do you have for that?" Gregory asked. "While it's true my mother was depressed, she has been since the beginning of April—"

"Oh, God!" Maggie said again. Andrew reached out for her, but she moved away from him.

Ivy knew what her mother was thinking. She remembered the scene a week earlier, when a picture of Caroline and Andrew had somehow turned up in the hall desk. Andrew had told Maggie to throw it in the trash. Maggie could not. She didn't want to think that she was the one who had "thrown Caroline out" of her home – years earlier, or now. Ivy guessed that her mother felt responsible for Caroline's unhappiness, and now her death.

"I'd still like to know," Gregory continued, "what makes you think that she killed herself. That doesn't seem like her. It doesn't seem like her at all. She was too strong a woman."

Ivy could hardly believe how clearly and steadily Gregory could speak.

"First, there is circumstantial evidence," said the policeman. "No actual note, but photographs that were torn and scattered around the body." He glanced toward Maggie.

"Photographs of . . . ?" Gregory asked.

Andrew sucked in his breath.

"Mr. and Mrs. Baines," said the officer. "Newspaper photos from their wedding."

Andrew watched helplessly as Maggie bent over in her chair, her head down, wrapping her arms around her knees.

Ivy let go of Gregory's hand, wanting to comfort her mother, but he pulled her back.

"The gun was still twisted around her thumb. There were powder burns on her fingers, the burns one gets from firing such a weapon. Of course, we'll be checking the gun for prints and the bullet for a match, and we'll let you know if we find something unexpected. But her doors were locked – no sign of forced entry – her air-conditioning on and windows secure, so . . ."

Gregory took a deep breath. "So I guess she wasn't as tough as I thought. What – what time do you think this happened?"

"Between five and five-thirty P.M., not that long before we got there."

An eerie feeling washed over Ivy. She had been driving through the neighborhood then. She had been watching the angry sky and the trees lashing themselves. Had she driven by

Caroline's house? Had Caroline killed herself in the fury of the storm?

Andrew asked if he could talk later with the police and guided Maggie out of the room. Gregory stayed behind to answer questions about his mother and any relationships or problems he knew about. Ivy wanted to leave; she didn't want to hear the details of Caroline's life and longed to be with Tristan, longed for his steadying arms around her.

But Gregory again held her back. His hand was cold and unresponsive to hers and his face still expressionless. His voice was so calm she found it spooky. But something inside him was struggling, some small part of him admitted the horror of what had just happened, and asked for her. So she stayed with him, long after Tristan had gone and everyone else was in bed.

10

"But you told me Gary wanted to go out on *Friday* night," Ivy said.

"He did," Tristan replied, lying back next to her in the grass. "But his date changed her mind. I think she got a better offer."

Ivy shook her head. "Why does Gary always chase the golden girls?"

"Why does Suzanne chase Gregory?" he countered.

Ivy smiled. "Same reason Ella chases butterflies, I guess." She watched the cat's leaping ballet. Ella was very much at home in Reverend Carruthers's garden. In the midst of snapdragons, lilies, roses, and herbs, Tristan's father had planted a little patch of catnip.

"Is Saturday night a problem?" Tristan asked.

"If you're working, we could make it a late movie."

Ivy sat up. Tristan came first with her, always. But with their plans set for Friday night and Sunday too – well, she might as well blurt it out, she thought. "Gregory has invited Suzanne, Beth, and me out with some of his friends that night."

Tristan didn't hide his surprise or his displeasure.

"Suzanne was so eager," Ivy said quickly. "And Beth was really excited, too – she doesn't go out very much."

"And you?" Tristan asked, propping himself up on one elbow, twisting a long piece of grass.

"I think I should go – for Gregory's sake."

"You've been doing a lot for Gregory's sake in the last few weeks."

"Tristan, his mother killed herself!" Ivy exploded.

"I know that."

"I live in the same house with him," she went on. "I share the same kitchen and hallways and family room. I see his moods, his ups and downs. Lots of downs," she added softly, thinking about how some days Gregory did nothing but sit and read the newspaper, thumbing through it as if in search of something, but never finding it.

"I think he's very angry," she went on. "He tries to hide it, but I think he's furious at his mother for killing herself. The other night, one-thirty in the morning, he was out on the tennis court, banging balls against the wall."

That night, Ivy had gone out to talk to him. When she had called to him, he turned, and she had seen the depth of his anger and his pain.

"Believe me, Tristan, I help him when I can, and I'll keep on helping him, but if you think I have any special feelings for him, if you think he and I— That's ridiculous! If you think— I can't believe you'd—"

"Whoa, whoa." He wrestled her down in the grass with him. "I'm not worried about anything like that."

"Then what's bugging you?"

"Two things, I guess," he replied. "One, I think you may be doing a lot out of guilt."

"Guilt!" She pushed him back and sat up again.

"I think you've picked up your mother's attitude, that she and her family are responsible for Caroline's unhappiness."

"We're not."

"I know that. I just want to make sure you do – and that you're not trying to make it up to someone who is milking it for all it's worth."

"You don't know what you're talking about,"

Ivy said, pulling up tufts of grass. "You really don't know what he's going through. You haven't been around Gregory. You—"

"I've been around him since first grade."

"People can change from first grade."

"I've known Eric for that long, too," Tristan continued. "They've done some pretty wild, even dangerous things together. And that's the other thing that worries me."

"But Gregory wouldn't try stuff with my friends and me around," Ivy insisted. "He respects me, Tristan. This is just his way of reaching out, after the last three weeks."

Tristan didn't look convinced.

"Please don't let this come between us," she said.

He reached up for her face. "I wouldn't let anything come between us. Not mountains, rivers, continents, war, floods—"

"Or dire death itself," she said. "So you did read Beth's latest story."

"Gary ate it up."

"Gary? You're kidding!"

"He kept the copy you gave me," Tristan said, "but I swore to him that I'd tell you I lost it."

Ivy laughed and lay down close to Tristan, resting her head on his shoulder. "You understand, then, why I said yes to Gregory."

"No, but it's your choice," he said. "And that's that. So what are you doing *next* Saturday night?"

"What are *you* doing?" Ivy asked back.

"Dining at the Durney Inn."

"The inn! Well, we must be earning big bucks giving swimming lessons this summer."

"We're earning enough," he said. "You don't happen to know of a beautiful girl who likes to be treated to candlelight and French food, do you?"

"Yeah, I do."

"Is she free that night?"

"Maybe. Does she get an appetizer?"

"Three, if she likes."

"How about dessert?"

"Raspberry souffle. And kisses."

"*Kisses . . .*"

"Well, that was fun," Ivy remarked dryly.

"I was bored anyway," Eric said.

"I wasn't," Beth told them. She was the last one to leave the party at the campus sorority house that Saturday night. Borrowing paper from one of the sorority sisters, she had interviewed just about everyone there. When the other high-schoolers had been thrown out, she was invited to stay. Sigma Pi Nu was flattered that she would put them in a story.

"Eric, you're going to have to learn to keep

your cool," Gregory said, clearly irritated. He had been in the corner with some redhead (which had prompted Suzanne to go body to body with a bearded guy) when Eric decided to pick a fight with a giant wearing a varsity football shirt. Not smart.

Now Eric stood on the steps of a pillared building, staring up at a statue and cocking his head left and right, as if he were conversing with it.

Suzanne lay on her back on a stone bench in the college quad, laughing softly to herself, her bare knees up, her skirt fluttering back provocatively. Gregory eyed her.

Ivy turned away. She and Will were the only ones who hadn't been drinking. Will had seemed at home at the campus party scene, but restless. Perhaps the rumors at school were true: he had seen it all and nothing much impressed him.

Like Ivy, Will had been a newcomer in January. His father was a television producer in New York, however, which scored big points with the kids at school. Upon arrival, he had been immediately taken up by the fast crowd, but his silent manner kept everyone from getting a real fix on him. It was easy to imagine a lot of things about Will, and most people that Ivy knew imagined he was very cool.

"Where'sss your old man?" Eric suddenly

shouted. He was still peering up at the statue on the steps. "G.B., where's your old man?"

"That's my old man's old man," Gregory replied.

Ivy realized then that it was a statue of Gregory's grandfather. Of course. They were in front of Baines Hall.

"Why isssn't your old man up there?"

Gregory sat down on a bench across from Suzanne. "I guess because he's not dead yet." He took a deep swig from a beer bottle.

"Then why isssn't your old lady up there? Huh?"

Gregory didn't reply. He took another long drink.

Eric frowned up at the statue. "I miss her. I misssss old Caroline. You know I do."

"I know," Gregory said quietly.

"Ssso, let's put her up there." He winked at Gregory.

Gregory didn't say anything, and Ivy went to stand behind him. She rested one hand lightly on Gregory's shoulder.

"I got Caroline right here in my pocket," Eric said.

All of them watched as he patted and searched his shirt and pants. Finally he pulled out a bra. He held it up to his cheek. "Still warm."

Ivy laid her other hand on Gregory's shoulder. She could feel the tension in him.

Eric wrapped the bra around his arm and struggled to climb up on the statue.

"You're going to kill yourself," Gregory told him.

"Like your mother," said Eric.

Gregory made no response except to take another drink. Ivy turned his head away from Eric. Gregory let his face rest against her then, and she felt him relax a little. Both Suzanne and Will watched the two of them, Suzanne with flashing eyes.

But Ivy stayed where she was while Eric put the bra on Judge Baines. Then she confiscated a few unopened beers and walked over to Suzanne. "Gregory could use some hand-holding," she said to her friend.

"Even after you and the redhead."

Ivy ignored the comment. Suzanne had also had too much to drink.

Eric gave a sudden yelp, and they turned quickly to see him sliding off the statue. He landed in the gravel and rolled up like a snail. Will hurried over to him. Gregory laughed.

"Nothing broken but my brain," Eric muttered as Will pulled him to his feet.

"I think we should get back to the car," Will said coolly.

"But the party's just begun," Gregory protested, rising to his feet. The alcohol was obviously kicking in. "I haven't felt this good since who knows when."

"I know when," said Eric.

"The party will be over soon enough if the campus police catch us," Will pointed out.

"My father's the prez," said Gregory. "He'll get us off the hook."

"Or hang us from a higher one," said Eric.

Ivy looked at her watch: 11.45. She wondered where Tristan was and what he was doing. She wondered if he missed her. She could have been sitting next to him at that moment, enjoying the soft June night.

"Come on, Beth," she said, sorry she had gotten her friends into this situation. "Suzanne," she commanded.

"Yes, *mother,*" Suzanne replied.

Gregory laughed, which stung Ivy a little. They're both wasted, she reminded herself.

It took a long time for the six of them to find Gregory's car again. When they did, Will held out his hand for Gregory's keys. "How about if I drive?"

"I can handle it," Gregory told him.

"Not this time." Will's tone was easygoing, but he reached determinedly for the keys.

Gregory yanked them away. "Nobody drives this Beamer but me."

Will glanced over at Ivy.

"Come on, Gregory," she said. "Let me be the D.D."

"If someone else drives," Will pointed out to Gregory, "you can drink all you want."

"I'll drink all I want *and* I'll drive all I want," Gregory shouted, "and if you don't like it, walk."

Ivy thought about walking – to the nearest phone and calling for a ride. But she knew Suzanne would stay with Gregory, and she felt responsible for her safety.

Will asked Ivy if he could borrow her sweater, then stuffed that and his jacket between the two front seats, making a seat in the middle. He pulled Eric into the front of the car with him, so that Gregory, he, and Eric sat three across. Ivy climbed into the middle of the backseat, with Beth and Suzanne on either side.

"Why, Will," Gregory said, observing the way he was squeezed in next to him, "I didn't know you cared. Suzanne, get up here!"

Ivy pulled Suzanne back.

"I said, get up here. Let Will sit back there with the girl of his dreams."

Ivy shook her head and sighed.

"Anybody likely to throw up has to sit by a window," Will said.

Ivy buckled Suzanne's seat belt.

Gregory shrugged, then started the car. He drove fast, too fast. The tires squealed on turns, the rubber barely holding the road. Beth closed her eyes. Suzanne and Eric hung their heads out the window as the car lurched sickeningly from side to side. Ivy stared straight ahead, her muscles contracting each time Gregory had to brake or turn the car, as if she were driving the route for him. Will actually did help drive. Ivy realized then why he had placed himself in a dangerous spot without a seat belt.

They were snaking south on the back roads, and when they finally crossed the river into town, Ivy let out a sigh of relief. But Gregory made a sharp turn north again, taking the road that ran along the river and beneath the ridge, past the train depot, beyond town limits.

"Where are we going?" Ivy asked as they followed a narrow road, their headlights striping the trees.

"You'll see."

Eric lifted his head off the door. "Chick, chick, chick," he sang. "Who's a chick, chick, chick?"

The ridge, looming high and dark on their

right, crowded the road closer and closer to the train tracks on the left. Ivy knew they must be getting near to the point where the tracks crossed over the river.

"The double bridges," Beth whispered to her, just as they ran out of road. Gregory cut the engine and lights. Ivy couldn't see a thing.

"Who's a chick chick chick?" Eric said, swinging his head back and forth.

Ivy felt ill from the fumes of the car and the alcohol. She and Beth climbed out of one side. Suzanne sat with the door open on the other. Gregory popped open the trunk. More beer.

"Where did you get all this?" Ivy demanded.

Gregory grinned and put a heavy arm around her. "Something else for you to thank Andrew for."

"Andrew bought it?" she said incredulously.

"No, his credit card did."

Then he and Eric each reached for a six-pack.

Though Ivy understood Gregory's need to blow off steam, though she knew how tough it had been for him since his mother's death, she had been growing angrier by the minute. Now her anger began to ebb, giving way to a slow tide of fear.

The river wasn't far away; she could hear it rushing over rocks. As her eyes adjusted to the country dark she traced the high wires of the electric train line. She remembered why kids came here: to play chicken on the railroad bridge. Ivy didn't want to follow Gregory as he led them single file to the bridges. But she couldn't stay behind, not with Suzanne unable to take care of herself.

Eric was pushing her from behind, singing in a high, weird voice, "Who's a chick, chick, chick?"

Small round stones rolled under their feet. Eric and Suzanne kept tripping on the railroad ties. The six of them walked the avenue that sliced sharply through the trees, a path made by the trains rushing between New York City and towns north of it.

The avenue opened out and Ivy saw the two bridges side by side, the new one built about seven feet from the old. Two gleaming steel rails penciled the path of the new one. There was no railing or restraining fence. The fretwork beneath it stretched like a dark and sinister web across the river. The older bridge had collapsed in the middle. Each side was like a hand extending from the river banks, fingers of metal and rotting wood reaching toward but unable to grip the others.

Far below both bridges, the water rushed and hissed.

"Follow the leader, follow the leader," Eric said, prancing ahead of them. He stumbled toward the newer bridge.

Ivy looped two fingers through the waistband of Suzanne's skirt. "Not you."

"Let go of me," Suzanne snapped.

Suzanne tried to follow Eric onto the bridge, but Ivy pulled her back.

"Let go!"

They struggled for a moment, and Gregory laughed at the two of them. Then Suzanne slipped out of Ivy's grasp. Desperate, Ivy reached forward and caught Suzanne's bare leg, causing her to trip over the rail and tumble down the track's bed of stone into some brush. Suzanne tried to pull herself up but couldn't. She sank back, her eyes blazing at Ivy, her hands curled with anger.

"Beth, you'd better see if she's all right," Ivy said, and turned her attention back to Eric He was fifteen feet out now and over the water. His too-thin body skipped and turned along the track like a dancing skeleton.

"Chick, chick, chicken," he taunted the others. "Look at all you chick, chick, chickens."

Gregory leaned against a tree and laughed. Will watched, his expression guarded.

Then everyone's head turned as the whistle sounded from across the river.

It was the whistle of the late-night train that Ivy had heard so often from their house high on the ridge, a streamer of sound that wrapped around her heart every night as if it wanted to take her with it.

"Eric!" she and Will shouted at the same time. Beth held Suzanne, who was leaning over the bushes and throwing up.

"Eric!"

Will started after him, but Eric took off, crazily bobbing over the tracks. Will pursued.

They'll both be killed, thought Ivy. "Will, come back! Will! You can't!"

The train made its swing onto the bridge, its bright eye throwing back the night, burning the two boys into paper-thin silhouettes. Ivy saw Eric tottering on the very edge of the bridge. Water and rocks lay far below him.

He's going to jump to the old bridge, she thought. He'll never make it.

Angels, help us! she prayed. Water angel, where are you? Tony? I'm calling you!

Eric leaned down, then suddenly dropped over the side.

Ivy screamed. She and Beth screamed and screamed.

Will was running back now, stumbling and running. The train wasn't slowing down. It was huge and dark. It was as large as night itself, bearing down on him behind one bright, blind eye. Twenty feet, fifteen feet – Will wasn't going to make it! He looked like a moth being drawn into its light.

"Will! Will!" Ivy shrieked. "Oh, angels—"

He leaped.

The train rushed by, the ground thundering beneath it, the air burning with metal smells. Ivy took off down the steep hill, crashing through the brush in the direction that Will had leaped.

"Will? Will, answer me!"

"I'm here. I'm okay."

He stood up in front of her.

By the hands of the angels, she thought.

They held on to each other for a moment. Ivy didn't know if it was he or she who was shaking so violently.

"Eric? Did he—"

"I don't know," she answered quickly. "Can we get down to the river from here?"

"Try the other side."

They clawed their way up the bank together. When they got to the top, they both stopped and stared. Eric was walking toward them along the new bridge, a thick rope and a bungee cord slung casually over his shoulder.

It took them a moment to figure out what had occurred. Ivy spun around to look at Gregory. Had he been in on the trick?

He was smiling now. "Excellent," he said to Eric. "Excellent."

11

"You know what I don't understand?" Gregory said, cocking his head, studying Ivy in her short silk skirt. A mischievous smile spread over his face. "I don't understand why you never wear that nice bridesmaid's dress."

Maggie looked up from the plate of snacks she was carrying upstairs to Andrew. Everyone was going out that evening.

"Oh, it's much too formal for the Durney Inn," Maggie said, "but you're right, Gregory, Ivy should find someplace to wear her dress again."

Ivy smiled briefly at her mother, then shot Gregory an evil look. He grinned at her.

After Maggie had left the kitchen, he said, "You look hot tonight." He said it in a matter-of-fact way, though his eyes lingered on her. Ivy no longer tried to figure out what Gregory meant by some of his comments – whether he was truly giving a compliment or subtly mocking her. She let a lot of what he said roll right on by. Maybe she had finally gotten used to him.

"You're getting used to making excuses for him," Tristan had said after she told him what had happened on Saturday night.

Ivy had been furious at Eric for his stupid trick. Gregory wouldn't admit to being in on the stunt. He had shrugged and said, "You never know what Eric's up to. That's what makes him fun."

Of course, she had been angry at Gregory too. But living with him day after day, she saw how he struggled. Since his mother's death there were hours when he seemed completely lost in his own thoughts. She thought about the day he had asked her to go for a ride and they had driven through his mother's old neighborhood. She had told him that she had been there that stormy night. He had barely spoken after that and wouldn't meet her eyes the rest of the way home.

"I'd have to be a stone not to feel for him," Ivy had told Tristan, and ended the discussion there.

Both Gregory and Tristan were inclined to avoid each other. As usual, Gregory disappeared as soon as Tristan drove up that evening.

Tristan always came early to play for a few minutes with Philip. Ivy saw, with some satisfaction, that this time Tristan couldn't concentrate, though the home team was down by two in the rubber match of the series with Derek Jeter coming to bat. Second base was stolen while the pitcher was sneaking peeks at Ivy.

Philip grew frustrated the third time that Tristan couldn't remember how many outs there were, and stomped off to call Sammy. Ivy and Tristan seized the opportunity to slip out of the house. On the way to the car, Ivy noticed that Tristan seemed unusually quiet.

"How's Ella?" she asked.

"Good."

Ivy waited. Usually he told her a funny Ella story. "Just good?"

"Very good."

"Did you get a new bell for her collar?"

"Yes."

"Is something wrong, Tristan?"

He didn't answer right away. It's Gregory, she thought. He still has himself all wound up about Gregory and last weekend.

"Tell me!"

He faced her. With one finger he touched the back of her neck. Her hair was pinned up that night. Her shoulders were bare, except for two thin little straps. The top she wore was a simple camisole, with small buttons down the front.

Tristan ran his hand down her neck, then across her bare shoulder. "Sometimes it's hard to believe you're real," he said.

Ivy swallowed. Ever so gently he kissed her throat.

"Maybe . . . maybe we should get in the car," she suggested, glancing up at the windows of the house.

"Right."

He opened the door. There were roses on the seat, lavender roses. "Whoops, I forgot," said Tristan. "Do you want to run them back inside?"

She picked them up and held them close to her face. "I want them with me."

"They'll probably wilt," he told her.

"We can stick them in a water glass at the restaurant."

Tristan smiled. "That will show the maitre d' what kind of class we have."

"They're beautiful!"

"Yeah," he said softly. His eyes ran all over her, as if he were memorizing her. Then he kissed her on the forehead and held the roses while she got in the car.

As they drove they talked about their plans for the summer. Ivy was glad Tristan took the old routes rather than the highway. The trees were cool and musky with June. Light dappled their branches like gold coins slipping through angels' fingers. Tristan drove the winding roads with one hand on the steering wheel, the other reaching out for hers, as if she might slip away.

"I want to go to Juniper Lake," Ivy said. "I'm going to float out there in the deepest part, float for an hour, with the sun shooting sparkles at my fingers and toes—"

"Till along comes a big fish," Tristan teased.

"I'll float in the moonlight too," she went on.

"The moonlight? You'd swim in the dark?"

"With you I would. We could skinny-dip."

He glanced over at her and their eyes held for a moment.

"Better not look at you and drive at the same time," he said.

"Then stop driving," she replied quietly.

He glanced quickly at her, and she put her hand over her mouth. The words had escaped, and she suddenly felt shy and embarrassed. Couples dressed up and on their way to expensive restaurants didn't pull over to make out.

"We'll be late for our reservation," she said. "You should keep going."

Tristan eased the car off the road.

"There's the river," he said. "Do you want to walk down to it?"

"Yes."

She laid the roses in the back of the car. Tristan came around to open Ivy's door

"Are you going to be able to walk in those shoes?" Tristan asked, glancing down at Ivy's high heels.

She stood up. Both heels sank straight down in the mud.

Ivy laughed, and Tristan picked her up. "I'll give you a lift," he said.

"No, you'll drop me in the mud!"

"Not till we get there," he said, and hoisted her up higher till he held her legs, letting the top half of her fall over his shoulder as if he were carrying a sack.

Ivy laughed and pounded him on the back. Her hair was coming out of its pins. "My hair! My hair! Let me down!"

He pulled her back, and she slid down the front of him, her skirt riding up, her hair tumbling down.

"Ivy."

He held her so tightly against him, she could feel the trembling up and down his body.

"Ivy?" he whispered.

She opened her mouth and pressed it against his neck.

At the same time, they both reached for the handle and pulled open the car's back door.

"I never knew how romantic a backseat could be," Ivy joked a while later. She rested against the seat, smiling at Tristan. Then she looked past him at the pile of junk on the car floor. "Maybe you should pull your tie out of that old Burger King cup."

Tristan reached down and grimaced. He tossed the dripping thing into the front of the car, then sat back next to Ivy.

"Ow!" The smell of crushed flowers filled the air.

Ivy laughed out loud.

"What's so funny?" Tristan asked, pulling the smashed roses from behind him, but he was laughing, too.

"What if someone had come along and seen your father's Clergy sticker on the bumper?"

Tristan tossed the flowers in the front seat and pulled her toward him again. He traced the silk strap of her top, then tenderly kissed her shoulder. "I'd have told them I was with an angel."

"Oh, what a line!"

"Ivy, I love you!" Tristan said, his face suddenly serious.

She stared back at him, then bit her lip.

"This isn't some kind of game for me. I love you, Ivy, and one day you're going to believe me."

She put her arms around him and held him tightly. "Love *you*," she whispered into his neck. Ivy did believe him, and she trusted him as she trusted no one else. One day she'd have the nerve to say it, all of the words out loud. I love you, Tristan. She'd shout it out the windows. She'd string a banner straight across the school pool.

It took a few minutes to straighten themselves up and clamber into the front of the car. Ivy started laughing again. Tristan smiled and watched her try to tame her gold tumbleweed of hair – a useless effort. Then he started the car, urging it over the ruts and stones and onto the narrow road.

"Last glimpse of the river," he said as the road made a sharp turn away from it.

The June sun, dropping over the west ridge of the Connecticut countryside, shafted light on the very tops of the trees, flaking them with gold. The winding road slipped below, into a tunnel of maples, poplars, and oaks. Ivy felt as if she were sliding under the waves with Tristan, the setting sun glittering on top, the two of them moving together through a chasm of blue, purple, and deep green. Tristan flicked on his headlights.

"You really don't have to hurry," said Ivy, "I'm not hungry any more."

"I ruined your appetite?"

She shook her head. "I guess I'm all filled up with happiness," she said softly.

The car sped along and took a curve sharply.

"I said, we don't have to hurry."

"That's funny," Tristan murmured. "I wonder what's—" He glanced down at his feet. "This doesn't feel . . ."

"Slow down, okay? It doesn't matter if we're a little late— Oh!" Ivy pointed straight ahead. "Tristan!"

Something had plunged through the bushes and into the roadway. She hadn't seen what it was, just the flicker of motion among the deep shadows. Then the deer stopped. It turned its head, its eyes drawn to the car's bright headlights.

"Tristan!"

They were rushing towards the shining eyes.

"Tristan, don't you see it?"

Rushing still.

"Ivy, something's—"

"A deer!" she exclaimed.

The animal's eyes blazed. Then light came from behind it, a bright burst around its dark

149

shape. A car was coming from the opposite direction. Trees walled them in. There was no room to veer left or right.

"Stop!" she shouted.

"I'm—"

"Stop, why don't you stop?" she pleaded. "Tristan, *stop!*"

12

It was dazzling: the eye of the deer like a dark tunnel, the center of it bursting with light. Tristan braked and braked, but nothing would stop the rushing, nothing could keep him from speeding through the long funnel of darkness into an explosion of light.

For a moment he felt a tremendous weight, as if the trees and sky had collapsed on him. Then, with the explosion of light, the weight was lifted. Somehow he had gotten free.

She needs you.

"Ivy!" he called out.

The darkness swirled in again, the road around him like a kaleidoscope, black spinning with red, night swirling with the pulsing blue light of an ambulance.

She needs you.

He did not hear it, but he understood it Did the others? "Ivy! Where's Ivy? You have to help Ivy!"

She was lying still. Bathed in red.

"Somebody help her! You've got to save her!"

But he could not hold on to the paramedic, could not even pull on his sleeve.

"No pulse," a woman said. "No chance."

"Help her!"

The swirling ran long and streaky now. Ribbons of light and dark rushed past him horizontally. Was she with him? The siren wailed: *I-veee. I-veee.*

Then he was in a square room. It was day there, or as bright as. People were rushing around. Hospital, he thought. Something was laid over his face, and the light was blocked out. He wasn't sure how long it was out.

Someone leaned over him. "Tristan." The voice broke.

"Dad?"

"Oh, my God, why did you let this happen?"

"Dad, where's Ivy? Is she okay?"

"My God, my God. My child!" his father said.

"Are they helping her?"

His father did not speak.

"Answer me, Dad! Why don't you answer me?"

His father held his face. His father was leaning over him, tears falling down on his face—

My face, Tristan thought with a jolt. That's *my* face.

And yet he was watching his father and himself as if he were standing apart from himself.

"Mr. Carruthers, I'm sorry." A woman in a paramedic's uniform stood next to him and his father.

His father would not look at her. "Dead at the scene?" he asked.

She nodded. "I'm sorry. We didn't have a chance with him."

Tristan felt the darkness coming over him again. He struggled to hold on to consciousness.

"And Ivy?" his father asked.

"Cuts and bruises, in shock. Calling for your son."

Tristan had to find her. He focused on a doorway, concentrated with all his strength, and passed through it. Then another, and another – he was feeling stronger now.

Tristan hurried down the corridor. People kept coming at him. He dodged left and right. He seemed to be going so much faster than they were, and none of them bothered to move out of his way.

A nurse was coming down the hall. He stopped to ask her help in finding Ivy, but she walked past him. He turned a corner and found himself facing a cart loaded with linens. Then he faced the man pushing it. Tristan spun around. The cart and the man were on the other side of him.

Tristan knew that they had passed through him as if he were not there. He had heard what the paramedic said. Still, his mind searched for some other – any other – explanation. But there was none.

He was dead. No one could see him. No one knew he was there. And Ivy would not know.

Tristan felt a pain deeper than any he had ever known. He had told her he loved her, but there had not been time enough to convince her. Now there was no time at all. She'd never believe in his love the way she believed in her angels.

"I said, I can't speak any louder."

Tristan glanced up. He had stopped by a doorway. An old woman was lying in the bed within. She was tiny and gray with long, thin tubes connecting her to machines. She looked like a spider caught in its own web.

"Come in," she said.

He looked behind him to see whom she was talking to.

No one.

"These old eyes of mine are so dim, I can't see my own hand in front of my face," the woman said, "But I can see your light."

Tristan again looked behind him. Her voice sounded certain of what she saw. It seemed much bigger and stronger than her little gray body.

"I knew you would come," she said. "I've been waiting very patiently."

She has been waiting for somebody, Tristan thought, a son or a grandson, and she thinks I'm him. Still, how could she see him if no one else could?

Her face was shining brightly now.

"I've always believed in you," she said. She extended a fragile hand toward Tristan. Forgetting that his hand would pass through hers, he instinctively reached out to her. She closed her eyes.

A moment later, alarms went off. Three nurses rushed into the room. Tristan stepped back as they crowded around the woman. He suddenly realized that they were trying to resuscitate her; he knew they would not. Somehow he knew that the old woman did not want to come back.

Maybe somehow the old woman had known about him.

What did she know?

Tristan could feel the darkness coming over him again. He fought it. What if this time he didn't come back? He had to come back, he had to see Ivy one last time. Desperately he tried to keep himself alert, focusing on one object after another in the room. Then he saw it, next to a small book on the woman's tray: a statue, with a hand outstretched to the woman and angelic wings spread.

For days after, all Ivy could remember was the waterfall of glass. The accident was like a dream she kept having but couldn't remember. Asleep or awake, it would suddenly take over. Her whole body would tense, and her mind would start reeling backward, but all she could remember was the sound of a windshield exploding, then a slow-motion waterfall of glass.

Every day people came and went from the house, Suzanne and Beth, and some other friends and teachers from school. Gary came once; it was a miserable visit for both of them. Will ducked in and out on another day. They brought her flowers, cookies, and sympathy. Ivy couldn't wait until they left, couldn't wait until she could sleep again. But when she lay down at night, she couldn't sleep, and then she had to wait forever until it was day once more.

At the funeral they stood around her, her mother and Andrew on one side, Philip on the other. She let Philip do all the sobbing for her. Gregory stood behind her and from time to time laid his hand on her back. She'd lean against him for a moment. He was the only one who didn't keep asking her to talk about it. He was the only one who seemed to understand her pain and didn't keep telling her that remembering was good for her.

Little by little she did remember – or was told – what had happened. The doctors and police prompted her. The undersides of her arms were full of cuts. She must have held her hands up in front of her face, they said, protecting it from the flying glass. Miraculously, the rest of her injuries were just bruises from the impact and the seat belt restraint. Tristan must have swerved, for the car had swung around to the right, the deer coming in on his side. To protect her, she thought, though the police didn't say that. She told them he had tried to stop but couldn't. It had been twilight. The deer had appeared suddenly. That's all she remembered. Someone told her the car had been totaled, but she refused to look at the newspaper photo.

A week after the funeral, Tristan's mother came to the house and brought a picture of him. She said it was her favorite one. Ivy cradled it in her hands. He was smiling, wearing his old baseball cap, and a ratty school jacket, looking as Ivy had seen him look so many times. It seemed as if he were about to ask her if she wanted to meet for another swimming lesson. For the first time since the accident, Ivy began to cry.

She didn't hear Gregory come into the kitchen, where she and Tristan's mother were sitting. When he saw Dr. Carruthers, he demanded to know why she was there.

Ivy showed him Tristan's picture, and he looked angrily at the woman.

"It's over now," he said. "Ivy is getting over it. She doesn't need any more reminders."

"When you love someone, it's never over," Dr. Carruthers replied gently. "You move on, because you have to, but you bring him with you in your heart."

She turned back to Ivy. "You need to talk and remember, Ivy. You need to cry. Cry hard. You need to get angry, too. I am!"

"You know," said Gregory, "I'm getting tired of listening to all this crap. Everyone is telling Ivy to remember and talk about what happened. Everyone has a pet theory on how to mourn, but I wonder if they're really thinking of how it feels for *her*."

Dr. Carruthers studied him for a moment. "I

wonder if you have really mourned your own loss," she said.

"Don't tell me you're a shrink!"

She shook her head. "Just a person who, like you, has lost someone I loved with all my heart."

Before she left, Tristan's mother asked Ivy if she wanted Ella back.

"I can't have her," Ivy said. "They won't let me!"

Then she ran up to her room, slammed the door, and locked it. One by one, those she loved were being taken away from her.

Picking up an angel statue, one that Beth had just brought her, Ivy hurled it against the wall.

"Why?" she cried out. "Why didn't I die, too?"

She picked up the angel and threw it again.

"You're better off, Tristan. I hate you for being better off than me. You don't miss me now, do you? Oh, no, *you* don't feel a thing!"

On the third try, the angel shattered. Another waterfall of glass. She didn't bother to pick it up.

After dinner that evening, Ivy found the glass cleaned up and the picture of Tristan sitting on her bureau. She didn't ask who had done it. She didn't want to speak to any of them. When Gregory tried to come into her bedroom, she slammed the door in his face. She slammed it in his face again the next morning.

That day, she was barely civil to the customers at 'Tis the Season. When she arrived home, she went straight to her room. Opening the door, she found Philip there, spreading out his baseball cards. She had noticed that he no longer called out the play-by-play for his games, just moved the players silently from base to base. But when he looked up at Ivy, he smiled at her for the first time in days. He pointed to her bed.

"Ella!" Ivy exclaimed. "Ella!"

She hurried in and dropped to her knees beside the bed. Immediately the cat began to purr. Ivy buried her face in the cat's soft fur and started to cry.

Then she felt a light hand on her shoulder. Drying her cheeks on Ella, she turned to Philip. "Does Mom know she's here?"

He nodded. "She knows. It's okay. Gregory said it was. Gregory brought her back to us."

13

When Tristan awakened, he tried to remember which day of the week it was and what lessons he would be giving at the swim camp. Judging by the dim light in his room, it was too early to rise and dress for work. Lying back, he dreamed of Ivy – Ivy with her hair tumbling down.

Slowly he became aware of footsteps outside the door and a sound like something being wheeled by. He leaped up. What was he doing there – lying on the hospital floor in the room of a man he had never seen before? The man yawned and glanced around the room. He did not appear at all surprised by Tristan's presence; he acted as if he didn't even see him.

Then it came back to Tristan: the accident, the ambulance ride, the paramedic's words. He was dead. But he could think. He could watch other people. Was he a ghost?

Tristan remembered the old lady. She had said she saw his light, which was why, he thought, she had mistaken him for an—

"No, no." He said it aloud, but the man didn't hear him. "I can't be that."

Well, whatever he was, he was something that could laugh. He laughed and laughed, almost hysterically. He cried too.

The door behind him swung open suddenly. Tristan quieted himself, but it didn't matter. The nurse who entered was not aware of him, though she stood so close her elbow passed through his as she filled out the man's chart. July 9, 3.45 A.M., Tristan read.

July 9? It couldn't be! It had been June when he'd last been with Ivy. Had he been unconscious for two weeks? Would he black out again? Why was he conscious and there at all?

He thought about the old woman who had reached out to him. Why had she noticed him, but the nurse and others had seen nothing? Would Ivy see him?

Hope surged through Tristan. If he could find Ivy before he fell into the darkness again, he'd have another chance to convince her that he loved her. He would always love her.

The nurse left, shutting the door behind her.

Tristan reached to open it, but his fingers slipped through the handle. He tried again, and again. His hands had no more strength than shadows. Now he'd have to wait for the nurse to come back. He didn't know how long he would stay conscious or whether, like ghosts in old tales, he'd melt away at dawn.

He tried to remember how he had gotten this far and pictured the halls he had traveled down from the emergency room. He could see very clearly the corner where the orderly had gone through him. Suddenly he was traveling the halls to that spot. That was the trick. He had to project a route in his head and focus on where he wanted to go.

Soon he was out on the street. He had forgotten he was at County Hospital and had to get himself all the way home to Stonehill. But he had driven the route a thousand times to pick up his parents. At the thought of them, Tristan slowed down. He remembered his father in the emergency room, leaning over him and weeping. Tristan longed to assure him that everything was all right, but he didn't know how much time would be given to him. His parents had each other; Ivy was alone.

The night sky was just starting to fade into dawn when he arrived at her house. Two rectangles of light glimmered softly in the west wing. Andrew must have been working in his office. Tristan went around the back and found the office's French doors thrown open to the cool night air. Andrew was at his desk, deep in thought. Tristan slipped in unseen.

He saw that Andrew's briefcase was open and papers with the college insignia were scattered about. But the document he had been reading was a police report. Tristan realized with a jolt that it was the official report on his and Ivy's accident. Next to it was a newspaper article about them.

The printed words should have made his death more real to him, but they didn't. Instead, they made things that had once counted – his appearance, his swimming record, his school achievements – seem meaningless and small. Only Ivy was important to him now.

She had to know he loved her and that he always would.

He left Andrew to pore over the report, though he didn't understand why he would be so interested in it, and took the back stairs. Slipping past Gregory's room, which was above the office, he crossed the gallery to the hall that led to Ivy's room. He could hardly wait to see her, hardly wait for her to see him. He trembled as he had done before their first swimming lesson. Would they be able to speak to each other?

If anyone could see him and hear him, Ivy could- – her faith was strong! Tristan focused on her room and passed through the wall.

Ella sat up immediately. She had been sleeping on Ivy's bed, her thick black fur balled close to Ivy's golden head. Now the cat blinked and stared at him, or at the empty air – after all, cats did that, he thought. But when he moved toward the other side of Ivy's bed, Ella's green eyes followed him.

"Ella, what do you see, Ella?" he asked quietly.

The cat began to purr, and he laughed.

He stood by Ivy's side now. Her hair was tumbled over her face. He tried to brush it back. More than anything he longed to see her face, but his hands were useless.

"I wish you could help me, Ella," he said.

The cat walked over the pillows toward him. He kept very still, wondering what exactly she perceived. Ella leaned as if she would rub against his arm. She fell over sideways and yelped.

Ivy stirred then, and he called her name softly.

Ivy rolled onto her back and he thought she was going to answer him. Her face was a lost moon, beautiful, but pale. All of her light lay in the golden lashes and her long hair spread out like rays from her face.

Ivy frowned. He wanted to smooth the frown away but couldn't. She began to toss and turn.

"Who's there?" she asked. "Who's there?"

He leaned over her. "It's me. Tristan."

"Who's there?" she asked again.

"Tristan!"

Her frown deepened. "I can't see."

He laid his hand on her shoulder, wishing she would awaken, certain that she would see him and hear him. "Ivy, look at me. I'm here!"

Her eyes fluttered open for a moment. Then he saw the change come over her face. He saw the terror take over her. She began to scream.

"Ivy!"

She screamed and screamed.

"Ivy, don't be afraid."

He tried to hold her. He wrapped his arms around her, but their bodies slipped through each other. He could not comfort her.

Then the bedroom door flew open. Philip rushed in. Gregory was close behind him.

"Wake up, Ivy, wake up!" Philip shook her. "Come on, Ivy, please."

Her eyes opened wide now. She gazed at Philip, then glanced around the room. She did not pause at Tristan; she looked straight through him.

Gregory rested his hands lightly on Philip's shoulders and moved him aside. He sat down on the bed, then pulled Ivy close to him. Tristan could see that she was shaking.

"Everything is going to be all right," Gregory said, smoothing back her hair. "It was just a dream."

A terrifying dream, thought Tristan. And he couldn't help her, couldn't comfort her now.

But Gregory could. Tristan was overcome with jealousy.

He couldn't stand to see Gregory holding her that close.

And yet he couldn't stand to see Ivy so frightened and upset. Gratitude to Gregory, as powerful as his jealousy, swept through him. Then jealousy again. Tristan felt weak from this war of feelings and backed away from the three of them, moving toward Ivy's shelves of angels. Ella followed him cautiously.

"Was your dream about the accident?" Philip asked.

Ivy nodded, then dropped her head, running her hands over and over the twisted sheets.

"You want to talk about it?" Gregory asked.

Ivy tried to speak, then shook her head and turned one hand over, palm up. Tristan saw the jagged scars running up her arm like the traces of lightning strikes. For a moment the darkness came up from behind him, but he fought it back.

"I'm here. Everything's okay," Gregory said, and waited patiently.

"I – I was staring at a window," she began. "I saw a large shadow in it, but I wasn't sure who, or what, it was. 'Who's there?' I called out. 'Who's there?'"

From across the room, Tristan watched, her pain and fear pressing upon him.

"I thought it might be someone I knew," she continued. "The shadow looked familiar somehow. So I walked closer, and closer. I couldn't see." She stopped and glanced around the bedroom.

"You couldn't see," prompted Gregory.

"There were other images on the glass, reflections that made it confusing. I got closer. My face was almost against the glass. Suddenly it exploded! The shadow turned into a deer. It crashed through the window and raced away."

She fell silent. Gregory cupped her chin in his hand and pulled it up toward him, gazing deeply into her eyes.

From across the room, Tristan called to her. "Ivy! Ivy, look at me," he begged.

But she looked back at Gregory, her mouth quivering.

"Is that the end of the dream?" Gregory asked.

She nodded.

With the back of his hand he gently stroked her cheek.

Tristan wanted her to be comforted, but—

"You don't remember anything else?" Gregory said.

Ivy shook her head.

"Open your eyes, Ivy! Look at me!" Tristan called to her.

Then he noticed Philip, who was staring at the angel collection – or perhaps at him; he wasn't sure. Tristan put his hand around the statue of the water angel. If only he could find a way to give it to Ivy. If he could send her some sign—

"Come here, Philip," Tristan said. "Come get the statue. Carry it to Ivy."

Philip walked toward the shelves as if drawn by a magnet. Reaching up, he put his hand over Tristan's.

"Look!" Philip cried. "Look!"

"At what?" asked Ivy.

"Your angel. It's glowing."

"Philip, not now," said Gregory.

Philip took the angel down from the shelf and carried it over to her.

"Do you want her by your bed, Ivy?"

"No."

"Maybe she'll keep away bad dreams," he persisted.

"It's just a statue," she said wearily.

"But we can say our prayer, and the real angel will hear it."

"There *are* no real angels, Philip! Don't you understand? If there were, they would have saved Tristan!"

Philip fingered the wings of the statue. He said in a stubborn, little voice, "Angel of light, angel above, take care of me tonight, take care of everyone I love."

"Tell her I'm here, Philip," Tristan said. "Tell her I'm here."

"Look, Ivy!" Philip pointed toward the statues, where Tristan stood. "They're shining!"

"That's enough, Philip!" Gregory said sternly. "Go to bed."

"But—"

"Now!"

When Philip passed by, Tristan held out his hand, but the little boy did not reach back to him. He stared with wonder, not recognition.

What did Philip see? Tristan wondered. Maybe what the old woman had seen: light, some kind of shimmering, but not a shape.

Then he felt the darkness coming on once more. Tristan fought it. He wanted to stay with

Ivy. He could not stand to lose her now. He could not stand to leave her before Gregory did.

What if this was his last time with her? What if he was losing Ivy forever? He struggled desperately to keep back the darkness, but it was rising on all sides now, like a black mist, before him, behind him, closing over his head, and he succumbed.

14

When Tristan awoke from his dreamless dark, the sun was shining brilliantly through Ivy's windows. Her sheets were pulled up and smoothed over with a light comforter. Ivy was gone.

It was the first time Tristan had seen daylight since the accident. He went to the window and marveled at the details of summer, the intricate designs of leaves, the way the wind could run a finger through the grass and send a green wave over the top of the ridge. The wind. Though the curtains were moving, Tristan couldn't feel its cool touch. Though the room was streaked with sun, he couldn't feel its warmth.

Ella could. The cat was lying on a T-shirt of

Ivy's tucked in a bright corner. She greeted Tristan by opening one eye and purring a little.

"Not much dirty laundry lying around here for you, is there?" he asked, thinking of the cat's fondness for his smelliest socks and sweats. The stillness of the house made him speak quietly, though he knew he could shout loud enough to – well, loud enough to wake the dead, and only he would hear.

The loneliness was intense. Tristan feared that he would always be alone this way, wandering and never seen, never heard, never known as Tristan. Why hadn't he seen the old lady from the hospital after she died? Where had she gone?

Dead people went to cemeteries, he thought as he crossed the hallway to the stairs. Then he stopped in his tracks. He had a grave somewhere! Probably next to his grandparents. He hurried down the steps, curious to see what they had done with him. Perhaps he'd also find the old woman or someone else recently dead who could make sense of all this.

Tristan had visited Riverstone Rise Cemetery several times when he was a little boy. It had never seemed a sad place to him, perhaps because the sites of his grandparents' graves had always inspired his father to tell Tristan interesting and funny stories about them. His mother had spent the time trimming and planting. Tristan had run and climbed stones and broad-jumped the graves, using the cemetery as a kind of playground and obstacle course. But that seemed centuries ago.

It was strange now to slip through the tall iron gates – gates he had swung on like a little monkey, his mother always said – in search of his own grave. Whether he moved from memory or instinct, he wasn't sure, but he found his way quickly to the lower path and around the bend marked by three pines. He knew it was fifteen feet farther and prepared himself for the shock of reading his own name on the stone next to his grandparents'.

But he didn't even glance at it. He was too astonished by the presence of a girl who had stretched out and made herself quite at home on the freshly upturned dirt.

"Excuse me," he said, knowing full well that people didn't hear him. "You're lying on my grave."

She glanced upward then, which made him wonder if he was shimmering again. The girl was about his age and looked vaguely familiar to him.

"You must be Tristan," she said. "I knew you'd show up sooner or later."

Tristan stared at her.

"You're him, right?" she said, sitting up, indicating his name with a jab of her thumb. "Recently dead, right?"

"Recently alive," he said. There was something about her attitude that made him want to argue with her.

She shrugged. "Everybody has his own point of view."

He couldn't get over the fact that she could hear him. "And you," he said, studying her rather unusual looks, "what are you?"

"Not so recently."

"I see. Is that why your hair is that color?"

Her hand flew up to her head. "Ex*cuse* me?"

The hair was short, dark, and spiky, and had a strange magenta tinge, a purplish hue, as if the henna rinse had gone wrong.

"That's what color it was when I died."

"Oh. Sorry."

"Have a seat," she said, patting the newly mounded earth. "After all, it's your resting place. I was just crashing for a while."

"So you're a . . . a ghost," he said.

"Ex*cuse* me?"

He wished she'd stop using that annoying tone.

"Did you say 'ghost'? You *are* recent. We're not ghosts, sweetie." She tapped his arm several times with a long, pointed, purplish-black nail.

Again he wondered if this was from being "not recently" dead but was afraid she'd puncture him if he asked.

Then he realized that her hand did not pass through his. They were indeed made of the same stuff.

"We're angels, sweetie. *That's right.* Heaven's little helpers."

Her tone and tendency to exaggerate certain words were starting to grate on his nerves.

She pointed toward the sky. "Someone's got a wicked sense of humor. Always chooses the least likely."

"I don't believe it," Tristan said. "I don't believe it."

"So this is the first time you've seen your new digs. Missed your own funeral, huh? *That,*" she said, "was a very big mistake. I enjoyed *every minute* of mine."

"Where are you buried?" Tristan asked, looking around. The stone on one side of his family plot had a carving of a lamb, which hardly seemed right for her, and on the other side, a serene-looking woman with hands folded over her breasts and eyes lifted toward heaven – an equally bad choice.

"I'm not buried. That's why I'm subletting from you."

"I don't understand," said Tristan.

"Don't you recognize me?"

"Uh, no," he said, afraid she was going to tell him she was related to him somehow, or maybe that he had chased her in sixth grade.

"Look at me from this side." She showed him her profile.

Tristan looked at her blankly.

"Boy, you didn't have much of a life, did you, when you had a life," she remarked.

"What do you mean?"

"You didn't go out much."

"All the time," Tristan replied.

"Didn't go to the movies."

"I went all the time," Tristan argued.

"But you never saw any of Lacey Lovitt's films."

"Sure I did. Everybody did, before she— You're Lacey Lovitt?"

She rolled her eyes upward. "I hope you're faster at figuring out your mission."

"I guess it's just that your hair color is different."

"We've already talked about my hair," she said, scrambling up from the grave. It was odd to see her standing against the background of trees. The willows waved ropes of leaves in the breeze, but her hair lay as still as a girl's in a photograph.

"I remember now," Tristan said. "Your plane

went down over the ocean. They never found you."

"Imagine how pleased I was to find myself climbing out of New York Harbor."

"The accident was two years ago, wasn't it?"

At that, she ducked her head. "Yeah, well . . ."

"I remember reading about your funeral," Tristan said. "Lots of famous people went."

"And lots of almost-famous. People are always looking for publicity." There was a bitter edge to her voice. "I wish you could have seen my mother, weeping and wailing." Lacey struck a pose like the marble figure of a woman weeping in the next row over. "You would have thought she had lost someone she loved."

"Well, she did if you're her daughter."

"You *are* naive, aren't you." It was a statement rather than a question. "You could have learned something about people if you had gone to your own funeral. Maybe you still can learn. There's a burial on the east side this morning. Let's go," she said.

"Go to a burial? Isn't that kind of morbid?"

She laughed at him over her shoulder. "Nothing can be morbid, Tristan, once you're dead. Besides, I find them highly entertaining. And when they're not, I make them so, and you look like you could use some cheering up. Come on."

"I think I'll pass."

She turned and studied him for a minute, perplexed. "All right. How about this: I saw a group of girls come in earlier, headed for the ritzy side of town. Maybe you'd enjoy that more. Good audiences, you know, are hard to come by, especially when you're dead and most of them can't see you."

She began pacing around in a circle.

"Yeah, that'll be much better." She seemed to be talking to herself as much as him. "It will score me some points." She glanced over at Tristan. "You see, fooling around with funeral parties doesn't really meet with approval. But with this, I'll be performing a service. Next time those girls will think twice about respect for the dead."

Tristan had hoped that another person like him would clear things up a bit, but—

"Oh, cheer up, Dumps!" She started down the road.

Tristan followed slowly and tried to remember if he had ever read that Lacey Lovitt was crazy.

She led him to an older section of the cemetery where there were family plots owned by longtime, wealthier residents of Stonehill. On one side of the road, mausoleums with facades like miniature temples sank their backs into the hill. On the other side were gardenlike squares with tall, polished monuments and a variety of marble statues. Tristan had been there before. At Maggie's request, Caroline had been buried in the Baines family plot.

"Swanky, huh?"

"I'm surprised you sublet from me," Tristan remarked.

"Oh, I made millions in my time," said Lacey. "Millions. But at heart I'm a simple girl from New York's Lower East Side. I started with the soaps, remember, and then – but no need to go into all that. I'm sure, now that you recognize me, you know all about me."

Tristan didn't bother to correct her.

"So, what do you think those girls had in mind?" she asked, stopping to look around. There was no one in sight, just smooth stones, bright flowers, and a sea of lush grass.

"I was wondering the same thing about you," he replied.

"Oh, I'll just improvise. I doubt you'll be much help. You couldn't have any real skills yet Probably all you can do is stand there and shimmer, like some kind of freakin' Christmas ornament – meaning only a believer or two will see you."

"Only a believer?"

"You mean you still haven't figured out *that?*" She shook her head in disbelief.

But he had figured it out; he just didn't want to admit it, just didn't want it to be true. The old lady had been a believer. So was Philip. Both of them had seen him shimmering. But Ivy had not. Ivy had stopped believing.

"You can do something more than shimmer?" Tristan asked hopefully.

She looked at him as if he were utterly stupid. "What on earth do you think I've been doing for the last two years?"

"I have no idea," Tristan said.

"Don't tell me, *puh-lease* don't tell me I'm going to have to explain to you about missions."

He ignored the melodramatics. "You mentioned that before. What missions?"

"Your mission, my mission," she replied quickly. "We each have a mission. And we have to fulfill it if we want to get on to where everyone else has gone." She started walking again, rather quickly, and he had to hurry to catch up.

"But what is my mission?"

"How should I know?"

"Well, somebody has to tell me. How can I fulfill it if I have no idea what it is?" he said, frustrated.

"Don't complain to me about it!" she snapped. "It's your job to find out." In a quieter voice she added, "It's usually some kind of unfinished business. Sometimes it's someone you know who needs your help."

"So I have at least two years to—"

"Well, no, that's not exactly how it works," she said, making that funny ducking motion with her head that he had seen before. She moved ahead of him, then passed through a black iron fence whose curled and rusted spikes made odd designs against the walls of an old stone chapel. "Let's find the kids."

"Wait a minute," he said, reaching for her arm. She was the one thing that he could grab hold of. "You've got to tell me. How *exactly* does this mission thing work?"

"Well . . . well, you're supposed to find out and complete your mission as soon as possible. Some angels take a few days, some angels take a few months."

"And you've been at it for two years," he said. "How close are you to completing yours?"

She ran her tongue over her teeth. "Don't know."

"Great," he said. "Great! I don't know what I'm doing, and I've finally found myself a guide, only she's taking eight times as long as everybody else."

"Twice as long!" she said. "Once I met an angel who took a year. You see, Tristan, I get a little distracted. I'm going about my business, and I see these opportunities that are just too good to pass by. Some of them don't really meet with approval."

"Some of them? Like what?" Tristan asked suspiciously.

She shrugged. "Once I dropped a stage chandelier on my jerky ex-director's head – just missing, of course. He always was a big fan of *Phantom of the Opera* – that's what I mean by an opportunity just too good to pass by. And that's how it usually goes for me. I'm two points closer, then something comes up, and I'm three points back and never quite getting to figuring out my mission.

"But don't worry – you probably have more discipline than me. For you, it'll be a snap."

I'm going to wake up, Tristan thought, and this nightmare will be over. Ivy will be lying in my arms—

"How much do you want to bet that those girls are in the chapel?"

Tristan eyed the gray stone building. Its doors had been bound with heavy chains since he was a little boy.

"Is there a way in?"

"For us, there is always a way in. For them, a broken window in the back. Any special requests?"

"What?"

"Anything you'd like to see me do?"

Wake me up, thought Tristan. "Uh, no."

"You know, I don't know what's on your mind, Trist, but you're acting deader than dead."

Then she slipped through the wall. Tristan followed.

The chapel was dark except for one square of luminescent green where the window was broken in the back. Dry leaves and crumbling plaster were scattered over its floor, along with broken bottles and cigarettes. Wooden benches were carved over with initials and blackened with symbols that Tristan couldn't decipher.

The girls, whom he judged to be about eleven or twelve, were seated in a circle in the altar area and giggling with nervousness.

"Okay, who are we going to call back?" one of them asked. They glanced at one another, then over their shoulders.

"Heath Ledger," said a girl with a brown ponytail.

"Kurt Cobain," another suggested.

"My grandmother."

"My great-uncle Lennie."

"I know!" said a tiny, freckle-faced blonde. "How about Tristan Carruthers?"

Tristan blinked.

"Too bloody," said the leader.

"Yeah," said the brunette, pulling her ponytail up into two long pieces. "He'd probably have antlers coming out of the back of his head."

"Ew, gross!"

Lacey snickered.

"My sister had the biggest crush on him," the freckled blonde said.

Lacey batted her eyelashes at Tristan.

"One time, like, when we were fooling around at the pool, he, like, blew the whistle at us. It was cool."

"He was hot!"

Lacey stuck her finger down her throat and rolled her eyes.

"Still, he might be bloody," said a redhead. "Who else can we call for?"

"Lacey Lovitt."

The girls looked around at each other. Which one of them had said it?

"I remember her. She was in *Dark Moon Running.*"

"*Dark Moon Rising.*"

It was Lacey's voice, Tristan realized, sounding the same but different, the way a televised voice was the same but different than a live one. Somehow she was producing it in a way that they all could hear.

The girls looked around, a little spooked.

"Let's join hands," the leader said. "We're calling back Lacey Lovitt. If you're here, Lacey, give us a sign."

"I never liked Lacey Lovitt."

Tristan saw Lacey's eyes spark.

"Shhh. The spirits are around us now."

"I see them!" said the little blonde. "I see their light! Two of them."

"So do I!"

"I don't," said the girl with the brown pony-tail.

"Let's get somebody other than Lacey Lovitt."

"Yeah, she was obnoxious."

It was Tristan's turn to snicker.

"I like that new girl in *Dark Moon*. The one who took her place."

"Me too," the redhead agreed.

"She's a much better actress. And she has better hair."

Tristan's laughter softened. He glanced warily at Lacey.

"Well, she's not dead," said the leader. "We're calling Lacey Lovitt. If you're here, Lacey, give us a sign."

It began with a slow whirling of dust. Tristan saw that Lacey herself became faint as the dust whirled upward. Then the dust drifted off and she was there again, running around the outside of the circle, pulling hair.

The girls shrieked and held their heads. She pinched two of them, then picked up their sweaters and hurled them this way and that.

By this time the girls were on their feet, still screaming, and running for the open window.

Empty bottles flew over their heads and smashed against the chapel wall.

In a moment the girls were gone, their screams trailing behind them like thin, birdlike calls.

"Well," said Tristan when it was quiet again, "I guess everyone should be glad that there wasn't a chandelier in here. Feeling better?"

"Little snips!"

"How did you do that?" he asked.

"I've seen that new actress. She stinks."

"I'm sure," said Tristan, "that she can't be nearly as dramatic as you. You were pulling and throwing. How did you do that? I can't use my hands at all."

"Figure it out for yourself!" She was still fuming. "Better hair!" She pulled on strands of the purplish stuff. "This is my own personal style." She glared at Tristan.

He smiled back.

"As for how I use my hands," she said, "do you really think I'd take up *my* precious time to teach *you?*"

Tristan nodded. "Good audiences are hard

to come by," he reminded her, "especially when you're dead and most of them can't see you."

Then he left her sulking in the chapel. He figured she'd know how to locate him and would when she was ready.

Out in the noonday sun again, Tristan blinked. While he did not feel changes in temperature, he did seem very sensitive to light and darkness. In the darkened chapel he had seen auras around the girls, and now, in the tree-shaded landscape, splotches of sunlight seemed dazzlingly bright.

Perhaps that was why he mistook the visitor for Gregory. The way he moved, the dark hair, and the shape of his head convinced Tristan that Gregory was walking away from the Baines family plot. Then the visitor, as if he sensed someone watching him, turned around.

He was much older than Gregory, forty or so, and his face was twisted with grief. Tristan reached out a hand to him, but the man turned away and continued on.

So did Tristan, but not before he noticed, on the fresh green belly of Caroline's grave, a long-stemmed red rose.

15

Lacey found Tristan again late that afternoon. She called his name, startling him as he walked along the edge of the ridge. He looked up to see her sitting in a tree.

"Nice view, isn't it?" said Lacey.

Tristan nodded, and gazed again down the stony drop. The land fell away steeply there for two or three hundred feet He remembered seeing in the early spring the silver tracks and the roof of the one-room train station in the valley below, but now they were hidden. Only small flecks of river could be seen flashing blue through the trees. "I don't know why I'm so drawn to this place."

Lacey cocked her head. "I'm sure that it has *nothing* to do with the fact that Ivy lives here," she said sarcastically.

"How did you know about Ivy?"

The girl did a neat skin-the-cat and dropped down from the tree.

"Read about her, of course." Lacey walked along next to him. "Read all about your accident. I make it a habit to drop by the station every morning and read the paper with the commuters. Don't like to be out of the skinny. Besides, it helps me to keep the date straight."

"Today's Sunday, July tenth," Tristan said.

"Brrrrrr!" She made a sound like a gameshow buzzer, and snapped a twig from the tree. "Tuesday, July twelfth."

"Couldn't be," Tristan said. He reached up but couldn't pull off a leaf, much less snap a branch.

"Did you fall into the darkness in the last couple of days?"

"Last night," he replied.

"More like three nights ago," she told him. "That will happen, but eventually you'll build up your strength and need less and less rest. Except, of course, when you do fancy jobs."

"Fancy jobs. Like what?"

She waited till she had his full attention, then said, "Look at me."

"What do you think I'm doing?"

"Stand back a little and look harder. What am I missing?"

"Do you promise not to pull my hair?"

She scowled at him. It was a fine scowl, but it passed quickly – she was just acting.

"Look at that cat," she said.

He glanced over his shoulder. "Ella!"

"Look at the grass next to the cat and look at the grass next to me."

He saw it then. "You have no shadow."

"Neither do you."

"You're talking out loud," he observed. "I recognize that sound and saw Ella's ears flick in your direction."

"Now watch the grass behind me," she instructed, and closed her eyes. Slowly, like dark water seeping over the lawn, her shadow grew. Just as slowly she lost her shimmering quality. Ella cautiously circled her once, twice. Then she rubbed against Lace's leg and didn't fall over.

"You're solid!" Tristan exclaimed. "Solid! Anybody could see you! Teach me how to do it. If I can make myself solid, Ivy will see me, she'll know I'm here for her, she'll know—"

"Whoa," Lacey cut in. Then her projected voice began to fade. "I'll be with you in a minute."

Her shadow disappeared. Then she did – completely.

"Lacey?" Tristan spun around. "Lacey, where are you? Are you all right?"

"Just tired." Her voice was small. Her body appeared again but was almost translucent. She lay curled in a ball on the ground. "Give me a few minutes."

Tristan paced back and forth, eyeing her worriedly.

Suddenly she sprang up, looking like herself again. "It's like this," she said. "For transient angels – that's you and me, sweetie – it takes all the energy we have and a lot of experience to materialize completely. To speak at the same time – well, only a professional can do that."

"Meaning you," he said.

"Usually I just materialize part of myself, such as my fingers, when I want to do something – pull hair or turn the paper to the movie reviews."

"Teach me!" Tristan said fervently. "Will you show me how?"

"Maybe."

They had come around to a full view of the back of the house. Tristan gazed up at the dormer window that looked out from Ivy's music room.

"So this is where the chick lives," Lacey said. "I suppose I should think it refreshing that a guy would let himself be such a fool over a girl."

He saw Lacey's lips curl back in distaste.

"I don't see why you should think anything. It's got nothing to do with you," Tristan replied. "Are you going to teach me?"

"Oh, why not? I have time to kill."

They searched out a hidden nook in the trees and sat down, Ella following slowly behind them. Lacey began to pet the cat, and Ella rewarded her with a small, polite purr. When Tristan looked closely, he could see that the tips of her fingers did not glow. They were quite solid.

"All it requires is concentration," said Lacey. "Intense concentration. Look at your fingertips, stare at them as a way of maintaining your focus. You almost will them into being."

Tristan extended his hand toward Ella. He forced everything else out of his mind, focusing on his fingertips. He felt a slight tingling sensation, the kind of pins-and-needles feeling he used to get when his arm fell asleep. The sensation grew stronger and stronger in his fingers. Then another kind of tingling began in his head, a feeling he did not like. He started to grow faint. His whole self, except for his fingers, felt like it was melting away. He pulled back.

Lacey clucked at him. "Lost your nerve."

"I'll try again."

"Better rest for a sec."

"I don't need rest!"

It was humiliating, after being strong and smart all his life – the swimming teacher, the maths tutor – to accept lessons from this know-it-all girl on something as simple as petting a cat.

"Looks like I'm not the only one around here with a big ego," Lacey observed with satisfaction.

Tristan ignored the comment. "What was happening to me?" he asked.

"All your energy was being rerouted to your fingertips," she said, "which made the rest of you feel faint, or like you were dissolving or something."

He nodded.

"As you build up your strength that won't be a problem," she added. "If you ever get to the point of materializing your whole self and projecting your voice – though, frankly, I doubt you will – you'll have to learn to draw energy from your surroundings. I just suck it right out of there."

"You sound like an alien in a sci-fi horror movie."

She nodded. *Lips of Planet Indigo.* You know, I came this close to winning an Oscar for that."

Funny, Tristan remembered it as a box-office bomb.

"Want to try again now?"

Tristan extended his hand. In a way, it was like finding his pulse, like lying on a bed and hearing his own heart: he suddenly became aware of the way energy traveled through him, and he directed it, this time coolly and calmly, to his fingertips. They lost their shimmer.

Then he felt her. Soft, silky, deep fur. Ella began to purr loudly as he traced out all her favorite places to be petted. She rolled on her back. Tristan laughed. When he scratched her belly, her "motor" seemed as loud as a small prop plane's.

Then he lost the touch. The sunlit day went gray. Ella stopped purring. All he could do was hold still and wait, sucking on the air around him like someone trying to catch his breath, though he had none.

"Excellent!" said Lacey. "I had no idea I was such a good teacher."

Color returned to the grass and trees. The sky burned blue again. Only Ella, scrambling to her feet and sniffing the air, showed signs that something wasn't quite right.

Tristan turned to Lacey, exhausted. "I won't be able to reach her. If that is as much as I can do, I won't be able to reach her."

"Are we talking about the chick again?"

"You know her name."

"Ivy. Symbol of faithfulness and remembering. Is there some message you're trying to send her?"

"I have to convince her that I love her."

"That's it?" Lacey made a face. *That's it?*

"I think it's probably my mission," Tristan said.

"Oh, *puh-lease.*"

"You know, I'm getting pretty tired of your sarcasm," Tristan told her.

"I don't much enjoy your silliness," she replied. "Tristan, you are naive if you think the Number One Director would go to all the trouble of making you an angel so you could convince some chick that you love her. Missions are never that simple, never that easy."

He wanted to fight with her, but her melodramatic hand-waving had ceased. She was serious.

"I still don't get it," he said. "How am I supposed to discover my mission?"

"You watch. You listen. You stay close to the people you know or the people you feel yourself drawn to – they're probably the people you've been sent back to help."

Tristan began to wonder who in his life might need special help.

"It's sort of like being a detective," Lacey said. "The hitch is, it's not just a whodunit. It's a who-done-*what*. Often you don't know what the problem is that you've been sent to solve. Sometimes the problem hasn't happened yet – you have to save the person from some disaster that is going to occur in the future."

"You're right," said Tristan. "It's not simple."

They had walked their way past the tennis court and around to the front of the house. Ella, who had been following them, scurried ahead and up the front steps.

"Even if it is something that will happen in the future," Lacey went on, "the key is often hidden in your own past. Fortunately, time travel is not that hard."

Tristan raised his eyebrows. "Time travel?"

Lacey hopped up on Gregory's car, which had been left in the driveway in front of the house.

"Traveling backward in your mind, I mean. There are a lot of things we forget if we remember only in the present. There may be clues that we didn't pick up in the past, but they're still there and can be found again by traveling backward in our minds."

As Lacey spoke she stretched out on the hood of the BMW. She looked to Tristan like Morticia Addams doing a car ad.

"Maybe," she baited him, "I'll teach you how to travel through time, too. Of course, traveling backward in someone *else's* mind, that's not something for an amateur like you to fool around with. There is some danger in all of this," she added. "Oh, cheer *up,* Dumps."

"I'm not down. I'm thinking."

"Then *look* up," she said.

Tristan glanced toward the front door. Ivy stood there, looking out toward the driveway, as if waiting for someone.

"'It is my lady, O, it is my love! O, that she knew she were!'" said Lacey.

Tristan kept his eyes on Ivy. "What?"

"Romeo and Juliet. Act two, scene two. I auditioned for it, you know, for Shakespeare in the Park. The casting director wanted me."

"Good," Tristan said vaguely. He wished she'd leave him alone now. All he wanted was to be alone, to revel in the sight of Ivy, Ivy stepping out onto the porch, Ivy with her hair blowing gold as she gracefully moved to the top of the steps and picked up Ella.

"The director said my kind of talent was to die for."

"Great," said Tristan. If only cats could talk, he thought. Tell her, Ella, tell her what you know.

"The producer, a *major artsy-fartsy,* said he wanted someone who had a 'more classic' face, someone with a voice that wouldn't lapse into New Yorkese."

Ivy was still standing on the porch, cuddling Ella and looking toward him. Maybe she did believe, Tristan thought. Maybe she had a faint sense of his presence.

"That producer is in New York for a couple of weeks, getting a road show ready. I thought I'd pay him a visit."

"Great," Tristan repeated. He turned his head when Ivy did, hearing the whine of a small car climbing to the top of the hill.

"I thought I'd murder him," Lacey added, "'cause a traffic accident that would kill him on the spot."

"Terrific."

"You're pathetic!" she said. "You're really pathetic! Were you this gaga in life? I can only imagine you when you still had hormones pumping through you."

He turned to her angrily. "Look," he said, "you're no better than I am. I'm in love with Ivy, you're in love with you. We're both obsessed, so back off."

For a moment Lacey didn't say anything. Her eyes changed ever so slightly. A camera would not have caught the flicker of hurt feelings. But Tristan did, and knowing that this time she wasn't acting, he regretted his words.

"I'm sorry."

Lacey had turned away from him. He figured she'd be off anytime now, leaving him to fumble his way through his mission.

"Lacey, I'm sorry."

"Well, well, well," she said.

"It's just that—"

"Who is this?" she interrupted him. "Tweedledee and Tweedledum come to mourn with your lady?"

He turned to watch Beth and Suzanne get out of the car. As it happened, they were both wearing black, but Suzanne had always liked black, especially scanty black, which was what she was wearing – a cool halter-top dress. Beth, on the other hand, was wearing clothes typical of Beth: a long, loose dress with white details around the neckline. The hem grazed the ankles, where her gladiator sandals were tied.

"They're her friends, Beth and Suzanne."

"That one is definitely a radio," said Lacey.

"A radio?"

"The one who looks like she's wearing a kaftan."

"Beth," he said. "She's a writer."

"What'd I tell you? A born radio."

Tristan watched Ivy greet her friends and lead them into the house.

"Let's go," Lacey said, springing forward. "This is going to be fun."

He hung back. He had seen her kind of fun earlier.

"Do you want to tell her you love her, or don't you? This will be good training for you, Tristan. You've got it made, the girl's an absolute radio. Good radios don't even have to believe," she added. "They are receptive to all kinds of things, one of those things being angels. You can speak through her – at least, you can write through her. You know what automatic writing is, don't you?"

He had heard of it. Mediums did it, their hands supposedly writing at the will of someone else, relaying messages from the dead.

"You mean Beth is like a medium?"

"An untrained one. A natural radio. She'll broadcast you – if not today, then tomorrow. We've just got to establish the link and slip into her mind."

"Slip into her mind?" he asked.

"It's pretty simple," Lacey said. "All you need to do is think exactly like her, see the world the way Beth sees it, feel as Beth feels, love whomever she loves, desire her deepest desires."

"No way," said Tristan.

"In short, you have to adopt the radio's point of view, and then you slip right in."

"You obviously don't know the way Beth's mind works," said Tristan. "You've never seen her stories. She writes these torrid romances."

"Oh. . . you mean the kind where the lover stares longingly at his beloved, his eyes soulful, his heart aching so that he cannot see or hear anyone else?"

"Exactly."

She tilted back her head and smirked. "You're right. You and Beth are certainly different."

Tristan didn't say anything.

"If you really loved Ivy, you'd try. I'm sure the lovers in Beth's stories wouldn't let a little challenge like this stop them."

"How about Philip?" said Tristan. "He's Ivy's brother. And he can see me shimmering."

"Ah! You've found a believer," she said.

"A radio, I'm sure," Tristan told her.

"Not necessarily. There's no real connection between believing and being a radio."

"Can't we try him first?"

"Sure, we can waste time," she said, and slipped inside the house.

Philip was in the kitchen making microwave brownies. On the counter next to his bowl were a few sticky baseball cards and a catalogue opened to a picture of kids' mountain bikes. Tristan was confident. This was a point of view he knew well.

"Stay behind him," Lacey advised. "If he notices your glow, it will distract him. He'll start searching and trying to understand. He'll focus outward so hard that he won't be open to letting anything else in."

Actually, staying behind Philip helped in other ways. Tristan read the box directions over Philip's shoulder. He thought about what step he should do next and how the brownies would smell as they baked, how they would taste, warm and crumbly, just out of the oven. He wanted to lick the spoon, with its raw, runny chocolate. Philip did lick it.

Tristan knew who he was, and at the same time he was someone else too, the way he'd felt sometimes when reading a good story. This was easy. "Philip, it's me—"

Wham! Tristan reeled backward, as if he had walked into a glass wall. He hadn't seen it, had been totally unaware of it, till it slammed him in the face. For a few moments, he was stunned.

"It can get pretty rough sometimes," Lacey said, observing him. "I guess it's clear to you now. Philip doesn't want you in."

"But I was his friend."

"He doesn't know it's you."

"If he'd let me talk to him, then he would know," Tristan argued.

"It doesn't work that way," she said. "I warned you. I'm getting good at telling radios from non-radios. You can try him again, but he'll be ready for you this time, and it will be even tougher. You don't want a radio who fights you. Let's try Beth."

Tristan paced around. "Why don't *you* try Beth?"

"Sorry."

"But" – he thought fast – "you're such a great actress, Lacey. That's why this kind of thing comes easily to you. An actress's job is to take on a role. The really great ones, *like you,* don't just imitate. No, they *become* the other person. That's why you do it so well."

"Nice try," she said. "But Beth is your radio to the one you're messaging. You have to do it yourself. That's just the way it works."

"It never seems to work the way I want it to," he complained.

"You've noticed that too," she remarked. "I assume you know how to get up to your lady's bower."

Tristan led the way to Ivy's bedroom. The door was open a crack. Ella, who was still following them, nudged it open and entered; they passed through the walls.

Suzanne was sitting in front of Ivy's mirror, rifling through an open jewelry box, trying on Ivy's necklaces and earrings. Ivy was sprawled out on her bed, reading a sheaf of papers – one of Beth's stories, Tristan figured. Beth was pacing around the room.

"At least get yourself a jewel-encrusted pencil," Suzanne said, "if you're going to continue to wear it in your hair like that."

Beth reached up to the knot of hair wound high on her head and plucked out a pencil. "I forgot."

"You're getting worse and worse, Beth."

"It's just all so interesting. Courtney swears her little sister is telling the truth. And when some of the guys went back to the chapel, they found one of the girls' sweaters hung high up on a sconce."

"The girls could have thrown it up there themselves," Suzanne pointed out.

"Mmm. Maybe," Beth said, and pulled a notebook out of her purse.

Lacey turned to Tristan. "There's your entrance. She's thinking about this morning Couldn't have been laid out easier for you."

Beth rolled her pencil back and forth between her fingers. Tristan moved close to her. Guessing that she was trying to picture the scene, he recalled the way the chapel had looked, moving from the bright light outside into its tall shadowiness. He saw the girls settling themselves in the altar area. Beth's stories always had a million details. He recalled the crumbling debris on the floor and imagined how the damp stone might feel beneath the girls' bare legs, how their skin might prickle if a draft came through the broken window, or how they'd twitch if they thought they felt a spider on their legs.

He was in the scene, slipping out of himself and into— Whoa! She didn't slam down like Philip, but he was pushed back swiftly and firmly. Beth stood up, moved several feet away, and looked back at the spot where she had been writing.

"Does she see me?" Tristan asked Lacey. "Does she see my glow?"

"I don't think so – she's not paying any attention to mine. But she knows something's going on. You came on too strong."

"I was trying to think the way she would think, giving her some details. She loves details."

"You rushed her. She knows it doesn't feel right. Back off a little."

But Beth started writing then, describing the girls in the circle. Some of his details were there – whether by his suggestion or her own creation, he wasn't sure – but he couldn't resist pushing further.

Slam! This time it came down hard, so hard that Tristan actually fell backward.

"I warned you," said Lacey.

"Beth, you are as nervous as a cat," Suzanne said.

Ivy looked up from her story. "As nervous as Ella? She's been acting really funny lately."

Lacey shook her finger at Tristan. "Listen to me. You've got to go easy. Imagine Beth is a house and you're a thief breaking in. You have to take your time. You have to creep. Find what you need in the basement, in her unconscious, but don't disturb the person living upstairs. Got it?"

He got it, but he was reluctant to try again. The strength of Beth's mind and the directness of her blow was much greater than Philip's.

Tristan felt frustrated, unable to send the simplest message to Ivy. She was so close, so close, yet . . . He could pass his hand through hers, but never touch. Lie next to her, but never comfort. Say a line to make her smile, but never be heard. He had no place in her life now, and perhaps that was better for her, but it was life in death for him.

"Wow!" said Beth. "Wow – if I do say so myself! How's this for the first line of a story: 'He had no place in her life now, and perhaps that was better for her, but it was life in death for him.'"

Tristan saw the words on the page as if he were holding the notebook in his own hands. And when Beth turned to gaze at the picture of him on Ivy's bureau, he turned, too.

If only you knew, he thought

"'If only'" she wrote. "If only, if only, if only . . ." She seemed to be stuck.

"That is a good beginning," Ivy said, setting aside the typed story. "What comes after it?"

"'If only.'"

"If only what?" Suzanne asked.

"I don't know," Beth said.

Tristan saw the room through her eyes, how pretty it was, how Ella was staring at her, how Suzanne and Ivy exchanged glances, then shrugged.

If only Ivy knew how I love her. He thought the words as clearly as possible.

"'If only I freed—'" She stopped writing and frowned. He could feel the puzzlement like a crease in his own mind.

"Ivy, Ivy, Ivy," he said. "If only Ivy."

"Beth, you look so pale," Ivy observed. "Are you okay?"

Beth blinked several times. "It's as if someone else is making up words for me."

Suzanne made little whistling sounds.

"I am not cuckoo!" said Beth.

Ivy walked over to Beth and looked into her

eyes; she gazed straight in at him. But he knew she didn't see.

"'But she didn't see,'" Beth wrote. Then she scratched out and rewrote, reading aloud as she went: "'He had no place in her life, and perhaps that was best for her, but it was a miserable life in death for him. If only she'd free . . . him from his prison of love. But she didn't know, didn't see the key that was in her hands only—' Beth lifted her pencil for a moment. "I'm on a roll now!" she exclaimed.

She started writing again. "'In her gentle, loving, caring, caressing, hands, in hands that held, that healed, that hoped—'"

Oh, come on, thought Tristan.

"Shut up," Beth answered him.

"What?" said Ivy, her eyes opening wide.

"You're glowing."

Everyone turned to look at Philip, who was standing outside Ivy's door.

"You're glowing, Beth," Philip said.

Ivy turned away. "Philip, I told you I don't want to hear any more about that."

"About me glowing?" Beth asked.

"He's into this angel stuff," Ivy explained. "He claims he sees colors and things, and thinks they're angels. I can't stand it anymore! I don't want to hear it anymore! How many times do I have to tell you that?"

Hearing her words, Tristan lost heart. His effort had taken him well past exhaustion; hope was all that had been sustaining him. Now that was gone.

Beth jerked her head, and he was outside of her once more. Philip kept his eyes on Tristan, following him as he joined Lacey.

"Gee," said Suzanne, winking at Beth, "I wonder where Philip learned about angels."

"They've helped you in the past, Ivy," Beth said gently. "Why can't they help him now?"

"They didn't help me!" Ivy exclaimed. "If angels were real, if angels were our guardians, Tristan would be alive! But he's gone. How can I still believe in angels?"

Her hands were curled into two tight fists. The stormy look in her eyes had become an intense green, burning with certainty, the certainty that there were no angels.

Tristan felt as if he were dying all over again.

Suzanne looked at Beth and shrugged. Philip said nothing. Tristan saw that familiar set in his jaw.

"He's a stubborn little bugger," Lacey remarked.

Tristan nodded. Philip was still believing. Tristan let himself hope just a little.

Then Ivy pulled a plastic bag out of her

trash can. She started clearing off her shelves of angels.

"Ivy, no!"

But his words wouldn't stop her.

Philip tugged on her arm. "Can I have them?"

She ignored him.

"Can I have them, Ivy?"

Tristan heard glass breaking inside the bag. Her hand moved steadily, relentlessly down the line, but she hadn't touched Tony or the water angel yet.

"Please, Ivy."

At last she stopped. "All right. You can have them," she said, "but you have to promise me, Philip, that you will never speak to me about angels again."

Philip looked up thoughtfully at the last two angels. "Okay. But what if—"

"No," she said firmly. "That's the deal.'

He carefully took down Tony and the water angel. "I promise."

Tristan's heart sank.

When Philip had left, Ivy said, "It's getting late. The others will be here soon. I'd better change."

"I'll help you pick out something," Suzanne said.

"No. Go on down, I'll be with you in a few minutes."

"But you know how I like to pick out clothes for you—"

"We're going," Beth said, pushing Suzanne toward the door. "Take all the time you want, Ivy. If the guys get here, we'll stall." She pulled the door closed behind Suzanne.

Ivy looked across her room at the photograph of Tristan. She stood as still as a statue, tears running down her cheeks.

Lacey said softly, "Tristan, you need to rest now. There's nothing you can do until you rest."

But he could not leave Ivy. He put his arms around her. She slipped through him and moved toward the bureau, taking the picture in her hands. He wrapped her in his arms again, but she only cried harder.

Then Ella was set lightly on the bureau top. Lacey's hands had done it. The cat rubbed up against Ivy's head.

"Oh, Ella. I don't know how to let go of him."

"Don't let go," Tristan begged.

"In the end, she must," Lacey warned.

"I've lost him, Ella, I know it. Tristan is dead. He can't hold me ever again. He can't think of me. He can't want me now. Love ends with death."

"It doesn't!" Tristan said. "I'll hold you again,

I swear it, and you'll see that my love will never end."

"You're exhausted, Tristan," Lacey told him.

"I'll hold you, I'll love you forever!"

"If you don't rest now," Lacey said, "you'll become even more confused. It'll be hard to tell real from unreal, or to rouse yourself out of the darkness. Tristan, listen to me . . ."

But before she finished speaking, the darkness overtook him.

16

"Well," said Suzanne as the group of them filed out of the movie theater, "in the last few weeks, I think we've seen at least as many films as Siskel and Ebert."

"I'm not sure they went to see that one," Will observed,

"It's the only flick I've liked so far," Eric said. "Can't wait till they do *Bloodbath IV.*"

Gregory glanced over at Ivy. She turned her head.

Ivy was the one who suggested a movie whenever someone told her she needed to get out, which was often lately. If it had been up to her, she'd sit through a triple feature. Occasionally she lost herself in the story, but even if she didn't, it was a way of looking sociable without having to talk. Unfortunately, the easiest part of the evening was over now. Ivy winced when they came out of the cinema's cool, dark otherworld and into the hot, neon-lit night.

"Pizza?" Gregory asked.

"I could use a drink," said Suzanne.

"Well, Gregory's buying, since he wouldn't let me stock the trunk," Eric told her.

"Gregory's buying pizza," Gregory said.

More and more, Ivy thought, Gregory was coming to resemble a camp counselor, shepherding around this odd flock of people, acting responsible. It was a wonder that Eric put up with it – but she knew that Gregory, Will, and Eric still had their own nights out, nights with wilder girls and guys.

On these group dates Ivy played a game with herself, seeing how long she could go without thinking about Tristan, or at least without missing him terribly. She worked at paying attention to those around her. Life went on for them, even if it didn't for her.

That night they headed for Celentano's, a popular pizza parlor. Their chairs wobbled and the tablecloths were squares of torn-off paper – Crayons and Pencils Provided, a sign said – but the owners, Pat and Dennis, were gourmet all the way. Beth, who loved anything with chocolate, adored their famous dessert pizzas.

"What's it going to be tonight?" Gregory teased her. "Brownies and cheese?"

Beth smiled, two pink streaks showing high in her cheeks. Part of Beth's prettiness was her openness, Ivy thought, her way of smiling at you without holding back.

"I'm getting something different. Something healthy. I've got it! Brie with apricots and shavings of bitter chocolate!"

Gregory laughed and laid his hand lightly on Beth's shoulder. Ivy thought back to the time when she had been mystified by some of Gregory's comments and convinced that he could only mock her and her friends.

But now she found him pretty easy to figure out. Like his father, he had a temper and he needed to be appreciated. At the moment, both Beth and Suzanne were appreciating him, Suzanne watching him more shrewdly, glancing over the top of her menu.

"All I want is pepperoni," Eric complained. "Just pepperoni." He was running his finger up and down and across the list of pizzas, up and down and across, like a frustrated mouse that couldn't find its way out of a maze.

Will had apparently made up his mind. His menu was closed and he had begun drawing on the paper tablecloth in front of him.

"Well, Rembrandt returns," said Pat, passing

by their table, nodding toward Will. "Here for lunch three times this week," she explained to the others. "I'd like to think it's our cooking, but I know it's the free art materials."

Will gave her a smile, but it was more with his eyes, which were deep brown, than with his mouth. His lips turned up slightly at just one corner of his mouth.

He was not easy to figure out, thought Ivy.

"O'Leary," said Eric when the owner had passed by, "have you got the hots for Pat, or what?"

"Likes those older women," Gregory teased. "One at UCLA, one doing Europe instead of college . . ."

"You're kidding," said Suzanne, obviously impressed.

Will glanced up. "We're friends," he said, and continued sketching. "And I work next door, at the photo lab."

That was news to Ivy. None of Gregory's friends had real jobs.

"Will did that portrait of Pat," Gregory told the girls.

It was tacked up on the wall, a piece of cheap paper worked over with wax crayons. But it was Pat all right, with her straight, soft hair and hazel eyes and generous mouth – he had found her beauty.

"You're really good," said Ivy.

Will's eyes flicked up and held hers for a second, then he continued his drawing. For the life of her she didn't know if he was trying to be cool or if he was just shy.

"You know, Will," said Beth, "Ivy keeps wondering if you're really cool or just shy."

Will blinked.

"Beth!" said Ivy. "Where did that come from?"

"Well, haven't you wondered it? Oh, well, maybe it was Suzanne. Maybe it was me. I don't know, Ivy, my mind's a muddle. I've had a kind of headache since I left your house. I think I need caffeine."

Gregory laughed. "That chocolate pizza should do the job."

"For the record," Will said to Beth, "I'm not really cool."

"Give me a break," Gregory said.

Ivy sat back in her chair and glanced at her watch. Well, it had been eight whole minutes that she had thought about other people. Eight whole minutes without imagining what it would have been like if Tristan had been sitting beside her. That was progress.

Pat took their order. Then she dug in her pocket and handed some forms to Will. "I'm doing this in front of your friends, so you can't back out, Will. I've been saving your tablecloths—I'm planning to sell them once your paintings are hanging in the Metropolitan Museum. But if you don't enter some of your work in the festival, I'm entering the tablecloths."

"Thanks for letting me choose, Pat," he said dryly.

"Do you have any more of those forms?" asked Suzanne. "Ivy needs one."

"You've been saving my tablecloths, too?" Ivy asked.

"Your *music,* girl. The Stonehill Festival is for all kinds of artists. They set up a stage for live performances. This will be good for you."

Ivy bit her tongue. She was so tired of people telling her what would be good for her. Every time somebody said that, all she could think was, Tristan is good for me.

Two minutes this time, two minutes without thinking of him.

Pat brought more festival forms along with their pizzas. The others reminisced about the summer arts festivals of the past.

"I liked watching the dancers," Gregory said.

"I was once a young dancer," Beth told him.

"Till an untimely accident ended her career," Suzanne remarked.

"1 was six," Beth said, "and it was all quite magical – flitting around in my sequined costume, a thousand stars sparkling above me. Unfortunately, I danced right off the stage." Will laughed out loud. It was the first time Ivy had heard him laugh like that.

"Do you remember when Richmond played the accordion?"

"Mr. Richmond, our principal?"

Gregory nodded. "The mayor moved a stool out of his way."

"Then Richmond sat down," said Eric.

"Yow!"

Ivy laughed with everyone else, though mostly she was acting. Whenever something did interest her or make her laugh, the first second it held her attention, and the next second she thought, I'll have to tell Tristan.

Four minutes this time.

Will was drawing funny little scenes on the tablecloth: Beth twirling on her toes, Richmond's legs flying upward. He put the scenes together like a comic strip. His hands were quick, his strokes strong and sure. For a few moments, Ivy watched with interest.

Then Suzanne breathed out with a hiss. Ivy glanced sideways, but Suzanne's face was a mask of friendliness. "Here comes a friend of yours," she said to Gregory.

Everyone turned around. Ivy swallowed hard. It was Twinkie Hammonds, the "little, petite" brunette, as Suzanne called her – the girl that Ivy had talked to the day she first saw Tristan swim. And with her was Gary.

Gary was staring at Ivy. Then he checked out Will, who was seated next to her, then Eric and Gregory. Ivy prickled. It wasn't as if she were on a date; still, she felt Gary's eyes accusing her.

"Hi, Ivy."

"Hi."

"Having a good time?" he asked.

She toyed with a crayon, then nodded her head. "Yes."

"Haven't seen you for a while."

"I know," she said, though she had seen him – at the mall once, and another time in town. She had quickly ducked inside the nearest doorway.

"Getting out a lot now?" he asked.

"Pretty much, I guess."

Each time she saw him, she expected Tristan to be nearby.

Each time she had to go through the pain all over again.

"Thought you were. Twinkie told me."

"You got a problem with that?" asked Gregory.

"I was talking to her, not you," Gary replied coolly, "and I was just wondering how she was doing." He shifted his weight from foot to foot. "Tristan's parents were asking about you the other day."

Ivy lowered her head.

"I visit them sometimes."

"Good," she said. She had promised herself a hundred times that she would go see them.

"They get lonely," Gary said.

"I guess they do." She made dark little *X*'s with her crayon.

"They like to talk about Tristan."

She nodded silently. She couldn't go to that house again, she couldn't! She laid the crayon down.

"They still have your picture in his room."

Her eyes were dry. But her breath was ragged. She tried to suck it in and let it out evenly, so no one would notice.

"Your picture has a note tucked under it." Gary's voice wavered with a kind of tremulous laughter. "You know the kind of parents they are — were. Always respecting Tristan and his privacy. Even now they won't read it, but they know it's your handwriting and that he saved it. They figure it's some kind of love note and should stay with your picture."

What had she written? Nothing valuable enough to save. Just notes confirming the time they would meet for their next lesson. And he had saved such a scrap.

Ivy fought back the tears. She should never have gone out with the others that night. She couldn't keep her act together long enough.

"You jerk!" It was Gregory's voice.

"It's okay," said Ivy.

"Get out of here, jerk, before I make you!" Gregory ordered.

"It's okay!" She meant it. Gary couldn't help how he felt, any more than she could.

"I told you, Gary," Twinkie said, "she's not the kind to wear black for a year."

Gregory's chair fell back as he rose, and he kicked it away.

Dennis Celentano collared him just before he got to the other side of the table. "What's the trouble here, guys?"

Ivy sat still with her head down. At one time she would have prayed to her angels for strength, but she couldn't anymore. She held herself still, wrapping her arms around herself. She shut down all thoughts, all feelings; she blocked out all the angry words that whirled around her. Numb, she would stay numb; if only she could stay numb forever.

Why hadn't she died instead of him? Why had it happened the way it did? Tristan had been all his parents had. He had been all she wanted. No one could take his place. She should have died, not him!

The room was suddenly quiet, deathly quiet around her. Had she said that out loud? Gary was gone now. She couldn't hear anything but the scratching of a pencil. Will's hand moved quickly, with strokes strong and even more certain than before.

Ivy watched with numb fascination. Finally Will drew back his hand. She stared at the drawings. Angels, angels, angels. One angel that looked like Tristan, his arms wrapped around her lovingly.

Fury rushed through her. "How dare you!" she said. *"How dare you, Will!"*

His eyes met hers. There was confusion and panic in them. But she did not relent. She felt nothing but fury.

"Ivy, I don't know why . . . I didn't mean . . . I'd never want to, Ivy, I swear I never would—"

She ripped the paper off the table.

He stared at it in disbelief. "I'd never hurt you," he said quietly.

It had been so easy. In less than a millisecond, it seemed, Tristan had slipped inside Will. There was no struggling to communicate: the angel pictures had come quickly, as if their minds were one. He had shared Will's amazement at the sight of the image his pencil had drawn; if only Will could make it real for them, his comforting Ivy.

"What do I do now, Lacey?" Tristan asked.

"How can I help Ivy, when all I do is keep hurting her?"

But Lacey wasn't around to give advice.

Tristan wandered the streets of the silent town long after Ivy and her companions had left. He needed to think things out. He was almost afraid to try again. Statues of angels, pictures of angels, just mentioning angels stirred up in Ivy nothing but pain and anger – but that's what he was now, her angel.

His new powers were useless, completely useless. And there was still the question of his mission, about which he was totally ignorant. It was so hard to think about that, when all he could think about was reaching Ivy.

"What do I do now, Lacey?" he asked again.

He wondered if Lacey was being overly dramatic when she had said that his mission could be to save somebody from disaster. But what if she was right? And what if he was so caught up in his and Ivy's pain that he failed someone?

Lacey had said to stay close to the people he knew, which was why, as soon as he awakened from the darkness, he'd sought out Gary and followed him to Celentano's that evening. She'd also told him that the clue to his mission might be in the past, some problem he saw but did not recognize as such. He needed to figure out how to travel back in time.

He imagined time as a whirling net that held thoughts and feelings and actions together, a net that had held him until he suddenly broke away. It seemed that the easiest point of entry would be his point of exit. Would it help to go to the place itself?

He quickly made his way along the dark, winding back roads. It was quite late now and no cars were on the road. An eerie kind of feeling, the sense that at any moment a deer might leap out in front of him, made him slow down, but only for a moment.

It was strange how easily he found the spot and how certain he was that it *was* the spot, for each turn and twist in the road looked the same. The moon, though it was full, barely filtered through the heavy leaves. There was no silver splash of light here, just a lightening of the air, a kind of ghostly gray mist. Still, he found the roses. Not the ones he had given her, but roses like them. They lay on the side of the road, completely wilted. When he picked them up, their petals fell off like charred flakes; only their purple satin ribbon had survived.

Tristan looked down the road as if he could look back into time. He tried to remember the last minute of being alive. The light. An incredible light and voice, or message – he wasn't sure if it was actually a voice and couldn't remember any words. But that had come after the explosion of light. He returned to the light again and focused his mind on it.

A pinpoint of light – yes, before the tunnel, before the dazzling light at the end, there had been a pinpoint of light, the light in the deer's eye.

Tristan shuddered. He braced himself. Then his whole self felt the impact. He felt as if he were collapsing in on himself. He fell back. The car was rushing backward, like an amusement park ride suddenly thrown in reverse. He was caught in a tape running backward, with words of gibberish and frantic motions. He tried to stop it, willed it to stop, every bit of his energy bent on stopping the backward-racing time.

Then he and Ivy sat side by side, absolutely still, as if frozen in a movie frame. They were in the car and eased slowly forward now.

"Last glimpse of the river," he said as the road made a sharp turn away from it.

The June sun, dropping over the west ridge of the Connecticut countryside, shafted light on the very tops of the trees, flaking them with gold. The winding road slipped below, into a tunnel of maples, poplars, and oaks. It was like slipping under dark green waves. Tristan flicked on his headlights.

"You really don't have to hurry," said Ivy, "I'm not hungry any more."

"I ruined your appetite?"

She shook her head. "I guess I'm all filled up with happiness," she said softly.

The car sped along and took a curve sharply.

"I said, we don't have to hurry."

"That's funny," he murmured. "I wonder what's—" He glanced down at his feet. "This doesn't feel . . ."

"Slow down, okay? It doesn't matter if we're a little late— Oh!" Ivy pointed straight ahead. "Tristan!"

Something had plunged through the bushes and into the roadway. He saw it, too, a flicker of motion among the deep shadows. Then the deer stopped. It turned its head, its eyes drawn to the car's bright headlights.

"Tristan!" she shouted.

He braked harder. They were rushing toward the shining eyes.

"Tristan, don't you see it?"

"Ivy, something's—"

"A deer!"

He braked again and again, the pedal pressed flat to the floor, but the car wouldn't slow down.

The animal's eyes blazed. Then light came from behind it, a burst of headlights – a car was coming from the opposite direction. Trees walled them in. There was no room to steer to the left or the right, and the brake pedal was flat against the floor.

"Stop!" she shouted.

"I'm—"

"Stop, why don't you stop?" she pleaded. "Tristan, *stop!*"

He willed the car to stop, he willed himself back into the present, but he had no control, nothing would stop him from speeding into the whirling funnel of darkness. It swallowed him up.

When he opened his eyes, Lacey was peering down at him.

"Rough ride?"

Tristan looked around. He was still on the wooded road, but it was early morning now, gold light fragile as spiderwebs netting the trees. He tried to remember what had happened.

"You called me, hours ago, asked me what to do next," she reminded him. "Obviously you couldn't wait to find out."

"I went back," he said, and then in a rush he remembered. "Lacey, it wasn't just the deer. If it hadn't been the deer, it would have been a wall. Or trees or the river or the bridge. It could have been another car."

"Slow down, Tristan! What are you saying?"

"There was no pressure, no fluid. It went all the way down to the floor."

"What did?" Lacey asked.

"The pedal. The brake. It shouldn't have given out like that." He grabbed Lacey. "What if . . . what if it wasn't an accident? What if it only looked like one?"

"And you only look dead," she replied. "Sure fooled me."

"Listen to me, Lacey. Those brakes were in perfect shape. Somebody must have messed with them. Somebody cut the line! You have to help me."

"But I don't even know how to pump gas," she said.

"You have to help me reach Ivy!" Tristan started down the road.

"I'd rather work on the brakes," Lacey called after him. "Slow down, Tristan. Before you knock off another deer."

But nothing would stop him. "Ivy has to believe again," Tristan said. "We have to reach her. She has to know that it wasn't an accident. Somebody wanted me – or Ivy – dead!"

17

"This time I'll reach her!" Tristan said. "I have to warn Ivy, I have to tell her that the crash wasn't an accident. Lacey, help me out! You know this angel stuff doesn't come naturally to me."

"You can say that again," Lacey replied, leaning back against Tristan's tombstone.

"Then you'll come with me?"

Lacey checked her nails, long purple nails that wouldn't chip or break any more than Tristan's thick brown hair would grow again. At last she said, "I guess I can squeeze in a pool party for an hour. But listen, Tristan, don't expect me to be a perfect, angelic guest."

Ivy stood at the edge of the pool, her skin prickling from the cold water that occasionally splashed her. Two girls brushed past her, chased by a guy with a water gun. The three of them tumbled into the pool together, leaving Ivy drenched by a shower of icy drops. If this had been the year before, she would have been trembling, trembling and praying to her water angel. But angels weren't real. Ivy knew that now.

The previous winter, when she had dangled from a diving board high above the school pool, frozen with a fear she had known since childhood, she had prayed to her water angel. But it was Tristan who had saved her, then taught her to swim. She had loved him, even when he argued that angels weren't real.

Tristan had been right. And now Tristan was gone, along with her belief in angels.

"Going for a swim?"

Ivy turned quickly and saw her own suntanned face and tumbleweed of gold hair reflected in Eric Ghent's sunglasses. His wet hair was slicked back, almost transparent against his head.

"I'm sorry we don't have a high dive," Eric said.

She ignored the little jab. "It's a beautiful pool anyway."

"It's pretty shallow at this end," he said, pulling off his sunglasses, letting them dangle from their cord against his bony chest. Eric's eyes were light blue, and his lashes were so pale he looked as if he didn't have any. "I can swim – either end," Ivy told him.

"Really." One side of Eric's mouth curled up. "Let me know when you're ready," he told her, then walked away to talk to his other guests.

Ivy hadn't expected Eric to be any nicer than that. Though he had invited her and her two closest friends to his midsummer pool party, they weren't members of Stonehill's fast crowd. Ivy was sure that Beth, Suzanne, and she were there only at the request of Eric's best friend and Ivy's stepbrother, Gregory.

She gazed across the pool at a line of sunbathers, searching for her friends. In the midst of a dozen oiled bodies and bleached heads sat Beth, wearing a huge hat and a long tunic. She was talking a mile a minute to Will O'Leary, another one of Gregory's friends. Somehow Beth Van Dyke, who had never even dreamed of being cool, and Will, who was thought to be ultracool, had become friends.

The girls around them were arranging themselves to show the sun – or Will – their best angle, but Will didn't notice. He was nodding encouragingly to Beth, who was probably telling him her newest idea for a short story. Ivy wondered if, in his quiet way, Will enjoyed Beth's writings – poems and stories, and, once for history class, a biography of Mary, Queen of Scots – which somehow always turned into steamy bare-every-emotion tales of romance. The thought made Ivy smile.

Will glanced across the pool just then and

caught the smile. For a moment his face seemed alight. Perhaps it was only the flicker of sun flashing off the water, but Ivy took a self-conscious step back. Just as quickly, he turned his face into the shade of Beth's hat.

As Ivy stepped back she felt the bare skin of a cool, hard chest. The person did not move out of the way, but rather lowered his face over her shoulder, brushing her ear with his mouth.

"I think you have an admirer," said Gregory.

Ivy did not move away from him. She had gotten used to her stepbrother, his tendency to lean too close, his way of showing up behind her unexpectedly. "An admirer? Who?"

Gregory's gray eyes laughed down at her. He had a deep tan from spending hours a day playing tennis.

In the last month, he and Ivy had spent a lot of time together, though back in April she would never have believed it possible. Then, all that she and Gregory had in common was shock at their parents' decision to marry, and anger at and distrust of each other.

When two people live in the same house, Ivy discovered, they share some of their deepest feelings, and, surprisingly enough, she had come to trust Gregory with hers. He was there for her when she missed Tristan the most.

"An admirer," Ivy repeated, smiling. "Sounds to

me like you've been reading Beth's romances." She moved away from the pool, and Gregory moved with her like a shadow. Quickly Ivy scanned the patio area for Suzanne. For Suzanne's sake, Ivy wished Gregory would not stand so close. She wished he wouldn't whisper to her as if they shared some secret.

Suzanne said she and Gregory were officially dating now; Gregory smiled and admitted to nothing. Just as Ivy laid a light hand on Gregory to push him back a little, a glass door slid open and Suzanne emerged from the pool house. She paused for a moment, as if taking in the scene – the long sapphire oval of the pool, the marble sculptures, the terraces of flowers. The pause conveniently gave all the guys a chance to look at her. With her shimmering mane of black hair and a tiny bikini that seemed more like jewelry than clothing, she outshone all the other girls, including the ones who had been longtime members of Eric and Gregory's crowd.

"If anyone has admirers," Ivy said, "it's Suzanne. And if you're smart, you'll get over there before twenty other guys line up."

Gregory just laughed and brushed back a tangle of golden hair from Ivy's cheek. He knew, of course, that Suzanne was watching. Both Gregory and Suzanne were into playing games, and Ivy was often caught in the middle.

Suzanne moved with catlike grace, reaching them quickly, yet never appearing to move faster than a leisurely stroll.

"Great suit!" she greeted Ivy.

Ivy blinked, then stared down at her one-piece in surprise. Suzanne had been with her when she bought the suit and had urged her to find something that plunged even further. But of course this was just a setup to turn Gregory's attention to Suzanne's . . . jewelry.

"It really looks terrific on you, Ivy."

"That's what I told her," Gregory said in an overly warm voice.

He had never said a thing about Ivy's suit. His white lie was intended to make Suzanne jealous. Ivy flashed him a look and he laughed.

"Did you bring any sunblock?" Suzanne asked. "I can't believe I forgot mine."

Ivy couldn't believe it, either. Suzanne had been working that line since they were twelve and vacationing at the Goldsteins' beach house.

"I know my back is going to fry," Suzanne said.

Ivy reached for her bag, which was on a nearby chair. She knew that Suzanne could stretch out on a sheet of foil at high noon and still never burn. "Here. Keep it. I've got plenty."

Then she placed the tube in Gregory's hands. She started off, but Gregory caught her by the arm.

"How about you?" he asked, his voice low and intimate.

"How about me what?"

"Don't you need some lotion?" he asked.

"Nope, I'm fine."

But he wouldn't let her go. "You know how you forget the most obvious places," he said as he smoothed the lotion at the base of her neck and across her shoulders, his voice as silky soft as his fingers. He tried to slip a finger under one strap. Ivy held the strap down. She was getting mad. No doubt Suzanne was burning up, too, she thought – though not from the sun.

Ivy pulled away from Gregory and quickly put on her sunglasses, hoping they would mask her anger. She walked away briskly, leaving them to tease and antagonize each other.

Both of them were using her to score points. Why couldn't they leave her out of their stupid games?

You're jealous, she chided herself. You're just jealous because they have each other, and you don't have Tristan.

She found an empty lounge chair at the edge of a small crowd and dropped down into it. The guy and girl next to her watched with interest as Suzanne led Gregory to two loungers in a corner apart from the others. They whispered as Gregory spread lotion over her perfectly shaped body.

Ivy closed her eyes and thought about Tristan, about their plans to run off to the lake together, to float out in the middle of it with the sun sparkling at their fingertips and toes. She thought about the way Tristan had kissed her in the backseat of the car the night of the accident. It was the tenderness of his kiss that she remembered, the way he had touched her face with wonder, almost reverence. The way he had held her made her feel not only loved, but sacred to him.

"You still haven't gone in the water."

Ivy opened her eyes. It seemed pretty clear that Eric wouldn't let her alone until she proved she would not freak out in the pool.

"I was just thinking about it," she said, removing her sunglasses. He waited for her by the pool's edge.

Ivy was glad that, at his own party, Eric had stayed sober. But perhaps this was how he made up for it. Without alcohol, without drugs, this was how Eric entertained himself: testing people on their most vulnerable points.

Ivy slipped into the water. In the first few moments the old fear washed over her as the water crept up her neck, and she was terribly afraid. "That's what courage is," Tristan had said, "facing what you're afraid of." With each stroke, she grew a little more comfortable.

She swam the length of the pool, then stopped

and waited for Eric in the deep end. He was a poor swimmer.

"Not bad," Eric said when he caught up with her. "You're not bad for a beginner."

"Thanks," said Ivy.

"You're not even out of breath."

"I guess I'm in good shape."

"Not out of breath at all," he said. "You know, there's a game Gregory and I played at camp when we were little kids."

He paused, and Ivy guessed that he was going to suggest they play it now. She wished they were hanging on to the wall at the other end of the pool, where it was shallow and the trees didn't crowd out the sun, and most everyone else now waded and sat.

"It's a test to see how long each of us can hold our breath," he told her. He spoke without looking at her; Eric rarely looked anyone in the eye.

"You have to duck under the water and stay under for as long as possible while the other person times it."

Ivy thought it was a dumb game, but she went along with it, figuring that the sooner they played it, the sooner she could get rid of him.

Eric quickly went under, holding his arm above the surface so she could read his watch. He stayed under for one minute and five seconds, surfacing with a rasping gasp. Then Ivy took a deep gulp of air and dropped down. She counted slowly to herself – (one one thousand, two one thousand) – determined to beat him. While she held her breath she watched her loose hair swirl around her. The chlorine was strong, and she wanted to close her eyes, but something told her not to trust Eric.

When she finally surfaced he said, "I'm impressed! One minute and three seconds."

She had counted one minute and fifteen.

"Here's the next step," he said. "We see if we can stay under longer by going down together. It's like we encourage each other. Ready?"

Ivy nodded reluctantly. After this, she was getting out of the pool. Eric stared at his watch. "On the count of three. One, two—" He suddenly pulled her under.

Ivy hadn't gotten her breath. She pulled back, but Eric wouldn't let go. She waved her hands at him underwater but he gripped her upper arms.

Ivy began choking. She had swallowed some water as Eric dragged her down, and she couldn't help coughing, trying to clear her lungs – but each time she did, she swallowed more water. Eric held her tight.

She tried to kick him but he moved his legs out of the way and smiled a close-lipped smile.

He's enjoying this, she thought. He thinks this is fun. He's crazy!

Ivy struggled to get away from him. Her stomach tightened with cramps, and her knees drew up. Her lungs felt as if they would burst.

Suddenly Eric grimaced. He pulled to one side so swiftly that he swung Ivy around with him. Then he let go. They both came to the surface, gasping and sputtering.

"You jerk. You stupid jerk!" Ivy yelled. But her coughing stopped her from going on.

Eric pulled himself up onto the wall, his face pale, his fingers still clutching his side. When his hand dropped, she saw the red marks, thin bloody stripes, as if someone had scratched his back and side with long, sharp fingernails.

Eric glanced around quickly with pale, unfocused eyes, then turned to her. His face seemed almost as distorted as it had underwater. "I was only playing," he said.

Someone called him from the opposite end of the pool. People were starting to move inside. He got up slowly and headed in the direction of the pool house. Ivy stayed by the side of the pool, taking deep breaths. She knew she had to stay in the pool. She had to wait till she was breathing normally again, then swim some laps. Tristan had led her past her fear. She was not going to let Eric take her back again. She began to swim.

When Ivy reached the end of the pool and made her turn for another lap, Beth reached down and grabbed her ankle. Ivy looked over her shoulder and saw Beth teetering on the edge of the pool, her large-brimmed hat coming down over her eyes. Will moved quickly to anchor Beth from behind.

"What's up?" Ivy asked, smiling at Beth, glancing quickly, self-consciously at Will.

"Everyone's going inside to watch videos," Beth told her enthusiastically, "some that were taken at school this year, and after school at basketball games and—" Beth stopped.

"Swim meets," Ivy finished the sentence for her. Perhaps she could see, one more time, Tristan swimming the butterfly.

Beth took a step back from the edge of the pool and turned to Will. "I'm going to stay outside for a while."

"Don't stay outside for me, Beth," Ivy said. "I—"

"Listen," Beth interrupted her, "with everybody inside, I can finally bare this beautiful white bod and not worry about giving them all snow blindness."

Will laughed softly and said something intended for Beth's ears only.

Will was a sweet guy, but Ivy wouldn't have blamed him if he were furious at her, not after the scene she had made the previous Saturday night when he had drawn pictures of angels – one of Tristan as an angel with his arms wrapped around Ivy – and she had ripped it to shreds.

"Go in and watch the videos, Beth," Ivy said firmly. "I just want to swim a little."

Will leaned forward then. "You shouldn't swim by yourself, Ivy."

"That's what Tristan used to say."

In response, Will gazed back at her with eyes that spoke a language of their own. They were brown pools, deep enough to drown in, Ivy thought. Tristan's had been hazel, and yet there was something similar about his eyes and Will's, something that drew her to him.

She turned away quickly, then caught her breath. With a soft flash of colorful wings, a butterfly landed on her shoulder.

"A flyer," Beth said. Perhaps because they were all thinking about Tristan, Beth had used the word for a swimmer who did the butterfly.

Ivy tried to brush off the insect. Its wings fluttered, but it surprised her by staying put.

"It's mistaken you for a flower," Will said, smiling, his eyes full of light.

"Maybe," Ivy replied, anxious to get away from him and Beth. Pushing off from the side of the pool, she began to swim.

She did lap after lap, and when she was finally tired, she swam to the middle of the pool and flipped over to float.

"It's such a great feeling, Ivy. Do you know what it's like to float on a lake, a circle of trees around you, a big blue bowl of sky above you? You're lying on top of the water, sun sparkling at the tips of your fingers and toes."

The memory of Tristan's voice was so strong it was as if she heard it now. It seemed impossible that the big blue bowl of sky stayed up; it should have shattered like the car windshield the night of the accident, but there it was.

She remembered lying back in the water, feeling his arm beneath her as he taught her to float. "Easy now, don't fight it," he'd said.

She didn't fight it. She closed her eyes and imagined being in the center of a lake. When she had opened her eyes, he was looking down on her, his face like the sun, warming her.

"I'm floating," Ivy had whispered, and whispered it now.

"You're floating."

"Floating." They had read it off each other's lips, and for a moment now she felt as if he were bending over her still – "Floating" – their lips close, so close . . .

"Give 'em back!"

Ivy pulled her head up quickly, and her feet sank straight down beneath her. She quickly wiped the water out of her eyes.

The door of the pool house had been flung open, and Gregory was racing across the lawn, carrying a small piece of dark clothing in his hands.

Odd globs of white, foamy stuff flew from his hair. Eric came streaking after him, one hand clutching Beth's hat – his only bit of cover – and the other wielding a long kitchen knife. "You're dead meat, Gregory."

"Come get them." Gregory egged him on, holding up Eric's trunks. "Come on. Give it your best shot."

"I'm going to—"

"Sure, sure," Gregory baited.

Eric suddenly stopped running. "I'll get you, Gregory," he warned. "When you least expect it."

18

Lacey sat back in the café chair, smiling at Tristan and looking very pleased with herself. Apparently she had forgiven him for dragging her away from the pool house free-for-all at Eric's party. Now she hooked her thumbs together and flapped her hands, rippling her fingers like wings. "You have to admit, landing that butterfly on Ivy was a nice touch."

Tristan eyed her shimmering fingers and long nails, and responded with something between a grimace and a smile

"The butterfly was nice," he began, "but—"

"You're wondering how I did it," she interrupted. "I guess I'll have to teach you about using force fields." She eyed the dessert tray as it went by – not that she, or he, could actually eat.

"But—" Tristan said again.

"You're wondering how I knew about the butterfly," she said. "I told you, I read all about Stonehill High's hero, the great swimmer, Tristan Carruthers, in the local paper. I knew the butterfly was your stroke. I knew it would make Ivy think of you."

"What I was wondering was this: Couldn't you have left the pies alone?"

Her eyes slid over to the dessert tray again.

"Don't even think about it," he said.

There were only a handful of customers sitting at the town's outdoor café at four-thirty in the afternoon, but he knew Lacey could create chaos with very little. Two pies and some whipped cream – that's all it had taken earlier at Eric's. "I mean, isn't that kind of stunt a little old, Lacey? It was old when the Three Stooges did it."

"Oh, lighten up, Dumps," she replied. "Everyone at the party enjoyed it. Okay, okay," she said, "*some* people enjoyed it, and a few, like Suzanne, got fussy about their hair. But *I* had a good time."

Tristan shook his head. Lacey had been lightning-quick, moving around the pool house, invisibly picking fights. She had obviously enjoyed yanking at Gregory's swimming trunks whenever Eric was close by. "Now I know why you never complete your mission," Tristan said.

"Well, *excu-u-use* me! *Please* remind me of that next time you *beg* me to come with you and help you reach Ivy." She stood up abruptly and stomped out of the café. Tristan was used to her dramatics and followed her slowly onto Main Street.

"You've got nerve, Tristan, criticizing my little bit of fun. Where were you when Ivy started making faces like a goldfish down in the deep end of the pool? Who took care of Eric?"

"You did," he said, "and you know where I was."

"All tangled up inside of Will."

Tristan nodded. The truth was embarrassing.

He and Lacey moved silently down the brick sidewalk, passing a row of shops with bright striped awnings. Windows full of antiques, art books and soft furnishings showed off the taste of the wealthy Connecticut town. Tristan still walked as if he were alive and solid, moving out of the way of shoppers. Lacey went straight through them.

"I must be doing something wrong," Tristan said at last. "One moment I'm inside Will, so much a part of him that when he looks at Ivy, I do, too. It's like he feels what I feel for her. Then all of a sudden he pulls back."

Lacey had stopped to look in the window of a dress shop.

"I must be pushing too hard," Tristan continued. "I need Will to speak for me. But I think he's discovered me prowling around in his mind, and now he's afraid of me."

"Or maybe," said Lacey, "he's afraid of *her*."

"Of Ivy?"

"Of his feelings for her."

"*My* feelings for her!" Tristan said quickly.

Lacey turned to look at him, her head cocked. Tristan feigned a sudden interest in an ugly black sequined dress hanging in the window. He couldn't see a reflection of Lacey's face in the glass, any more than he could see his own. Just a shimmer of gold and wisps of soft color shone against the window; he guessed that it was what a believer would see when looking at them.

"Why?" Lacey asked. "I want to know *why* you assume that you're the only guy in the world in love with—"

Tristan cut in. "I entered Will, and since he's a good radio, he started to feel my feelings and think my thoughts. That's how it works, right?"

"Didn't it ever occur to you that the reason it was so easy for an amateur like you to enter Will was because he was *already* feeling your feelings and thinking your thoughts, at least when it comes to Ivy?"

It had, but Tristan had done his best to squelch the idea.

"I got inside Beth's mind, too," he reminded her.

"You got inside, but it was tougher for you," Lacey pointed out. "You bumbled a lot, remember? And besides, Beth also loves Ivy."

She turned back to the window. "A killer dress,"

she said, then walked on. "What I really want to know is what everyone sees in this chick."

"It was nice of you to save a chick you think so little of," Tristan remarked dryly.

They passed the photo lab where Will worked and stopped in front of Celentano's, the pizza parlor where Will had drawn the angels on the paper tablecloth.

"I didn't save her," Lacey replied. "Eric was just playing – but you'd better figure out what kind of game it is. I've known some real creeps in my life, and I've got to say, he's not someone *I'd* like to party with."

Tristan nodded. He had so much to learn.

"Do you think Eric did it?" he asked.

"Went after your brakes?" Lacey twisted a spike of purple hair around a daggerlike fingernail. "That's a leap, from being a bully in the deep end to committing murder. What did he have against you and Ivy?"

Tristan lifted his hands, then let them drop. "I don't know."

"What did anybody have against you or her? They could have been after just one of you. If it was you they wanted to get rid of, she's safe now."

"If she's safe, why was I brought back on a mission?"

"To annoy me," Lacey said. "Obviously you're

some kind of penance for me. Oh, cheer up, Dumps! Maybe you just got your mission wrong."

She slipped through the door of Celentano's without opening it, then reached up mischievously and jangled the three little bells over it. Two guys in T-shirts and grass-stained cutoffs stared at the door. She jangled them a second time, and the guys, unable to see either Lacey or Tristan, looked at each other.

Tristan smiled, then said, "You're going to scare away business."

Lacey climbed up on the counter next to Dennis Celentano. He had rolled out some dough and was expertly flipping it above his head – until it didn't come back down. It hung like a wet washrag in midair. Dennis gaped up at it, then leaned from one side to the other, trying to figure out what was holding up the dough.

Tristan guessed that the dough was going to be one more pie in the face. "Be nice, Lacey."

She dropped the dough neatly on the counter. They left Dennis and his customers to look at one another and wonder. "With you around," she complained to Tristan, "I'll be earning gold stars and finishing up my mission in no time."

Tristan doubted it. "Maybe you can earn some more stars by helping me with mine," he told her. "Didn't you tell me there was a way to travel back in time through somebody else's mind? Didn't you say I could search the past through someone else's memory?"

"No, I said *I* could," she replied.

"Teach me."

She shook her head.

"Come on, Lacey."

"Nope."

They were at the end of the street now, standing in front of an old church with a low stone wall around it. Lacey hopped up on the wall and began to walk it.

"It's too risky, Tristan. And I don't think it's going to help you any. Even if you could get inside a mind like Eric's, what do you think you'd find? That guy's circuits have been curled and fried. It could be – to use one of his terms – a very bad trip for you."

"Teach me," he persisted. "If I'm going to learn who cut the brakes, I'm going to have to go back to that night in the mind of everybody who might have seen something, including Ivy."

"Ivy! You'll *never* get in! That chick's got you and everyone else closed out cold."

Lacey paused, waiting till she had Tristan's full attention, then lifted up one leg as if she were doing a balance-beam routine. She's never lost her appetite for an audience, Tristan thought.

"I tried Ivy myself at the pool party this afternoon," Lacey went on. "I can't imagine how, even when you were alive, you and that chick ever got it on."

"Do you think you could come up with a way to give advice without making sarcastic remarks about 'that chick'?"

"Sure," she answered agreeably, and started walking the wall again. "But it wouldn't be half as much fun."

"I'll try Philip again," Tristan said, more to himself than to her. "And Gregory—"

"Now, *Gregory's* a tough nut to crack. Do you trust him? Stupid question," she said before he could answer. You don't trust anyone who's got eyes for Ivy."

Tristan's head bobbed up. "Gregory's dating Suzanne."

She laughed down at him. "You're so naive! It's refreshing, for a jock-hunk type like you, but it's kind of pitiful, too."

"Teach me," he said for the third time, then reached up and caught her hand. "I'm worried about her, Lacey, I'm really worried."

She looked down at him.

"Help me."

Lacey stared at her long fingers caught by his. She pulled her hand away very slowly, then reached down and patted him on the head. He hated the way she could patronize him, and he didn't like begging, but she knew things that would take a long time for him to learn on his own.

"Okay, okay. But listen up, because I'm only telling you once."

He nodded.

"First you have to find the hook. You have to find something that the person saw or did that night. The best kind of hook is an object or action that is connected with that night only, but avoid anything that might threaten your host. You don't want to set off alarm bells in his head."

She stepped carefully along a crumbling section of wall. "It's sort of like Google. If you pick a term that's too general, you'll call up all kinds of junk you don't want."

"Easy enough," he said with confidence.

"Uh-huh," she said, and rolled her eyes. "Once you've got your hook, you enter the person, like you've already done with Will and Beth, only you have to be more careful than ever. If your host feels you prowling around, if something feels strange to him, he's going to be on guard. Then he'll be too alert to let his mind wander back through memories."

"They'll never guess I'm there."

"*Uh-huh*," she said again. "Be patient. Creep." She crept along the wall in slow motion. "And slowly bring into focus whatever image you're using for the hook. Remember to see it the same way that your host would."

"Of course." It was simple. He probably could have figured it out on his own, he thought. "And then?"

She jumped down from the wall. "That's it."

"That's it?"

"That's when the fun begins."

"But tell me what it's like, Lacey, so I know what to expect. Tell me how it feels."

"Oh, I think you probably could figure it out on your own."

He stopped short. "Can you read minds?"

She turned to look him straight in the eye. "No, but I'm pretty good at reading faces. And yours is like a large-print book."

He glanced away.

"You need me, Tristan, but you don't take me seriously. I met a lot of people like you when I was alive."

He didn't know what to say.

"Listen, I've got my own mission to work on. It's time I start poking around New York City, going back to the beginning and figuring out what I'm supposed to be figuring out. Thanks to you, I'm already late for the train."

"Sorry," he said.

"I know you can't help it. Listen, if you should finish up your mission before I get back, can I have your grave? I mean, me not having one, unless you count my airplane seat at the bottom of the Atlantic, and you wouldn't be needing one after that—"

"Sure, sure."

"Of course, I might finish up my mission first."

After two years of procrastinating? he thought, but didn't dare say it aloud.

"I swear your face is like one of those large-print books my mother used to read."

Then she laughed and hurried off in the direction of the station that was at the edge of town, nestled between the river and the ridge.

Tristan turned the opposite way to climb a road that would take him to the top of the ridge, where the Baines house was. Philip might be home, he thought. And Ella would be there.

He was able to pet Ella when he materialized the tips of his fingers. That was about as much as he could do now: pet a cat, pick up a piece of paper. Tristan longed to touch Ivy, to be strong enough to hold her in his arms.

He'd go straight to the house now and wait for her to come home from the party. He'd watch for Gregory, too. While he did, he'd figure out whose mind might hold the clue he needed – and how, please tell me how, he prayed, to reach Ivy!

19

Suzanne swatted back a piece of hanging plant that needed clipping, then stretched out luxuriously on her sofa. She wore a pale-pink silk robe and had wrapped a pink towel around her head like a turban. Everything in the room – the large, round tub, the pillows, the luxurious carpeting and silk-grained wallpaper – was pink or white.

The first time Ivy had walked into this room at Suzanne's house, her eyes had popped open. She was seven years old then. The sumptuous bath, the elegant child's bedroom, and the velvet-lined trunks containing twenty-six Barbie dolls immediately convinced Ivy that Suzanne was a princess, and Suzanne didn't act otherwise. She was a remarkable princess who cheerfully shared all her toys and had a nice streak of wildness in her.

That day Ivy and Suzanne had snipped off small

hunks of their own hair and made little wigs for the dolls. Twenty-six dolls required a lot of hair. Ivy figured she'd never get invited back, but soon she was being picked up by Mrs. Goldstein all the time, because Suzanne said she wanted to play with Ivy even more than she wanted her allowance or a pony.

Suzanne sighed, adjusted her turban, and opened her eyes. "Are you warm enough, Ivy?"

Ivy nodded. "Perfect." After bringing Suzanne home from the party, Ivy had changed from her wet bathing suit to a T-shirt and shorts. Suzanne had lent her a pale blue, satiny robe, which was needed in the air-conditioned house. It made Ivy feel like part of the princess scene.

"Perfect," Suzanne repeated, lifting a long, tan leg, pointing her toes. She took a sudden ungraceful swat at the plant hanging over her sofa, then dropped her leg and laughed. Now that the pie and whipped cream had been washed out of her hair, she was in a much better mood.

"He is . . . perfect. Tell me the truth, Ivy," she said. "Does Gregory think about me often?"

"How would I know, Suzanne?"

Suzanne turned on her side to face Ivy. "Well, does Gregory talk about me?"

"He has," Ivy said cautiously.

"A lot?"

"Naturally he wouldn't say a lot to me. He knows I'm your best friend and would pass it along to you, or at least have it tortured out of me." Ivy grinned.

Suzanne sat up and whipped the towel off her head. A tumble of jet black hair fell over her shoulders.

"He's a flirt," she said. "Gregory will flirt with anyone – even you."

Ivy didn't take offense at the words *even you*. "Of course he will," she said. "He knows it gets to you. He likes to play games, too."

Suzanne dropped her chin and smiled up at Ivy through wisps of damp hair.

"You know," Ivy went on, "you two are supplying Beth with a ton of material. She'll have written five Harlequins before we graduate from high school. If I were you, I'd ask for a cut."

"Mmm." Suzanne smiled to herself. "And I've only just begun."

Ivy laughed and stood up. "Well, I've got to go now."

"You're going? Wait! We've hardly talked about the other girls at the party."

They had dissected the other girls all the way home, and shouted a dozen more catty comments over the loud drumming of Suzanne's shower.

"And we haven't talked about *you*," said Suzanne.

"Well, when it comes to me, there's really nothing to talk about," Ivy told her. She took off the robe and started folding it.

"Nothing? That's not what I heard," Suzanne said slyly.

"What did you hear?"

"Well, first off, I want you to know that when I heard it—"

"Heard what?" Ivy asked impatiently.

"—I told them all that, as someone who has known you a long time, I thought it unlikely."

"Thought what unlikely?"

Suzanne started combing her hair. "I may have even said *very* unlikely – I can't remember."

Ivy sat down. "Suzanne, what are you talking about?"

"At least I told them I was very surprised to hear that you were making out in the deep end with Eric."

Ivy's mouth dropped. "Making out with Eric! And you told them it was *unlikely?* More like totally impossible! Suzanne, you know I wouldn't!"

"I don't know anything for sure about you anymore. People do strange things when they're mourning. They get lonely. They try different ways to forget . . . What exactly were you doing?"

"Playing a game."

"A kissing game?"

Ivy blew out through her lips. "A stupid game."

"Well, I'm glad to hear it," Suzanne said. "I don't think Eric's right for you. He's much too fast, and he plays around with some weird stuff. But of course you *should* start dating again."

"No."

"Ivy, it's time you started living again."

"Living and dating aren't the same thing," Ivy pointed out.

"They are to me," Suzanne replied.

They both laughed.

"What about Will?" Suzanne asked.

"What about him?"

"Well, he's kind of a newcomer to Stonehill, like you, and an artsy type – like you. Gregory said that the paintings he's entering in the festival are awesome."

Gregory had told Ivy the same thing. She wondered if the two of them were conspiring to get her and Will together.

"You're not still angry about him drawing those angels, are you?" Suzanne asked.

Drawing a picture of Tristan as an angel wrapping his arms around me, Ivy corrected silently. "I know he thought it would make me feel better," she said aloud.

"So cut him a break, Ivy. I know what you're thinking. I know exactly how you feel. Remember when Sunbeam died, and I said, 'That's it for

Pomeranians. I never want another dog again'? But I've got Peppermint now and—"

"I'll think about it, okay?"

Ivy knew Suzanne meant well, but losing Tristan wasn't quite like losing a fourteen-year-old half-blind and completely deaf dog. She was tired of dealing with people who meant well and said ridiculous things.

Fifteen minutes later Ivy was headed home, her old Dodge climbing the long drive up the ridge. Several months earlier she would not have believed it possible, but she had grown fond of the low stone wall and the patches of trees and runs of wild flowers she passed – her stepfather Andrew's wall and trees and flowers. The large white house on top of the hill actually seemed like home now. The high ceilings did not look so high to her, the wide hall and center staircase no longer intimidated her, though she still usually scooted up the back steps.

It was about an hour before dinner and Ivy looked forward to some time by herself in her music room. It had been four weeks exactly since Tristan died – though no one else seemed to have noticed the date – and four weeks exactly since she had stopped playing the piano. Her nine-year-old brother, Philip, had begged her to play for him as she once did. But every time she sat down on the bench she went cold inside. The music was frozen somewhere within her.

I have to get past this block, Ivy thought as she pulled her car into the garage behind the house.

The Stonehill Arts Festival was two weeks away. If Ivy didn't practice soon, she and Philip would have to do their famous "Chopsticks" duet.

Ivy paused outside the garage to watch Philip play beneath his tree house. He was so involved in his game, he didn't notice her.

But Ella did. It was as if the cat had been waiting for her, her green eyes wide and staring expectantly. She was purring even before Ivy rubbed her around her ears, her favorite spot, then she followed Ivy inside.

Ivy called hello to her mother and Henry, the cook, who were sitting at a table in the kitchen. Henry looked weary, and her mother, whose most complicated recipes were copied off soup cans, looked confused. Ivy guessed that they were planning another menu for a dinner entertaining benefactors of Andrew's college.

"How was the party, dear?" her mother asked.

"Good."

Henry was busily scratching items off Maggie's list. "Chicken à la king, chocolate pie with whipped cream," he said, sniffing with disapproval.

"See you later," Ivy said. When neither of them looked up, she headed for the back stairs.

A narrow gallery lined by pictures connected the family room to the wing occupied by Andrew's office on the first floor and Gregory's bedroom on the second. Ivy took the small staircase that ran up from the gallery, then crossed through the passage that led back into the main part of the house, into the hall with her room and Philip's. As soon as she entered her room she smelled something sweet.

She gasped with surprise. On her bureau, next to the photo of Tristan, were a dozen lavender roses. Ivy walked toward them. Tears rose quickly in her eyes, as if the salty drops had been there all along without her knowing.

There was a note next to these roses. Gregory's jagged handwriting was never easy to decipher, and less so through tears. She wiped her eyes and tried again.

"I know these have been the hardest four weeks of your life," the note said.

Ivy lifted down the vase and laid her face lightly against the fragrant petals. Gregory had been there for her, looking out for her, since the night of the accident. While everyone else was encouraging her to remember that night and talk about the accident – because, they said, it would help her heal – he'd let her take her time, let her find her own way of healing. Perhaps it was his own loss, his mother's suicide, that had made him so understanding.

His note fluttered to the floor. Ivy quickly leaned over and picked it up. It fluttered down a second time. When she tried to pick it up again, the paper tore a little in her fingers, as if it had caught on something. Ivy frowned and gently smoothed the note. Then she set it back on the bureau, slipping one corner under the heavy vase.

Despite the tears, she felt more peaceful now. She decided to try playing the piano, hoping she'd be able to find the music within her. "Come on, Ella. Upstairs. I need to practice."

The cat followed her, scurrying ahead of her into the room and leaping up onto the piano.

"So, you're sure I'm going to play today," Ivy said.

The cat still had her wide-eyed look and stared just beyond Ivy, purring.

Ivy pulled out music books, trying to decide what to play. Anything, anything, just to get her fingers going. For the festival she would do something from one of her past recitals.

She reached for Liszt and opened the score. Her hands trembled as they touched the smooth keys and she started her scales. Her fingers liked the familiar feel of the stretches; the repetitive rise and fall of notes soothed her. She glanced up at the opening measures of "Liebestraum" and willed herself to play. Her hands took over then, and it was as if she had never stopped playing. For a month she had been holding herself so tightly; now she gave in to the music that swirled up around her. The melody wanted to carry her, and she let it, let it take her wherever it would lead.

"I love you, Ivy, and one day you're going to believe me."

She stopped playing. The sense of him overwhelmed her. The memory was so strong – him standing behind her in the moonlight, listening to her play – that she could not believe he was gone. Her head fell forward over the piano. "Tristan! I miss you, Tristan!"

She cried as if someone had just now told her that he was dead. It will never get easier, she thought. Never.

Ella crowded close to her head, nosing her. When Ivy's tears stopped flowing, she reached for the cat. Then she heard a sound: three distinct notes. Ella's feet must have slipped, Ivy thought. She must have stepped down on the piano keys.

Ivy blinked back the wetness and cuddled the cat in her arms. "What would I do without you, Ella?"

She held the cat until she was breathing normally again. Then she set her gently on the bench and got up to wash her face. Ivy was halfway across the room, with her back to the piano, when she heard the same three notes again. This time the identical set of three was struck twice.

She turned back to the cat, who blinked up at her. Ivy laughed through a fresh trickle of tears.

"Either I'm going crazy, Ella, or you've been prac-ticing." Then she descended the stairs to her bedroom.

She wanted to pull the shades and sleep now, but she didn't let herself. She didn't believe the pain would ever lessen, but she had to keep going, keep focusing on the people around her. She knew that Philip had given up on her. He had stopped asking her to play with him three weeks ago. Now she'd go outside and ask him.

From the back door she saw him performing some kind of magic cooking ritual beneath two large maples and his new tree house. Sticks were arranged in a pile and an old crockpot sat on top.

It's only a matter of time, Ivy thought, before he decides to light one of these piles and sets fire to Andrew's landscaped yard.

She watched him with some amusement, and as she did the six notes floated back into her head. The repeated triplets were familiar to her, from some song she had heard long ago. Suddenly words attached themselves to the notes. "When you walk through a storm . . ."

Remembering the words slowly, Ivy sang, "When you walk through a storm . . . keep your head up high." She paused. "And don't be afraid of the dark." The song was from the musical *Carousel.* She couldn't recall much about the play except that at the end, a man who had died returned with an angel to someone he loved. The title of the song floated into her mind.

"'You'll Never Walk Alone,'" she said aloud.

She put her hand up to her mouth. She was going crazy, imagining Ella playing certain notes, imagining music with a message. Still, Ivy found some comfort in remembering that song.

Across the lawn Philip was chanting his own soft song over a pot of weedy greens. Ivy approached him quietly. When he looked up and waved a wand at her, she could tell he was making her a character in his game. She played along.

"Can you help me, sir?" she said. "I've been lost in the woods for days. I'm far from home, with nothing to eat."

"Sit down, little girl," Philip said in a quivery old-man voice.

Ivy bit her lip to keep from giggling.

"I will feed you."

"You're not – you're not a witch, are you?" she asked with dramatic caution.

"No."

"Good," she said, sitting down by the "campfire," pretending to warm her hands.

Philip carried the pot of leaves and weeds to her. "I'm a wizard."

"Eiii!" She jumped up.

Philip exploded with laughter, then quickly

assumed his serious, wizardly look again. "I'm a good wizard."

"Phew!"

"Except when I'm mean."

"I see," said Ivy. "What's your name, wizard?"

"Andrew."

The choice took her aback for a moment, but she decided not to say anything about it. "Is that your house, Wizard Andrew?" she asked, pointing to the tree house above them.

Philip nodded.

The other Andrew, the one who did magic with his credit cards, had hired carpenters to rebuild the tree house Gregory had played in as a child. It was more than doubled in size now, with a narrow boardwalk leading to the maple next to it, where more flooring and railings had been hammered into place. In both trees, upper levels had been added. A rope ladder dangled from one maple, and a thick rope that ended in a knot beneath a swing seat hung from the other. It was everything a kid could want, and more – Gregory and Ivy had agreed on that after climbing around in it one day when Philip was out.

"Do you want to come up to my hideout?" Philip asked her now. "You'll be safe from all the wild beasts, little girl."

He scampered up the rope ladder and Ivy followed, enjoying the physical effort, the hard rub of the rope against her palms, and the way the wind and her own motion made the ladder sway. They climbed up two levels from the main floor, then stopped to catch their breath.

"It's nice up here, Wiz."

"It's safe," Philip replied. "Except when the silver snake comes." Far below the Baines property was Stonehill's tiny railroad station, but from the tree house one could hear only the whistles of the trains as they ran between the river and the ridge.

Farther to the north, Ivy could see a twisting piece of blue, like a ribbon cut from the sky and dropped between the trees, and, next to it, a train crawling along, flashing back the sunlight.

She pointed to it. "What's that, Wizard Andrew?"

"The silver snake," he replied without hesitation.

"Will it bite?"

"Only if you stand in its way. Then it will gobble you up and spit you out in the river."

"Ugh."

"Sometimes at night it climbs up the ridge," Philip said, his face absolutely serious.

"It couldn't."

"It does!" he insisted. "And you have to be very careful. You can't make it angry."

"Okay, I won't say a word."

He nodded approvingly, then warned, "You

can't let it know you're afraid. You have to hold your breath."

"Hold my breath?" Ivy studied her brother.

"It will see you if you move. It watches you even when you don't think it's watching. Day and night."

Where was he getting this stuff from?

"It can smell you if you're afraid."

Was he really frightened of something, or was this just a game? she wondered. Philip had always had an active imagination, but it seemed to her it was becoming overactive and darker. Ivy wished his friend Sammy would return from summer camp. Her brother had everything he could want now, but he was too isolated from other kids. He was living too much in his own world.

"The snake won't get me, Philip," she told him, almost sternly. "I'm not afraid of it. I'm not afraid of anything," she said, "because we're safe in our house. All right?"

"All right, little girl, you stay here," he said. "And don't let anyone else in. I'm going over to my other house and get some magic clothes for you. They will make you invisible."

Ivy smiled a little. How would she play invisible? Then she picked up a battered broom and began to sweep off the flooring.

Suddenly she heard Philip yelp. She spun around and saw him tottering on the edge of the narrow boardwalk, sixteen feet above the ground. She dropped the broom and rushed toward him, but knew she couldn't catch him in time.

Then, just as suddenly, he was balanced again. He dropped down on all fours and looked back over his shoulder. The rapt expression on his face stopped Ivy in her tracks. She had seen that look on his face before: the wonder, the glow of pleasure, his mouth half open in a shy smile.

"What happened?" Ivy asked, moving toward him slowly now. "Did you trip?"

He shook his head, then picked up the loose end of a board.

Ivy leaned down to study it. The bridge had been constructed like a miniature boardwalk, with two long, thin boards secured between the two trees and a series of short planks laid across them. The short planks overhung the boards a few inches on each side. This particular plank was nailed loosely on one side – Ivy could pull the nail out with her hands; on the other side there was a hole, but no nail.

"When I stepped here" – Philip pointed – "the other side came up."

"Like a seesaw," said Ivy. "It's a good thing you didn't lose your balance."

Philip nodded. "Good thing my angel was right here."

Ivy sucked in her breath.

"'Cause sometimes he isn't. Though he usually is when you're around."

Ivy closed her eyes and shook her head.

"He's gone now," said Philip.

Good, thought Ivy. "Philip, we've talked about this before. There are no such things as angels. All you have is a bunch of statues—"

"Your statues," he interrupted. "I'm taking good care of them."

"I told you," she said, her throat tightening and her head starting to throb, "I told you that if you wanted to keep those statues, you must never speak to me about angels again. Didn't I tell you that?"

He lowered his head and nodded.

"Didn't you promise?"

He nodded again.

Ivy sighed and pulled up the piece of wood. "Now slide around behind me. Before you go any farther, I want to check each board."

"But, Ivy," he said, "I saw my angel! I saw him catch the wood on the other side and push it down so I wouldn't fall. I saw him!"

Ivy sat back on her heels. "Don't tell me. Let me guess. He was wearing wings and a nightgown, and had a little saucer of light on his head."

"No, he was just light. He was just shining. I think he has sort of a shape, but it's always hard for me to see it. It's hard for me to see his face," Philip said. His own young face was earnest.

273

"Stop it!" said Ivy. "Stop it! I don't want to hear any more about it! Save it for when Sammy gets home, okay?"

"Okay," he said, the corners of his mouth stiff and straight. He slipped past her.

Ivy began to examine the boards and could hear her brother sweeping the tree house behind her. Then the broom stopped. She glanced over her shoulder. Philip's face was happy and bright again. He still clutched the broom, but he was standing on his tiptoes, stretching upward. "Thank you," he mouthed silently.

20

That evening Ivy wandered from room to room in the house, feeling restless and edgy. She didn't want to go out or call up a friend, but she could find nothing to do at home. Each time she heard the clock chime in the dining room, she couldn't stop her mind from turning back to the night Tristan died.

When Maggie and Andrew went to bed, Ivy went up to her room to read. She wished that Gregory were home. In the last few weeks they had watched a lot of late-night TV together, sitting quietly side by side, sharing cookies, laughing at the dumb jokes. She wondered where he was now. Maybe he had helped Eric clean up after the party, then the two of them had gone out. Or maybe he had gone to Suzanne's. She could call Suzanne and say – Ivy caught herself before that thought went any further. What was she thinking? Call up Suzanne in the middle of a date?

I depend on Gregory way too much, Ivy thought.

She crept downstairs and took a flashlight from the kitchen drawer. Maybe a walk would make her sleepy; maybe it would get rid of that prickling feeling in the back of her mind. When Ivy opened the back door, she saw Gregory's BMW parked outside the garage. He must have brought back the car at some point and taken off again. She wished he were there to walk with her.

The driveway, a continuous curve down the side of the ridge, was three quarters of a mile long. Ivy walked it to the bottom. After the steep climb back, her body finally felt tired, but her mind was still awake and as restless as the tossing trees. It was as if there was something she had to remember, and she couldn't sleep until she remembered it – but she had no idea what it was.

When she arrived back at the house, the wind had changed and a sharp, wet smell swept over the ridge. In the west, lightning flashed, casting up images of clouds like towering mountains. Ivy longed for a storm with bright lightning and wind to release whatever it was that was pent up inside her.

At one-thirty she climbed into bed. The storm had skirted their side of the river, but there were more flashes in the west. Maybe they would get the next big gust of rain and wind.

At two o'clock she was still awake. She heard the long whistle of the late-night train as it crossed the bridge and rushed on through the little station far below the house. "Take me with you," she whispered. "Take me with you."

Her mind drifted after the lonely sound of the whistle, and Ivy felt herself slipping away, rocked by the low rumbling of thunder in the distant hills.

Then the rumbling became louder, louder and closer. Lightning quivered. The wind gusted up, and the trees that had been slowly swaying from side to side now lashed themselves with soaked branches. Ivy peered out through the storm. She could hardly see, but she knew something was wrong. She opened a door.

"Who is it?" she cried out. "Who's there?"

She was outside now, struggling against the wind and moving toward a window, with lightning streaking all around her. The window was alive with reflections and shadows. She could barely make out the figure on the other side, but she knew something or someone was there, and the figure seemed familiar to her.

"Who is it?" she called out again, moving closer and closer to the window.

She had done this before, she knew she had,

sometime, somewhere, perhaps in a dream, she thought. A feeling of dread washed over her.

She *was* in a dream, caught in it, the old nightmare. She wanted out! Out!

She knew it had a terrible end. She couldn't remember it, only that it was terrible.

Then Ivy heard a high whining sound. She spun around. The sound increased till it drowned out the storm. A red Harley roared up to her.

"Stop! Please stop!" Ivy cried. "I need help! I need to get out of this dream!" The motorcyclist hesitated, then gunned his engine and sped off.

Ivy turned back to the window. The figure was still there. Was it beckoning to her? Who or what could it be? Ivy put her face close to the window. Suddenly the glass exploded. She shrieked and shrieked as the bloody deer came crashing through.

"Ivy! Ivy, wake up!"

Gregory was shaking her. "Ivy, it's just a dream. Wake up!" he commanded. He was still fully dressed. Philip stood behind him, a little ghost in pale pajamas.

Ivy looked from one to the other, then sagged against Gregory. He put his arms around her.

"Was it the deer again?" Philip asked. "The deer coming through the window?"

Ivy nodded and swallowed hard several times. It was good to feel Gregory's arms strong and steady around her. "I'm sorry I woke you up, Philip."

"It's okay," he said.

She tried to still her trembling hands. Gregory's home now, she told herself, everything's okay.

"I'm sorry this keeps happening, Philip. I didn't mean to scare you."

"I'm not scared," he replied.

Ivy glanced up sharply at her brother's face and saw that, in fact, he wasn't.

"The angels are in my room," he explained.

"Then why don't you go back to them?" Gregory told him. Ivy felt the tightening muscles in his arms. "Why don't you—"

"It's all right, Gregory. Let Philip alone," she said with soft resignation. "He's dealing with this the best way he can."

"But he's making it harder on you," Gregory argued. "Can't you understand, Philip? I've tried a million times to—"

He stopped, and Ivy knew that Gregory saw it, too: the brightness in Philip's eyes, the certainty in his face. For a moment the little boy's will seemed stronger than both of theirs put together. It was impossible to argue him out of what he believed. Ivy found herself wishing that she could be so innocent again.

Gregory sighed and said to Philip, "I can take care of Ivy. Why don't you get some shut-eye? We've got a big day tomorrow – the Yankees game, remember?"

Philip glanced at Ivy and she nodded in agreement.

Then he gazed past her and Gregory in such a way that she instinctively turned around to look. Nothing.

"You'll be okay," he said confidently, and trotted off to bed.

Ivy sank back against Gregory. He wrapped his arms around her again. His hands were gentle and comforting. He brushed back her hair, then lifted her face up to his.

"How are you doing?" he asked.

"All right, I guess."

"You can't shake that dream, can you?"

She saw his concern. She saw how he searched her face for clues about what she was feeling.

"It was the same dream but different," Ivy told him. "I mean, there were things added to it."

His frown of worry deepened. "What was added?"

"A storm. There were all those mixed-up images on the window again, but this time I realized it was a storm I was seeing. The trees were blowing and lightning was flashing and reflecting off the glass. And there was a motorcycle," she said.

It was hard for her to explain the nightmarish feeling the motorcycle gave her, for that part of the dream was simple and ordinary. The motorcyclist had not harmed her. All he had done was refuse to stop to help her.

"A red motorcycle came rushing by," she continued. "I called out to the rider, hoping he would help me. He slowed down for a moment, then kept on going."

Gregory held her face against his chest and stroked her cheek. "I think I can explain that. Eric just dropped me off. He has a red Harley – you've seen it before. You must have heard the sound of it while you were sleeping and woven it into your dream."

Ivy shook her head. "I think there's more to it than that, Gregory," she said quietly.

He stopped stroking her cheek. He held very still, waiting for her to go on.

"Remember how it was storming the evening your mother ki— died?"

"Killed herself," he said clearly.

She nodded. "And I was in the neighborhood then, making a delivery for the store."

"Yes."

"I think that's part of the dream. I had completely forgotten about it. I had thought my nightmare was just about Tristan and the accident, with the deer crashing through the glass, crashing through our windshield. But it's not."

She paused and tried to sort things out in her mind.

"For some reason I put the two events together. The night your mother died, I couldn't find the right house. When I got out to check a street sign, someone on a red motorcycle came by. He saw me flagging him down and hesitated, but then rushed on past me."

She could feel Gregory's steady, rapid breathing on her forehead. He held her so close, she could hear the quick beat of his heart.

"Later I thought I had found the house – I had narrowed it down to two houses. One of them had a big picture window, and someone was standing inside, but I couldn't see who it was. I thought it might be the person who was waiting for my delivery. Then the door to the house next door opened – and that's where I was supposed to be."

It was strange the way the details of that night were slowly coming back to her.

"Don't you see, Gregory? That's the window I keep coming up to in the dream and trying to see through. I don't know why."

"Do you know if it was Eric you saw that night?" he asked.

Ivy shrugged. "It was a red motorcycle, and the rider had a red helmet. But then, I guess a lot of people do. If it had been Eric, wouldn't he have stopped for me?"

Gregory didn't answer.

"Maybe not," said Ivy. "I mean, I know he's your

friend, but he's never really liked me," she added quickly.

"As far as I know," Gregory said, "Eric's really liked only one person in his life. He can make things very hard for the people around him."

Ivy glanced up, surprised. Gregory saw Eric more clearly than she had realized. Still, he had remained a loyal friend to him, just as he was a friend to her now.

She relaxed against him. She was getting sleepy now, but was reluctant to pull away from the comfort of his arms.

"Isn't it strange," Ivy mused, "that I should put your mother's death and Tristan's together in one dream?"

"Not really," Gregory replied. "You and I have been through a lot of pain, Ivy, and we've been through it together, helping each other get by. It seems pretty natural to me that you would link those events in your dream." He lifted her face to his once again, looking deeply into her eyes. "No?"

"I guess so," she said.

"You really miss him, don't you? You can't help but keep remembering."

Ivy dropped her head, then smiled up at him through her tears. "I'll just have to keep remembering how lucky I am to have found a friend like you, someone who really understands."

*

"This is better than any flick coming out of Hollywood this summer," Lacey said.

"Who invited you in here?" Tristan asked.

He had been sitting by Ivy's bed watching her sleep – he didn't know for how long. At last Gregory had left him alone with her. At last Ivy looked at peace.

After Gregory left, Tristan had sorted through what he'd learned, and tried hard to keep himself conscious. The dreamless darkness had not come upon him for a while now. It did not come upon him as swiftly and as often as when he first became an angel, but he knew he could not keep going without rest. Still, as tired as he was, he could not bear to give up these moments alone with Ivy in the quiet of the night. He resented Lacey's intrusion.

"I was sent by Philip," she told him.

"By Philip? I don't understand."

"In Manhattan today I found this funky guardian angel statue, a baseball player with wings." She flapped her arms dramatically. "I got it for him as a little gift."

"You mean you stole it?"

"Well, how would you like me to pay for it?" she snapped. "Anyway, I was just dropping it off. He saw my glow and pointed, directing me in here. I guess he figured his sister needed all the help she could get."

"How long have you been here?" Tristan asked. He hadn't noticed Lacey's arrival.

"Ever since Gregory brushed back her hair and lifted her face up to his," she replied.

"You saw that?"

"I tell you, Hollywood could use him," Lacey said. "He's got all the right moves."

Lacey's view was both welcome and frightening to Tristan. On the one hand, he wanted Gregory to be doing nothing more than playing a romantic game with Ivy; he didn't want anything real to be happening between them. On the other hand, Tristan feared that there could be a darker reason behind such a game.

"So you heard it all. You've been here all this time."

"Yep." Lacey climbed up on the headboard of Ivy's bed. Her brown eyes glinted like shiny buttons, and her spikes of purple hair were pale and feathery in the moonlight. She perched above Ivy's head.

"I didn't want to disturb you. You were so deep in thought," she said. "And I figured you wanted time alone with her."

Tristan cocked his head. "Why are you suddenly being so thoughtful? Have you finished your mission? Are you getting ready to leave?"

"Finished?" She almost choked on the word. "Uh . . . no," she said, glancing away from him. "I doubt I'll be shoving off to the next realm anytime soon."

"Oh," he said. "So, what happened in New York?"

"Uh . . . I don't think I should tell you. It'll probably be in the papers tomorrow, anyway."

Tristan nodded. "So you're earning back a few points now."

"Take advantage of me while you can," she urged.

Tristan smiled.

"I get points for that," she said, just touching his lips with the tip of a long nail, but his smile had already disappeared. "You're really worried."

"You heard the dream," he said. "It's pretty obvious. There's some connection between Caroline's death and mine."

"Tell me about Caroline. How'd she croak?" Lacey asked.

"Shot herself, in the head."

"And they're sure it was a suicide?"

"Well," said Tristan, "the police found only her fingerprints on the gun, and her fingers were still twisted around it. She left no note, but she had torn up photographs of Gregory's father and Ivy's mother."

Lacey sprang off the headboard and began to pace the room in a circle.

"I suppose someone could have set it up to look

like a suicide," Tristan said slowly. "And Ivy was in the neighborhood that night. She could have seen something. Lacey! What if she saw something she shouldn't have—"

"Did I ever tell you I was in *Perry Mason?*" Lacey interrupted.

"—and what if she didn't even realize it?" Tristan exclaimed.

"Of course, Raymond Burr is dead now," Lacey continued.

"I need to check out the address of Gregory's mother," Tristan told her, "and the address where Ivy made the delivery that night."

"As soon as I read the obit, I looked Raymond up," Lacey said.

"Listen to me, Lacey."

"I was sure he would be assigned some kind of mission."

"Lacey, please," he begged.

"I thought we could pal around together."

"Lacey!" he shouted.

"I mean, Raymond would make an awesome angel."

Tristan dropped his head in his hands. He needed time to think about what was going on and how he could keep Ivy safe.

"But he must have whisked right on," Lacey said.

"Must have," Tristan mumbled. He could feel

his mind growing dim. He needed rest before he could figure things out.

"I can't tell you how disappointed I was!"

"You just did," Tristan observed wearily.

"Raymond said he'd never forget the episode I did with him."

There could be a lot of reasons for that, Tristan thought.

"Raymond always appreciated my talent."

Ivy was in danger, and he didn't know how to warn her or whom to warn her against, and Lacey was going on and on about a dead actor.

"So what I am saying is that I can probably help you on this matter," Lacey said.

Tristan stared at her. "Because you played a supporting role in one episode with another actor who pretended he was a lawyer who somehow ended up solving television crimes?"

"Well, if you're going to put it that way, don't expect my help!"

She stalked across the room, then paused theatrically and looked over her shoulder.

Tristan wished she'd keep right on going. The room was washed in the palest of morning light now, and the first birds were up, their flickering song being passed along from one tree to the next. He wanted the last bit of time he could have alone with Ivy. He turned toward her, longing to touch her.

"I wouldn't do that if I were you."

"You don't know what I'm going to do," Tristan replied.

"Oh, I can guess," she said to his back. "And you're too exhausted."

"Leave me alone, Lacey."

"I just thought I'd warn you."

"Leave me alone!"

She did.

As soon as she left he stretched out his hand. Ivy slept quietly beneath it. He wanted so badly to touch her, to feel her warmth, to know her softness just one more time. Gathering all his strength, Tristan focused on the tips of his fingers. He knew he was tired, too tired, but still he concentrated with his last bit of energy. The ends of his fingers stopped shimmering. They were solid now.

Slowly, gently, he ran his fingers down her cheek, feeling the silk of her, the wonder of her. He traced Ivy's mouth.

If only he could kiss those lips! If only he could hold Ivy, fold all of her in his arms . . .

Then he began to lose the sense of her.

He reached again, but he was losing touch. "No!" he cried out. It felt like he was dying all over again. The pain of losing her was so intense, so unbearable, that when the dreamless darkness came, he gave himself over to it willingly.

21

"Well, hello, sleepyhead," said the girl sitting on the mall bench.

Tristan jumped, startled out of deep thought. He had emerged from the darkness about fifteen minutes before and immediately tracked Ivy to her job at 'Tis the Season. For the last few minutes he'd been trying to piece together the fragments of Ivy's dream and what those pieces meant, but his mind still felt dark and muddled.

Lacey laughed at him. "Know what day it is?"

"Uh, Monday."

"*Brrtt.*" She did her obnoxious imitation of a game-show buzzer, then gestured to the seat next to her.

Tristan sat down. "It's Monday," he insisted. "When I came into the mall, I checked a newspaper, just like you told me to do."

"Maybe you should have checked the *latest* one," Lacey observed. "It's Tuesday, and nearly one o'clock. Ivy should be taking her break soon."

He looked across the mall toward the shop. Ivy was busy with two customers, a bald old man trying on a Superman cape and a grandmotherly type holding a pink basket and wearing bunny ears. He knew that 'Tis the Season sold costumes and holiday items — most of which were out of season. But the recent darkness, the two customers in their odd outfits, and the presence of a very large woman carrying a bagel and coffee who had just sat down on Tristan made it all very confusing.

Lacey patted his arm. "I told you that you were too tired. I warned you."

"Move over," he grunted. He couldn't feel the woman's weight, but it seemed a little weird having her wide, striped dress flowing over him.

Lacey slid down a little and said, "I have something to tell you. While you were in the darkness, I've been busy."

"I already know."

The Monday paper had caught his attention because of an article on people gathering to pray in Times Square after an image of Mariah Carey, projected on an electronic billboard, grew a chubby, pink angel body and flitted around.

"Does this have anything to do with the traffic jams on Forty-second Street?" he asked.

She dismissed the event with a wave of her hand.

"I read something about Carey considering a lawsuit, and how the New York cabbies—"

"Mariah should never have said I honked like a goose. Not that I couldn't have used a few more voice lessons—"

"Lacey, how are you ever going to complete your mission?"

"My mission? Today I'm helping you with yours," she said, then sprang up from the bench.

Tristan shook his head and followed her.

"I went to the cemetery Sunday to pay a visit to Gregory's mother," Lacey said as they walked along with the shoppers. "While I was there, somebody came by, a tall, thin guy, dark-haired. About forty, I think. He left Caroline some flowers."

"He's been there before," Tristan said. "I saw him the day we were in the chapel." He remembered watching the visitor from behind, mistaking him for Gregory until he turned around. He could still see the man's face, full of anguish.

"What's his name?" she asked.

"I don't know."

They were heading away from 'Tis the Season. Tristan looked back longingly at Ivy, but Lacey marched on.

"We should find out. He might be able to help us."

"Help us what?" Tristan asked.

"Figure out what happened the night Caroline died."

They stopped by the fountain to watch cascades of water fall in pink and blue drops. One day, when nobody was looking, Tristan had made a wish here, a wish that Ivy would be his.

"I looked up Caroline's address in the phone book," Lacey went on. "Five twenty-eight Willow. Her date of death was written on her tombstone. I came here this morning to check out the shop records for that day." She paused and looked at Tristan expectantly.

When he didn't say anything, she said, "What an angel you are, Lacey, helping me out like this."

"What did you find out?" he asked, ignoring her sarcasm.

"For one thing, that Lillian and her sister haven't a clue about how to keep business books. But after a lot of hunting and squinting I did find it: a delivery on May twenty-eighth to a Mrs. Abromaitis on Willow Street – no house number given. I looked it up in the phone book. Guess what? Five thirty Willow."

"Right next door," Tristan said, his voice a whisper, his mind prickling with fear. "I knew it. Ivy saw something."

"Looks that way," Lacey agreed. She caught a coin that a woman had tossed toward the fountain and flipped it back at her. The woman stared down at it, then stuck the unlucky penny in a pot of ferns.

"Ivy saw something at Caroline's," Tristan said, "and it wasn't a suicide."

"We can't assume that," Lacey replied. "Caroline still could have killed herself, and someone could have been there afterward, taking something or hiding something. I mean, there are a lot of things Ivy could have seen—"

"That she shouldn't have," Tristan finished Lacey's sentence. "I have to reach her, Lacey!"

"I thought we should check out the house today."

"I have to warn her now!"

"I remember how we did a search on *Perry Mason*," Lacey said. She started pulling Tristan toward the mall exit, but he was intent on heading back to 'Tis the Season, and he was stronger. "Tristan, listen to me! There's nothing you can do to protect Ivy. You and I weren't given that kind of power. The best you can do is combine the powers you do have with someone else and make that person stronger. But you yourself can't stop anyone who wants to harm her."

Tristan stood still. He had never feared for his own life the way he now feared for Ivy's.

"As long as she's in a crowd, she's safe," Lacey added. "So let's check out the house and—"

"As soon as she gets in her car tonight, she'll be

alone," Tristan pointed out. "As soon as she goes for a walk, as soon as she goes up to her music room, she'll be in danger."

"There are other people at home with her," Lacey pointed out. "She's probably safe there. So let's find out who she has to watch out for and then—"

But Lacey was left to talk to herself. Beth and Suzanne had just entered the mall. Spotting them, Tristan turned quickly and began to walk with them. He figured they were meeting Ivy for lunch. This time he would get through.

Ivy was standing by the shop entrance, and for a moment Tristan forgot she was seeing only the girls. When he saw the look of welcome on her face, he hurried toward her, only to find she was now looking past him at Suzanne and Beth. It never got easier – the pain of being close to her, but far away, never seemed to lessen.

"Now, take your time over lunch," Lillian was saying to the girls. "It's a slow day, so do a little shopping. Be sure to take a peek in that new gift shop. I'll bet they don't have glow-in-the-dark wind chimes."

"Not in the shape of leprechauns and fairies," Beth said. Whenever she came to the shop, she got a look of total wonder on her face. Suzanne had to reach back and pull her out the door.

Tristan followed the girls through the mall. They

stopped at one store window after another, and he began to grow impatient. He wanted Beth to sit down right away and start scribbling in her notebook. He thought they'd never get out of the Beautiful You shop, with all those bottles and tubes and little pots of color.

He began to pace from one side of the store to the other and ran head-on into Lacey. He hadn't realized that she had come along.

"Chill out, Tristan," Lacey said. "Ivy's safe for now, unless someone runs her through with a nail file."

Then she wandered off to a corner, as mesmerized as the others by the hundreds of colors – which all looked pretty much like red and pink to him. Tristan wondered whether, if he ever made it to the next realm, some mysteries about girls would be explained.

Suzanne, now wearing stripes of tester lipstick all the way up her arm, was talking about a wedding in Philadelphia that she was going to that weekend.

"I wish you were coming with us, Ivy," she said. "I showed my cousin your picture. He's definitely interested, and he's so perfect for you."

Terrific, thought Tristan.

"So you decided to go to the lake after all?" Beth asked. She was trying on a shower cap that looked like a silver mushroom.

"The lake!" Suzanne said, surprised. "She's staying home, and you're staying with her, Beth."

Beth frowned. "Suzanne, you know I can't miss my family reunion. I thought she was going to Philly with you."

Ivy had turned away from both of them.

"Ivy!" Suzanne commanded.

"What?" She started sorting through a bin of barrettes and didn't look up.

"What are you doing this weekend?"

"Staying home."

Suzanne raised her perfectly shaped black eyebrows. "Your mother's letting you stay alone?"

"She thinks that you and Beth will be with me. And I'm counting on you two to cover for me," Ivy added.

Lacey glanced over at Tristan.

"I don't know what the big deal is," Ivy went on. "I'd like to have the house to myself for a change. I'll have plenty of time to practice for the festival, and Ella will keep me company."

"But Ella can't protect you," Tristan protested.

"I just don't like the idea of you moping around all weekend by yourself," Suzanne said.

"That house is too big, too lonely," Beth added.

"Listen to them, Ivy," Tristan urged.

"I told you both, I won't go to Juniper Lake! I can't!"

"This is some kind of Tristan thing, isn't it?" Suzanne said.

"I don't want to talk about it," Ivy replied.

It was. Tristan remembered the plans they had made the night he died. Ivy had told him how she was going to float in the sunlight in the deepest part of Juniper Lake. "I'll swim in the moonlight, too."

"The moonlight?" he'd said. "You'd swim in the dark?"

"With you I would."

Lacey touched Tristan on the arm. "You've got to get through to her this time."

He nodded.

They followed the girls out of the store. Tristan was tempted to slip inside Beth's mind right then, to direct her toward a table where she could take out her writing pad, but he didn't want to give her too many instructions. She might begin to resist.

Beth stopped suddenly in front of Electronic Wizard, and Tristan followed her eyes to a display of computers inside.

"Look at her. Look at her!" Suzanne said, nudging Ivy. "You'd think Beth was checking out guys."

"There's the laptop I want," Beth said.

Then Lacey came up quickly behind her. Tristan saw that the tips of her fingers had stopped shimmering. She gave a swift push. Beth stumbled through the door and looked back in surprise at

Suzanne and Ivy. They followed Beth inside, with Tristan and Lacey right behind them.

"Can I help you?" asked a salesman.

"Uh, I'm just looking," Beth said, blushing. "Can I try out your display models?"

He flicked his hand in their direction and walked away.

"You're on, Tristan," Lacey said.

It didn't take Beth long to find the word-processing program. Tristan had to struggle to keep up with her, to think what her next thought might be, which was the way Lacey had taught him to slip into the minds of others.

When a writer looked at an empty computer screen, what did she see? Tristan wondered. A movie screen ready to be lit with faces? A night sky with one small star blinking at the top, a universe ready to be written on? Endless possibilities. Love's endless twists and turns – and all love's impossibilities.

Beth started typing:

Impossibilities
What did she see when she looked out every night at the lonely black screen of sky? Possibilities. Love's endless twists and turns, and, oh, bitter heart, all love's impossibilities.

Phew! Tristan thought.

"Phew!" Beth typed, then squinted at the screen.

"Stay with her, Tristan," Lacey said. "Keep your focus."

Back up. Delete word. Oh, bitter heart, Tristan prompted Beth.

"Oh, bitter heart, lonely heart," Beth typed, then paused.

They were both stuck, then Tristan saw the connection: You should not stay home alone.

"You should not stay home alone," Beth typed.

It's not safe alone, he thought.

"It's not safe alone," she typed.

Then, before he could send her a message about anything else, she wrote on: "But is my heart safe alone *with him?*"

No, he thought.

"Yes," Beth replied.

No!

"Yes!"

No!

"Yes!" Beth frowned.

Tristan sighed. Of course, she wanted the romance to work out and have the girl who was gazing at the night sky not be lonely anymore. But Tristan wanted to issue a warning. If Ivy was alone with the wrong guy . . .

"What's wrong?" asked Ivy.

"I've got that funny feeling again," Beth said.

"It's really strange, like there's someone inside my head, saying things."

"Oh, you writers." Suzanne snorted.

Ivy bent down to look at the screen. "No! Yes! No! Yes!" she read, then laughed a little sadly. "It sounds like me when I first met Tristan."

"It's Tristan," Beth typed quickly.

Ivy stopped smiling.

Tristan pressed on, and Beth typed as fast as he thought: "Be careful, Ivy. It's dangerous, Ivy. Don't stay alone. Love you. Tristan."

Ivy straightened up. "That's not funny, Beth! That's stupid, and mean!"

Beth stared at the screen, her mouth open in disbelief.

Suzanne leaned down to read it. "Beth!" she said. "How could you? Ivy, wait!"

But Ivy was already halfway out of the store. Suzanne ran after her. Beth stared at the screen, her entire body shaking. Tristan slipped out of Beth's mind, exhausted.

"Would you like to print that out now?" the salesman asked, walking toward her.

Beth shook her head slowly and pressed delete. "Not this time," she said with tears in her eyes.

Every effort Tristan made to reach Ivy that week failed. What was worse, his attempts at warning her had pushed her further away from him and from those who cared for her. She was avoiding Beth, and now Philip too, after the little boy told her his angel said she must not stay alone. Tristan could have tried once more through Will, but he knew Ivy would just build another wall, a higher one.

Thursday night he headed for Riverstone Rise Cemetery, planning to get some rest, hoping to stave off the dreamless darkness so that he could keep watch over Ivy through the long weekend. On the way to his own grave, Tristan decided to go by Caroline's plot and see if fresh roses had been left there. He thought that Lacey was right: they had to find out who Caroline's visitor was and what he knew about her death.

Tristan crept along the cemetery road as if he were still flesh and blood, afraid of rousing the peaceful dead. In the moonlight, the white stones made a stark cityscape: obelisks towering like sky-scrapers, mausoleums standing as mansions, the low rounded stones and shiny rectangular blocks marking neighborhoods of ordinary people. It was a still and eerie city, the city of the dead – my city, he thought grimly. Then he recognized the stone that marked one corner of the Baines family plot.

It was a well-kept plot with some ornate statu-ary, figures that seemed to watch Tristan as he approached Caroline's grave from behind. When he walked past her marker, he spun around with sur-prise. Sitting on Caroline's grass, lying back against her stone as if he were lounging in bed, was Eric. His arms and legs were limp, and his head was turned sideways, his cheek flat against the stone. For a moment Tristan wasn't sure if Eric was breathing. Moving closer, he saw that Eric's pale eyes were open, his pupils so dilated they looked as if he had drunk up two pools of night.

He was breathing softly, and he was mumbling something – something that made sense only to a mind high on drugs. Tristan wondered if Eric was capable of certain actions in this state. Could he stand up, could he walk? With his mind messed up like this, could he do something he'd wish later on that he hadn't done? Materializing his fingers, Tristan ran them across Eric's upturned palm.

Eric grabbed Tristan's fingers and for a moment Tristan was caught. Then he let his fingers dissolve and pulled himself free.

"Been a while," Eric said, flexing the hand that had grabbed hold of Tristan. "Been too long, Caroline, sorry about that. A lot's been going on, a lot more than anybody knows." He laughed quietly and pointed, as if he could see her directly in front of him. "Of course, you know."

"I don't know," Tristan replied. "What's going on? Tell me."

Eric cocked his head, and for a moment Tristan thought he had heard the question.

"Yeah . . . probably," Eric said, answering some

other question. "But it could be, you know, messy. I don't like things . . . messy."

Messy? Tristan wondered. What did that mean? Complicated? Bloody?

Eric sat straight up now, blinking his eyes, attentive to the voice he was hearing in his head. His hair was almost white in the moonlight, and his shadowed eyes stared holes through Tristan.

"You mean Ivy. Her name's Ivy," Eric said, waving his bony hand in the air. It passed directly through Tristan, chilling him like the touch of a skeleton.

"Well, what can I do?" Eric said. "You know where I'm at, Caroline. Don't push me! Back off!" He jumped to his feet and stood there, teetering.

Then he started to laugh low in his throat. "Yeah, yeah," he said. "This weekend everyone's going to the lake but Ivy." Eric smiled as if he'd just heard something funny. "Now, that's not a very nice thing to say!"

What, in his drug-crazed mind, did he think Caroline had said?

"Hey!" Eric shouted. "I *said* don't push me." He took two steps sideways. "Back off, Caroline. I don't want to listen to you anymore. *Back off!*"

Eric started running then, stumbling into markers and lurching from side to side, shrieking in a weird, high-pitched voice, "Back off, Caroline! Back off! Back off!"

Tristan watched him until he disappeared down the road. He tried to imagine the other half of Eric's conversation. What did Eric think Caroline wanted him to do?

Terrifying thoughts flooded Tristan's mind. Then he calmed himself and, focusing all his energy, called out, "Caroline, are you there?" He called her three times, hoping each time that she'd answer back. But his angel senses had already told him what the silence proved: There was nothing there but a cold body, and its answers were rotting with it.

22

On Friday morning Gregory waved a piece of paper with a phone number on it at Ivy. "Promise me," he said.

She shrugged, then nodded halfheartedly.

"Juniper Lake is an hour and a half away, and the way I drive, just an hour," he added with a grin. "Promise me, Ivy."

"I can take care of myself," she told him, and rearranged the food in the ice chest for the fourth time. Maggie was feeding Andrew, Gregory, Philip, and herself that weekend but had packed enough additional food for a family of bears.

"I know you can take care of yourself," Gregory said, "but you still might get down or freaked out. This place can be pretty scary when you're alone." He rattled the paper. "If you need me – I don't care if it's in the middle of the night – call me."

Ivy gave a little duck of her head, which didn't mean that she would or wouldn't, then started packing the variety of cookies and chips that her mother had set out on the kitchen counter. "I hope you're ready to eat twenty-four hours a day," she told Gregory.

He laughed and opened one of the bags she was holding, snagging two cookies. He held one up to her mouth, and she bit it.

"I told you, Ivy, I won't squeal about you being alone here," Gregory said, "but the deal is that you have to call me once each day." He held her with his eyes. "Okay?"

She nodded.

"Promise," he said, his face close to hers. He held her with one finger hooked through her belt loop. "Promise."

"Okay, okay, I promise," she said, laughing.

He let her go. For a moment she wished that Gregory would stay home.

"I know what you're really up to," he teased. "As soon as we clear out of here, you'll be calling up people from all over and throwing a big bash."

"That's it," said Ivy, tossing a pack of napkins on top of the snack bag. "You've got me figured out."

"Have you thought about calling Will?" Gregory was still smiling, but his suggestion was serious.

"No," she said firmly.

"Why don't you like him?" he asked. "Not because of those angel drawings—"

"No, it's not that." Ivy checked the packs of paper plates and cups. They were from 'Tis the Season and decorated with Thanksgiving turkeys and Valentine hearts. "I like him all right. He just makes me uncomfortable. I can't quite explain it. When I look at him, there's something in his eyes . . ."

Gregory laughed out loud. "Love? Or is it just raging hormones?"

"Right, right," Ivy said. "That must be it."

"I think so." He put his hands on her shoulders and would not let her turn away. "One of these days you'll realize that there are guys you don't even suspect who are looking at you . . . with something in their eyes."

Ivy looked down at her feet.

He laughed again and dropped his hands. "Be nice to Will," he said. "He's had some rough times in the past."

Before Ivy could ask what kind of rough times, Maggie and Philip came into the kitchen. Philip was wearing the Yankees cap and T-shirt that Gregory had bought him at the game.

Little by little, Philip was warming up to Gregory, and Gregory seemed pleased by it. Philip's talk of angels still annoyed him, but that was probably because it upset Ivy.

Philip gave Ivy a light punch in the arm. She had noticed lately that when others were around, her little brother wouldn't hug her. Maggie, who was dressed for the great outdoors from the neck down and made up for a photo session from the neck up, gave Ivy a squeeze and a kiss.

Gregory and Philip immediately rubbed their faces in the same place. Ivy grinned at them but left the fresh, red print of lips on her cheek.

"That's my girl," Maggie said. "Got us all packed up. I swear, I raised you to be a better mother than me."

Ivy laughed.

Gregory carried out the ice chest, and the others followed with bags and suitcases, putting them in Maggie's car. Gregory planned to take his own car, and Andrew, who had been held up by a late-afternoon meeting, would drive up to the lake afterward.

There was a lot of car door banging and loud spurts of music. Philip, who wanted to ride with Gregory, was fooling around with his stereo. At last both cars drove off, and Ivy stood alone, cherishing the silence. The afternoon was warm and still, and only the trees, the very tops of them, rustled dryly. It was one of the few moments of real peace that she had felt since Tristan's death.

She went inside and grabbed a book, one that Beth had given her, so it was sure to be a torrid romance. Beth had sent it via Suzanne with a note of apology, afraid to face Ivy and afraid to call her up. Ivy had telephoned Beth to let her know she wasn't angry anymore.

She was still mystified, however. It was such an odd thing for Beth to have done – creating computer messages from "Tristan." Beth was usually so sensitive to other people's feelings. Well, she had thought that Will was sensitive, too, and look what he had done: put a pair of wings on Tristan.

In spite of the pain of that memory, Ivy smiled a little. What would Tristan have thought about Will turning him into an angel?

She read for more than an hour and a half up in the tree house, occasionally gazing out through the branches at the distant glittering strip that was the river. Then she stuck the book in the waistband of her jeans and swung down on the rope. In the mood for a walk, Ivy circled around the front of the house and headed down the winding drive. She quickened her pace, and kept it up as she climbed the hill again, returning to the top, sweaty and exhilarated.

Maybe she could finally play "Liebestraum," she thought. With all this quiet around her, maybe she'd play up a storm, and work all the way through the love song. She had been practicing for the festival every day but hadn't been able to get to the end of the piece. At some point the memories always came back to her, a slow tide turning in her, and washed out all her music. Maybe that day she could hold on to the notes.

Ivy grabbed a soda from the kitchen and hurried upstairs to take a shower. Halfway through it, she wondered if she should have locked the back door. Don't be silly, she told herself. No one ever comes up on this hill. She intended to enjoy these days of peace and wouldn't let the worrying of Suzanne, Beth, and Gregory put her on edge.

When Ivy climbed the steps to her music room, Ella scooted ahead of her and leaped up onto the piano bench.

Ivy smiled. "You're practicing for the festival, too?"

She thought about the triplets of notes that Ella had "played" the week before, then pushed it out of her mind; the song would make her start thinking of Tristan.

Ivy began her warm-ups, then played melodies that were Philip's favorites, and finally began "Liebestraum." She was pleased by her playing, her fingers flying over the keys, caught up completely in the vibrant cadenza. Just before she returned to the opening theme, in the moment she paused to turn the page, she heard a noise.

Immediately she thought of glass shattering. Her flesh turned to goose bumps, but she fought against her fear. She reminded herself that breaking glass was a sound from her nightmares. If anyone really wanted to get in, all the person had to do was open the back door. The noise wasn't a window breaking, she told herself. A tree branch fell against the house, or something had blown over downstairs.

Still, Ivy felt uneasy. She glanced around the room and saw that Ella was gone. Maybe the cat had knocked over something. The best thing to do would be to investigate and prove to herself that it was nothing. Ivy went to the top of the attic stairs and listened.

She thought the noise had come from the west wing, by Andrew's office. Maybe it was Andrew, out of his meeting early, stopping by the house to pick up something.

Ivy crept down the steps to her bedroom and stopped just inside the door that led to the hall. She wished Ella were with her; the cat could warn her with a prick of her ears or a twitch of her tail.

The house seemed suddenly huge, twice its real size, pocked with a hundred hiding places and far away from anyone who could hear her scream. Ivy stepped back and picked up the telephone in her room, then put it down.

Get ahold of yourself, she thought. You can't drag the police all the way out here for nothing.

"Andrew?" she called. "Andrew, is that you?"

No answer.

"Ella, come here. Where are you, Ella?"

The house was deafeningly silent.

Ivy tiptoed into the hall and decided to go down the center stairway rather than the narrower one that led into the west wing. There was a phone on the table in the lower hall. If she noticed that anything had been disturbed, she'd immediately make a call from there.

At the bottom of the stairs Ivy looked quickly left and right. Maybe she should just run out the front door, she thought.

And then what? Let someone take what he wanted? Or better yet, let him find a snug spot to lie in wait for her?

Don't let your imagination run away with you, she chided herself.

The rooms on the east side of the house – the living room, library, and solarium – were closed up, still shuttered against the early sunlight. Ivy turned the other way, peeking around the corner into the dining room. She walked through it, tensing at the creak of old boards, and pushed open the door to the kitchen. Across from her was the door she had left unlocked, still closed. After quickly checking two closets, she locked the outside door.

But what about the basement? She bolted the door on the kitchen side. She could check the outside entrance to it later, she thought, then headed into the family room. Nothing had been disturbed.

Just as she stepped into the gallery that led to Andrew's office, Ella came trotting toward her.

"Ella!" Ivy breathed out with relief. "What have you been up to?"

Ella swished her tail fiercely back and forth.

"First it was his chair," Ivy said, shaking her finger at the cat, though she was gasping with relief. "Now what, a Waterford vase?"

She marched into the room and stopped.

A windowpane was smashed in, the door next to it ajar. Ivy stepped back.

She stepped into him. "Wha—?"

Before she could turn around, a sack was pulled over her head. Ivy screamed and fought to get free, ripping at the sack with her hands, clawing it like a cat. The more she yanked at the cloth, the tighter it was pulled around her. She felt as if she were suffocating.

She fought to keep herself from panicking, struggling against someone much stronger than she. Think! Think! she told herself.

Her feet were still free. But she knew that if she kicked and lost her balance, he'd have her. She began to use her weight, swinging her whole body from side to side. She swung hard. He lost his grip, and Ivy spun away.

Then he grabbed her again. He was pushing her now, toward a wall or a corner, she thought. She couldn't see a thing inside the dark bag and had lost track of where she was. Even if she could get free of him, she didn't know which way to run.

The sack was so rough that each time he pulled it the threads burned against her face. She wanted to lift her hands and claw her way through so she could see her attacker's face.

He made no sound. She felt him shift his grip, holding her now with just one arm. Then she felt it, something pressed against her head, something hard and round – like the barrel of a gun.

She began to kick and kick, and shriek.

Then she heard a pounding sound from somewhere else in the house. Someone was pounding and calling, "Ivy! Ivy!"

She tried to answer.

She was hurtled forward and could not stop herself from falling. She slammed against something as hard as rock and slid down it. Metal things tumbled and clattered around her. Then everything went black.

"Ivy! Ivy!" Tristan called.

"Ivy! Ivy!" Will shouted, pounding on the front door. Then he raced around the outside of the house, looking for some other way in.

He saw Gregory's car parked in the back. He stopped – Tristan stopped – at the broken window and the door that opened into Andrew's office.

"Ivy, what the— Who did this?" Gregory was saying, bending over her, gently pulling off the sack. "Are you okay? Easy now. You're safe now."

Fireplace tools were scattered on the floor. Ivy rubbed her head and stared up at Gregory. Then they both turned to look at Will, who was framed by the open door. Tristan had just slipped out of Will, but he saw the fear and mistrust in Ivy's face and the angry flush on Gregory's.

"What are you doing here?" Gregory demanded.

Will was speechless, and even if Tristan had stayed inside him, he couldn't have given an answer that would have satisfied Gregory or Ivy.

"I don't know," Will said. "I just thought— I just knew I had to be here. I felt something was wrong and that I had to come."

With the angry color draining out of Gregory's face, his skin looked paler than normal. He looked almost as shaken as Ivy.

"Are you all right, Ivy?" Will asked.

She nodded and turned away, resting her head against Gregory's chest.

"Is there anything I can do?" Will asked.

"No."

"I'd better call the police," he said.

"You'd better," Gregory said, his voice cold and unfriendly.

When Will placed the call, he spoke calmly, but Tristan knew that his partner was as shaken and bewildered as he. Tristan knew little more than Will about how he had first sensed that Ivy was in danger.

She needs you. The message had come to Tristan, though whether he'd heard it or simply understood it, he couldn't say. But knowing that something was about to happen, and remembering that Lacey had said he could not rescue her himself, that he had to combine his powers with someone else's, he had rushed right to Will, urging him to go to Ivy, to help her.

It had been a struggle, especially at the beginning. Tristan had to learn to channel his energy, and gradually Will gave himself over to his direction. Tristan wondered if Will realized he had driven up the hill at eighty miles per hour, despite the upgrade and turns. Did Will remember racing around from the front to the back of the house faster than was humanly possible?

But still not fast enough to catch Ivy's attacker, thought Tristan. Until he knew who the attacker was, there was no way of guessing when he'd strike next, or how Will and he could protect Ivy.

Will and he. He and Will. There was no denying now that Will cared for Ivy – and that Tristan needed him to.

Tristan watched as Gregory picked up Ivy and carried her to the sofa. Ella crouched under Andrew's desk, her eyes glowing like embers.

"Who was it, Ella?" Tristan asked. "You're the only one who saw it. Who did this?"

Will left the room and came back with an icepack.

Gregory held it gently against Ivy's head. "I'm here. Everything's going to be all right," he said over and over, continually rubbing her back and soothing her.

Before long they heard the whine of a siren. A police car swung into the driveway, followed unexpectedly by another car. Andrew's.

"What happened?" Andrew cried, rushing into the house with the officers. "Ivy, are you all right?"

He looked at the broken window, then at Will, and finally turned his attention to Gregory. "Why are you here?" he asked. "You're supposed to be with Maggie and Philip."

"Why are *you?*" Gregory asked back.

Andrew glanced quickly at the police, then gestured toward his desk. "I left some papers behind, some reports I wanted to work on at the lake."

"I came because Ivy called me," Gregory said. "I'd told her earlier today that she should call me if she needed anything." He gazed down at her. Ivy met his eyes with a puzzled expression.

"It was you who called me, wasn't it?" he asked. "No."

Gregory looked surprised, then squeezed her hands hard and dropped them. "Whew," he said softly. "You owe somebody big time."

He turned to the others. "When we got to the lake, I had to run out to the store. Maggie had remembered everything for our trip, except toilet paper.

"When I returned, the man at the lodge said someone had called three times, asking for me, but didn't leave a message. I figured it was Ivy. It's been rough for her lately – you know that," he said, appealing to his father. "I didn't waste any time. I came right home."

"Lucky girl," remarked one of the police officers.

The police began to ask questions then. Tristan moved slowly around the room, studying faces and reading what the police were scribbling down.

Was it jealousy that he felt every time he saw Gregory touch Ivy? Or was it some kind of intuition? he wondered. Was Ivy really safe in Gregory's arms?

Had Gregory told Eric that Ivy would be alone all weekend? If Eric was responsible for this, would Gregory cover for him?

And why had Gregory questioned his father? Did he think Andrew's excuse for returning to the house was a little too convenient?

The police stayed a long time that afternoon and asked lots of questions, but it seemed to Tristan they were all the wrong ones.

23

When Ivy answered the door on Tuesday morning, she knew that Beth had read the local paper. Her friend stepped inside with a quick, shy "How're you doing?" She hugged Ivy, nearly squeezing the breath out of her, then backed off, blushing.

"I'm fine," said Ivy. "I'm really fine."

"Are you?" Beth looked like a worried mother owl, her eyes wide, her light-brown hair falling out of its knot in soft feathers. She stared at Ivy's bruised cheek.

"It's the newest thing since tattoos," Ivy said, smiling and touching her face lightly.

"Your face looks like . . . a pansy."

Ivy laughed. "Purple and yellow. I'm going to look great for the festival. You got anything that matches?"

Beth tried to smile, but ended up biting her lip.

"Come on back," Ivy said, leading her to the kitchen. "Let's get something to drink. We have to stick around here for a few minutes. I'm getting interviewed for the third time."

"By a newspaper?"

"By the police."

"The police! Ivy, did you tell them—" Beth hesitated.

"Tell them what?"

"About the computer messages," Beth said quietly.

"No." Ivy pulled out a bar stool for Beth to sit on. "Why should I? It was nothing more than a strange coincidence. You were just fooling around and—"

The look in Beth's eyes stopped her. "I wasn't fooling around."

Ivy shrugged a little, then measured out some coffee beans. Since Friday evening she had been acting as if nothing much had happened, as if she had already gotten over the scare. She felt bad about ruining everyone's weekend and tried to keep them from worrying and fussing over her. But the truth was, she was glad to have her family home with her. She was starting to get spooked.

Philip was convinced an angel had sent Gregory to save her – the same angel who had prevented him from tumbling out of the tree house, he said. Recently he had found a statue of an angelic baseball player and claimed it had been delivered to him by a glowing friend of his own guardian.

Ivy knew her brother was talking like this because he was frightened. Maybe, Ivy thought, having lost Tristan, Philip was scared of losing her, too. Maybe that was why he had warned her several times about the train climbing up the ridge to get her.

How could she blame him? With the car accident, then Friday's close call, Ivy herself imagined hidden dangers wherever she looked. And if there was one thing she didn't need just then, it was Beth looking at her as if she had glimpsed something frightening from beyond.

"Beth, you're my friend, and you were worried about me being alone, the same way Suzanne and Gregory were worried. The difference is, you're a writer and – and you've got a very active imagination," Ivy added, smiling. "It's only natural that when you worry, it comes out in a story."

Beth didn't look convinced.

"In any case, you're not responsible. Even if you were psychic, psychics only know about things, they don't make them happen."

The doorbell rang, and Ivy quickly dried her hands. "So there's no reason to tell the police."

"Tell them what?" Gregory asked, coming into the kitchen.

He was up earlier than usual, dressed for a day in New York City with Suzanne.

"Tell Gregory about it, Beth, if it would make you feel any better," Ivy advised, then went to answer the door.

A redheaded man sucking on a breath mint was pacing the front porch as if he had been waiting for hours. He identified himself as Lieutenant Donnelly and asked Ivy if he could speak with her in the office where the assault had occurred.

"I'll see," Ivy replied. "My stepfather didn't go to the college today, and if he's working—"

"Is he in? Good," the detective said briskly. "He's on my list, too."

A few minutes later they were joined in Andrew's office by Gregory. The detective had questions for all of them, but most of what they talked about were facts they had gone over before.

When they were finished, the lieutenant said, "Our reason for questioning you again is that we had a similar incident late last night in Ridgefield. Same style of break-in, victim a high-school girl, got a bag pulled over her head. If our friend is embarking on a series of such attacks, we want to find as many similarities as possible. That way we can establish a pattern, predict him – and nail him."

"Then you've concluded that the attack on Ivy

was a random act," Andrew said, "rather than something done by someone who knows her?"

"We haven't concluded anything," the detective replied, leaning forward, raising his bushy red eyebrows, "and I'm always interested in other people's theories."

"I have no theories," Andrew said crisply. "I just want to know if she is safe now."

"Is there some reason you think she isn't? Is there anyone you know who would want to hurt a member of your family?"

"No," Andrew replied. Then he turned to Gregory. "Not that I can think of," he said slowly. "Do you know of anyone, Gregory?"

Gregory let the question hang in the air for a moment. "Nope."

Andrew turned back to the detective. "We just want to know if we can assume that Ivy is safe."

"Of course. I understand, sir," Donnelly said. "And of course you understand that I can't assure you of that." He handed Ivy his card. "If you remember anything else, give me a call."

"About the girl in Ridgefield," Ivy said, catching the detective's sleeve. "Is she okay?"

The man's mouth formed a grim line. He shook his head twice. "Dead," he said quietly, then pushed open the door next to the newly fixed windowpane. "I can let myself out."

As soon as he'd left, Ivy hurried out of the room,

not wanting the others to see her tears. Gregory caught her halfway up the back stairs. She scrambled away from him and went down on all fours. He pulled her to him.

"Ivy. Talk to me. What is it?"

She pulled away from him and pressed her lips together.

"What is it?"

"It could have happened to me!" she blurted. "If you hadn't come at that moment, if you hadn't scared him away—" Tears tumbled down her cheeks.

"It didn't happen," he said gently but firmly, and sat her down on the steps.

Don't leave now, Ivy begged silently. Don't go out with Suzanne today. I need you more than she does.

Immediately she felt guilty about those thoughts.

Gregory wiped away her tears.

"Sorry," Ivy said.

"Sorry for what?"

"For acting so – so—"

"Human?"

She rested against him.

He brushed the hair back from her face and let his fingers stay tangled in it.

"My father was right, you know. For once, old Andrew got it right. I feel sorry for the other girl's family, but I'm pretty relieved. Now we know it wasn't someone out to get you." He pulled his head back to look at her. "And that lets Will off the hook," he joked.

Ivy didn't laugh.

"Unless Will has a career we don't know about. He can be awfully silent and mysterious . . ."

Ivy still didn't smile. She breathed as evenly as possible, trying to stifle her hiccoughs. "You'd better get going, Gregory," she advised. "Do you realize what time it is? Suzanne doesn't like her dates to be late."

"I know," he said, and held Ivy apart from him, studying her.

Does he look at Suzanne that way, she wondered, so intently, as if he's searching out her thoughts? Does he look into her eyes the way he looks into mine? Does he care about her as much as he cares about me?

Another wave of guilt washed over Ivy; her face must have revealed it.

"What?" he asked. "What are you thinking?"

"Nothing. You'd better get going."

He continued to look at her uncertainly.

"On your way out, would you stop and tell Beth I'll be down in a minute?"

He shrugged, then let go of her. "Sure."

Ivy hurried up the steps. She was glad she'd be spending most of her day off with Beth. If Ivy told her she didn't want to talk about something, Beth would drop the subject. Unfortunately, she had already agreed to meet Suzanne for dinner that evening, after Gregory and she returned from New York. Ivy wasn't looking forward to hashing over the details of Gregory's heroic rescue and every "he said, I said" of Suzanne's date.

Ivy had just passed Gregory's room when his phone rang. She wondered if she should pick it up for him or let the answering machine take a message.

It's probably Suzanne, Ivy thought, calling to find out where he is. She stopped to listen; if it was her friend, she'd pick up the phone and tell her that Gregory was on his way.

The machine beeped. There was a moment of silence, then a voice said, "It's me. I need the money, Gregory. You know I don't like to go to your old man. And you know what will happen if I don't get the money. I need the money, Gregory, now."

The caller hung up without identifying himself, but she recognized his voice. Eric.

Ivy drummed her fingers on the wicker chair, looked out at the pond behind the Goldsteins' house, and checked her watch once more. Obviously Suzanne had forgotten about their plans.

They were to meet there at six-thirty. It was now twenty-five minutes past seven.

Ivy was annoyed that she had waited this long, especially since she didn't even want to see Suzanne that night. But she thought that as a loyal best friend she should stick it out.

"Always your best friend," she murmured. At home she had a large box of tattered letters, notes that Suzanne had started writing in fourth grade whenever she got bored in class. All the letters were signed, "Always your best friend."

Always – but the truth was, with Gregory around, things were changing between the two of them. And Suzanne was as guilty as she. Ivy got up from the chair abruptly and started down the porch steps.

From the other side of the house came the sound of a car in the driveway. A door slammed. Ivy circled around the house, then stopped. Gregory and Suzanne were walking slowly toward the house, their arms around each other, Suzanne's head on his shoulder. Ivy wished she had left earlier, much earlier.

Gregory spotted her first and stopped walking. Then Suzanne looked up. "Hi, Ivy!" she said with surprise. A moment later, her hand flew up to her head. "Oh, no, I totally forgot! I'm so sorry. I hope you haven't been waiting too long."

Since six-thirty, and you know it, and I'm

starved, Ivy wanted to say, but didn't. But she also didn't play Suzanne's game by reassuring her in some way: No, no, I just got here myself. That's what she was supposed to say, wasn't it? Ivy just looked at her friend and let her figure it out.

Perhaps Gregory picked up on some of the tension between them. He jumped in quickly. "We decided at the last minute to get a pizza at Celentano's. I'm sorry we didn't know you were here, Ivy. It would have been great if you'd come with us."

He was rewarded with two glares: Suzanne's, for implying that dinner would have been great if Ivy had come; Ivy's, for suggesting that she'd enjoy being with them on a date. Hadn't he ever heard that three's a crowd?

Gregory unwrapped himself from Suzanne, then retreated toward the car. Slipping one hand in his pocket, he propped the other on the open door, trying to look casual.

"I can see there's going to be some talking here tonight, some dirt-dishing. Maybe I should leave before I get hooked by the soap opera."

You are the soap opera, Ivy thought.

"You may as well," Suzanne replied. "Most guys are amateurs at talking."

Gregory laughed – not as much at ease as he pretended, Ivy thought – then rattled his keys at them and left.

"I'm beat," Suzanne said, throwing herself down

on the front steps and pulling Ivy down next to her. "Manhattan in the summer – I tell you, it brings out the crazies. You should have seen all the people at Times Square, waiting for another vision of—"

She stopped herself, but Ivy knew what she was about to say. She had already read about the angelic Mariah Carey.

Suzanne reached out then and touched Ivy's face very, very gently. "Aren't they getting tired of seeing you in the emergency room?"

Ivy laughed a little.

"How're you feeling?" Suzanne asked.

"All right . . . really," she added when she saw the doubt in Suzanne's eyes.

"Are you dreaming about this now, too?"

"I haven't so far," said Ivy.

"You're tough, girl," Suzanne said, shaking her head. "And I bet you're hungry and ready to kill me."

"Very hungry and almost ready," Ivy replied as Suzanne pushed herself up from the steps and dug in her purse for her house keys. Peppermint, Suzanne's Pomeranian, greeted them with yaps of joy, anticipating dinner. They headed straight for the kitchen.

While Suzanne fed Peppermint, Ivy explored the Goldsteins' refrigerator, which was always well stocked. She settled for a large bowl of homemade soup. Suzanne set a pan of brownies and some lemon frosted cupcakes on the table between them. She cut herself a brownie, then swiveled back and forth in her chair. "I've got him, Ivy," she said. "Gregory's definitely hooked. Now all I have to do is reel him in."

"I thought you were going to reel him in last week, or maybe the week before," Ivy recalled.

"That's why I need your help," Suzanne said quickly. "I'm never sure with Gregory. I have to know, Ivy – did he go out with any girls this weekend? I mean, with me being away and him having to come home because of you, I wondered whether he got out his little date book and . . ."

Ivy chased noodles around with her soup spoon. "I don't know," she said.

"How can you not know? You live with him!"

"He was home Saturday morning. In the afternoon we played tennis and went shopping. At night he went to a movie with Philip and me. He was out for a while on Sunday afternoon, but the rest of the time he was with Philip and me."

"*And you*. It's a good thing you're my best friend and Gregory's stepsister," Suzanne remarked, "or else I'd be insanely jealous and suspicious. Lucky for both of us, isn't it?"

"Yeah," Ivy replied without enthusiasm.

"How about Monday? Did he go out then?"

"For a while in the morning, then late last night.

Suzanne, I don't feel right reporting on him to you."

"Well, whose side are you on?" her friend asked.

Ivy crumbled a cracker in her soup. "I didn't know there were sides."

"Who do you feel most loyal to, me or Gregory?" Suzanne persisted. "You know, in the beginning I thought you didn't like him. In fact, I thought you couldn't stand him but didn't say anything because you didn't want to hurt my feelings."

Ivy nodded. "I didn't know him very well then. But I do now, and since I care about him and I care about you, and since you're chasing him—"

"I've caught him, Ivy."

"Since you've caught him, and you hooked *me* years ago, how can there be sides?"

"Don't be so naive," Suzanne replied. "There are always sides in love." She chopped away at the brownies in the pan. "Love is war."

"Don't, Suzanne."

She stopped chopping. "Don't what?"

"Don't do what you're doing to him."

Suzanne sat back in her chair. "Just what are you saying?" There was a noticeable chill in her voice.

"I'm saying don't play games with him. Don't push him around the way you've pushed around the other guys. He deserves better treatment, much better."

Suzanne was silent for a moment. "You know what you need, Ivy? A boyfriend of your own."

Ivy stared down at her soup.

"And Gregory agrees with me on that."

Ivy glanced up sharply.

"He thinks Will is perfect for you."

"Tristan was perfect for me."

"*Was*," said Suzanne. "*Was*. Life goes on, and you've got to go on with it!"

"I will when I'm ready," Ivy replied.

"You've got to let go of the past." Suzanne laid her hand on Ivy's wrist. "You've got to stop acting like a little girl, holding on to the hand of big brother Gregory."

Ivy looked away.

"You've got to start getting out and seeing other guys. Will's a start."

"Butt out, Suzanne."

"Gregory and I can set you up."

"I said, butt out!"

"All right!"

Suzanne sliced an ultrathin piece of brownie, then pointed the knife at Ivy. "But you butt out, too, and don't tell me what to do. I'm warning you now, don't interfere with me and Gregory."

What did she mean by interfere? Ivy wondered. Don't give her advice – or stop holding on to Gregory's hand?

They both stared down at their food in silence.

Peppermint sat between their chairs, looking from one to the other. Then somehow, after what seemed an interminable silence, they found their way onto safer ground, talking about the wedding Suzanne had been to. But as Suzanne talked on and Ivy nodded, all Ivy could think of was that one way or the other, she was going to lose someone who meant a lot to her.

24

"Give us a few more minutes, Philip," Ivy said. "We want to look at the rest of these paintings."

"I think I'll go find Gregory."

Ivy reached out quickly and caught her brother by the back of his T-shirt. "Not today. You're stuck with Beth and me."

For the last four days Ivy had spent little time with Gregory, seeing him only at occasional family meals and in chance passings in the hall. Whenever their paths did cross, she'd been careful not to start a long conversation with him. When he'd sought her out – and the more she'd avoided him the more he had sought her out – she'd claimed she was on her way up to the music room to practice.

Gregory looked puzzled and a little angry about the distance she was putting between them. But what else could she do? They had grown too close.

Without meaning to, Ivy had come to depend on him. If she didn't back off now, she might lose Suzanne as a friend.

Suzanne and Beth had met Gregory, Philip, and Ivy in town that afternoon, at the bottom of Main Street, where the festival began. Suzanne had immediately draped her arm across Gregory's back and slipped her hand into his back pocket, walking him away from Ivy and Philip. Ivy had responded by steering Philip in another direction. Beth was left standing on the street corner.

"Come with us," Ivy had called to her. "We're going to see the art."

The display was set up along a narrow lane of old shops that ran back from Main Street. An assortment of townspeople – women pushing baby strollers, old ladies in straw hats, kids with their faces painted, and two guys dressed as clowns – walked along looking at the pictures, trying to guess who the artists were. Each picture was titled and numbered, but the artists' names were masked for the judging that would take place later that day.

Ivy, Beth, and Philip were almost at the end of the display when Philip had started fussing about finding Gregory.

Now Ivy pointed to a strange painting, trying to distract him. "What do you think that is?" she asked.

"*Things.*" He read the title with a scowl.

"Looks to me like a row of lipsticks," Beth said, "or trees in the fall or Christmas candles or catsup bottles or missiles at sunset—"

Philip screwed up his face. "It looks to me like it's stupid," he said loudly.

"Shh! Philip, keep your voice down," Ivy warned. "For all we know, the artist is right behind us."

Philip turned around to look. Suddenly the scowl was gone. His face lit up. "No," he said, "but there's an—" He hesitated.

"What?" Beth asked.

Ivy glanced quickly behind her. No one was there.

Philip gave a little shrug. "Never mind." He sighed.

They moved on to the last entry, a panel with four watercolors.

"Wow!" Beth said. "These are fabulous! Number thirty-three, whoever you are, you're my winner."

"Mine, too," Ivy agreed. The artist's colors were almost transparent and infused with a light of their own.

Ivy pointed to a painting of a garden. "I wish I could sit there, for hours and hours. It makes me feel so peaceful."

"I like the snake," Philip observed.

Only a little boy would have found that snake, Ivy thought, painted in so slyly.

"I want to talk to the woman in the last picture," Beth said.

The woman sat under a tree with her face turned away from the painter. Blossoms were streaming down on her, luminous apple blossoms, but they made Ivy think of snow. She looked at the title: *Too Soon.*

"There's a story behind that one," Beth said softly.

Ivy nodded. She knew the story, or one like it, about losing someone before you had a chance to—

For a moment her eyes stung. Then she blinked and said, "Well, we've seen everything in the show. Let's go spend money."

"Yeah!" Philip shouted. "Where're the rides?"

"There aren't any rides, not at a festival like this."

Philip stopped short. "No rides?" He couldn't believe it. "No rides!"

"I think we're in for a long afternoon," Ivy told Beth.

"We'll just keep feeding him," Beth replied.

"I want to go home."

"Let's walk back to Main Street," Ivy suggested, "and see what everyone is selling."

"That's boring." Her brother was getting that stiff-jawed look that meant trouble. "I'm going to find Gregory."

"No!" She said it so sharply that Beth glanced over at her.

"He's on a date, Philip," Ivy reminded him quietly, "and we can't bother him."

Philip started dragging his feet as though he had been walking for miles. Beth was walking slowly, too, studying Ivy.

"It's just that it's really not fair to Gregory," Ivy told Beth, as if she had asked for an explanation. "He's not used to a nine-year-old tagging along everywhere."

"Oh." The way Beth glanced away told Ivy that her friend knew this wasn't the whole truth.

"And of course, Suzanne's not used to it at all."

"I guess not," Beth replied mildly.

"This is boring, boring, boring," Philip complained. "I want to go home."

"Then walk!" Ivy snapped.

Beth glanced around. "How about getting our picture taken?" she suggested. "Every year there's a stand called Old West Photos. They have different costumes you can dress up in. It's fun."

"Great idea!" Ivy replied. "We'll take enough for an album," she added under her breath, "if it keeps him occupied."

The canopied stand was set up in front of the photo shop and looked like a small stage set. There were several backdrops to choose from, trunks of clothes that kids and adults were sorting through, and props scattered about—pistols, wooden mugs, a fake-fur buffalo head. Tinkly piano music gave the tent a saloon atmosphere.

The photographer himself was dressed up in a cowboy hat, vest, and tight cowhide pants. Beth eyed him from behind. "Cute," she observed. "Very cute."

Ivy smiled.

"I like anything in boots," Beth said, a little too loudly.

The cowboy turned around.

"Will!"

Will laughed at Beth, who flushed with embarrassment. He put a reassuring hand on her arm, then nodded at Ivy. Philip had already strayed toward the costume trunks.

"How are you?" Will asked.

Beth banged herself on the head. "I completely forgot that with your job, you'd be doing this."

He smiled at her – a big and easy smile. It was impossible to see Will's eyes under the shadow of his hat, but Ivy could tell when he glanced from Beth to her, because the smile became not so big, and not so easy.

"Thinking about having your picture done?" he asked.

Philip was already elbow-deep in clothes.

"Looks like our date wants to," Beth said to Ivy.

"Your date?"

"My brother, Philip," Ivy explained. He had wedged himself in between two guys big enough to play pro football. "The short one."

Will nodded. "Maybe I should steer him toward another trunk. Ladies' costumes are over there," Will added over his shoulder, pointing toward trunks where a flock of girls were gathered.

A few of the girls were older than Ivy and Beth. Others looked two or three years younger. All of them kept turning around, looking at Will and giggling.

"Hey, cowboy," Beth called softly after him. "I bet *they'd* like your help, even more than Philip."

"They're doing fine," he said, and continued on.

"Love those buns."

Will stopped.

Ivy looked at Beth, and Beth looked at Ivy. Ivy knew she hadn't said it, but Beth acted as if she hadn't, either. Her blue eyes were brimming with laughter and surprise.

"I didn't say it."

"Neither did I."

Will just shook his head and walked on.

"But you were thinking it," someone said. Ivy glanced around.

"Well, maybe I was, Ivy," Beth admitted, "but—"

Will turned around.

"I didn't say it!" Ivy insisted.

"Say what?" Will asked, cocking his head.

Ivy was sure he had heard. "That you have— That I thought— That—" Ivy looked sideways at Beth. "Oh, never mind."

"What is she talking about?" Will asked Beth.

"Something about your buns," said Beth.

Ivy threw up her hands. "I don't care about his buns!"

The buzz of voices beneath the canopy ceased. Everyone looked at Will, then Ivy.

"Would you like to see mine?" asked one of the football types.

"Oh, jeez," Ivy said.

Will laughed out loud.

"Your cheeks are pink," Beth told Ivy.

Ivy put her hands up to her face.

Beth pulled them away. "It's a much better color for you than purple and yellow."

Fifteen minutes later, Ivy grimaced as Beth zipped her up in front of the dressing room mirror.

"If I lean over, Will's going to get a fine shot."

"He's going to get a fine shot even with you straightened up," Beth observed.

They had decided to dress as saloon girls in identical red-and-black dresses, "floozy frocks," as Beth called them. She smoothed her hands over her ample hips. "I don't care if my man's law-abiding," she said with a Western twang, "so long as he abides by *my* laws."

Ivy laughed, then gave a backward glance at herself in the mirror. Beth had given her the smaller dress to wear; there wasn't a curve that didn't show. Ivy was reluctant to step through the dressing room curtains, though Beth informed her that the two football types had left. Ivy could deal with the Brothers Macho; it was Will she felt shy around.

Maybe he sensed that. He stretched out his hand to Beth, as she and Ivy stepped out of the dressing room. "Oh, Miss Lizzie," he said, "you do look mighty fine today. You too, Miss Ivy," he added quietly.

"How about me?" Philip asked. He came out in fringed pants and a vest that almost fit him. But the ten-gallon hat was about nine gallons too big.

"Fearsome," Will said. "Fearsome and awesome, if only I could see your chin."

Ivy laughed, feeling more comfortable again. "How about if we try a different size?"

"Make it black," said Philip.

"Right, Slim."

Will found a hat and got the three of them lined up in front of the camera, angling them just right. Then he pushed his hat back and went behind the camera. It was a digital camera in the body of an old one, rigged up to give off a big puff of smoke – that was part of the show. But after the flash and the smoke, Will's head shot up from behind the equipment. He looked almost comical, and at first

Ivy thought that too was part of the show. But the way Will was staring made all three of them turn to look behind them.

"I – uh – I'm going to take another," he said. "Can you set yourselves just like before?"

They did, and a second puff of smoke was sent up.

"What went wrong the first time?" Beth asked.

"I'm not sure." A look Ivy couldn't interpret passed between him and Beth. He shook his head. Then the hat was back over his eyes again. "These will take a few minutes to print. Do you want two or three copies?" Will asked them.

"Two's fine," Ivy replied. "One for Beth and one for us."

"I want my own copy," said Philip.

"So do I," said another voice.

Everyone turned.

"Howdy, pardner," Gregory said, holding his hand out to Philip. "Ladies." His eyes lingered on Ivy, traveling down her slowly.

Suzanne gave her a quicker look. "You sure squeezed yourself into that one," she remarked. "It's a wonder a crowd hasn't gathered."

Will pulled on his tight pants. "Are you talking about her or me?" he asked lightly.

Gregory laughed. Beth laughed after Gregory did, then glanced uncomfortably at Suzanne. Suzanne wasn't amused.

Will set up for his next group of customers.

"Suzanne, there were only two dresses alike," Ivy said quickly, "and Beth and I wanted to match, so she took that one and I took— Tell her, Beth."

But as Beth repeated the explanation, Ivy said to herself, Why bother? Until Gregory learns to keep his eyes from wandering to other girls, it's hopeless. I wish he'd wander them over to Beth, though.

She turned toward the dressing room.

Gregory caught her by the arm. "We'll wait for you," he said. "We're going to check out Will's paintings."

Ivy saw Suzanne out of the corner of her eye, drumming her fingers on the top of a trunk.

"We've already seen them," Ivy told him.

"Though we didn't know which were his," Beth said. "The artists' names are still covered."

"They're watercolors," Gregory told them.

"Watercolors?" Ivy and Beth repeated at the same time.

"Will," Gregory called out. "What's your entry number?"

"Thirty-three," he replied.

Beth and Ivy exchanged glances.

"You painted the garden where Ivy wants to sit for hours," Beth said.

"And the snake," Philip said.

"And the woman with blossoms falling around her like snow," Ivy added.

346

"That's right." Will continued to work, arranging his customers before the camera.

"They were amazing!" Beth said.

"I like the snake," said Philip.

Ivy watched Will without saying anything. He was being the cool Will O'Leary again, acting as if his paintings and what they said about them didn't matter to him. Then she saw the quick turn of the head, as if he were checking to see whether she was still there. She realized then that he had wanted her to make a comment.

"Your paintings are really . . . uh . . ." All the words she could think of sounded flat.

"That's okay," he said, cutting her short before she could come up with the right description.

"Are you coming along for a second look?" Gregory asked impatiently.

"Be out in a minute," Beth replied, hurrying toward the dressing room.

Philip was walking to the dressing room and undressing at the same time.

"I can't," Ivy said to Gregory. "I play at five o'clock and I need to—"

"Practice?" His eyes flashed.

"I need time to collect myself, to think through what I'm playing, that's all. I can't do that with everyone around."

"I'm sorry you can't come," Suzanne said, and

Ivy knew she was making progress. Still, it hurt her to see Gregory turn away.

She dawdled in the dressing room long enough for the others to go. When she came out, there were only two customers left, trying on hats and laughing.

Will was relaxing in a canvas chair with one leg propped up on a trunk, studying a photograph in his hands. He turned it facedown when he saw her. "Thanks for stopping by," he said.

"Will, you didn't give me a chance to tell you what I liked about your paintings. I couldn't find the right words at first—"

"I wasn't fishing for compliments, Ivy."

"I don't care whether you were or weren't," she said, and plopped down in the chair across from him. "I have something to say."

"All right." His mouth curved up slightly. "Shoot."

"It's about the one called *Too Soon*."

Will took off his hat. She wished he had kept it on. Somehow – more and more, it seemed – looking into his eyes made it difficult for her to speak. She told herself they were just deep brown eyes, but whenever she looked into them she felt as if she were going into free fall.

The eyes are windows to the soul, she'd read once. And his were wide open.

She focused on her hands. "Sometimes, when

something touches you, it's hard to find the words. You can say things like 'beautiful,' 'fabulous,' 'awesome,' but the words don't really describe how you feel, especially if you were feeling all that, but the picture made you – made you hurt some, too. And your picture did." She flexed her fingers. "That's all."

"Thanks," Will said.

She looked up at him then, which was a mistake.

"Ivy—"

She tried to look away, but couldn't.

"—how are you?"

"I'm fine. Really, I am." Why did she have to keep telling people that? And why, when she said it to Will, did it feel as if he could see straight through the lie?

"I have something to say, too," he told her. "Take care of yourself."

She could feel him looking at her cheek, the one that had been bruised during the assault. There was still a pale wash of color there, though she had done her best to disguise it with makeup.

"Please take care of yourself."

"Why wouldn't I?" she snapped.

"Sometimes people don't."

Ivy wanted to say, You don't know what you're talking about, you've never lost anyone you loved. But then she remembered Gregory's words about

Will having gone through a tough time. Maybe Will did understand.

"Who's the person in your painting?" Ivy asked. "Is it someone you knew?"

"My mother. My father still won't look at the picture." Then he waved that thought away and leaned forward. "Be careful, Ivy. Don't forget that there are other people who will feel that they have lost everything if they lose you."

Ivy looked away.

He reached for her face. She pulled back instinctively when he touched the bruised side. But he didn't hurt her, and he didn't let go. He cupped one hand around the back of her head. There was no escaping him.

Maybe she didn't want to escape him.

"Be careful, Ivy. Be careful!" His eyes shone with a strange intensity. "I'm telling you – *be careful!*"

Ivy blinked. Then she broke away from Will and ran.

25

Tristan lay back in the grass, exhausted. The park at the end of Main Street was filling up with people. Their picnic blankets looked like bright-colored rafts on a green sea. Kids rolled around and punched each other. Dogs pulled against their leashes and touched noses. Two teenagers kissed. An older couple flipped down their sunglasses and watched, the woman smiling.

Lacey returned from her exploration of the park's stage, which was set up for the five o'clock performance. She dropped down next to Tristan. "It was a silly thing to do," she chided.

He had expected her to say something like that.

"Which part?" he asked. After all, the afternoon had been long and eventful.

"Trying to get inside Gregory's head." She

snorted. "It's a wonder he didn't knock you as far as Manhattan. Or L.A.!"

"I was desperate, Lacey! I've got to know what kind of game he's playing with Ivy and Suzanne."

"And you thought you needed a trip inside his head to find that out?" she asked incredulously. "You should have asked me. His game's no different than the kind I've seen a lot of guys play with girls. He's taking the easy one for a ride and chasing Miss Hard-to-Get." She moved her face close to Tristan's. "Am I right?"

Tristan didn't reply. It wasn't just a romantic game that was worrying him. Ever since he had made the connection between Caroline's death and Ivy's delivery to the house next door, he had wondered about the hidden purpose behind Gregory's new closeness to Ivy.

"Well, I hope you learned your lesson today," Lacey said.

"I have a pounding headache," he replied. "Are you satisfied?"

She laid her hand lightly on his forehead and said in a quieter voice, "If it makes you feel any better, Gregory probably has one, too."

Tristan squinted up at her, surprised by this small bit of gentleness.

She removed her hand and squinted back. "And why were you chasing Philip around, getting inside *his* mind?" she demanded. "Seems to me like another waste of energy. He already sees us glow – and gets in trouble every time he mentions it. That little conversation put Gregory in a *real* good mood this afternoon."

"I had to tell Philip who I was. Beth signed my name on the computer message. If Philip tells her he sees me, or my light, sooner or later she is going to have to believe."

Lacey shook her head doubtfully.

"And speaking of Philip," Tristan said, pulling himself up on one elbow, "I noticed how Gregory's mood got even better when Philip stopped talking about angels and pulled out an actual photograph of one. What mission were *you* working on today when you jumped into that picture?"

Lacey didn't answer him right away. She gazed up at three women in leotards who had just been introduced onstage. "What do you suppose they're going to do?"

"Dance or aerobics. Answer my question."

"If I were them, I'd wear veils."

"Try again," Tristan said.

"I was working on my semi-materializing process," she told him, "solidifying myself enough to show a general shape but not become an actual body. You never know – I might need to do something like that sometime in the future. To complete my mission, of course."

"Of course. And projecting your voice, so that

everyone at Old West Photos could hear you – I guess you needed to practice that some more, too."

"Oh, well, that," she said with a flick of her hand. "I was working on *your* mission then."

"My mission?"

"In my own way," she replied. "You and I have very different styles."

"True. I'd never have thought of telling Will he has nice buns."

"Terrific buns," Lacey corrected him. "The best I've seen in a long time . . ." She looked at Tristan thoughtfully. "Roll over."

"No way."

She laughed, then said, "That chick of yours, she wears her skin like a suit of armor. I thought that if I got a little joke going, I could get her to loosen up some, to open up to Will. I thought I had a chance, since she couldn't see his eyes beneath his hat. I think it's his eyes that get to her, that make her shut down like that."

"She sees me in them," Tristan said.

"Some guys will do that to you," Lacey went on. "They've got eyes a girl can drown in."

"She doesn't know it, but she sees me in them."

When Lacey did not confirm this, he sat all the way up. "Does Ivy see me looking out at her through Will's eyes?"

"No," Lacey said. "She sees another guy who's fallen in love with her, and it scares her to death."

"I don't believe it!" Tristan said. "You've got it wrong, Lacey."

"I've got it right."

"Will may have a crush, and she may find him sort of attractive, but—"

Lacey lay back in the grass. "Okay, okay. You're going to believe only what you want to believe, no matter what." She stuck one arm behind her head, propping it up a little. "Which isn't a whole lot different than the way Ivy believes – in spite of what's right in front of her nose."

"Ivy could never love anyone else," Tristan insisted. "I didn't know that before the accident, but I know it now. Ivy loves only me. I'm sure of that now."

Lacey tapped him on the arm with a long nail. "Excuse me for pointing out that you're dead now."

Tristan pulled his knees up and rested an arm on each one. He concentrated enough to materialize his fingertips, then dropped one of his hands and ripped up pieces of grass.

"You're getting good," Lacey observed. "That didn't take much effort."

He was too angry to acknowledge the compliment.

"Tristan, you're right. Ivy loves you, more than she loves anyone else. But the world goes on, and if you want her to stay alive, she can't stay in love with death. Life needs life. That's how the world goes."

Tristan didn't reply. He watched the three leotard ladies bounce around, then plod off the stage, shining with sweat. He listened to a little girl dressed like Annie half-sing, half-scream "Tomorrow," over and over.

"It really doesn't matter who's right," he said at last. "I need Will. I can't help Ivy without him."

Lacey nodded. "He's just arrived. I guess he's taking a break from work – he's sitting by himself, not far from the park gate."

"The others are over there," Tristan said, pointing in the opposite direction.

Beth and Philip were lying on their stomachs on a big blanket, watching the performances and picking clover, weaving it into a long chain. Suzanne sat with Gregory on the same blanket, her arms wrapped around him from behind. She rested against his back, laying her chin on his shoulder. Eric had joined them, but was sitting on the grass just beyond the corner of the blanket, fidgeting with the end of it. He continually looked over the crowd, his body twitching at odd moments, his head turning to look quickly behind him.

They watched several more performances, then Ivy was introduced. Philip immediately stood up and clapped. Everyone started to laugh, including Ivy, who glanced over in his direction.

"That will help her," Lacey said. "It breaks the ice. I *like* that kid."

Ivy began to play, not the song she was scheduled to play, but "Moonlight Sonata," the music she had played for Tristan one night, a night that seemed as if it had been summers and summers ago.

This is for me, Tristan thought. This is what she played for me, he wanted to tell them all, the night she turned darkness into light, the night she danced with me. Ivy's playing for *me*, he wanted to tell Gregory and Will.

Gregory was sitting absolutely still, unaware of Suzanne's small movements, his eyes focused on Ivy as if he were spellbound.

Will also sat still in the grass, one knee up, his arm resting casually on it. But there was nothing casual about the way he listened and the way he watched her. He was drinking up every shimmering drop. Tristan rose to his feet and moved toward Will.

From Will's perspective Tristan watched Ivy, her strong hands, her tangle of gold hair in the late-afternoon sun, the expression on her face. She was in a different world than he was, and he longed with his whole soul to be part of it. But she didn't know; he feared she would never know.

In the blink of an eye, Tristan matched thoughts with Will and slipped inside him. He heard Ivy's music through Will's ears now. When she had finished playing, he rose up with Will. He clapped and clapped, hands high above his head, high above Will's head. Ivy bowed and nodded, and glanced over at him.

Then she turned to the others. Suzanne, Beth, and Eric cheered. Philip jumped up and down, trying to see over the heads of the standing audience. Gregory stood still. Gregory and Ivy were the only two people in that noisy park standing motionless, silent, gazing at each other as if they had forgotten everyone else.

Will turned abruptly and walked back toward the street. Tristan slipped out of him and sank down on the grass. A few moments later he felt Lacey next to him. She didn't say anything, just sat with him, shoulder touching shoulder, like an old team member on the swim bench.

"I was wrong, Lacey," Tristan said. "And so were you. Ivy doesn't see me. Ivy doesn't see Will, either."

"She sees Gregory," Lacey said.

"Gregory," he repeated bitterly. "I don't know how I can save her now!"

In a way, dealing with Suzanne after the performance had been easier than Ivy expected. As planned earlier, Ivy met Philip and her friends by the park gate. Before she got a chance to greet them, Suzanne turned away.

Ivy reached out and touched her friend on the arm. "How did you like Will's paintings?" she asked.

Suzanne acted as if she hadn't heard.

"Suzanne, Ivy was wondering what you thought of Will's paintings," Beth said softly.

The response came slowly. "I'm sorry, Beth, what did you just say?"

Beth glanced uneasily from Suzanne to Ivy. Eric laughed, enjoying the strain between the girls. Gregory seemed preoccupied and distant from both Suzanne and Ivy.

"We were talking about Will's paintings," Beth prompted.

"They're great," Suzanne said. She had her shoulder and head turned at an angle that cut Ivy out of her view.

Ivy waited for some kids with balloons to pass, then shifted her position and made another attempt to talk to Suzanne. This time she got Suzanne's back in her face. Beth stood between the two girls and began to chatter, as if words could fill up the silence and distance between them.

As soon as Beth paused for breath, Ivy said she had to go, so that she could get Philip to his friend's house on time. Perhaps Philip saw and understood more than Ivy had realized. He waited until they were a block away from the others before he said,

"Sammy just got back from camp and said not to come till after seven o'clock."

Ivy laid her hand on his shoulder. "I know. Thanks for not mentioning it."

On their way to the car, Ivy stopped at a small stand and purchased two bouquets of poppies. Philip didn't ask her why she bought them or where they were going. Maybe he had figured that out, too.

As Ivy drove away from the festival she felt surprisingly lighter. She had tried hard to reassure Suzanne, to please her friend by keeping her distance from Gregory. She had reached out to Suzanne several times, but each time her hand had been slapped back. There was no reason to keep trying now, to keep tiptoeing around Suzanne and Gregory. Her anger turned to relief; she felt suddenly free of a burden she hadn't wanted to carry.

"Why do we have two bouquets?" Philip asked as Ivy drove along, humming. "Is one of them going to be from me?"

He had guessed.

"Actually, they're both from us. I thought it would be nice to leave some flowers on Caroline's grave."

"Why?"

Ivy shrugged. "Because she was Gregory's mother, and Gregory has been good to both of us."

"But she was a nasty lady."

Ivy glanced over at him. *Nasty* wasn't one of the words in Philip's vocabulary. "What?"

"Sammy's mother said she was nasty."

"Well, Sammy's mother doesn't know every-thing," Ivy replied, driving through the large iron gates.

"She knew Caroline," Philip said stubbornly.

Ivy was aware that a lot of people hadn't liked Caroline. Gregory himself had never spoken well of his mother.

"All right, here's what we'll do," she said as she parked the car. "We'll make one bouquet, the orange one, from me to Caroline, and the other, the purple one, from me and you to Tristan."

They walked silently to the wealthy area of Riverstone Rise.

When Ivy went to lay the flowers on Caroline's grave, she noticed that Philip hung back.

"Is it cold?" he called to her.

"Cold?"

"Sammy's sister says that mean people have cold graves."

"It's very warm. And look, someone has left Car-oline a long-stemmed red rose, someone who must have loved her very much."

Philip wasn't convinced and looked anxious to get away. Ivy wondered if he was going to act funny around Tristan's grave, too. But as they walked toward it he started hopping over the stones and turned back into his old cheerful, chatterbox self.

"Remember how Tristan put the salad in his hair at Mom's wedding," Philip asked, "and it was all runny? And remember the celery he stuck in his ears?"

"And the shrimp tails in his nose," Ivy said.

"And those black things on his teeth."

"Olives. I remember."

It was the first time since the funeral that Philip had spoken to her about Tristan, the Tristan he had once played with. She wondered why her brother was suddenly able to do so.

"And remember how I beat him at checkers?"

"Two out of three games," she said.

"Yeah." Philip grinned to himself, then took off.

He ran up to the last mausoleum in a row of the elegant burial houses and knocked on the door. "Open up in there!" he shouted, then flapped his arms and flew ahead of Ivy, waiting for her at the next turn.

"Tristan was good at PlayStation games too," Philip said.

"He taught you some cool tricks, didn't he?"

"Yep. I miss him."

"Me, too," Ivy said, biting her lip. She was glad that Philip had rushed ahead again. She didn't want to ruin his happy memories with tears.

At Tristan's grave Ivy knelt down and ran her

fingers over the letters on the stone – Tristan's name and dates. She could not say the small prayer that had been carved on the stone, a prayer that put him in the hands of the angels, so her fingers read it silently. Philip also touched the stone, then he arranged the flowers. He wanted to shape them into a *T*.

He's healing, Ivy thought as she watched him. If he can, maybe I can, too.

"Tristan will like these when he comes back," Philip said, standing up to admire his own work.

Ivy thought she had misunderstood her brother.

"I hope he gets back before the flowers die," he continued.

"What?"

"Maybe he'll come back when it's dark."

Ivy put her hand over her mouth. She didn't want to deal with this, but somebody had to, and she knew that she couldn't count on her mother.

"Where do you think Tristan is now?" Ivy asked cautiously.

"I know where he is. At the festival."

"And how do you know that?"

"He told me. He's my angel, Ivy. I know you said never to say *angel* again" – Philip was talking very fast, as if he could avoid her anger by saying the word quickly – "but that's what he is. I didn't know it was him till he told me today."

Ivy rubbed her hands over her bare arms.

"He must still be there with that other one," Philip said.

"That other one?" she repeated.

"The other angel," he said softly. Then he reached in his pocket and pulled out a creased photograph. It was a picture of them that had been taken at Old West Photos, but not the same one she had been given. Something had gone wrong with the image. There was a cloudiness behind him.

Philip pointed to it. "That's her. The other angel."

Its shape vaguely resembled a girl, so Ivy could see why he might say that.

"Where did you get this?"

"Will gave it to me. I asked him for it because she didn't get into the picture he gave you. I think she's a friend of Tristan's."

Ivy could only imagine what Philip's active mind would create next – an entire community of angel friends and relatives. "Tristan is dead," she said. "Dead. Do you understand?"

"Yes." His face was somber and knowing as an adult's, but his skin looked baby smooth and golden in the evening sun. At that moment he reminded Ivy of a painting of an angel.

"I miss Tristan the way he used to be," Philip told her. "I wish he could still play with me. Sometimes I still feel like crying. But I'm glad he's my angel now, Ivy. He'll help you too."

She didn't argue. She couldn't reason with a kid who believed as strongly as Philip did.

"We need to go," she said at last.

He nodded, then threw his head back and shouted, "I hope you like it, Tristan."

Ivy hurried ahead of him. She was glad she was dropping him off at Sammy's for a sleepover. With Sammy back, maybe Philip would spend more time in the real world.

When Ivy arrived home she found a note from her mother reminding her that she and Andrew had gone to the dinner gala that was part of the arts festival.

"Good," Ivy said aloud. She'd had enough strained conversations for one day. An evening with just Ella and a good book was exactly what she needed. She ran upstairs, kicked off her shoes, and changed into her favorite T-shirt, which was full of holes and so big she could wear it like a short dress.

"It's just you and me, cat," Ivy said to Ella, who had chased her up the steps and down again to the kitchen. "Is mademoiselle ready to dine?" Ivy set two cans out on the counter. "For you, seafood nuggets. For me, tuna. I hope I don't get them mixed up."

Ella rubbed back and forth against Ivy's legs as Ivy prepared the food. Then the cat mewed softly.

"Why the fancy dishes, you ask?" Ivy got down a matched set of cut-glass plates, along with a crystal drinking glass and a crystal bowl. "We're celebrating. I played the piece, Ella, I played the movement all the way through!"

Ella mewed again.

"No, not the one I've been practicing – and not the one you've been practicing, either. The 'Moonlight.' That's right." Ivy sighed. "I guess I had to play it for him one last time before I could play for myself again. I think I could play anything now! Come on, cat."

Ella followed her into the family room and watched curiously as Ivy lit a candle and put it on the floor between them. "Is this classy, or what?"

The cat let out another soft meow.

Ivy opened the large French doors that led out to the patio at the back of the house, then put on a CD of some soft jazz.

"Some cats don't have Saturday nights like this, you know."

Ella purred through dinner. Ivy felt just as content as she watched Ella clean herself, then settle down by the tall screen doors, her nose and ears positioned to catch all the smells and tiny sounds of twilight.

After a few minutes of keeping vigil with Ella, Ivy dug a book out from underneath the chair cushion, a collection of stories Gregory had been reading. Moving the candle out of the draft, she rolled over on her stomach next to it and began to read.

It wasn't till then that she realized how tired she was. The words kept blurring before her eyes, and the candle cast a hypnotic flicker across the page. The story was some kind of mystery, and she tried to concentrate, not wanting to miss any of the clues. But before the killer struck a second time, her eyes closed.

Ivy didn't know how long she had been sleeping. It had been a dreamless sleep. Her mind had jerked awake suddenly, alerted by some sound.

Before she opened her eyes, she knew that it was late. The CD had ended and she could hear the crickets outside, a full choir of them. From the dining room came the soft bonging of the mantel clock. She lost count of the hours – eleven? twelve?

Without lifting her head, she opened her eyes in the dark room and saw that the candle, though still burning, was a stub. Ella had left, and one screen door gaped open, silvery in the moonlight.

A cool breeze blew in. The fine hairs along Ivy's arms stirred, and her skin felt suddenly chill. It was Ella who had slipped through the door, she told herself. Probably the screen had been unlatched, and Ella pushed it open to let herself out. But the draft was strong, drawn across the room to the door behind Ivy. That door, which led to the gallery, had been closed when Ivy fell asleep.

It was open now – without turning around, she knew it. And she knew that someone was there watching her. A board creaked in the doorway, then another, much closer to her. She could feel his dark presence hovering above her.

Ivy quietly sucked in her breath, then opened her mouth and screamed.

26

Ivy screamed and fought him, kicking behind her with all her strength. He held her down on the floor, his hand pressed over her nose and mouth. She screamed into his hand, then she tried to bite it, but he was too quick for her. She started rolling her body back and forth. She'd roll him into the candle flame if she had to.

"Ivy! Ivy! It's me! Be quiet, Ivy! You'll scare Philip. It's just me."

She went limp beneath him. "Gregory."

He slowly lifted himself off her. They stared at each other, sweating and out of breath.

"I thought you were asleep," he said. "I was trying to see if you were all right without waking you."

"I – I just – I didn't know who you were. Philip

is out. He's staying over at Sammy's tonight, and Mom and Andrew are at the gala."

"Everybody's out?" Gregory asked sharply.

"Yes, and I thought—"

Gregory rammed his fist into his palm several times, then stopped when he saw the way she was looking at him.

"What's wrong with you?" he demanded. "What's wrong with you, Ivy?" He held her by both arms. "How can you be so stupid?"

"What do you mean?" she asked.

He stared deep into her eyes. "Why have you been avoiding me?"

Ivy looked away.

"Look at me! Answer me!"

She swung her head back. "Ask Suzanne, if you want to know why."

She saw the flicker in his eyes then, as if he suddenly understood. It was hard to believe that he hadn't guessed what was going on. Why else would she avoid him?

He loosened his grip. "Ivy." His voice was softer now, wavering. "You're home alone, late at night, in a house where you were attacked last week, with the door wide open. You left the door wide open! Why would you do something so dumb?"

Ivy swallowed hard. "I thought the screen was latched. But it wasn't, I guess, and Ella must have pushed it open."

Gregory leaned back against the sofa, rubbing his head.

"I'm sorry. I'm sorry I upset you," she said.

He took a deep breath and laid one hand over hers. He was much calmer now. "No, I scared you. I should be the one apologizing."

Even in the flickering candlelight, Ivy could see the weariness around his eyes. She reached up and touched the temple he had been rubbing. "Headache?"

"It's not as bad as it was earlier today."

"But it still hurts. Lie down," she said. She set a pillow on the floor for his head. "I'll get you some tea and aspirin."

"I can get it myself."

"Let me." She put her hand lightly on his shoulder. "You've done so much for me, Gregory. Please let me do this for you."

"I haven't done anything I didn't want to."

"Please."

He lay back.

Ivy got up and put on some piano music. "Too loud? Too soft?"

"Perfect," he said, closing his eyes.

She made a pot of tea, put some cookies on the tray along with aspirin, and brought it back to the candlelit room.

They sipped awhile in silence and munched

cookies. Then Gregory playfully clinked his cup against hers in a silent toast.

"What is this stuff? I feel like I'm drinking a garden."

She laughed. "You are – and it's good for you."

He took another sip and looked at her through the wispy steam. "You're good for me," he said.

"Do you like to have your back scratched?" Ivy asked. "Philip loves to."

"Have it scratched?"

"Rubbed. When you were a little boy, didn't your mother ever rub your back trying to get you to sleep?"

"*My* mother?"

"Turn over."

He looked at her, somewhat amused, then set down his tea and rolled over on his stomach.

Ivy began to rub his back, running her hand over it in small and big circles, the way she did with Philip. She could feel the tension in him; every muscle was tight. What Gregory really needed was a massage, and it would feel better if he removed his shirt, but she was afraid to suggest this.

Why? He's just my stepbrother, Ivy reminded herself. He's not a date. He's a good friend and kind of a brother—

"Ivy?"

"Yes?"

"Would it be all right with you if I took off my shirt?"

"It would be better," she said.

He removed it and lay down again. His back was long and tan and strong from playing tennis. She began to work again, pushing hard this time, moving her hands up his spine and across his muscular shoulders. Ivy kneaded the back of his neck, her fingers working up into his dark hair, then she ran her hands down to his lower spine. Slowly but surely she felt him relax beneath her fingers.

Without warning he rolled over and looked up at her.

In the candlelight, his features cast rugged shadows. Golden light filled a little hollow in his neck. She was tempted to touch that hollow, to lay her hand on his neck and feel where his pulse jumped.

"You know," Gregory said, "last winter, when my father told me he was marrying Maggie, the last thing I wanted was you in my house."

"I know," Ivy replied, smiling down at him.

He reached up and touched her on the cheek.

"Now . . ." he said, spreading his fingers, letting them get tangled in her hair. "Now . . ." He pulled her head down closer to his.

If we kiss, thought Ivy, if we kiss and Suzanne—

"Now?" he whispered.

She couldn't fight it anymore. She closed her eyes.

With both hands, he pulled her face swiftly down to his. Then his rough hands relaxed, and the kiss was long and light and delicious. He lifted her face and kissed her softly on the throat.

Ivy moved her mouth down and they started kissing again. Then they both froze, startled by the sound of a motor and the sweep of headlights on the driveway outside. Andrew's car.

Gregory rolled his head back and laughed a little. "Unbelievable." He sighed. "Our chaperons have arrived."

Ivy felt how slowly and reluctantly his fingers let her go. Then she blew out the candle, turned on the light, and tried not to think about Suzanne.

Tristan wished he knew some way to soothe Ivy. Her sheets were twisted and her hair a tangle of gold that had been tossed back and forth. Had she been dreaming again? Had something happened since he left her at the festival?

After the performance, Tristan knew he had to find out who wanted to hurt Ivy. He also knew he was running out of time. If Ivy fell for Gregory, then Tristan would lose Will as a way of reaching her and warning her.

Ivy stirred. "Who's there? Who's there?" she murmured.

Tristan recognized the beginning of the dream. A sense of dread washed over him, as if he himself were being drawn into the nightmare. He couldn't stand to see her that frightened again. If only he could hold her, if only he could take her in his arms—

Ella, where was Ella?

The cat sat purring in the window. Tristan quickly moved toward her, materializing his fingers. He marveled at his growing strength, how he could pick up the cat by the scruff of her neck for a few seconds and carry her to the bed. He put her down and, just before the strength went out of him, used his fingertips to nudge Ivy awake.

"Ella," she said softly. "Oh, Ella." Her arms wrapped around the cat.

Tristan stepped back from the bed. This was how he had to love her now, one step removed from her, helping others to comfort and care for her in his place.

With Ella snuggled next to her, Ivy settled into a more peaceful sleep. The dream was gone, pushed deeper into the recesses of her mind, deep enough not to trouble her for a while. If only he could get to that dream. Tristan was sure that Ivy had seen something she shouldn't have the night Caroline died – or that someone thought she had seen something. If he knew what it was, he'd know who was after her. But he couldn't get inside her any more than he could get inside Gregory.

He left her sleeping there. He had already

decided what to do, and planned to do it in spite of all of Lacey's warnings: time-travel back in Eric's mind. He had to find out if Eric was the one riding his motorcycle through Ivy's dream, and if he had been to Caroline's the evening she died.

As Tristan moved toward Eric's house he tried to recall all the details he had seen earlier that night. After the festival, Lacey had accompanied him to Caroline's house. While she had opened closets, looked behind pictures, and poked through things that were in the process of being boxed up, he'd studied the details of the house, outside and in. These would be the keys, the objects he could meditate on once inside someone's head, giving him his chance to trigger the right string of memories.

"If you're going to go through with this stupid plan of yours," Lacey had said while digging between the sofa cushions, "go prepared. And get some rest first."

"I'm ready now," he had argued, his glance sweeping the living room where Caroline had died.

"Listen, jock angel," Lacey replied, "you're starting to feel your strength now. That's good, but don't let yourself get carried away. You're not ready for the heavenly Olympics, not yet. If you insist on trying to slip inside Eric, then get some hours of darkness tonight. You'll need it."

Tristan hadn't answered her right away. Standing by the picture window, he had noticed that there was a clear view of the street and anyone coming up the walk. "Maybe you're right," he'd said at last.

"No maybe about it. Besides, Eric will be most vulnerable to you at dawn or just after, when he's sleeping lightly," she had told him. "Try to get him just conscious enough to follow your suggestion, but not so awake that he realizes what he's doing."

It had sounded like good advice. Now, with the sky starting to glow in the east, Tristan found Eric asleep on the floor of his bedroom. The bed was still made, and Eric was still dressed in his clothes from the day before, lying on his side, curled in a corner next to his stereo. Magazines were scattered nearby. Tristan knelt down next to him. Materializing his fingers, he paged through a motorcycle magazine till he found a picture of a machine similar to Eric's. He focused on it and nudged Eric awake.

Tristan was admiring the cycle's clean, curved lines, imagining its power, and suddenly he knew he was seeing it through Eric's eyes. It had been as easy as slipping inside Will. Maybe Lacey was wrong, he thought. Maybe she didn't realize just how well he had developed his powers. Then the picture softened at the edges.

Eric's eyes shut. For a moment there was nothing but dark around Tristan. Now was the time for him to think about Caroline's street, to take Eric on a slow ride up to her house, to get him started on a memory.

But suddenly the blackness opened out, as if a dark wall had been unzipped, and Tristan went hurtling forward. Road came at him out of nowhere and kept coming like the road in a video racing game. He was moving too quickly to respond, too quickly to guess where he was going.

He was on a motorcycle, racing over a road through brilliant flashes of light and dark. He lifted his eyes from the road and saw trees and stone walls and houses. The trees were so intensely green they burned against Tristan's eyes. The blue sky was neon. Red felt like heat.

They were racing up a road, climbing higher and higher. Tristan tried to slow them down, to steer one way, then another, to exert some control, but he was powerless.

Suddenly they screeched to a halt. Tristan looked up and saw the Baines house.

Gregory's home – it was and it wasn't. He stared at the house as they walked toward it. It was like looking at a room reflected in a Christmas orna-ment; he saw objects he knew well stretched by a strange perspective, at once familiar and weird.

Was he in a dream, or was this a memory whose edges had been burned and curled by drugs?

They knocked, then walked through the front door. There was no ceiling, no roof. In fact, there wasn't a furnished room, but a huge playground, whose fence was the shell of the house. Gregory was there, looking down at them from the top of a very tall sliding board, a silver chute that did not stop at ground level but tunneled into it.

There was a woman also. Caroline, Tristan realized suddenly.

When she saw them she waved and smiled in a warm and friendly way. Gregory stayed on top of his sliding board, looking down at them coldly, but Caroline beckoned them over to a merry-go-round, and they could not resist.

She was on one side, they were on the other. They ran and pushed, ran and pushed, then hopped on. They whirled around and around, but instead of slowing down, as Tristan expected, they went faster and faster. And faster and faster still – they hung by their fingertips as they spun. Tristan thought his head would fly off. Then their fingers slipped and they went hurtling into space.

When Tristan looked up, the world still spun for a moment, then stopped. The playground had disappeared, but the shell of the house remained, enclosing a cemetery.

He saw his own grave. He saw Caroline's. Then he saw a third grave, gaping open, a pile of freshly dug earth next to it.

Was it Eric who started shaking then, or was it himself? Tristan didn't know, and he couldn't stop it

– he shook violently and fell to the ground. The ground rumbled and tilted. Gravestones rolled around him, rolled like teeth shaken out of a skull. He was on his side, shaking, curled in a ball, waiting for the earth to crack, to split like a mouth and swallow him.

Then it stopped. Everything was still. He saw in front of him a glossy picture of a motorcycle. Eric had awakened.

It was a dream, thought Tristan. He was still inside, but Eric didn't seem to notice. Maybe he was too exhausted, or maybe his fried brain was too used to strange feelings and thoughts to respond to Tristan.

Did the bizarre events of the dream mean anything? Was there some truth hidden in them, or were they the wanderings of a druggie's mind?

Caroline was a mysterious figure. He remembered how they had no will to resist her invitation to a ride on the merry-go-round. Her face was so welcoming.

He saw it again, the welcoming face. It was older now. He imagined her standing at the door of her own house. Then he walked through that door with her. This time he was in Eric's memory!

Caroline looked around the room, and they did, too. The blinds were opened in the big picture window; he could see dark clouds gathering in the western sky. In a vase was a long-stemmed rose, still tightly curled in a bud. Caroline was sitting across from him, smiling at him. Now she was frowning.

The memory jumped, like a badly spliced movie, frames dropping out of it. Smiling, frowning, smiling again. Tristan could barely hear the words being spoken; they were drowned out by waves of emotion.

Caroline threw back her head and laughed. She laughed almost hysterically, and Tristan felt an overwhelming sense of fear and frustration. She laughed and laughed, and Tristan thought he'd explode with the force of Eric's frustration.

He grabbed Caroline's arms and shook her, shook her so hard her head rolled backward and forward like a rag doll's. Suddenly he heard the words being screamed out at her:

"Listen to me. I mean it! It's not a joke. Nobody's laughing but you. It's not a joke!"

Then Tristan felt a pressure squeezing his head, compressing his mind so intensely he thought he would dissolve. Caroline and the room dissolved, like a scene from a movie disintegrating in front of his eyes; the screen went black. Eric had pressed down on the memory. His own bedroom suddenly came back into focus.

Tristan got up and moved with Eric across the room. He watched his fingers open a knapsack and pull out an envelope. Eric shook brightly colored pills into his quivering hand, lifted them to his mouth, and swallowed.

Now, Tristan thought, was the time to take seriously Lacey's warnings about a drug-poisoned mind. He cut out of there fast.

27

"Capes and teeth are selling big," Betty said, glancing through the sales receipts for 'Tis the Season. "Is there a convention for vampires at the Hilton this week?"

"Don't know," Ivy murmured, counting out a customer's change for the third time.

"I think you need a break, dear," Lillian observed.

Ivy glanced at the clock. "I just had dinner an hour ago."

"I know," said Lillian, "but since you'll be closing up for Bet and me, and since you just sold that sweet young man who bought the Dracula cape a pair of wax lips . . ."

"Wax lips? Are you sure?"

"The Ruby Reds," Lillian said. "Don't worry, I caught him at the door and got him to trade them for a nice set of fangs. But I do think you should take a little break."

Ivy stared down at the cash register, embarrassed. She had been making mistakes for three days now, though the sisters had graciously pretended not to notice. She wondered if the cash box had come out right Sunday and Monday. She was amazed that they would trust her to close up that night.

"The last time I saw you like this," Betty said, "you were falling in love."

Lillian shot her sister a look.

"I'm not this time," Ivy said firmly. "But maybe I could use a break."

"Off you go," Lillian said. "Take as long as you need."

She gave Ivy a gentle push.

Ivy walked the top floor of the mall from one end to the other, trying once more to sort things out. Since Saturday she and Gregory had been doing a sort of shy dance around each other: hands brushing, eyes meeting, greeting each other softly, then backing away. Sunday night her mother had set the table for a family dinner and lit two candles. Gregory looked at Ivy from across the table as he'd often done before, but this time Ivy saw the flame dancing in his eyes. Monday Gregory had slipped away without speaking to anyone. Ivy didn't know where he had gone and didn't dare ask. Maybe to

Suzanne's. Maybe Saturday night had been just a moment of closeness – a single moment, a single kiss, after all the hard times they had shared.

Ivy felt guilty.

But was it so wrong, caring for someone who cared for her? Was it wrong, wanting to touch someone who touched her gently? Was it wrong, changing her mind about Gregory?

Ivy had never felt so mixed up. Only one thing was clear: she was going to have to get her act together and concentrate on what she doing, she told herself – just as she ran into a baby stroller.

"Oops. Sorry."

The woman pushing the stroller smiled, and Ivy returned the smile, then backed into a cart selling earrings and chains. Everything jingled.

"Sorry. Sorry."

She narrowly avoided a trash can, then headed straight for the Coffee Mill.

Ivy took her cup of cappuccino to the far end of the mall. The two big stores that had been there were closed, and several lights had burned out. She sat on an empty bench in the artificial twilight, sipping her drink. Voices from shoppers at the other end of the mall lapped toward her in soft waves that never quite reached her.

Ivy closed her eyes for a moment, enjoying the solitude. Then she opened them, turning her head quickly, surprised by three distinct voices to the right of her. One of them was very familiar.

"It's all there," he said.

"I'm going to count it."

"Don't you trust me?"

"I said I'm going to count it. You figure out whether I trust you."

In a dimly lit tunnel that led to the parking garage, Gregory, Eric, and a third person were talking, unaware that anyone was watching. When the third person turned his head into the light, Ivy could hardly believe her eyes. She had seen him outside the school and knew he was a drug dealer. But when she saw Gregory hand the dealer a bag, what she really couldn't believe was how she had forgotten about the other side of Gregory.

How had she gotten so close to a guy whose friends were rich and fast? How had she come to rely on someone who, bored with what he had, took stupid risks? Why did she trust a person who played dangerous games with his friends, no matter who it hurt?

Tristan had warned her once, before that night at the train bridges, before the night that Will was almost killed. But Ivy thought that Gregory had changed since then. In the last four weeks he'd – Well, obviously, she was wrong.

She got up abruptly from the bench, spilling cappuccino down the front of her.

Tristan! she cried out silently. Help me, Tristan! Help me get my head straight!

She ran down the hall to the brighter area of the mall. She was hurrying for the escalator when she slammed into Will.

The girl with him, an auburn-haired girl whom Ivy recognized from Eric's party, swore softly.

Will stared at Ivy, and she stared back. She could hardly stand it, the way he looked at her, the way he could hold her captive with his eyes.

"What are you doing here?" Ivy demanded.

"What's it to you?" the girl snapped.

Ivy ignored her. "Don't tell me," she said to Will, "you just had the feeling, you just thought – somehow you just knew—"

She saw a flicker of light in his eyes, and she glanced away quickly.

The girl with him was squinching up her face, looking at Ivy as if she were crazy; Ivy *felt* a little crazy. "I – I have to get to work," she said, but he held her still with his eyes.

"If you need me," Will told her, "call me." Then he turned his head slightly, as if someone had spoken over his shoulder.

Ivy brushed past him and hurried up the escalator, climbing faster than the steps moved, and rushed to the shop.

"Oh, dear," Lillian said when Ivy burst through the door.

"Oh, my!" said Betty.

Ivy was panting, from anger as much as running. Now she stopped to look down the front of her pale green dress. It was mud-colored.

"We should soak that right away."

"No, it's okay," she said, trying to catch her breath, breathing slowly and deeply to calm herself down. "I'll just sponge it off." She moved toward the rest room in the back, but Betty was already going through one rack of costumes, and Lillian was gazing thoughtfully at another.

"I'll just sponge it off," Ivy repeated. "I'll be out in a minute."

Lillian and Betty hummed to themselves.

"It's an old dress anyway," Ivy added.

Sometimes the old ladies played deaf.

"Something simple," she finally begged. Last time she had ended up as an alien – enhanced with batteries that made her blink and beep.

The sisters did keep it simple, giving her a soft white blouse, gathered and worn off the shoulders, and a colorful skirt.

"Oh, what a lovely gypsy she makes," Lillian said to Betty.

"We should dress her up every day," Betty agreed.

They smiled at her like two doting great-aunts.

"Don't forget to turn out the light in the back,

love," Betty said, then the sisters went home to their seven cats.

Ivy breathed a sigh of relief. She was glad to be running the shop alone for the next two hours. It kept her busy enough to keep her mind off what she had just seen.

She was angry – but at herself more than at Gregory. He was who he was. He hadn't changed his ways. It was she who had made him into the perfect guy.

At 9.25, Ivy was finished with her last customer. The mall had become virtually empty. Five minutes later she dimmed the lights in the shop, locked the door from the inside, and started counting the money and adding up receipts.

She was startled by someone knocking on the glass. "Gypsy girl," he called.

"Gregory."

For a moment she considered leaving him out there, putting back the glass wall that he had erected between them last January. She walked toward him slowly, unlatched the store door, and cracked it open three inches.

"Am I disturbing you?" he asked.

"I have to total the register and close up."

"I'll keep quiet," he promised.

Ivy opened the door a few inches more and he entered.

She started toward the cash register, then turned

back quickly. "I may as well get this out of the way now," she said.

Gregory waited; he looked as if he knew something big was coming.

"I saw you and Eric and the other guy – that dealer – making an exchange."

"Oh, that," he said, as if it were nothing.

"Oh, that?" she repeated.

"I thought you were going to tell me something like, from now on, we were never to see each other alone."

Ivy looked down, pulling and twisting a tassel on her skirt. It would probably be better if they didn't.

"Oh," he said, "I see. You were going to say that, too."

Ivy didn't answer him. She didn't honestly know.

Gregory walked over to her and laid his hand on top of hers, keeping her from yanking off the tassel.

"Eric does drugs," he said, "you know that. And he's gotten himself in deep, real deep, with our friendly neighborhood dealer. I bailed him out."

Ivy looked up into Gregory's eyes. Against his tan, they looked lighter, like a silver sea on a misty day.

"I don't blame you, Ivy, for thinking I'm doing the wrong thing. If I thought Eric would stop when he ran out of money, I wouldn't pay up for him. But he won't stop, and they'll go after him."

He let go of her hand. "Eric's my friend. He's been my friend since grade school. I don't know what else to do."

Ivy turned away, thinking about how loyal Gregory was to Eric and how disloyal she had been to Suzanne.

"Go ahead. Say it," Gregory challenged her. "You don't like what I'm doing. You think I should find myself better friends."

She shook her head. "I don't blame you for what you're doing," she said. "Eric's lucky to have you for a friend, as lucky as I am. As lucky as Suzanne is."

He turned her face toward him with just one finger. "Finish up your work," he said, "and we can talk some more. We'll go out somewhere, not home, okay?"

"Okay."

"Are you going to wear that?" he asked, smiling.

"Oh! I forgot. I spilled cappuccino on my dress. It's soaking in the basin."

He laughed. "I don't mind. You look . . . uh, exotic," he said, his eyes dropping down to her bare shoulders.

She tingled a little.

"I guess I'll have to find a costume for me."

He started looking over the wall of hats and wigs. A few minutes later he called out to her, "How's this?"

Ivy looked up from behind the register and laughed out loud.

He was wearing a frizzy red wig, a top hat, and a polka-dotted bow tie.

"Dashing," she said.

Gregory tried on one costume after another – a Klingon mask, King Kong's head and chest, a huge flowered hat and boa.

"Clown!" said Ivy.

He grinned at her and waved his feathery stole.

"If you want to try on a whole outfit, there are fitting rooms in the back. The one on the left is large, with mirrors everywhere. You get all angles," she told him. "I'm really sorry Philip isn't here to play with you."

"When you're done, you can play with me," Gregory replied.

Ivy worked a little longer. When she finally closed the books, she saw that he had disappeared into the back.

"Gregory?" she called.

"Yes, my sveet," he answered with an accent.

"What are you doing?"

"Come here, my sveet," he replied. "I've been vaiting for you."

She smiled to herself. "What are you up to?"

Ivy tiptoed to the dressing room and slowly pushed open the swinging door. Gregory had flattened himself against the wall. Now he turned quickly, jumping in front of her.

"Oh!" she gasped. She wasn't acting; Gregory made a startlingly handsome vampire in a white shirt with a deep V-neck and a high-collared black cape. His dark hair was slicked back, and his eyes danced with mischief.

"Hello, my sveet."

"Tell me," she said, recovering from the surprise, "if you put in your fangs, will you be able to pronounce *w*'s?"

"No vay. Thees is how I speak." He pulled her into the room. "And may I say, my sveet, vat a lovely neck you have!"

Ivy laughed. He put in his long teeth and began to nuzzle her neck, tickling her.

"Where do I thrust in the wooden stake?" she asked, pushing him back a little. "Right there?" She poked him lightly where his shirt gaped.

Gregory caught her hand and held it for a long moment. Then he took out his teeth and lifted her hand to his mouth, kissing it softly. He pulled her closer to him. "I think you've already done it, thrust it straight through my heart," he told her.

Ivy looked up at him, barely breathing. His eyes burned like gray coals beneath his lowered lashes.

"What a lovely neck," he said, bending his head, his dark hair falling forward. He kissed her softly on the throat. He kissed her again and again, slowly moving his mouth up to hers.

His kisses became more insistent. Ivy answered with gentler kisses. He pressed her to him, held her tightly, then suddenly released her, dropping down before her. He knelt in front of her, reaching up to her, his strong, caressing hands moving slowly over her body, pulling her down to him. "It's okay," he said softly. "It's okay."

They clung to each other and swayed. Then Ivy opened her eyes. To the left, to the right, reflected in front of her, reflected from behind her – from every angle in the mirrored dressing room – she could see herself and Gregory wrapped around each other.

She pulled herself free of him and leapt up. "No!" Her hands went up to her face, covering her eyes.

Gregory tried to pull her hands away from her face. She turned to the wall, cowering in the corner, but she couldn't get away from the reflection of the girl who had been kissing Gregory.

"This isn't right," she said.

"Isn't *right?*"

"It isn't a good thing. For you, or me, or Suzanne."

"Forget Suzanne! What matters is you and me."

"Don't forget Suzanne," Ivy pleaded softly. "She's wanted you for a long time. And I, I want to be near you, I want to talk to you, I want to touch you. And kiss you. How could I help it, when you've been so wonderful to me? But, Gregory, I know—" She took a deep breath. "I know I'm still in love with Tristan."

"And you think I *don't* know that?" He laughed. "You've made it kind of obvious, Ivy."

He took a step closer to her and reached out for her hand. "I know you're still in love with him and still hurting for him. Let me help ease the pain."

He held her hand softly in both of his.

"Think about it, Ivy. Just think about it," he said.

She nodded silently, her free hand toying with the tassel on her skirt.

"I'll change my clothes now," he told her, "and we'll go home in our own cars. I'll take a long route so we don't arrive at the same time. We won't even see each other going up to our rooms. So—" He lifted her hand to his mouth. "This is my good-night kiss," he said, gently touching his lips to her fingertips.

When Tristan awoke, only his soft glow lit the dressing room, shining back at him from each of the mirrors. But the darkness that he felt surrounding him in the empty room was more than the absence of light. The darkness felt like something real in itself, a soft and ominous shape, a presence that angered and frightened Tristan.

"Gregory," he said aloud, and the scenes he had witnessed hours earlier flashed through his mind. For a moment he thought the room was lit. Had Gregory really fallen in love with Ivy? Tristan wondered. And was he telling the truth about Eric and the dealer? Tristan had to know, had to get inside his head. "You're next, Gregory," he said. "You're next."

"Would you stop talking to yourself? How's a girl supposed to get her beauty sleep?"

Tristan pushed through the dressing room door into the shop, which was lit by two dim nightlights and an exit sign. Lacey was stretched out at the feet of King Kong.

"I waited for you at your Riverstone Rise condo," she said, then held up a dead flower. "Brought you this. There were others, just as dead, forming a *T* on your grave. Figured you hadn't been there for a while."

"I haven't."

"I checked out Eric," she continued, "just in case you'd gotten lost in that fun house otherwise known as his mind. Then I checked out Ivy, who's not having a good night – so what else is new?"

"Is she okay?" Tristan asked. He had wanted to follow her home and get the rest he needed there. Then he could have made sure that Ella was close by; he could have summoned Philip if she needed him. But he knew if he had gone with her, he'd have stayed up all night watching. "Is she okay?"

"She's Ivy," Lacey replied, fluffing up her hair. "So tell me, what did I miss in this soap opera? Gregory's just as restless as she is. What's eating him?"

Tristan told Lacey what had happened earlier that evening, as well as what he had experienced inside Eric's head – the memory of the scene at Caroline's house, with its overwhelming feelings of frustration and fear. Lacey listened for a bit, then paced around the shop. She materialized her fingers, and tried on a mask, turning to face Tristan for a moment, then trying on another.

"Maybe this isn't the first time Eric's gotten himself in deep," Lacey said. "What if Eric used to hit on Caroline for drug money – the way he now hits on Gregory? And what if that night, when he needed a payment, Caroline didn't come through?"

"No, it's not that simple," Tristan replied, a little too quickly. "I know it's not that simple."

She raised an eyebrow at him. "You *know* that, or you just want to *believe* that?" she asked.

"What do you mean?"

"Seems to me you'd find it just a tiny bit satisfying to prove Gregory guilty. Poor, innocent, handsome Gregory," she said, baiting Tristan. "Maybe the only things he's guilty of are playing games with girls and falling for *your* girl – and your girl falling for him," she added slyly.

"You can't really believe that!" Tristan said.

She shrugged. "I'm not saying Gregory isn't a jerk sometimes, but other times, at least one time, he had a good enough heart to save the neck of his messed-up friend." She ran her tongue over her teeth and smiled. "I think he's rich, good-looking, and innocent."

"If he's innocent, his memory will prove it," Tristan said.

Lacey shook her head, suddenly serious. "This time he may throw you as far as the moon."

"I'll take my chances, and I'll succeed, Lacey. After all, I've had such an excellent teacher."

She squinted at him.

"You were right. Eric was easier to slip into when he was sleeping lightly. I'm going to try the same thing with Gregory."

"That will teach me not to teach you!"

Tristan cocked his head. "It ought to get you some points, Lacey – angel points for helping me complete my mission."

She turned away.

"And those points might help you finish yours. Isn't that what you want?"

Lacey shrugged, keeping her back turned to him.

Tristan looked at her, puzzled. "Is there something I don't get?"

"A lot, Tristan." She sighed. "What do you want me to do with this flower?"

"Leave it, I guess. It was nice of you to bring it, but I'll use up too much strength trying to carry it. Listen, I've got to get going."

She nodded.

"Thanks, Lacey."

She still didn't turn around.

"You're an angel!" he said.

"Mmm."

Tristan hurried off and arrived in Ivy's bedroom just as the sky was beginning to lighten. It was so tempting to materialize one finger and run it along her cheek.

I love you, Ivy. I've never stopped loving you.

Just one soft touch, that's all he wanted. What would it cost, one soft touch?

He left her before he gave in to the temptation and used up energy that he needed for Gregory.

Gregory was sleeping restlessly. Tristan looked quickly through his music collection and found a CD he was familiar with. Materializing two fingers, he slipped the disk into the player and turned the volume on low. He nudged Gregory, then he began to follow the music himself, saying the words, concentrating on the song's images.

But for some reason, Tristan kept getting mixed

up. He'd thought he knew the lyrics by heart. He refocused, then realized his images were intermixing with other images – Gregory's.

I'm in! Lacey, I'm in!

Suddenly he could feel Gregory searching for him, reaching out blindly, desperately, the way a sleeper gropes for a clock when an alarm goes off. Tristan held himself still, absolutely still, and the music floated Gregory away from him.

Tristan sagged with relief. How far could Gregory blast him from his mind? he wondered.

But every thought like that was a thought different from Gregory's and would only alert him again. Tristan couldn't think about what he was doing but simply had to do it.

He had chosen to focus on the floor lamp in Caroline's living room. The day he and Lacey searched the house, he had noticed it standing next to the chair where the police had found Caroline's body. The halogen lamp, with its long pole and metal disk at the top, was so common it wouldn't create suspicion, but it might trigger a visual memory of Caroline sitting in the chair on that late-May afternoon.

Tristan focused on it. He circled it with his mind. He reached out for it as if he would switch it on.

And he found himself standing in Caroline's living room. She was sitting in the chair, looking back at him, slightly amused. Then she suddenly got up. The color was high in her cheeks, long red fingers of it, rising as it did in Gregory's cheeks when he was angry. But there was also a victorious gleam in her eyes.

She walked toward a desk. Tristan, inside Gregory's memory, stayed where he was, close to the lamp. Caroline picked up a piece of paper and waved it at him, as if she was taunting him. He felt Gregory's hands draw up into fists.

Then she walked toward him. He thought she was telling him to look at the paper, but he couldn't hear the words clearly. His anger had grown so quickly, the fury in him was so great, that his heart pounded, his blood rushed through him, singing in his ears.

Then his hand rose up. He slammed it into the lamp, slammed the lamp toward her. He saw her go reeling back, flying backward like a cartoon figure into the bright blue square of the picture window.

He shouted out. Tristan, himself, shouted out when he saw Caroline pitching backward, a long stripe of blood on her face.

Gregory suddenly jerked, and Tristan knew that Gregory had heard him. He was the one who'd get slammed next. He scrambled to get out. But images were swirling around him now like pieces of sharp, colored glass in a kaleidoscope. He felt dizzy and sick. He couldn't separate his own mind from

Gregory's. He ran a maze through endless, circling, insane thoughts. He knew he was trapped.

Then suddenly there was a voice calling to Gregory, pleading with him to wake up. Ivy.

He saw her through Gregory's eyes, wrapped in her robe, leaning over him. Her hair tumbled down and touched his face. Her arms went around him, comforting him. Then Gregory stilled his whirling thoughts, and Tristan slipped out.

28

"That's it, Philip!" Gregory said, lifting up his shirt, wiping the sweat from his face. "I'm not giving you any more tennis lessons. You're going to beat me every time."

"Then I'll have to give *you* lessons," Philip replied, extremely pleased with himself.

Gregory finished taking off his damp shirt and swatted Philip lightly. "Brat."

Ivy and Maggie, who had been watching Thursday morning's lesson, laughed.

"This is how I'd always hoped it would be," Maggie said.

It was a perfect summer day, the sky postcard blue, the pine trees stirring with a light breeze. They were sitting together by the tennis court, Ivy sunbathing, her mother occupying the shady half of the blanket.

Maggie sighed contentedly. "We're a family at last! And I can go away knowing my chickens are happy and safe at home."

"Don't spend one moment thinking about us, Mom," Ivy said. "You and Andrew deserve some time alone at the lake."

Maggie nodded. "Andrew needs the time away, that's for sure. Something's been on his mind lately. Usually, before bed, he tells me everything that's happened that day – every detail of everything. That's how I get to sleep."

Ivy laughed.

"But I can tell," Maggie continued, "something's worrying him, and he's keeping it to himself."

Ivy laid her hand over her mother's. "You guys really need to get away from us and from the college, too. I hope you have a great time, Mom."

Her mother kissed her, then rose to say goodbye to Philip.

She put her arm around his shoulder. "You be good, pumpkin."

Philip made a face.

"Okay," Gregory answered cheerfully.

Maggie laughed. She planted a big, pink kiss on Philip, hesitated, then shyly kissed Gregory, too.

"Take care of my baby," Ivy heard her mother say quietly. "Take care of my big baby and my little one."

Gregory smiled. "You can count on me, Maggie."

Ivy's mother walked off happily, her huge hand-bag swinging behind her. The car was already packed; she was picking up Andrew after his morning meeting.

Gregory smiled down at Ivy, then stretched out on the blanket next to her. "For the next three days," he said, "we can eat whatever we want, whenever we want."

"I'm going to make a sandwich now," Philip told them. "Want one?"

Ivy shook her head. "I have to go to work soon. I'll pick up something at the mall."

"What kind are you making?" Gregory asked.

"Cream cheese, cinnamon, and sugar."

"Think I'll pass on that."

Philip started for the house, but not before wiping his face on his shirt, then pulling it off and swatting a tree with it.

When her brother had disappeared behind the grove of pines separating the house from the tennis court, Ivy said, "You know, he's imitating you. How do you like being a role model?"

"I don't know." Gregory smiled a lopsided smile. "I guess I'm going to have to clean up my act."

Ivy laughed and settled back on the blanket. "Thanks for being nice to my mom," she said.

"Promising to take care of her baby? That won't

be a hard one to keep." Gregory lay back close to Ivy. He glanced at her, then ran a light hand over her bare midriff. "Your skin's so warm."

Ivy felt warm all over. She laid her hand on top of Gregory's.

"How come you didn't wear that bikini to Eric's party?" he asked.

Ivy laughed. "I only wear it where I feel comfortable."

"And you're comfortable with me?" He pulled himself up on one elbow and looked into her eyes, then let his gaze pass slowly down her.

"Yes and no," she replied.

"You're always so honest," he said, bending over her, smiling.

Without touching her, he lowered his mouth to hers. She kissed him. He pulled up for a moment, then lowered his mouth again, still not touching her except with his lips.

They kissed a third time. Then Ivy reached up and slipped her hands around his neck, pulling him down to her.

She didn't hear the soft footsteps in the grass.

"I was waiting for you at the park since ten."

Gregory's head jerked up, and Ivy grabbed the edge of the blanket.

"Looks like you found something better to do," Eric said, and nodded at Ivy.

Gregory lifted himself off her. Ivy pulled the

blanket around her, as if Eric had caught her without any clothes. The way he looked at her, she felt naked. She felt exposed.

Eric laughed.

"I saw a movie about a sister who couldn't keep her hands off her brother."

"It's *step*brother," Gregory told him.

Ivy huddled inside the blanket.

"Whatever. I guess you're over Tristan, huh?" Eric said. "Gregory's cured you?"

"Lay off, Eric," Gregory warned.

"Is he better at it than Tristan?" Eric asked, his voice low and soft. "He's sure got all the moves." His words were like snakes working their way into Ivy's mind.

"Shut up!" Gregory shouted, jumping to his feet.

"But you knew that, didn't you?" Eric continued in a silky voice. "You knew about Gregory because girls talk."

"Get out of here!"

"Suzanne would have told you," Eric went on.

"I'm warning you—"

"Suzanne would have told her best friend just how hot Gregory is," Eric said, wriggling his hips.

"Get off my property!"

Eric turned to Gregory and laughed. "*Your* property?" He stretched his lips into an exaggerated smile. "Yours? Maybe one day, *if* you're lucky."

Gregory was silent for a moment, then spoke with a voice that was cool but threatening. "You'd better hope I am, Eric. Because if I'm out of luck, you're out, too." He took several steps closer to his friend.

Eric took off. He looked over his shoulder and laughed, like a kid skipping away and daring others to catch him, but there was a maniacal edge to his laughter that made Ivy's blood run cold.

Philip, who had come out of the house when he heard the shouting, now raced across the lawn to them.

"What's wrong?" he asked. He looked from Gregory to Ivy, who was standing next to him, still wrapped in the blanket. "What happened?"

"Nothing," Gregory said. "Nothing for you to worry about."

Philip looked at him doubtfully, then turned to Ivy. "Are you okay?"

She nodded silently.

Gregory put his arm around Ivy. "Eric said some mean things to her."

"Mean things like what?"

"Just mean things," Gregory replied.

"Like what?"

"I don't want to talk about it right now," Ivy said.

Philip bit his lip. Then he turned and started to walk away from them.

Ivy knew that he felt left out. She slipped out from under Gregory's protective arm. "Can I have a hug, Philip? I know you're getting big now, but I'm feeling kind of bad. Can I have a hug?"

Her brother turned back and wrapped his arms around her, squeezing her tight.

"We'll take care of you," he whispered.

"Will you?" she whispered back.

"Gregory and me," he assured her, "and angel Tristan."

Ivy quickly let go of him. She tried hard to keep her mouth from quivering. "Thanks," she said, then ran into the house.

When Tristan heard the shouting, he rushed to the window to see what was going on. Gregory and Eric were hidden behind the trees. The sound of their voices carried, but he couldn't catch the words. The angry exchange was over almost as quickly as it had begun.

Tristan debated what to do. He wanted to make sure Ivy was all right, but he couldn't leave Gregory's bedroom as it looked now. He had spent the morning searching it, and drawers were still open, papers spread around, the pockets of pants and jackets pulled inside out. If Gregory discovered that someone had been looking through his things, he would become much more cautious, and that would make it harder to figure out what was going on.

The last time Ivy had needed help, she had called out to Tristan – silently – but he had heard her. He kept very still for a few moments now, listening. When he didn't sense that she was in danger, he decided to stay where he was and began to straighten up.

A few minutes later he heard Ivy running upstairs, then Philip and Gregory talking as they approached the house. Tristan began to work more quickly, but he was rapidly losing his strength. His fingers, having materialized repeatedly for short periods of time, were growing tired and clumsy. He could barely open and close Gregory's desk.

There was an old school magazine on top of the desk, anchoring newspaper articles Gregory had saved. Earlier, Tristan had skimmed the news stories, trying to figure out why they interested Gregory. Now they were blowing around. He snatched at one of them and knocked over a stack of boxes containing DVDs.

Several of the boxes had come open, and Tristan hurried to pick them up. He could hear Gregory talking to Philip at the bottom of the back stairway, but the more he hurried, the more he bungled. One of the DVDs wouldn't slip back into its box – something was sticking.

Tristan focused all his energy and yanked it out again. That's when he saw it, cellophane taped along one side of the black casing, with three bright red capsules inside.

He heard the steps creak. Gregory was coming up. Tristan ripped off the plastic, slid the DVD back in its box, and set it on top of the stack. He knew that Gregory would not be able to see him, but he'd spot the red capsules. With his last bit of energy, Tristan threw them behind the bureau. A half second later Gregory entered the room.

Tristan sank back, exhausted. He saw that everything was in place except a train schedule that lay on the floor where the boxes had fallen.

No problem, he told himself. Gregory would think it had blown off the desk, since it wasn't anchored by anything.

In fact, Gregory didn't notice the schedule, though he went directly to his desk and sat down. There were beads of sweat on his forehead, and his skin had turned a strange color, paling beneath his tan. He dropped his head in his hands. For several minutes, he rubbed his temples, then he sat back in the chair.

Suddenly his head jerked around. Gregory stared at the train schedule on the floor, then glanced slowly, suspiciously around the room. He reached for the DVD and pulled it out of the box. His jaw dropped.

He checked the label, then yanked out one DVD after another. He ripped cellophane off a second box – it contained three more capsules – and again glanced around the room.

"Philip!" He stood up abruptly, knocking his chair back on the floor. He started for the door, then stopped and slammed his palm against the wall. He stood there, motionless, staring at the door to the hall, one hand still clutching the drugs.

"Damn you, brat!"

He shoved the capsules deep in his pocket, then slipped his wallet in after them. Returning to his desk, he picked up the chair, then sat down to read the train schedule.

Tristan read over his shoulder and watched as Gregory circled the time of the last train running after midnight. It left Tusset at 1.45 A.M., but didn't make a stop at Stonehill's little station. Gregory did some quick calculations, wrote down 2.04, circled it twice, then slipped the schedule under a book. He sat for fifteen minutes more, his chin resting on his hands.

Tristan wondered what was going through Gregory's mind, but he was much too weak to attempt an entrance. Gregory seemed much calmer now – so calm it was eerie. He sat back slowly and nodded to himself as if he had made some big decision. Then he reached for his car keys and started toward the door. Halfway down the steps, Gregory began to whistle.

29

"I think its blooming days are over," Beth said, eyeing the dead poppy that Ivy had placed in the water glass on the table between them.

When Lillian and Betty opened the shop Thursday morning, they had found the purple flower in King Kong's mouth, poking out like a rose between a dancer's teeth. Later that day Ivy had repeatedly denied being the joker who had placed it there.

"Why are we trying to revive it?" Beth asked. She swirled her tongue around her ice cream cone. "Can't we buy King Kong another one?"

"They were selling poppies at the festival Saturday," Ivy replied. "I bought some purple ones for Tristan. Philip and I took them to the cemetery."

"I'm glad Philip went with you," Beth said. "He misses Tristan, too."

"He made a *T* with them on the grave," Ivy told her, smiling a little.

Beth nodded, as if it were perfectly clear now why Ivy would bother with a wilted poppy left in the shop.

"I'm going crazy, aren't I?" Ivy said suddenly. "I'm supposed to be getting better! I'm supposed to be getting over Tristan! And here I am, saving this stupid flower like a souvenir because it looks like one that I—"

She plucked the poppy out of the glass and tossed it on a tray of dirty dishes that a waitress was carrying by.

Beth slipped out of the booth, chased down the waitress, and returned with the poppy.

"Maybe it will seed," she said, sticking it back in the water glass.

Ivy shook her head and sipped her tea in silence. Beth munched her cone for a few minutes.

"You know," Beth said at last, "I'm always prepared to listen."

Ivy nodded. "I'm sorry, Beth. I call you in a panic at nine o'clock at night, drag you away from your writing to get a snack with the over-fifty-but-still-swinging bowling league at Howard Johnson's" – she glanced around the crowded green and orange room – and now I can't seem to talk."

"That's okay," Beth said, waving her cone at Ivy. "I'm having a triple dip of double fudge – for that, you could have called me at three in the morning. But how'd you know I was writing?"

Ivy smiled. Beth had met her in the parking lot wearing cutoff jeans, no makeup, and an old pair of glasses, which she wore only when she was glued to a computer screen. A scribbled note on a yellow Post-it was still stuck to her T-shirt, and her hair was pulled back in a binder clip.

"Just a hunch," Ivy said. "What's Suzanne up to tonight?"

Ivy and Suzanne had not spoken since the festival.

"She's out with somebody."

"Gregory?" Ivy asked, frowning. He had promised to stay with Philip till she got home that night.

"No, some guy who's supposed to make Gregory unbelievably jealous."

"Oh."

"She didn't tell you?" Beth asked with surprise. "That's all Suzanne could talk about." Seeing the look on Ivy's face, she added quickly, "I'm sure Suzanne thought she did. You know how it is – you say something to one person, and you think you've said it to the other."

Ivy nodded, but both of them knew that wasn't the case.

"Gregory hasn't spent much time with Suzanne lately," Beth said, pausing to chase drips of chocolate around her cone, "but you know that."

Ivy shrugged. "He goes out, but I don't ask him where."

"Well, Suzanne is sure he's seeing someone else."

Ivy began to trace the pictures on her place mat.

"At first Suzanne thought he was just playing around. She wasn't worried because it wasn't anyone special. But now she thinks he's seeing just one person. She thinks he's really hooked on somebody."

Ivy glanced up and saw Beth studying her. Can Beth actually read minds, she wondered, or is it my face that always gives me away?

"Suzanne keeps asking me what I think is going on," Beth continued, her brow slightly puckered.

"And what do you tell her?" Ivy asked.

Beth blinked several times, then looked away. She watched a silver-haired waitress flirt with two bald men in burgundy satin bowling shirts.

"I'm not a good person to ask," she said at last. "You know me, Ivy, I'm always watching people and adding stuff to what I see to make stories out of them. Sometimes I forget what part I've made up and what part is really true."

"What do you think is really true about Gregory?" Ivy persisted.

Beth waved her cone around. "I think he gets around. I think that, uh, lots of different girls like him. But I can't guess who he's really interested in and what he's actually thinking. I just can't read him very well."

Beth took a crunching bite out of her cone and chewed thoughtfully. "Gregory's like a mirror," she said. "He reflects whoever he's with. When he's with Eric, he seems to act like Eric. When he's with you, he's thoughtful and funny like you. The problem for me is that I can't ever really see who Gregory is, any more than I can see what a mirror by itself looks like, because he reflects whoever's around him. Know what I mean?"

"I think I do."

"What should I say, Ivy?" Beth asked, the tone of her voice changing. She was pleading for an answer. "You're both my friends. When Suzanne asks me what's going on, what should I say?"

"I don't know." Ivy started examining her place mat again, reading all the descriptions of Hojo's desserts. "I'll tell you when I do know, okay? So, how's your writing going?"

"My writing?" Beth repeated, struggling to shift gears with Ivy. "Well, I've got good news."

"Yeah? Tell me."

"I'm going to be published. I mean, in a real magazine." Beth's blue eyes sparkled. "*True-Heart Confessions.*"

"Beth, that's great! Which story?"

"The one I did for drama club. You know, it was in the lit mag at school last spring."

Ivy tried to recall it. "I've read so many now."

"'She clutched the gun to her breast,'" Beth began. "'Hard and blue, cold and unyielding. Photos of him. Frail and faded photos of him – of him with *her* – torn up, tear-soaked, salt-crusted photos,' et cetera, et cetera."

Two waitresses, carrying full trays, had stopped to listen.

"What is it?" Beth asked Ivy. "You've got a really funny look on your face."

"Nothing . . . nothing, I was just thinking," Ivy replied.

"You've been doing a lot of that lately."

Ivy laughed. "Maybe I can keep it up next month when school starts."

Their check was dropped on the table. Ivy reached for her purse.

"Listen," Beth said, "why don't you sleep over at my house tonight? We don't have to talk. We'll watch DVDs, do our nails, bake cookies . . ." She popped the tip of her sugar cone into her mouth. "Low-cal cookies," she added.

Ivy smiled, then began digging in her purse for money. "I should get home, Beth."

"No, you shouldn't."

Ivy stopped digging. Beth had spoken with such certainty.

"I don't know why," Beth said, twisting a piece of her hair self-consciously. "You just shouldn't."

"I have to be home," Ivy told her. "If Philip wakes up in the middle of the night and finds I'm not there, he'll think something's wrong."

"Call him," her friend replied. "If he's asleep, Gregory can leave a note by his bed. You shouldn't go home tonight. It's . . . a feeling, a really strong feeling I have."

"Beth, I know you get these feelings, and one time before you were right, but this time it's different. The doors will be locked. Gregory is home. Nothing is going to happen to me."

Beth was looking past Ivy's shoulder, her eyes narrowing as if she was trying to focus on something.

Ivy turned around quickly and saw a curly-haired man in a shiny yellow bowling shirt. He winked at her, and Ivy turned back.

"Can I stay over with you?" Beth asked.

"What? No. Not tonight," Ivy said. "I need some sleep, and you need to finish that story I interrupted. This was my treat," she added, scooping up the check.

In the parking lot Ivy said goodbye several times, and Beth left her reluctantly.

As Ivy drove home she thought about Beth's story. The details of Caroline's suicide had not been made public, so Beth didn't know about the photos that Caroline had torn up the day she shot herself. It was funny the way Beth came up with things in her writing that seemed farfetched and kind of melodramatic, until some version of them came true.

When Ivy arrived home, she saw that all the lights in the house were out except one, a lamp in Gregory's room. She hoped he hadn't noticed her car coming up the drive. She left it outside the garage. That way, if he got worried, he could see that she had arrived home safely. Ivy planned to go up the center stairs so she wouldn't have to pass his room. In the afternoon Gregory had called the shop twice. She knew he wanted to talk, and she wasn't ready.

It was a warm evening, with no moon up yet, only stars sequining the sky. Ivy gazed up at them for a few moments, then walked quietly across the grass and patio.

"Where have you been?"

She jumped. She hadn't seen him sitting in the shadow of the house.

"What?"

"Where have you been?"

Ivy prickled at his tone. "Out," she said.

"You should have called me back. Why didn't you call me back, Ivy?"

"I was busy with customers."

"I thought you'd come home right after work."

Ivy dropped her keys noisily onto a cast-iron table. "And I thought I wouldn't be questioned about going out for an hour – not by you. I'm getting tired of it, Gregory!"

She could hear him shifting in the chair, but couldn't see his face.

"I'm getting tired of everyone watching out for me! Beth isn't my mother, and *you're* not my big brother!"

He laughed softly. "I'm glad to hear you say that. I was afraid that Eric had gotten you mixed up."

Ivy dropped her head a little, then said, "Maybe he did." She took a step toward the house.

Gregory caught her wrist. "We need to talk."

"I need to think, Gregory."

"Then think out loud," he said.

She shook her head.

"Ivy, listen to me. We're not doing anything wrong."

"Then why do I feel so – so confused? And so disloyal?"

"To Suzanne?" he asked.

"Suzanne thinks you're seeing someone else," Ivy told him.

"I am," he replied quietly. "I'm just not sure if she's seeing me . . . Are you?"

Ivy bit her lip. "It isn't just Suzanne I'm thinking of."

"Tristan."

She nodded.

He tugged on her arm, pulling her closer to him. "Sit down."

"Gregory, I don't want to talk about it."

"Then just listen. Hear me out. You love Tristan. You love him like you love no one else."

Ivy pulled away a little, but he held her fingers tightly. "Listen! If you had been the one killed in the accident, what would you have wanted for Tristan? Would you want no one else to love him? Would you want him to be alone the rest of his life?"

"No, of course not," she said.

"Of course not," he repeated softly.

Then he pulled her down into the chair with him. The metal was cold and hard.

"I've been thinking about you all day and all night," he said.

He caressed her lightly, his fingers tracing her face and the bones of her neck. He kissed her as gently as he would a child. She let him, but she didn't kiss him back.

"I've been waiting here all night," he said. "I need to get out. How about going for a ride with me?"

"We can't leave Philip," Ivy reminded him.

"Sure we can," Gregory replied softly. "He's sound asleep. We'll lock up the house and turn on the outside alarm. We can drive around for a little while. And I won't talk any more, promise."

"We can't leave Philip," she said a second time.

"He'll be all right. There's nothing wrong with riding around, Ivy. There's nothing wrong with blasting the stereo and driving a little fast. There's nothing wrong with having a good time."

"I don't want to go," she said.

She felt his body go rigid.

"Not tonight," she added quickly. "I'm tired, Gregory. I really need to go to bed. Another night, maybe."

"All right. Whatever you want," he said, his voice husky. He sagged back against the chair. "Get some sleep."

Ivy left him there and felt her way through the dark house. She checked on Philip, then walked through the adjoining bath to her own bedroom, where she was greeted by Ella's glowing eyes. Ivy switched on a small bureau lamp, and Ella began to purr.

"Is that purr for me," Ivy asked, "or him?"

Tristan's picture, the one his mother had given her, sat within the yellow circle of light.

Ivy took the picture in her hands. Tristan smiled up at her, wearing his old baseball cap. His school jacket flapped open, as if he were walking toward her. Sometimes she still couldn't believe that he was dead. Her head knew that he was, knew that in one sudden moment Tristan had stopped existing, but her heart just wouldn't let go.

"Love you, Tristan," she said, then kissed the photograph. "Sweet dreams."

Ivy woke up screaming. Her voice was hoarse, as if she had been screaming for hours. The clock said 1.15 A.M.

"It's okay! You're safe! Everything's okay, Ivy."

Gregory had his arms around her. Philip stood next to the bed, clutching Ella.

Ivy stared at them, then sank back against Gregory. "When will it stop? When will this nightmare end?"

"Shh, shh. Everything's okay."

But it wasn't. The nightmare kept growing. It kept adding on details, continually sending out tendrils of fear that curled into the dark places of her mind. Ivy closed her eyes, resting her head against Gregory.

"Why does she keep dreaming?" Philip asked.

"I'm not sure," Gregory said. "I guess it's part of getting over the accident."

"Sometimes dreams are messages from angels," Philip suggested. He said *angels* quickly, then glanced at Ivy, as if he thought she'd yell at him for mentioning them again.

Gregory studied Philip for a moment, then asked, "Angels are good, aren't they?"

Philip nodded.

"Well, if angels are good," Gregory reasoned, "do you think they'd be sending Ivy bad dreams?"

Philip thought about it, then slowly shook his head. "No . . . but maybe it's a bad angel doing it."

Ivy felt Gregory stiffen.

"It's just my mind doing it," she said quietly. "It's just my mind getting used to what happened to Tristan and me. In a while, the nightmares will stop."

But she was lying. She was afraid the dreams would never stop. And she was starting to think that there was something more to them than her getting over Tristan's death.

"I have an idea, Philip," Gregory said. "Until Ivy's nightmares stop, we'll take turns waking her up and staying with her. Tonight's my turn. Next time it's yours, okay?"

Philip looked doubtfully from Gregory to Ivy. "Okay," he said at last. "Ivy, can I take Ella in my room?"

"Sure. She'd love to cuddle with you."

Ivy watched her brother as he carried Ella, his head bent over her, his brow furrowed.

"Philip," she called after him. "When I get home from work tomorrow, we'll do something, just you and me. Think about what you want it to be — something fun. Everything's all right Philip. Really. Everything will be all right."

He nodded, but she could tell that he didn't believe her.

"Sleep tight," Ivy said. "You've got Ella with you. And your angel," she added.

He looked at her, his eyes wide with surprise. "You saw him, too?"

Ivy hesitated.

"Of course not," Gregory answered for her.

Of course not, Ivy repeated to herself – and yet for a moment she almost thought she did. She could almost believe an angel existed for Philip, though not for herself.

"Good night," she said softly.

When he was gone, Gregory held Ivy close to him and rocked her for several minutes. "Same old dream?" he said.

"Yes."

"Is Eric still in it?"

"The red motorcycle is," Ivy replied.

"I wish I could stop your nightmares," Gregory said. "If I knew how, I'd dream them myself every night. If only I could keep you from going through this."

"I don't think anyone can stop them," she replied.

He lifted his head. "What do you mean?"

"There was something new tonight. The same way the motorcycle got added on before, something else was added this time. Gregory, I think I might be remembering things. And I think I might have to keep doing this until I remember – something." She shrugged.

He pulled his head back a little to look at her. "What was added to the dream?"

"I was driving. The window was there, the one I can't quite see through with the shadow on the other side. It was that same window, but this time I was driving toward it, not walking."

She paused. She didn't want to think about it, think what the new part could mean.

He held her close again. "And everything else was the same?"

"No. I was driving Tristan's car."

Ivy heard the sharp intake of breath.

"When I saw the window, I tried to stop the car. I stepped on the brake, but the car wouldn't slow down. Then I heard his voice. 'Ivy, stop! Stop! Don't you see, Ivy? Ivy, stop!' But I couldn't stop. I couldn't slow down. I pressed down the pedal over and over. I had no brakes!"

Ivy felt cold all over. Gregory's arms were around her, but his own skin was cold with sweat.

"Why were there no brakes?" she whispered. "Am I remembering, Gregory? *What* am I remembering?"

He didn't answer. He was shaking as much as she.

"Stay with me," she begged. "I'm afraid to go back to sleep."

"I'll stay, but you have to sleep, Ivy."

"I can't! I'm afraid I'll start dreaming again. It frightens me! I don't know what will happen next!"

"I'll be right here. I'll wake you as soon as you start dreaming, but you need to sleep. I'll get you something to help you."

He stood up.

"Where are you going?" she asked, panicky.

"Shh," he soothed. "I'm just going to fix you something to help you sleep."

Then he took Tristan's photo down from the bureau and set it on the night table next to her.

"I'll be right back. I won't leave you, Ivy, I promise I won't leave you." He smoothed her hair. "Not until these nightmares stop for good."

30

"Ivy, stop! Stop! Don't you see, Ivy? Ivy, stop!"

But she hadn't stopped. Ivy kept telling Gregory the dream, and now he knew that she was remembering more. Maybe next time she'd remember it all – whatever it was Gregory didn't want anyone to know. If there was a next time.

Tristan lay still in Ivy's room. He had gone crazy, shouting and screaming at her. He had used up huge amounts of energy. For what? She sat fidgeting, frightened – and hoping for Gregory's return.

Tristan pulled himself up. He rushed out of the bedroom and down the main stairway of the darkened house, turning instinctively toward the kitchen, where Gregory was. Only the small light over the stove was on. Water hissed in the teapot. Gregory sat on a stool at the counter, watching it, his skin pale and glistening.

He kept toying with a cellophane packet he had taken from his pocket. Tristan could guess what it contained and what Gregory planned to do next. And he knew that, even if he had his full strength now, he couldn't overcome him. He couldn't use Gregory's mind the way he could use Will's. Gregory would fight Tristan all the way, and his human body had a physical strength a hundred times greater than that of Tristan's materialized fingers.

But human fingers could still slip, Tristan thought. If a little red capsule – something that Tristan could manipulate – moved unexpectedly, Gregory might fumble.

Gregory had chosen raspberry tea, perhaps because its sharp flavor would cover the taste of a drug, Tristan thought. He moved steadily closer to Gregory. He'd have to materialize his fingers at just the right moment.

Gregory carefully undid the cellophane packet and picked up two of the three capsules. Tristan extended his glowing hand and began to focus on his fingertips. Gregory's hand hovered over the hot tea.

The moment he let go, Tristan flicked the capsules away. They skittered across the countertop. Gregory swore and flung out his hand, but Tristan was quicker and flicked them into the sink. The capsules stuck to the damp surface and Tristan had to work again to get them down the drain.

As he did Gregory dropped the third capsule into the tea.

Now Tristan reached for the mug, but Gregory wrapped his fingers firmly around it. He stirred the liquid with a spoon, and when the capsule had dissolved, he carried the cup upstairs.

Ivy looked so relieved to see him.

"This ought to help," Gregory said.

"Don't drink it, Ivy!" Tristan warned, though he knew she couldn't hear him.

She sipped, then set it down and laid her head against Gregory.

He picked the cup up again before Tristan could touch it. "Too hot?"

"No, it's good. Thank you."

"Stop!" Tristan cried.

She sipped again, as if to reassure Gregory that the tea was fine.

"I chose the right stuff, didn't I? You've got so many kinds down there."

"Put it down, Ivy."

"It's perfect," she said, and took longer drinks.

"Lacey, where are you when I need you? I need your voice, I need someone to tell her no!"

Whenever Ivy reached to put the drugged tea back on the table, Gregory took it from her and held it. He sat on the bed with her, one arm around her, the other lifting the cup to her lips.

"A little more," he coaxed.

"No more!" Tristan cried.

"How do you feel?" he asked several minutes later.

"Sleepy. Strange. Not scared . . . just strange. I feel like someone else is here, watching us," she said, glancing around the room.

"I'm here, Ivy!"

Gregory offered her the last mouthful of tea. "There's nothing to be worried about," he said. "I'm here for you, Ivy."

Tristan struggled to keep himself calm. One capsule probably wouldn't kill her, he reasoned. Had Gregory found the other pack that Tristan had thrown behind the bureau? Was he planning to dope her up a little, then give her the rest?

"Lacey, I can't save her by myself!"

Will, Tristan thought, find Will. But how long would that take? Ivy's eyes were slowly closing.

"Sleep," Gregory was saying over and over. "There's nothing to be afraid of. Sleep."

Ivy's eyes shut, then her head dropped. Gregory did not bother to catch her. He pushed her to the side and let her slump against the pillow.

Without realizing it, Tristan had begun to cry. He wrapped his arms around Ivy, though he could not hold her. She was far away from him, and drifting away from Gregory, too, sinking further and further into an unnatural sleep. Tristan cried helplessly.

Gregory got up abruptly and walked out of the room.

Tristan knew he had to get help, but he couldn't leave Ivy alone for long.

Philip. It was his only chance. Tristan hurried into the next room.

Ella became alert as soon as he entered.

"Help me out, Ella. We need to get him awake, just enough to let me in."

Ella climbed up on Philip's chest, sniffed at his face, then mewed.

Philip's eyes fluttered open. His small hand reached up and lazily scratched Ella. Tristan imagined how soft the cat felt to Philip. A second later, having shared his thoughts, he slipped inside the boy.

"It's me, Philip. Your friend, your angel, Tristan."

"Tristan," Philip murmured, and suddenly they were sitting across from each other with a checkerboard between them. Philip jumped Tristan's marker. "Crown me!"

Tristan had dropped into a memory or a dream woven from a memory. He struggled to get them out of it.

"Wake up, Philip. It's Tristan. Wake up. I need your help. Ivy needs your help."

Tristan could hear Ella purring again and saw her face peering into his, though everything was

433

blurry. He knew Philip was listening and waking up slowly.

"Come on, Philip. That's the way, buddy."

Philip was looking over at the angel statues now. He was wondering, but he was not afraid. His arms and legs still felt relaxed. So far, so good.

Then Tristan heard the noise in the hall. He heard footsteps – Gregory's – but Gregory was walking oddly, heavily.

"Get up, Philip! We have to see!"

Before Philip could rouse himself, Gregory was down the stairs. A moment later, an outside door banged.

"Put on your shoes. Your shoes!"

A car's engine sputtered. Tristan recognized it – Ivy's old Dodge. His heart sank. Gregory had Ivy with him. Where are you taking her? Where?

"I don't know," Philip said in a sleepy voice.

Think. What would be easy for him? Tristan said to himself.

"I don't know," Philip mumbled.

With Ivy drugged, it would be easy to stage an accident. What kind? How and where was he going to do it? There must have been clues in his room, a hint in the newspaper clippings.

Tristan suddenly remembered the train schedule. He recalled the strange look on Gregory's face when he found the timetable on the floor. Gregory had circled the late-night train, the one that stopped at Tusset. Then he had done some calculations, written down a time, and circled it twice. 2.04. That would be right – Tristan knew the train rushed through their station a few minutes after two each morning. Rushed through! It didn't stop at small stations such as Stonehill's, which would be deserted after midnight. They had to stop him!

He glanced at Philip's digital clock. 1.43 A.M.

"Philip, come on!"

The little boy was slumped down in the chair, with only one shoelace tied. His fingers were clumsy when he tried to tie the other one. He could barely stand up, and moved slowly down the hall with Tristan guiding him. Tristan chose the center staircase, where there was a railing to hang on to. They made it safely to the bottom, then Tristan guided him around to the back door, which Gregory had left open. As if he had a clock inside him, Tristan felt each second ticking away.

They'd never make it in time by foot; the long driveway down the ridge took them in the opposite direction from the station. Keys – could he find the keys for Gregory's car? If he did, he could materialize his fingers and— But what if they wasted all their time looking for keys that Gregory had with him?

"Other way, Philip." Tristan turned Philip around. It was a dangerous shortcut, but their only chance: the steep and rocky side of the ridge, which dropped to the station below.

After a couple of steps, the cool night air revived Philip. Through the boy's eyes and ears, Tristan became aware of the night's silvery shadows and rustling sounds. He too was feeling stronger. At Tristan's urging, Philip broke into a run across the grass. They raced past the tennis court, then forty yards more toward the boundary of the property, the edge where the land suddenly dropped off.

They were moving faster than a child could have, their powers combined. Tristan didn't know how long his renewed strength would hold out, and he wasn't certain that he could get them safely down the steep side of the ridge. It seemed to have taken forever just to get this far.

He felt a moment of resistance as he and Philip climbed the stone wall marking the end of the property.

"I'm not supposed to," Philip said.

"It's okay, you're with me."

Far below them he could see the train station. To get to it they'd have to climb down a hillside where the only toeholds were the roots of a few dwarfed trees and some narrow ledges of stone, with sheer drops beneath them. Occasionally patches of brush broke through the rocky surface, but mostly it was rutted earth with a cascade of tumbled rocks that would roll at the lightest touch of a foot.

"I'm not scared," Philip said.

"I'm glad that one of us isn't."

They picked their way slowly and carefully down the ridge. The moon had come up late and its shadows were long and confusing. Tristan had to continually check himself, reminding himself that the legs he was using were shorter, the arms unable to reach as far.

They were halfway down when he misjudged. Their jump was too short, and they leaned out too far from a narrow strip of rock. From their ledge, it was a straight drop down twenty-five feet, with nothing but stones to snag them at the bottom before another drop. They teetered. Tristan drew into himself, cloaking his thoughts and instincts, letting Philip take over. It was Philip's natural sense of balance that saved them.

As they descended, Tristan tried not to think about Ivy, though the image of her head hanging over her shoulder like a limp doll's kept passing through his mind. And all the while he was aware of time ticking away.

"What is it?" Philip asked, sensing Tristan's concern.

"Keep going. Tell you later."

Tristan couldn't let Philip know how much danger Ivy was in. He cloaked certain thoughts, hiding from Philip's consciousness both Gregory's identity and his intentions. He wasn't sure how

Philip would handle the information, whether he'd panic over Ivy or even try to defend Gregory.

They were at the bottom now, racing through the tall grass and weeds, getting tripped up by rocks. Philip's ankle twisted, but he kept going. Ahead of them was a high wire fence. Through it they saw the station.

The station had two tracks side by side, northbound and southbound, each with its own platform. The platforms were connected by a high bridge over the tracks. On the southbound side, which was farthest from Philip and Tristan, there was a wooden station house and a parking lot. Tristan knew that the late-night train ran southbound.

Just as they reached the fence Tristan heard the bells of a town church, tolling once, twice. Two o'clock.

"The fence is awfully high, Tristan."

"At least it's not electric."

"Can we rest?"

Before Tristan could answer, a train whistle sounded in the distance.

"Philip, we have to beat the train!"

"Why?"

"We have to. Climb!"

Philip did, digging his toes into the holes of the wire mesh, stretching and grasping with his fingers, pulling himself up. They were at the top of the fence, twenty feet high. Then Philip jumped. They slammed into the ground and rolled.

"Philip!"

"I thought you had wings. You're supposed to have wings."

"Well, *you* don't!" Tristan reminded him.

The whistle blew again, closer this time. They ran for the first platform. When they climbed up on it, they could see across the station.

Ivy.

"Something's wrong with her," Philip said.

She was standing on the southbound platform, leaning back against a pillar that was at the edge of the platform. Her head was hanging to one side.

"She could fall! Tristan, a train's coming and—" Philip began to shout. "Ivy! Ivy!"

She didn't hear him.

"The steps," Tristan told him.

They raced for them, then across the bridge and down the other side.

They could hear the train rumbling, getting closer. Philip kept calling to her, but Ivy stared across the track, mesmerized. Tristan followed her gaze – then he and Philip froze.

"Tristan? Tristan, where are you?" Philip asked in a panicky voice.

"Here. Right here. I'm still inside you."

But even to Tristan it looked as if he were out there, on the other side of the track. Tristan stared at the image of himself that stood in the shadows of the northbound platform. The strange figure was dressed in a school jacket, like the one Tristan wore in his photograph, and wore an old baseball cap. Tristan stared, as entranced by the figure as Ivy and Philip.

"That's not me," he told Philip. "Don't be fooled. It's someone else dressed like me." Gregory, he said to himself.

"Who is it? Why's he dressed like you?"

They saw a pale hand move out of the shadows into the clear moonlight. The figure beckoned to Ivy, encouraging her, drawing her across the track.

The train was rushing toward them now, its headlight whitening the track beneath them, its whistle blasting in a final warning.

Ivy paid no attention to it. She was drawn to the hand like a moth to a flickering fire. It kept reaching out to her. She suddenly reached out her own hand and took a step forward.

"Ivy!" Tristan shouted – Philip shouted. *"Ivy! Ivy, don't!"*

31

With her chin held high and her cloud of curly blond hair tossed back from her face, Ivy shut the school counselor's door and walked down the hall. Several guys from the swim team turned to stare as she moved toward her locker. Ivy forced herself to return their glances and to look confident. The jeans and top she wore for the first day of the school year had been selected by Suzanne, her oldest friend and fashion expert. Too bad Suzanne didn't pick out a matching bag to go over my head, Ivy thought. She walked past the senior class bulletin board. People whispered. People pointed her out with small nods. She should have expected it.

Anyone whom Tristan Carruthers had fallen for would be pointed out. Anyone who had been with Tristan the night he was killed would be whispered about. So naturally, anyone who had tried to kill herself because she couldn't get over Tristan's death would be pointed to and whispered about and watched very, very carefully. And that was what everyone said about Ivy: brokenhearted, she had taken some pills, then tried to throw herself in front of a train.

All she could recall from that night three weeks earlier was being comforted by her stepbrother, Gregory, then falling asleep, looking at Tristan's photo. That photo, her favorite picture of Tristan, in which he was wearing his old school jacket and a baseball cap, haunted her now. It had haunted her even before she'd heard her little brother's strange account of what had taken place.

Philip's story of an angel saving her hadn't convinced her family or the police that this wasn't a suicide attempt. And how could she deny taking a drug that had shown up in the hospital's blood tests? How could she argue against the train engineer's statement to the police that he wouldn't have been able to stop in time?

"Chick, chick, chick." A soft quivering voice interrupted Ivy's thoughts. "Who wants to play chick, chick, chick?"

He was calling to her from the shadowy space beneath the stairs. Ivy knew it was Eric Ghent. She kept on walking.

"Chick, chick, chick . . ."

When she didn't react he emerged from the dark

stairwell, looking like a skeleton startled out of his tomb. His wispy blond hair lay in strings across his high forehead, and his eyes looked like pale blue marbles set in bony sockets. Ivy had not seen Eric for the last three weeks; she suspected that Gregory had kept his jeering friend away from her.

Now Eric moved quickly enough to block her path. "Why *didn't* you do it?" he asked. "Lose your nerve? Why didn't you go ahead and kill yourself?"

"Disappointed?" Ivy asked back.

"Chick, chick, chick," he said softly, tauntingly.

"Leave me alone, Eric." Ivy walked faster.

"Uh-uh. Not now." He grabbed her wrist, his thin fingers wrapping tightly around her arm. "You can't blow me off now, Ivy. You and I have too much in common."

"We have nothing in common," she replied, pulling away from him.

"Gregory," he said, tapping one of his fingers. "Drugs." He ticked off a second item. "And we're both champions of the game of chicken." He grabbed a third finger and wiggled it. "We're buddies now."

Ivy kept walking, though she wanted to run. Eric bobbed along with her.

"Tell your good buddy," he said, "what made you want to do it? What were you thinking when you saw that train rushing down the track at you? Were you stoked? What kind of trip was it?"

Ivy felt repulsed by his questions. It seemed impossible to think she would have deliberately jumped in front of the train. She had lost Tristan, but there were still people in her life she cared deeply about – Philip, her mother, Suzanne and Beth, and Gregory. Gregory's mother had committed suicide the month before Tristan died. Ivy had seen the pain and anger caused by that death, and it seemed totally crazy to her that she would try the same thing.

But everyone said she had. Gregory said so.

"How many times do I have to tell you? I can't remember what happened that night, Eric. I can't."

"But you will," he said with a quiet laugh. "Sooner or later, you will."

Then he stepped away from her and turned back, like a dog that had reached the end of its territory. Ivy continued toward her and her friends' lockers, ignoring more curious stares. She hoped that Suzanne and Beth were finished with their senior orientation meetings.

Ivy didn't need to look at the locker numbers to find Suzanne's new nesting place. Suzanne wasn't there, but the locker was being fumigated with an open bottle of her favorite perfume, which guided Ivy – and all guys interested in leaving Suzanne a note – directly to the spot. Suzanne had found three new guys to date recently, but Beth and Ivy knew it was just a ploy to make Gregory jealous.

Beth's locker, which was close to Ivy's this year, already had a piece of paper sticking out of it, but it probably wasn't a note from an admiring hunk. More likely, she had shut the door on a scrap of a steamy romance, one of the many that filled her notebooks.

Ivy went ahead to her own locker to drop off her new books. Kneeling down, she dialed the combination and pulled open the door. She gasped. Taped inside her door was a photograph of Tristan, the same picture that had haunted her for the past three weeks. For a moment she couldn't breathe. How had it gotten there?

Frantically she recalled everything she had done that morning: roll call in homeroom, then a general assembly, then the school store, and finally a meeting with the counselor. She ran over the list twice, but she couldn't remember taping the photo to the door. Was she really losing her mind?

Ivy closed her eyes and leaned against the door. I'm crazy, she thought. I'm really crazy.

"Am I nuts, Gregory?" she had asked three weeks earlier as she stood in her bedroom on her first day home from the hospital. She held Tristan's photograph in her trembling hands. Gregory gently took the picture away from her, giving it to Philip, her nine-year-old savior.

"You're going to get better, Ivy. That much I'm

sure of," Gregory said, drawing her down on the bed next to him, putting his arm around her.

"Meaning I'm crazy now."

Gregory didn't answer right away. She had noticed the change in him when he came to see her at the hospital. His dark hair was combed perfectly, as always, and his handsome face was like a mask, just as it had been when she first met him, his light gray eyes hiding his deepest thoughts.

"It's a hard thing to understand, Ivy," he said carefully. "It's hard to know exactly what you were thinking at the time." He glanced over at Philip, who was setting the framed photo on the bureau. "And Philip's story sure doesn't help much."

Her brother responded with a stubborn glare.

"Maybe now that no one else is around, you can tell us what really happened, Philip," Gregory said.

Philip glanced up at the two empty shelves where Ivy's collection of angels had once stood.

"I already told you."

"Try again," Gregory said, his voice low and tense.

"Please, Philip." Ivy reached out for his hand. "It'll help me."

He let her hold his hand loosely. She knew he was tired of being interrogated, first by the police, then by the doctors at the hospital, then by their mother and Gregory's father, Andrew.

"I was sleeping," Philip told her. "After you had

your nightmare, Gregory said he'd stay with you. I was asleep again. But then I heard somebody calling me. I didn't know who it was at first. He told me to wake up. He said you needed help."

Philip stopped, as if that were the end of the story.

"And?"

He glanced up at the empty shelves, then pulled away from her.

"Go on," Ivy prompted.

"You're just going to yell at me."

"No, I won't," she said. "And neither will Gregory." She gave Gregory a warning look. "Just tell us what you remember."

"You heard a voice in your head," Gregory said, "and it was telling you that Ivy needed help. The voice sounded something like Tristan's."

"It was Tristan," Philip insisted. "It was angel Tristan!"

"Okay, okay," Gregory said.

"Did this voice tell you why I was in trouble?" Ivy asked. "Did the voice tell you where I was?"

He shook his head. "Tristan said to put on my shoes, go down the stairs, and go out the back door. Then we ran across the yard to the stone wall. I knew I wasn't supposed to go over it, but Tristan said it was okay because he was with me."

Ivy could feel Gregory's body tense next to hers, but she nodded encouragingly to Philip.

"It was scary, Ivy, climbing down the ridge. It was hard to hold on. The rocks were real slippery."

"It's impossible," Gregory said, sounding frustrated and perplexed. "A kid couldn't have done it. I couldn't have done it."

"I had Tristan with me," Philip reminded him.

"I don't know how you got to the station, Philip," Gregory said heatedly, "but I'm tired of this Tristan story. I don't want to hear it again."

"I do," Ivy said quietly, and heard Gregory draw in his breath. "Go on," she said.

"When we got to the bottom, we still had to get over another fence. I asked what was going on, but Tristan wouldn't tell me. He just said we had to help you. So I started climbing, then I kind of messed up. I thought because Tristan was an angel we could fly" – Gregory got up and started pacing around the bedroom – "but we couldn't, and we fell off the top of this high fence."

Ivy glanced down at her brother's wrapped ankle. His knees were cut and bruised.

"Then we heard the train whistle. And we had to keep going. When we got closer we saw you on the platform. We shouted to you, Ivy, but you didn't hear us. We ran up the steps and over the bridge. That's when we saw the other Tristan. The one in the cap and jacket, just like in your picture," he said, pointing to it.

Ivy shivered.

"So," Gregory said, "angel Tristan is in two places now – with you, and on the other side of the tracks as well. He's playing a trick on Ivy, calling her over to him. It wasn't a very nice trick."

"Tristan was with me," Philip said.

"Then who was across the tracks?" Gregory asked.

"A bad angel," Philip replied with complete certainty. "Someone who wanted Ivy to die."

Gregory blinked.

Ivy sank back against her headboard. As bizarre as Philip's story sounded, it seemed more real to her than the idea that she had taken drugs and thrown herself in front of a train. And the fact remained that somehow her brother had gotten there and he had pulled her back at the last moment. The engineer had seen the blur in front of his train and radioed in that he could not stop in time.

"I thought you saw Tristan," Philip said.

"What?" Ivy asked.

"You turned around. I thought you saw his light." Philip gazed at her hopefully.

Ivy shook her head. "I don't remember it. I don't remember anything from the train station."

Perhaps it would be easier if she never recalled what had happened, Ivy thought. But every time she looked at the photo now, there was a prickling in the back of her mind. Something wouldn't let her look away and forget. Ivy stared until the picture ran blurry. She didn't realize she had begun to cry.

"Ivy . . . Ivy, don't."

Suzanne's words jolted Ivy back into the present. As she lifted her head her friend crouched down next to the school locker. Her mouth was a grim, lipsticked line. Beth, who had also come back from orientation, stood above her, fumbling through her bag for tissues. She glanced down at Ivy, her own brimming eyes reflecting Ivy's tears.

"I'm okay," Ivy said, wiping her eyes quickly, looking from one to the other. "Really, I'm okay."

But she could tell they didn't believe her. Gregory had driven her to school that day, and Suzanne would be taking her home. It was as if they didn't trust her to drive herself, as if they thought that at any minute she'd lose it and steer right off a cliff.

"You shouldn't have that picture taped inside your locker," Suzanne said. "Sooner or later you're going to have to let go, Ivy. You're just making yourself—" She hesitated.

"Crazy?"

Suzanne smoothed back her mane of black hair, then toyed with a gold hoop earring. She had never been shy about speaking her mind before, but now she was being careful. "It's not healthy, Ivy," she said at last. "It's not good to have his picture here to remind you every time you open the door."

"But I wasn't the one who put it here," Ivy told her.

Suzanne frowned. "What do you mean?"

"Did you see me do it?" Ivy asked.

"Well, no, but you've got to remember—" her friend began.

"I don't."

Suzanne and Beth exchanged glances.

"So someone else must have," Ivy said, sounding a lot more certain than she was. "It's a school picture. Anyone could get a copy of it. I didn't tape it here, so someone else must have."

There was a moment of silence. Suzanne sighed.

"Did you see the counselor today?" Beth asked.

"I just came from there," Ivy told her, closing her locker, leaving the picture inside. She stood up next to Beth, whose outfit had also been selected by Suzanne. But Beth, no matter how fashionably dressed, would always look to Ivy like a wide-eyed owl, with her round face and light brown hair.

"What did Ms. Bryce say?" Beth asked as they started down the hall.

"Nothing much. I'm supposed to come talk to her twice a week and check in if I'm having a bad day. So you're both coming Monday?" Ivy asked, changing the subject.

Suzanne's eyes brightened. "To the Baines Bash? It's a Labor Day tradition!" She sounded relieved to be talking about a party.

Ivy knew that the last month had been hard on Suzanne. She'd been so jealous of the attention Gregory paid Ivy that she'd stopped speaking to her oldest friend. Later, when Gregory told Suzanne that Ivy had tried to commit suicide, she blamed herself for turning her back. But Ivy knew that she herself was partly to blame for the rift. She'd gotten too close to Gregory. In the three weeks since the incident at the train station, Gregory had cooled toward Ivy, treating her more like a sister than a girl he was romantically interested in. Suzanne had reached out to Ivy again, and Ivy was glad for the change in both of them.

"We've been going to the Baines Bash since we were kids," Beth told Ivy. "Everybody in Stonehill has."

"Except me," Ivy pointed out.

"And Will. He moved here last winter, like you," Beth said. "I told him about the party, and he's coming."

"Is he?" Ivy had noticed that Beth and Will were hanging around together more and more. "He's a nice guy."

"Real nice," Beth said enthusiastically.

They studied each other for a moment. Were Beth and Will getting to be more than friends? Ivy wondered. After writing all those romantic stories, maybe Beth had finally fallen. It wouldn't be hard to do: A lot of girls had crushes on Will. Ivy herself found that whenever she looked into his dark brown eyes— She caught herself and quickly shoved aside that thought. She would never let herself fall in love again.

The girls pushed through the school doors, and Suzanne led them on a roundabout route to their cars that conveniently ran past the field where the football team was practicing.

"I have to get a team program," Suzanne said after several minutes of watching. "What if I start drooling over number forty-nine and discover he's just a sophomore?"

"A hunk's a hunk," Beth replied philosophically. "And older women with younger guys are in."

"Don't tell Gregory I'm looking," Suzanne said in a stage whisper as they moved on toward their cars.

"Isn't looking allowed?" Beth asked innocently.

"On second thought, tell him, tell him!" Suzanne said, flinging her arms out dramatically. "Let him know, Ivy, I'm out and looking."

Ivy just smiled. From the beginning, Suzanne and Gregory had played mind games with each other.

"I mean, why should I tie myself down to one guy?" Suzanne continued.

Ivy knew this was just an act. Suzanne had been obsessed with Gregory since March and wanted desperately to tie him down to her.

"I'm going to start at the Baines Bash." She unlocked her car door. "That's where a lot of school romances have started, you know."

"How many are you planning for yourself?" Ivy teased.

"Six."

"Great," Beth said. "That's six more heartbreaks for me to write about."

"I'd settle for five romances," Suzanne added, giving Ivy a sly look, "if you'll take the other one and stop thinking about Tristan."

Ivy didn't reply.

Suzanne got in her car, closed the door, and reached across to unlock the passenger-side door. But before Ivy could open it, Beth caught her hand. She spoke quickly, quietly: "You can't forget, Ivy. Not yet. It would be dangerous to forget."

In the back of her mind, Ivy felt that prickling feeling again.

Then Beth yanked open her own car door, hopped in, and drove away fast.

Suzanne glanced in the rearview mirror, frowning. "I don't know what's gotten into that girl. Lately she's been hopping around like a scared rabbit. What did she just say to you?"

Ivy shrugged. "Just gave me a little advice."

"Don't tell me – she got another one of her premonitions."

Ivy remained silent.

Suzanne laughed. "You've got to admit, Ivy, Beth's flaky. I never take her 'advice' seriously. You shouldn't, either."

"I haven't so far," Ivy said. And both times, she thought, I've been sorry I didn't.

32

"Yo! Romeo! Where art thou? Rooo-me-ooo," Lacey called.

Tristan, who had been following Ivy down the wide center stair of the Baines home, stopped at the landing and stuck his head out an open window.

Lacey smiled up at him from the middle of a flower bed, the only piece of Andrew Baines's property that hadn't been overrun by the hundreds of guests with their picnic blankets and baskets. A Caribbean steel band was warming up on the patio. Paper lanterns hung from the pines around the tennis court; beneath them tables were laid out with refreshments.

Long before Tristan met Ivy, long before Andrew surprised everyone by marrying Maggie, Tristan had come to this annual party. He remembered how huge the white clapboard home had seemed to him as a little boy, with its east and west wings and double chimneys and rows of heavy black shutters – like a house that would be pictured in his mother's New England calendar.

"Ditch the chick, Romeo," Lacey called up to him. "You're missing a great party. Especially under some of the bushes."

Tristan's first instinct was to quiet her. But no one else could hear them, except when Lacey chose to project her voice. He gave her a lopsided smile, then withdrew from the window. At the same moment that Tristan turned back toward the stairs, Ivy stopped and turned toward the window.

Instantly he began hoping. She senses something, he thought.

But Ivy looked right through him, then without hesitation moved past him. She leaned upon the sill of the window, gazing wistfully at the scene before her. Tristan stood beside her and watched as torches were lit, flaring up suddenly in the summer twilight.

Ivy turned her head, and Tristan did, too, following her gaze to Will, who was standing at the edge of the crowd, surveying it. Suddenly Will looked up, meeting Ivy's eyes. Tristan knew what Will saw: brilliant green eyes and a tumbleweed of blond hair falling over her shoulders.

Ivy looked down at Will for what seemed like

forever, then stepped back abruptly, her hands going up to her cheeks. Tristan pulled back just as fast. Take a picture, Will, it lasts longer, he thought, then quickly descended the steps.

Lacey was waiting on the patio, amusing herself by hitting the drummer's cymbal every time he turned his back. Of course, the drummer didn't see her, not even the purple shimmer that some believers glimpsed. She winked at Tristan.

"I'm not here to fool around," he said.

"Okay, sweetie, let's get down to business," Lacey said, giving him a little push.

"I want to show you someone who's gulping down drinks over by the tennis court," Lacey told him, but first she headed for Philip's tree house. She simply couldn't resist the opportunity to knock away the tree's swing seat when a girl in a pink sundress tried to sit on it.

"Lacey, act your age."

"I will," she said, "just as soon as you decide to act like an angel."

"Seems to me I am," he said.

She shook her head. "Repeat after me," Lacey instructed in an obnoxious teacher voice. "Ivy's breathing, Will's breathing, *I'm not.*"

"It's just that she looked straight at me at the train station," Tristan said. "I was sure she believed again. When I pulled her and Philip back, I was sure Ivy saw me."

"If she did, she's forgotten it," Lacey said.

"I have to get her to remember. Beth—"

"Is feeling too rattled to help you out," Lacey cut in. "She predicted the break-in, then foresaw danger that night at the train station. She has a special gift, but she's too frightened to be an open channel anymore."

"Then Philip."

"Philip! Oh, *puh-lease.* How long do you think Gregory's going to put up with the kid who keeps talking about angel Tristan?"

Tristan knew she was right.

"That leaves Will," Lacey said. She walked backward and pointed a long purple nail at him. "So. Just how jealous are you?"

"Very," he replied honestly, then sighed. "You know how you feel about the actress who took your place in that film, the one you said stinks?"

"She *does* stink," Lacey said quickly.

"Multiply that feeling by a thousand. And the thing is, Will's not a bad guy. He'd be good for Ivy, and all I want is what's good for Ivy. I love her. I'd do anything for her—"

"Die, for instance," Lacey said. "But you've already tried that, and look where it got you."

Tristan grimaced. "Time with you."

She grinned, then nudged him. "Look over there. Next to the lady who looks like she got her perm and cut at the poodle parlor. Recognize him?"

"It's Caroline's friend," Tristan said, observing the tall dark-haired man. "The one who leaves roses on her grave."

"He creamed Andrew at tennis and looked like he enjoyed every minute of it."

"Did you find out his name?" Tristan asked.

"Tom Stetson. He's a teacher at Andrew's college. I tell you, who needs soap operas when you can hang around Stonehill? Do you think it was a long, torrid, secret affair? Do you think Andrew knew? Hey, Tristan!"

"I hear you," he said, but his eyes were focused on the crowd twenty feet away, where Ivy, Will, and Beth were talking.

"*Oh,* the *arrows of love,*" Lacey crooned. He hated it when she exaggerated her words like that. "I swear, Tristan, that girl's put so many holes in you, one day you're going to fold over like a slice of Swiss cheese."

He grimaced.

"It's pathetic, the way you look at her with those big puppy dog eyes. She doesn't even see you. I just hope that one day—"

"Know what I hope, Lacey?" Tristan asked, swinging around to her. "I hope you fall in love."

Lacey blinked with surprise.

"I hope you fall in love with a guy who looks right past you."

Lacey looked away.

"And I hope you do it soon, before I finish my mission," Tristan went on. "I want to be around to make lots of jokes about it."

He expected Lacey to make a snappy comeback, but she kept her eyes away from him, watching Ivy's cat, Ella, who had followed them through the crowd.

"I can't wait till the day," Tristan continued, "that Lacey Lovitt falls in love with some guy beyond her reach."

"What makes you think I haven't?" she muttered, then crouched down to scratch Ella. She petted the cat for several minutes.

After two years of procrastinating on her own mission, Lacey had developed more endurance and more powers than Tristan. He knew that she could keep the tips of her fingers materialized to scratch the cat much longer than he.

"Come on, Ella," Lacey said softly, and Tristan saw the cat's ears prick.

Ella followed Lacey, and Tristan followed Ella to a refreshment table. Eric and Gregory were standing there. Eric was arguing with Gregory and the bartender, trying to convince them to give him a beer.

Lacey gave Ella a nudge, and the cat leaped up lightly on the table. The three guys didn't notice her.

"A bowl of milk, please."

"Just a minute, miss," the bartender said, turning away from Gregory and Eric. His eyes widened as they fell upon Ella.

Ella winked.

The bartender turned back to the boys. "Did you hear that?"

"Milk, and hurry it up, please."

Now Eric and the bartender stared at the cat. Gregory craned his neck to glance behind Eric. "What's the problem?" he said impatiently. "Just fix an iced tea."

"I prefer milk."

The bartender lowered his face to Ella's. She meowed at him and leaped down from the table. Lacey snickered, but she had stopped projecting her voice, and only Tristan could hear her now.

The bartender, his brow still furrowed, poured the iced tea for Eric. Then Gregory flicked his head to the right, and he and Eric started off in that direction. Tristan trailed them as they wove their way through the crowd and beyond it, to the stone wall that marked the edge of the property.

Far below them was the tiny train station and the track that hugged the river. Even Tristan could hardly believe that he and Philip had made it down this side of the ridge.

"No way," Gregory muttered to himself. "That kid's lying to me, covering up. Who's in with him?"

462

"Just let me know when you're talking to me," Eric said cheerfully.

Gregory glanced at him.

"You've been doing it a lot lately, talking to yourself" – "Eric grinned – "or maybe to the angels."

"Screw the angels," Gregory said.

Eric laughed. "Yeah, well, maybe you should start praying to them. You've gotten yourself in deep, Gregory". His face grew serious, his eyes narrowing. "Real deep. And you're getting me in with you."

"You idiot! You're getting yourself in. You're always high – and you're always messing up. I'm asking you one more time, where're the clothes?"

"I'm telling you one more time, I don't have them."

"I want the cap and the jacket," Gregory said. "And you're going to find them for me, because if you don't, Jimmy's not getting the money you owe." Gregory tilted back his head. "And you know what that means. You know how touchy those dealers can be when they don't get their money."

Eric's mouth twitched. Without alcohol he could not stand up to Gregory. "I'm sick of it," he whined. "I'm sick of doing your dirty work."

He started to walk away, but Gregory yanked him back by the arm. "But you'll do it, won't you?

And you'll keep quiet about things, because you need me. You need your fix."

Eric struggled weakly. "Let me go. Someone's watching."

Gregory loosened his grip and looked around. Eric quickly stepped out of his reach. "Be careful, Gregory," he warned. "I can feel them watching."

Gregory arched his eyebrows and began to laugh menacingly. Even when Eric was out of sight, he continued to chuckle.

Lacey wriggled her shoulders. "Major creepo," she said.

They watched as Gregory worked his way back into the party, talking and smiling at the guests.

"What do you think Eric's dirty work was?" Lacey asked Tristan. "Knocking off Caroline? Cutting your brake line? Attacking Ivy in Andrew's office?" She materialized her fingers and hurled a stone as far as she could over the ridge. "Of course, we don't even know for sure if Caroline was murdered or if your brake line was deliberately cut."

Tristan nodded. "I'm going to have to time-travel through Eric's memories again."

Lacey had picked up another stone and now dropped it to her side. "You're going back through Eric's mind? You're crazy, Tristan! I thought you learned your lesson the first time. His circuits are fried, it's too dangerous, and his memories won't give you any proof."

"Once I know what is going on, I can find the proof," he reasoned.

Lacey shook her head.

"Right now," Tristan said, "I've got to get Ivy to remember what happened at the train station. I've got to find Will and convince him to help me."

"Gee, what a great idea," Lacey said. "I think someone else suggested that about fifteen minutes ago."

Tristan shrugged.

"That same someone will come with you, in case you need further help," she added.

"No jokes, Lacey," he warned.

"No promises, Tristan."

They found Will by the patio, dancing with Beth. Ivy and Suzanne were sitting next to Ivy's mother, watching kids from their class getting into the reggae music. Lacey started dancing by herself, swinging her hips, lifting her hands above her head, then dropping them to her waist. She's good at it, Tristan observed as she twisted and turned her way across the patio. Ella, seeing Lacey's light, began to follow her. Somebody stepped backward and fell over Ella, landing on his rear next to the cat.

"Would you like to dance?" It was Lacey's projected voice.

The guy stared at Ella for a moment, then scrambled to his feet

"Come here, Ella," Maggie called out, and the

cat sauntered toward Ivy's mother, with Lacey following. Ella leaped into Maggie's lap, and Ivy's mother settled back to watch the dancers.

"No one will ask me to dance, Maggie." Lacey again.

Maggie shifted the cat around, cupping Ella's chin in her perfectly manicured hand, staring at the cat as if she expected her to speak once more.

"Did you girls hear that?" Maggie asked, but neither replied. Suzanne was giving Ivy a detailed analysis of the relationships of all the couples on the patio.

Tristan left Lacey to her games and moved through the crowd toward Beth and Will. They were dancing with their heads as close as a romantic couple's, but he knew why Beth and Will were really together – Ivy.

"I'm afraid," Beth said. "I know things I don't want to know – I know them before they happen, Will. And I write things I never meant to write."

"I draw pictures I never meant to draw," Will replied.

"I wish someone would tell us what's going on. Whatever it is, it's not over yet – that much I know. I have this sense that things are terribly wrong, and they're going to get worse. I wake up scared, scared to death for Ivy. Sometimes I think I'm cracking up."

Will drew her closer. Tristan glanced over at Ivy and saw her quickly turn her head away.

"You're not cracking up, Beth. It's just that you have some kind of gift that—"

"I don't want this kind of gift!" she cried.

"Shhh. Shhh." With his hand, he smoothed Beth's hair.

"She's watching us," Beth said. "She'll get the wrong idea. You'd better ask her to dance."

Tristan knew at that moment what Will would be thinking. He gazed at Ivy and thought how it would feel to put his arms around her, to pull her to him, to let his fingers get lost in her bright hair. In that instant they matched thoughts, and Tristan slipped inside Will.

Will suddenly sagged against Beth. "It's that feeling again. I hate the feeling."

"I need to talk to Ivy," Tristan told him, and Will spoke the words aloud.

"What are you going to say to her?" Beth asked. Will shook his head, bewildered.

"Ask Ivy to dance," Tristan said, and once again Will spoke the words as if they were his own.

"You ask her," Beth replied.

Will's jaw tightened. Tristan could feel his struggle, how Will's instinct told him to thrust the intruder out of his mind, and how his curiosity fought back against this instinct. "Who are you?" Will wondered silently.

"It's Tristan. Tristan. You've got to believe me now."

"I can't believe," Beth said.

Will and she had stopped dancing and stood looking at each other, trying to understand.

"He's inside you, isn't he?" Beth asked, her voice shaking. "It's his words you're saying."

Will nodded.

"Can you make him leave?" she asked.

"Don't!"

"Why don't you leave us alone?" Beth cried.

"I can't. For Ivy's sake, I can't."

Will and Beth clung to each other. Then Will led her to the edge of the patio, where Ivy was sitting. "Will you dance with me?" he asked Ivy.

She glanced at Beth uncertainly.

"I'm beat," Beth said, pulling Ivy up out of the chair and taking her place. "Go on. I've got to give these dainty, size-nine feet a break."

Will walked quietly with Ivy to the least crowded part of the patio. Tristan felt him tremble as he put his arms around her. He felt each awkward step and remembered how he himself had felt the previous spring when he had first tried to get to know Ivy. Face-to-face with her, he couldn't manage a sentence with more than four words.

"How are you?" Will asked.

"Fine."

"Good."

A long silence followed. Tristan could feel questions forming in Will's mind. "If you're there," Will said silently to Tristan, "why aren't you telling me what to do?"

"I'm not that fragile," Ivy told him.

"What?"

"You're dancing with me as if you think I'll break," she said loudly, her green eyes shooting brilliant sparks.

Will looked at her, surprised. "You're angry."

"You noticed," she said sharply. "I'm tired of the way people are acting – everyone's being so careful around me! Tiptoeing, as though they're afraid they'll do something to set me off. Well, I've got news for you, Will, and everyone else. I'm not made of glass, and I'm not about to shatter. Got it?"

"I think so," Will said. Then, without warning, he spun her around twice, pushing her away from him and drawing her back like a yo-yo. He dropped his arm so she fell back, then he caught her at the last instant, leaning over her and pulling her up.

"Is that better?"

Ivy pushed back the hair that had tumbled over her face, and she laughed breathlessly. "A little."

Will grinned. Both of them were more relaxed now – it was time to speak to her, Tristan thought. But what could he say that wouldn't anger her again or scare her away?

"There's something I want to talk about," Will said, using Tristan's words.

Ivy pulled back a little to look into his eyes, then quickly glanced away. Eyes a girl could drown in – that was how Lacey had described Will's. And that's why Ivy looked away, Tristan thought, struggling to control his jealousy.

"It's about . . . Beth. She's kind of shaken up," Will said for Tristan. "You know how she has premonitions."

"I know I gave her a good scare a few weeks ago," Ivy said, "but that was just a—"

Will shook his head quickly, as Tristan did. "Beth is more afraid of the future than of what happened then."

"What do you mean?" Ivy asked. Her tone was indignant, but Tristan heard the slight tremor. "Nothing more is going to happen," she insisted. "What do I have to do to convince everyone that I'm okay?"

"You have to remember, Ivy."

"Remember what?" she asked.

"The night of the accident."

Tristan could feel Will pulling back now, wondering what his words were leading to. "What accident?" Will asked silently. "The one you died in?"

"The accident?" Ivy repeated. "Is that a nice, polite way of talking about my attempted suicide?"

"Ivy, you can't believe that! You know it's not true," Will said, passionately speaking each word Tristan gave him.

"I don't know anything anymore," she replied, her voice breaking.

"Try to remember," Will pleaded for Tristan. "You saw me at the train station."

"You were there?" she asked with surprise.

"I've always been there for you. I love you!"

Ivy stared at Will. Too late Tristan realized his mistake in speaking directly.

"You can't, Will."

Will swallowed hard.

"You should love someone else. I – I'll never love you."

Tristan felt Will take the blow.

"I'll never love anyone again," Ivy said, stepping back, "not the way I loved Tristan."

"Tell her it's me speaking," Tristan urged.

But Will stood still and said nothing. Other couples bumped into them, laughed, and danced around them. Will held Ivy at arm's length, and Ivy would not meet his gaze. She turned suddenly, and Will let her walk away.

"Go after her," Tristan ordered. "We're not finished."

"Leave me alone," Will muttered, and started off in the other direction, his head down.

Gregory, who was leading Suzanne into the

crowd of dancers, caught Will by the arm. "You're not giving up, are you?"

"Giving up?" Will repeated, his voice sounding hollow.

"On Ivy," Suzanne said.

"On the chase," Gregory said, grinning at Will.

"I don't think Ivy wants to be chased."

"Oh, come on," Gregory chided him. "My sweet and innocent stepsister loves to play games. And take it from me, she's a pro."

A pro at escaping you, Tristan thought as he moved out of Will.

"I'd never give up," Gregory said, glancing at Ivy, who was standing at the edge of the patio. His lingering smile made both Suzanne and Tristan turn toward Ivy uneasily. "There's nothing I like more than a girl who plays hard to get."

33

"Therefore," Philip told Ivy on Wednesday evening, "I can watch *X-men* again."

"Therefore?" Ivy repeated with a smile. Leaning over her mother's hand, she quickly repainted Maggie's nails. Her mother and Andrew were headed for another college fund-raiser.

"Andrew said so."

"So he's already checked your homework?" Ivy asked.

"He said my story about the party was highly imaginative and very fine."

"Highly imaginative and very fine," Maggie mimicked. "Before you know it, we're going to have a four-foot-tall professor walking around here."

Ivy smiled again. "Go set up the DVD player," she told Philip. "As soon as Mom and I are finished, I'll be down."

She lifted the scarlet brush just in time as Philip jumped off the bed, leaving her and her mother bouncing.

When he was outside the door, Maggie whispered to Ivy, "Gregory said he'd stay around tonight, so if Philip gives you any trouble—"

Ivy frowned. She had always been able to handle Philip much better than either her mother or Gregory could.

"—or if you start to feel, you know, under the weather . . ."

Ivy knew what her mother meant – depressed, crazy, suicidal. Maggie couldn't bring herself to say those words, but she had accepted what others told her about Ivy. There was no fighting it, so Ivy just ignored it. "It's nice of Andrew to help with Philip's schoolwork," she said.

"Andrew cares about both you and Philip," her mother replied. "I've been wanting to discuss this with you, Ivy, but with everything so, well, you know, in the last three weeks . . ."

"Spit it out, Mom."

"Andrew has filed adoption papers."

Ivy blobbed Scarlet Passion on her mother's knuckle. "You're kidding."

"We're going ahead with it for Philip," her mother said, wiping the knuckle off. "But you'll be eighteen soon. It's up to you to decide what you'd like to do."

Ivy didn't know what to say. She wondered if Gregory knew about this, and if he did, what he thought about it. Now his father would have two sons, and it was becoming more and more obvious that Andrew preferred Philip.

"Andrew wants you to know that you will always have a home here. We love you very much, Ivy. No one could love you more." Her mother spoke quickly and nervously. "Day by day, it's going to get better for you. It really will, honey. People fall in love more than once," Maggie went on, talking faster and faster. "Someday you'll meet someone special. You'll be happy again. Please believe me," she pleaded.

Ivy capped the bottle of polish. When she stood up, her mother remained sitting on the bed, looking up at Ivy with a concerned expression, her red fingernails spread out on her lap. Ivy leaned down and kissed her mother gently on the forehead, where all the lines of worry were. "It's already getting better," she said. "Come on, let me blast those beauties with the hair dryer."

After Maggie and Andrew left, Ivy settled down on the couch in the family room to watch *X-men* heroics. She stuck a pillow behind her head and propped her feet up on the stool that her brother was leaning against. Ella jumped up and stretched out on Ivy's long legs, resting a furry chin on Ivy's knee.

Elizabeth Chandler

Ivy petted the cat absentmindedly. Tired from her nonstop performance over the last few days, her cheerful effort to prove to everyone that she was okay, she felt her eyelids getting heavy. As Wolverine made his first appearance, Ivy was asleep.

Scenes from school ran together in a constantly shifting dream, with Ms. Bryce's pie face, her probing little counselor eyes, fading in and out. Ivy was in the classroom, then the school halls – walking down endless school halls. Teachers and kids were lined up on the sides watching her.

"I'm okay. I'm happy. I'm okay. I'm happy," she said over and over.

Outside the school, a storm was brewing. She could hear it through the walls, she could feel the walls shaking. Now she could see it, the fresh green leaves of May being torn off the trees, branches whipping back and forth against the inky sky.

She was driving now, not walking. The wind rocked her car, and lightning split the sky. She knew she was lost. A feeling of dread began to grow in her. She didn't know where she was going, yet the dread grew as if she were getting closer and closer to something terrible. Suddenly a red Harley came around the bend. The motorcyclist slowed down. For a moment she thought he'd stop to help her, but he sped by. She drove around the bend in the road and saw the window.

She knew that window, the great glass rectangle

with a dark shadow behind it. The car picked up speed. She was rushing toward the window. She tried to stop, tried to brake, pressed the pedal down again and again, but the car would not stop. It would not slow down! Then the door opened, and Ivy rolled out. She staggered. She could hardly hold herself up. She thought she'd fall into the great glass window.

A train whistle sounded, long and piercing. A dark shadow loomed larger and larger behind the glass. Ivy reached out with one hand. The glass exploded – a train burst through it. For a moment time froze, the flying glass hanging in the air like icicles, the huge train motionless, pausing before it slammed her to her death.

Then hands pulled her back. The train rushed by, and the shards of glass melted into the ground. The storm had passed, though it was still dark – the kind of sky one sees just before dawn. Ivy wondered whose hands had pulled her back; they were as strong as an angel's. Looking down, she found she was holding on to Philip.

She marveled at the peacefulness surrounding them now. Perhaps it really was dawn – she saw a faint glimmer of light. The light grew stronger. It became as long as a person, and its edges shimmered with colors. It wasn't the sun, though it warmed her heart to see it. It circled Philip and her, coming closer and closer.

"Who's there?" Ivy asked. "Who's there?" She wasn't afraid. For the first time in a long while, she felt full of hope. "Who's there?" she cried out, wanting to hold on to that hope.

"Gregory." He shook her awake. He rocked Ivy hard. "It's Gregory!"

He was sitting next to her on the couch, gripping her arms. Philip stood by her other side, clutching the DVD remote.

"You were dreaming again," Gregory said. His body was tense. His eyes searched hers. "I thought the dreams were over. It's been three weeks – I was hoping . . ."

Ivy shut her eyes for a moment. She wanted to see the light, the shimmering again. She wanted to get away from Gregory and back to the feeling of a powerful hope. His words ate away at the edges of it.

"What?" he asked her. "What is it, Ivy?"

She didn't answer him.

"Talk to me!" he said. "Please." His voice had softened to a plea. "Why are you looking that way? Was there something new in the dream?"

"No." She saw the doubt in his eyes. "Just at the beginning," she added quickly. "Before I was driving through the storm, I was walking down the halls at school, and everyone was staring at me."

"Staring," he repeated. "That's all?"

She nodded.

"I guess it's been hard for you the last few days," Gregory said, gently touching her cheek with his finger.

Ivy wished he would leave her alone. With each moment she spent near him, the dream's light and its feeling of hope faded.

"I know it's hard facing all the gossip at school," Gregory added, his voice full of sympathy.

Ivy didn't want to hear it. If she could find hope again, she didn't need his or anybody's sympathy. She closed her eyes, wishing she could block him out, but she could feel him staring at her, just like the others.

"I'm surprised your, uh, experience at the train station wasn't part of your dream," he said.

"Me too," she replied, opening her eyes, wondering if he knew she was holding back. "I'm fine, Gregory, really. Go back to whatever you were doing."

Ivy couldn't explain why she held back, except that the light seemed to be growing weaker and weaker in Gregory's presence.

"I was fixing a snack," he said. "You want anything?"

"No, thanks."

Gregory nodded and left the room, still looking concerned. Ivy waited till she heard him banging around in the kitchen, then dropped down on the floor next to her brother, who was watching the movie again.

"Philip," she said softly, "the night at the train station, after you saved me, was there some kind of shimmering light?"

Philip turned to her, his eyes wide. "You're remembering!"

"Shhh." Ivy glanced in the direction of the kitchen, listening to Gregory's movements. Then she sat back against the stool and tried to sort out the images in her mind. She saw the light from her dream as if it were in the train station, on the platform, not far from Philip and her. Had she made that up, or was she finally remembering?

"What did the light do?" she asked her brother. "Did it move?"

Philip thought for a moment. "He was walking around us, like in a circle."

"That's how it was in my dream," Ivy said. Then she turned her head and quickly put her finger to her lips.

When Gregory entered a minute later, Philip and she were sitting side by side, watching the movie intently.

"I thought some tea might help you calm down," Gregory said, crouching down next to her, handing her a warm mug. He handed Philip a Yoo-hoo.

"Hey, thanks," Philip said happily.

Gregory nodded and glanced back at Ivy. "Don't you want it?"

"Uh, sure. I — it's fine — great," she stammered, surprised by the double image that had just flashed before her eyes: Gregory as he was now and Gregory standing in her bedroom. When she took the drink from Gregory's hands, she saw him handing her another cup of steaming tea. Then she saw him as if he were sitting close to her, sitting on her bed and holding the cup to her lips, urging her to drink.

"Would you rather have something else?" Gregory asked.

"No, this is fine." Was she remembering that night? Could Gregory have given her drugged tea?

"You look pale," he said, and touched her bare arm. "You're ice cold, Ivy."

Her arm was covered with goose bumps. He ran his hand up and down it. Ivy became aware of just how strong his fingers were. Gregory had held her many times since Tristan's death, but for the first time Ivy noticed the power in his grip. He was staring beyond her now, at the television screen, at a fight scene.

"Gregory, you're hurting my arm."

He released her quickly and sat back on his heels to look at her. It was impossible to read the thoughts behind his light gray eyes.

"You still seem upset," he observed.

"Just tired," Ivy replied. "I'm tired of people

481

watching me, waiting for . . . for I don't know what."

"Waiting for you to crack up?" he suggested softly.

"I guess so," she said. But I won't, she thought. And I haven't yet, despite what you or anyone thinks.

"Thanks for the tea," she said. "I'm feeling better. I think I'll sit awhile with Philip and watch these guys become superhero punchboys."

One side of Gregory's mouth drew up a little.

"Thanks," Ivy repeated. "I don't know what I'd do without you."

He rested his hand on top of hers for a moment, then left her and Philip to watch the video. As soon as Ivy heard him climb the steps, she poured her tea into a potted plant. Philip was too engrossed in the film to notice.

Ivy sat back on the sofa and closed her eyes, trying to remember what the light was like, trying to hold on to the glimmer of hope her dream had given her.

Could it be true? Had Philip been seeing him all along? Was an angel there for her? Her eyes tingled with tears. Was it Tristan?

"Tristan?" Ivy called softly, and shivered with excitement. She had hidden in the school locker room on Thursday afternoon, waiting till the swimming pool was empty and the coach had left for a faculty meeting. Then, fully dressed, she had slipped off her shoes and climbed the thin silver ladder. Now she stood on the board high above the pool, just as she had the previous April.

Though Ivy could swim now, some of the old fear remained. She took three steps forward and felt the board flex beneath her. Gritting her teeth, Ivy stared down at the aqua water, streaked and spangled by the fluorescent lights. She would never love the water the way Tristan had, but this was where he had first reached out to her. This was where she had to try to reach back to him.

"Tristan?" she called softly.

The only sound was the steady buzzing of the fluorescent lights.

Angels, help me! Help me reach him.

Ivy didn't say the words out loud. After Tristan's death, she had stopped praying to her angels. After losing him, she couldn't find the words; she couldn't believe they would be heard. But this prayer felt as if it were burning its way out of her heart.

She took two more steps forward. "Tristan!" she cried out loud. "Are you there?"

She walked to the end of board and stood with her toes at the very edge. "Tristan, where are you?" Her voice echoed back from the concrete walls. "I love you!" she cried. "I love you!"

Ivy dropped her head. He wasn't there. He

couldn't hear her. She should get down before someone caught her up there, acting crazy.

Ivy took a step back from the edge. Watching her feet, she slowly and carefully turned around on the board. When she looked up, she gasped.

At the other end of the board, the air shimmered. It was like liquid light – a gold stem burning in the rough shape of a person. The glowing shape was surrounded by a mist of sheer and trembling colors. This was what she had seen at the train station.

"Tristan," she said softly. She reached out her hand and started walking toward him. She longed to be enveloped by his golden light, surrounded by the colors, embraced by all that Tristan was now.

"Tell me it's you. Speak to me," she begged. "Tristan!"

"Ivy!"

"Ivy!"

The two voices slammed off the walls – Gregory's and Suzanne's.

"Ivy, what are you doing up there?"

"She's cracking up, Gregory! I was afraid this would happen."

Ivy looked down and saw Gregory already two steps up the ladder and Suzanne looking about frantically. "I'll get help," Suzanne said. "I'll go get Ms. Bryce."

"Wait," Gregory said.

"But, Gregory, she's—"

"Wait." It was a command. Suzanne fell silent.

"There are enough stories about Ivy going around already. We can handle her ourselves."

Handle her? Ivy repeated silently. They were talking about her as if she were a mischievous child or maybe a crazy girl who couldn't take care of herself.

"I'll get her down," Gregory said calmly.

"I'll get myself down," Ivy said. "If I need any help, Tristan is here."

"I told you – she's gone, Gregory! Totally nuts! Don't you see—"

"Suzanne," Ivy shouted down at her, "can't you see his light?"

Now Gregory was scrambling up the ladder.

"There's nothing there, Ivy. Nothing," Suzanne moaned.

"Look," Ivy said, and pointed. "Right there!" Then she stared across the board at Gregory, who had pulled himself up on it. Suzanne was right. There was nothing there, no shimmering colors, no golden light.

"Tristan?"

"Gregory," he said in a hoarse whisper, then he held out his hand.

Ivy looked to either side of her. Was she going crazy? Had she had imagined it all? "Tristan?"

"That's enough, Ivy. Come down now."

She didn't want to go with him. She longed to go back to the golden light, to be surrounded by it again. She'd give anything to be held inside that moment with Tristan.

"Come here, Ivy. Don't make this difficult."

Ivy hated his patronizing tone.

"Come on!" Gregory ordered. "Do you want me to get Ms. Bryce?"

She glared at him, but she knew she couldn't fight him. "No," Ivy said at last. "I can get down by myself. Go ahead. Go ahead! I'll follow you."

"Good girl," Gregory said, then descended the ladder. Ivy walked to the end of the board and turned around. She was about to back down the first step when Suzanne called out, "Will! Over here! Hurry."

"Be quiet, Suzanne," Gregory said.

But Will, who had just come into the pool area, saw Ivy up on the board and ran toward Gregory and Suzanne. "Beth said you were looking for her," he said to them breathlessly. "Is she okay? What was she trying to do?"

The resentment burning in Ivy now flared into anger.

She. Her. They were talking about her as if she couldn't hear them, as if she couldn't understand.

"She and her are right here!" Ivy shouted down at them. "You don't have to talk about me as though my mind has gone."

"She thinks Tristan's up there and is going to help her," Suzanne told Will. "She said something about Tristan's light."

With that, Will gazed up at Ivy. Ivy glared down at him. Her furious stare was met with a look of wonder. His eyes traveled along the board behind her, searching. He glanced quickly around the pool, then up at her again. She saw the word "Tristan" on his lips, though he did not speak it aloud. At last he asked her, "Can you get down all right?"

"Of course I can."

Gregory and Suzanne stood on either side of the ladder as she climbed down, as if they might have to catch her. Will stood apart from them and continued to glance around the pool.

When Ivy reached the bottom, Suzanne hugged her, then held her at arm's length. "Girl, I could just shake you, shake you." She was laughing, but Ivy saw the tears in her friend's eyes and the relief in her face.

Gregory stepped in then and put his arms around Ivy, pulling her close. "You scared me, Ivy," he said. Ivy could barely breathe and tried to pull back, but he wouldn't let go.

Suzanne laid a hand on Gregory's arm. She was over her scare now and did not look happy about the long embrace. Will kept his distance, saying nothing.

"I'll take you home," Gregory said, freeing Ivy at last.

"No, I'm fine," she protested.

"I want to."

"Really, Gregory, I'd rather—"

"Am I supposed to walk?" Suzanne interrupted.

Gregory turned to her. "I'll take you first, Suzanne, and then—"

"But I'm all right," Ivy insisted.

"She's all right," Suzanne echoed. "She is, I can tell. And we had plans."

"Suzanne, after what just happened, you can't expect me to leave Ivy alone. If Maggie's at home, then we can—"

"Could I give you a ride home, Ivy?" Will cut in.

"Yes. Thanks," she replied.

Gregory looked irritated.

Suzanne smiled. "Well, then, big brother," she said, putting her arm around Gregory, "it's all worked out. You have nothing to worry about."

"You'll stay with her?" Gregory asked Will. "You'll take care of her until Maggie gets home?"

"Sure." Will glanced up at the diving board. "Either I will or Tristan will," he added.

Ivy cocked her head at him. Suzanne giggled, then covered her mouth with her hand. Gregory didn't crack a smile.

34

"Oh, hi!" Beth said a few minutes later, looking up to see Ivy and Will. She was sitting against Ivy's locker, pencil in hand, looking as if she had been busily writing a story. But when Ivy glanced down at Beth's notebook, she knew better.

"If you write that way, you're going to have the end of the story at the beginning," Ivy said, leaning down and turning the notebook around.

Will laughed lightly, and Beth blushed.

"I guess I'm not much of an actress," she said, standing up. "You okay?"

Ivy shrugged. "I don't know how to answer that question anymore – and when I do, no one believes me anyway."

"She's okay," Will said, laying his hand on Beth's shoulder, reassuring her. Oddly enough, his confident tone reassured Ivy too.

She gathered her books, and the three of them headed out to the parking lot. Beth walked between Ivy and Will, keeping the conversation going. But a few minutes later, when Beth drove off, Ivy and Will fell into an uncomfortable silence. Ivy climbed into his silver Prius and kept her eyes straight ahead. As they headed toward her house the only thing he asked was whether she wanted the windows up.

Since the party Will had been avoiding Ivy at school. She figured he was probably embarrassed about their strange conversation on the dance floor. And she was grateful to him for swallowing his pride enough to get her out of a jam with Gregory and Suzanne.

"Thanks again," Ivy said.

"No problem," Will replied, adjusting the sun visor.

Ivy wondered why he didn't ask for an explanation of what she had been doing up on the diving board. Maybe he just assumed it was what crazy people did. As he drove he kept his eyes on the traffic. When they stopped at an intersection, Will seemed unusually attentive to the people crossing in front of the car. Then he stole a sidelong glance at her.

"That was a joke, wasn't it?" Ivy blurted out. "When you told Gregory that you'd take care of me – or Tristan would – you were just making a joke."

The light changed, and Will drove a block before answering. "Gregory didn't laugh," he observed.

"Were you making a joke?" Ivy persisted, twisting around in her seat.

"What do you think?"

"What does it matter what I think?" Ivy exploded. "I'm the crazy girl who tried to kill herself."

Will turned the wheel suddenly and pulled over to the side of the road. "I don't believe that," he said quietly.

"Well, everyone else does."

He kept the motor running and rested his arms on the wheel. Ivy studied the flecks of paint on his hands. "Some people may have bought the rumors," he said, "but I'm surprised you would."

She didn't say anything.

"It seems to me" – his voice was calm and reasonable – "that *really* crazy people don't think they're crazy. Why would you?"

"Well, there is that little story about my showing up at a train station," Ivy replied, unable to stop the sarcasm in her voice, "just before the late-night express rushed through."

He turned to her, his dark eyes challenging her.

"Do you remember driving yourself there? Do you remember planning to jump in front of the train?"

Ivy shook her head. "No. None of that. I only remember the light afterward. The shimmering."

"Which is what you saw up on the diving board."

She nodded.

"I wonder why you see him and I hear him," Will said.

"You hear him?" Ivy reached over and switched off the motor. "You hear him?"

"So does Beth."

Ivy's mouth dropped open.

"She writes stories with messages that aren't hers. I draw angels I don't mean to draw." He drew an invisible image on the windshield. "We both thought we were losing it."

Ivy remembered the day at the electronics store, when Beth had typed on a computer: "Be careful, Ivy. It's dangerous, Ivy. Don't stay alone. Love you. Tristan." Ivy had run from the shop, furious at Beth for playing that trick. But she should have listened. Days later, she had been attacked at the house.

"He's warning you," Will continued. "Beth thinks it's something bigger than any of us can handle on our own, and she's scared to death."

Ivy felt the skin prickle on the back of her neck. Since the evening before, all she had thought about was reaching out toward the light that she believed was Tristan. She'd avoided the frightening question about why an angelic Tristan might be trying to reach her.

"You have to remember what happened," Will went on. "That's what Tristan was trying to tell you the night of the party, when we were dancing."

"He was with you then?" In her mind Ivy began to run through all the strange events of the past summer. "So the angels you drew, and that picture of an angel who looked like Tristan—"

"I was as amazed as you," Will said. "I tried to tell you, I'd never do something like that to hurt you. But I didn't know how to explain what happened. He got inside me. It was as if all I could do was draw those angels. My hands hardly felt like my own."

She reached over and laid her hand on his.

"I think he meant to comfort you," Will added.

Ivy nodded and blinked back tears. "I'm sorry I didn't understand then. I'm sorry I got so angry at you." She took a deep breath. "I have to remember. I have to go back to that night. Will, would you take me to the train station?"

He started the car immediately.

When they arrived, several people had just gotten off a commuter train from New York City. Will parked the car as the station emptied out. Then he walked with Ivy as far as the steps to the southbound platform. "I'm not going to say anything more," he said. "It's probably best if you poke around on your own and see what comes to you. But I'll be right here if you need me."

Ivy nodded, then climbed the steps. From the police report she knew which pillar Philip had found her leaning against – propped up against, she corrected herself: the one labeled D. But she had forgotten how close the metal pillars were to the edge of the platform and how close the platform was to the track. When she saw it, her stomach lurched.

She knew she should stand with her back against the pillar and try to remember how it had been that night, but she couldn't do it, not yet. She hurried along the platform to the steps that led to the bridge over the tracks. Then she crossed the bridge to the other side. From the northbound platform, Ivy looked back at Will, who was sitting on a bench, waiting patiently for her.

She began to pace around. Who could have been there that night? If Philip's story was true, someone had dressed up like Tristan. Almost anyone could have gotten their hands on a school jacket and baseball cap. And wearing them half in the shadows, anyone could have looked like Tristan – including Gregory.

She backed away quickly from that thought. She was getting paranoid, suspecting Gregory. But maybe it wasn't so paranoid to imagine Eric doing it. She remembered the night he had drawn Will onto the railroad bridge just before a train came. Eric got his kicks out of dangerous games. And Eric definitely had access to drugs.

A long, shrill sound broke in on Ivy's thoughts, a whistle from a train headed south, echoing against the steep wall of the ridge. She looked back over her shoulder at the rocky hillside. It seemed impossible that Philip could have made it down safely, but maybe if angels were real, if Tristan was there . . .

The whistle sounded again. Ivy started to run. She took the steps two at a time, then raced across the bridge and down the other side. She could hear the rumbling of the train before she saw its headlight, a pale, blind eye in the daytime. It was one of the big Amtraks that would rush straight through.

She ran to the pillar and stood with her back to it, close to the edge, transfixed by the train's white eye. Her heart beat faster and faster as the train sped toward her. She remembered Philip's old story about a train climbing up the hill – a train that was seeking her. It thundered toward her now, its lines sparking, the platform beneath her vibrating. She felt as if her shaking body would fly apart.

Then the train blew by her in one long blur.

Ivy didn't know how long he had been standing there, close behind her, letting her knot her fingers in his. She turned her head sideways, looking at Will over her shoulder.

"I'm glad you didn't jump," he said with a half smile. "We both would have gone."

Ivy loosened her fingers and turned to face him.

"Do you remember now?" Will asked.

She shook her head wearily. "No."

Will lifted his arm as if he might touch her cheek. She looked up at him, and he pulled his hand back quickly, digging it into his pocket. "Let's get out of here," he said.

Ivy followed him to the car, continually glancing back at the tracks.

What if Gregory and Eric had worked together? she thought. But she still couldn't believe that anybody, least of all Gregory, would want to hurt her. He cared about her – she'd thought he cared deeply.

They drove out of the parking lot silently, Will apparently as deep in thought as she. Then Ivy sat up quickly and pointed. About fifty yards past the exit, a red Harley was parked on the side of the road. "It looks like Eric's," she said.

"It is."

A long drainage ditch with high grass and shrubs bordered the road. Eric was searching the ditch and was so intent on his task that he didn't notice the car pulling over on the road's shoulder.

When Will opened the door, Eric's head bobbed

up. "Lose something?" Will asked, stepping out. "Need some help looking?"

Eric screened his eyes against the slant of the sun. "No, thanks, Will," he called back. "I'm just trying to find an old bungee cord I use to tie things down." Then he noticed Ivy in the car. He seemed startled, glancing from her to Will and back again. He waved them on. "I'm giving up in a minute," he said.

Will nodded and got back into the car.

"He was looking awfully hard for an old bungee cord," Ivy remarked as they drove away.

"Ivy," Will said, "is there any reason why somebody would want to scare you or hurt you?"

"What do you mean?"

"Is anyone holding a grudge against you?"

"No," she replied slowly. There isn't anyone now, she thought. The past winter had been a different story: Gregory hadn't been at all happy about his father's marriage to Maggie. But his resentment and anger had disappeared months ago, she reminded herself quickly. Gregory had been wonderful to her since Tristan died, comforting her, even rescuing her the day of the break-in. It was Gregory who had gotten there first, scaring off the intruder, pulling the bag off her head just when Will arrived.

Or had he? Maybe he had been there all along. His excuse for returning home that day had been an odd one. Suddenly Ivy felt cold all over. What if Gregory himself had attacked her, then changed plans when Will showed up?

The thought ran through her like an icy river, and her scalp and the skin on the back of her neck crawled. Ivy twisted her hands. Without realizing it, she bent a pen she had picked up from the car seat, cracking its plastic shell.

"Here," Will said, taking the pen away from her and offering her his hand. "I'll need my fingers back when we get to your house," he said, smiling, "but for now you won't get ink all over you."

Ivy gripped his hand. She held on tightly to Will and turned her head to watch bright patches of green flickering past them, the end of summer spliced with sharp shadows of fall.

"I've always been there for you. I love you." The words floated back to her. "Will, when we were dancing and Tristan was inside you, and you said—" She hesitated.

"And I said . . .?"

"I've always been there for you. I love you." She saw Will swallow hard. "It was Tristan speaking, right?" Ivy said. "It was just Tristan saying that, and I misunderstood. Right?"

Will watched a wishbone of geese flying across the sky. "Right," he said at last.

Neither of them spoke the rest of the way home.

35

Ivy stood next to Philip in his room, surveying a bookcase full of treasures: the angel statues she had given him after Tristan died, a stand-up paper doll of Derek Jeter, fossils from Andrew, and a rusty railroad spike.

Philip and Maggie had arrived home that afternoon just as Will was dropping off Ivy. After Ivy and Philip shared a snack, she'd scooped up his schoolbooks while he carefully carried his newest treasure, a moldy bird's nest, up to his room. Ivy watched him install the nest in a place of honor, then she ran her hand down the line of angel statues. She touched one that wasn't her own, an angel in a baseball uniform with wings.

"That's the statue Tristan's friend brought me," Philip told her. "I mean the girl angel. I've seen her a couple of times."

"You've seen another angel? Are you sure?" Ivy asked, surprised.

Philip nodded. "She came to our big party."

"How can you tell her apart from Tristan?" Ivy wondered.

Philip thought for a moment. "Her colors are more purplish."

"How do you know she's a girl?"

"She's shaped like one," he said.

"Oh."

"Like a girl your age," he added. From beneath a stack of comic books, Philip dug out the photograph with a strange pale blur in it that Will had taken of them at the arts festival.

Philip studied it and frowned. "I guess you can't see as much here," he said.

See as much what? Ivy wondered silently.

"Do you really want just your water angel back?" Philip asked.

Ivy knew he wanted to keep all the statues. "Just her," she assured him, then carried the porcelain angel into her own room. This was the statue Ivy loved most. Its swirling blue-green robe had prompted her to name it after the angel she had seen when she was four, the angel who had saved her from drowning. Ivy set the statue next to Tristan's picture, running her hand over the angel's smooth glazed surface. Then she touched Tristan's photo.

"Two angels – my two angels," she said, then headed up to her third-floor music room.

Ella followed her and leaped up into the dormer window across from Ivy's piano. Ivy sat down and began to work through her scales, sending out ripples of music. As her hands moved up and down the keyboard, she thought about Tristan, the way he'd looked when he swam, light scattered in the water drops around him, the way his light could shine around her now.

The late sunlight of September was a pure gold like his shimmer, and the sunset would have the same rim of colors. Ivy glanced toward the window and stopped playing abruptly. Ella was sitting up, her ears alert, her eyes big and shiny. Ivy turned quickly to look behind her. "Tristan," she said softly.

The glow surrounded her.

"Tristan," she whispered again. "Talk to me. Why can't I hear you? The others hear you – Will and Beth. Can't you speak to me?"

But the only sound was the light thump of Ella leaping down from her perch and trotting over to her. Ivy wondered if the cat could see Tristan.

"Yes, she saw me the first time I came."

Ivy was stunned by his voice. "It's you. You really are—"

"Amazing, isn't it?"

Within herself, Ivy could hear not only his voice

501

but also the laughter in it. He sounded just as he always had when something amused him. Then the laughing ceased.

"Ivy, I love you. I'll never stop loving you."

Ivy laid her face down in her hands. Her palms and fingers were bathed in pale golden light. "I love you, Tristan, and I've missed you. You don't know how much I've missed you."

"You don't know how often I've been with you, watching you sleep, listening to you play. It was like last winter all over again, waiting and wanting, hoping you'd notice me."

The yearning in his voice made Ivy quiver inside, the way his kisses once had.

"If I'd had the right angelic powers, I would have thrown some broccoli and carrots at you," he added, laughing.

Ivy laughed, too, remembering the tray of vegetables he'd overturned at her mother's wedding.

"It was the celery in your ears and the shrimp tails up your nose that made you irresistible to both Philip and me," she said, smiling. "Oh, Tristan, I wish we'd had this summer together. I wish we could have floated side by side in the center of the lake, letting the sun sparkle at our fingers and toes."

"All I want is to be close to you," Tristan told her.

Ivy lifted her head. "I wish I could feel your arms around me."

"You couldn't get any closer to my heart than you are now."

Ivy held out her arms, then folded them around herself like closed wings. "I've wished a thousand times that I could tell you I love you. But I never believed, I just never believed I'd be given a chance—"

"You have to believe, Ivy!" She heard the fear in his voice ringing inside her. "Don't stop believing, or you'll stop seeing me. You need me now, in ways that you don't know," he warned.

"Because of Gregory," she said, dropping her hands in her lap. "I do know. I just don't understand why he would want to" – she backed away from the most terrifying thought – "to hurt me."

"To *kill* you," said Tristan. "Everything that Philip described about that night happened, only 'the bad angel' was Gregory. And it wasn't the first time, Ivy. When you were alone that weekend—"

"But it doesn't make sense," she cried, "not after all he's done for me." She jumped up from the piano bench and began to pace around the room. "After the accident, he was the only one who understood why I didn't want to talk about it."

"He didn't want you to think too much," Tristan replied. "He didn't want you to remember that night and start asking questions – such as whether our accident was an accident."

Ivy paused by the window. Three stories below

her, Philip was kicking a soccer ball. Andrew, coming up the driveway, had stopped the car to watch. Her mother was walking across the grass toward him.

"It wasn't an accident," she said at last. She remembered her nightmare: she was in Tristan's car, and she couldn't stop – just like the night they'd hit the deer and couldn't stop. "Someone fooled with the brakes."

"It looks that way."

Ivy felt sick to her stomach at just the thought of Gregory touching her, kissing her, holding her close, close enough to kill her when the chance arose. She didn't want to believe it. "Why?" she cried.

"I think it goes back to the night of Caroline's murder."

Ivy walked back to the piano and sat down slowly, trying to sort things out. "You mean he blames me for his mother's – his mother's *murder?* It was suicide, Tristan." But as she said it she could feel a numbness in her chest and throat, a growing fear that threatened to shut down every reasonable thought.

"You were at the house next door on the night she died," Tristan told her. "I think you saw someone in the window, someone who knows what happened or was responsible for it. Try to remember."

Ivy struggled to separate her memory of the night from the nightmares that had followed. "All I could see was a shadow of a person. With all the reflections on the glass, I never saw who it was."

"But he saw you."

Bit by bit, the dream was unraveling. Ivy began to shake.

"I know," Tristan said gently. "I know."

Ivy longed to feel the touch that she had once felt when he spoke to her that way.

"I'm afraid, too," Tristan said. "I don't have the powers to protect you by myself. But believe me, Ivy, together we're stronger than he is."

"Oh, Tristan, I've missed you."

"I've missed you," he replied, "missed holding you, kissing you, making you mad . . ."

She laughed.

"Ivy, play for me."

"Don't – don't ask me that now. I just want to keep hearing your voice," she pleaded. "I thought I had lost you forever, but now you're here—"

"Shhh, Ivy. Play. I heard a noise. Someone's in your bedroom."

Ivy glanced at Ella, who stood at the top of the steps now, peering down into the darkness. The cat crept quietly down the stairs, her tail bristling. It's Gregory, Ivy thought.

She nervously opened a book and began to play. Ivy played loudly, trying to blot out the memories of Gregory's embraces, his urgent kisses, the night they had been alone in the store and the night they had been alone in the darkened house.

Trying to kill her? Killing his mother? It didn't make sense. She could almost understand how Eric could do it, half crazed with drugs. She remembered the message she'd overheard on Gregory's phone; Eric was always in need of drug money. Maybe he had tried to get some from Caroline, and things went wrong. But what motive would Gregory have had for such a terrible thing?

"That's what I've been trying to figure out."

Ivy stopped playing for a moment. "You can hear me?" she asked silently.

"You don't cloak your thoughts as well as Will."

So he had heard everything she had just thought, including the part about the urgent kisses. Ivy began playing again, banging on the piano.

Tristan sounded as if he were shouting in her head. "I guess I shouldn't have been listening in, huh?"

She smiled and softened the music.

"Ivy, we need to be honest with each other. If we can't trust each other, who else can we depend on?"

"I love you. That's honest," Ivy said, speaking all her words silently now, so only Tristan could hear. She finished the song and was about to start another.

"He's gone," Tristan told her.

Ivy breathed a sigh of relief.

"Listen to me, Ivy. You've got to get out of here."

"Get out? What do you mean?" she asked.

"You have to get as far away from Gregory as you can."

"That's impossible," Ivy said. "I can't just get up and leave. I have nowhere to go."

"You'll find somewhere. And I'll ask Lacey — she's an angel — to stay near you. Until I can figure out what's going on and come up with some evidence to take to the police, you have to get away from here."

"No," Ivy said, pushing back the piano bench.

"Yes," he insisted. Then he told her about what he had learned from time-traveling through the minds of Gregory and Eric. He recounted the angry scene between Gregory and his mother, how Caroline had taunted him with a piece of paper, and how he'd shoved the floor lamp at her, cutting her face. Then Tristan told Ivy about the memory he had experienced in Eric's mind, the intense scene between him and Caroline, which had taken place on a stormy evening.

"You're right about Eric," Tristan concluded. "He needs drug money and he's involved. But I still don't know exactly what he's done for Gregory."

"Eric was searching the gully by the station today," Ivy said.

"He was? Then he took Gregory's threat seriously," Tristan replied, and recounted the argument he had overheard at the party. "I'll watch both of them. In the meantime, you need to get away."

"No," Ivy repeated.

"Yes, as soon as possible."

"No!" This time the voice leaped out of her. Tristan fell silent.

"I'm not leaving," she said, speaking within her mind again. Ivy walked to the window and gazed out at the old and windblown trees that topped the ridge, trees that had become familiar to her in the last six months. She had watched them change from a spring mist of red buds to dense, green leaves to delicate shapes traced with the gold of the evening sun – the color of autumn. This was her home, this was where the people she loved were. She wasn't going to be chased away. She wasn't going to leave Philip and Suzanne alone with Gregory.

"Suzanne doesn't know anything," Tristan said. "After you left with Will today, I followed her and Gregory. She's innocent – confused about you and totally hooked on him."

"Totally hooked on Gregory, and you want me to leave her?"

"She doesn't know enough to get herself in trouble," Tristan argued.

"If I run away," Ivy persisted, "how do we know

what he'll do? How do we know he won't go after Philip? Philip may not understand what he saw, but he saw things that night, things that won't make Gregory very happy."

Tristan was silent.

"I can't see you," Ivy said, "but I can guess what kind of a face you're making."

Then she heard him laugh, and she started laughing with him.

"Oh, Tristan, I know you love me and are afraid for me, but I can't leave them. Philip and Suzanne don't know that Gregory's dangerous. They won't be on guard around him."

He didn't reply.

"Are you there?" she asked after a long silence.

"Just thinking," he said.

"Then you're cloaking," she said. "You're keeping your thoughts from me."

Suddenly Ivy was rocked with feelings of love and tenderness. Then intense fear rushed through her, and anger, and wordless despair. She was swimming in a churning sea of emotions, and for a moment she couldn't breathe.

"Maybe I should have lifted just one corner of the cloak," Tristan remarked. "I have to leave you now, Ivy."

"No. Wait. When will I see you again?" she asked. "How will I find you?"

"Well, you don't have to stand on the end of a diving board."

Ivy smiled.

"The end of a tree limb will do," he said. "Or the roof of any building three stories or higher."

"What?"

"Just kidding," he said, laughing. "Just call – anytime, anywhere, silently – and I'll hear you. If I don't come, it's because I'm in the middle of something that I can't stop, or I'm in the darkness. I can't control the darkness." He sighed. "I can feel it coming on – I can feel it right now – and I can fight it off for a while. But in the end I fall unconscious. It's how I rest. I guess one day the darkness will be final."

"No!"

"Yes, love," he said softly.

A moment later he was gone.

The emptiness he left inside her was almost unbearable. Without his light, the room fell into blue shadow and Ivy felt lost in the twilight between two worlds. She fought against the doubts that began to creep in. She hadn't imagined this – Tristan was there, and Tristan would come back again.

She worked through some Bach pieces, playing them mechanically one after another, and had just closed her music books when her mother called up to her. Maggie's voice sounded funny, and when Ivy reached the bottom of the steps she saw why. Maggie was standing in front of Ivy's bureau; the water angel lay shattered at her feet.

"Honey, I'm sorry," her mother said.

Ivy walked over to the bureau and got down on her knees. There were a few large pieces, but the rest of the statue had splintered into small fragments. It could never be repaired.

"Philip must have left it here," Maggie said. "He must have put it too close to the edge. Please don't let this upset you, honey."

"I brought it in here myself, Mom. And it's nothing to get upset about. Accidents happen," she said, marveling at her own calmness. "Please don't blame yourself."

"But I didn't do it," Maggie replied quickly. "I walked in to call you for dinner and saw it lying here."

Hearing their voices, Philip stuck his head in the door. "Oh, no!" he wailed. "She broke!"

Gregory came into the room behind him. He looked at the statue, then shook his head, glancing over at the bed. "Ella," he said softly.

But Ivy knew who had done it. It was the same person who had shredded Andrew's expensive chair months ago – and it wasn't Ella. She wanted to charge across the room. She wanted to back Gregory against the wall. She wanted to make him admit it in front of the others. But she knew she had to play along. And she would – till she got him to confess that he had broken more things than porcelain angels.

36

"'Tis the Season, Ivy speaking. How can I help you?"

"Did you find out?"

"Suzanne! I told you not to call me at work unless it's an emergency. You know we have a Friday night special," Ivy said, and glanced toward the door, where two customers had just come in. Betty was home sick, and Lillian and Ivy had their hands full.

"This *is* an emergency," Suzanne insisted. "Did you find out who Gregory's going out with tonight?"

"I don't even know if he's got a date. I came here right after school, so I have nothing new to tell you since we talked at three o'clock."

Ivy wished Suzanne hadn't called. In the twenty-four hours since Tristan had visited her, she had been on the alert no matter where she was. At home, Gregory's bedroom door was right down the hall from hers. At school, she saw him all the time. It had been a relief to come to work: she felt safe among the crowd of customers and was glad not to think about Gregory, even if it was for only six hours.

"Well, you sure are a lousy detective," Suzanne said, her laughter breaking in on Ivy's thoughts. "As soon as you get home tonight, start snooping. Philip may know something. I want to know who and where, for how long, and what she wore."

"Listen, Suzanne," Ivy said, "I don't want to be the one carrying stories back and forth between you and Gregory. Even if I knew that Gregory was with somebody else tonight, I wouldn't feel right telling you that, any more than I'd feel right telling him that you're with Jeff."

"But you've got to tell him, Ivy!" Suzanne exclaimed. "That's the whole point! How is he going to get jealous if he doesn't know?"

Ivy silently shook her head and watched three young boys jabbing pencils into the store's seven-foot model of King Kong. "I've got customers, Suzanne. I've got to go."

"Did you hear what I said? I want to make Gregory incredibly jealous."

"We'll talk later, okay?"

"Outrageously jealous," Suzanne said. "So jealous, he can't see straight."

"We'll talk later," Ivy said, hanging up.

Each time she finished with a customer that evening, Ivy's thoughts drifted back to Suzanne. If Suzanne made Gregory outrageously jealous, would he hurt her? She wished Suzanne and Gregory would lose interest in each other, but this on-again off-again stuff was just the kind of thing to keep the fire burning.

If I tell Suzanne he's going out with a hundred different girls, Ivy thought, she'll want him all the more. If I criticize him, she'll just defend him and get mad at me.

At closing time Lillian sat down wearily on the stool behind the cash register. She shut her eyes for a moment.

"You okay?" Ivy asked. "You look pretty tired."

The old woman patted Ivy's hand. Her mother's diamond ring, a pink healing crystal, and a Star Trek communicator glittered on her gnarled fingers. "I'm fine, dear, fine. I'm nothing but old," she said.

"Why don't you rest a few minutes? I can do the receipts," Ivy told her, taking the pile away from the owner. After they closed up, Ivy planned to walk Lillian to her car. Once the customers left and the lights were dimmed, the cavernous mall would be filled with shadows and small rustlings. That night Ivy would be as glad as Lillian to have some company.

"I'm nothing but ancient," Lillian said with a sigh. "Ivy, would you do me a favor? Would you close up tonight?"

"Close up?" Ivy was caught by surprise. Stay by myself? she thought. "Sure."

Lillian got up from the stool and put on her sweater. "Come in late tomorrow, lovey," she said as she walked toward the door. "Betty should be on her feet again, and we'll be all right. You're a dear."

"It's no trouble," Ivy said softly as she watched Lillian disappear into the mall. She wondered where Tristan was, and if she should call him.

Don't be such a coward, Ivy chided herself, and turned to open the wall box where the light switches were. She hit the switches, dimming all the store's lights, then changed her mind and turned half of them back on again. Ivy glanced toward the dressing rooms at the back of the store. She fought the urge to double-check and make sure everyone was out. Don't be so paranoid, she told herself. But it wasn't hard to imagine someone lurking in a fitting room, and it wasn't hard to picture someone waiting for her in the shadows of the mall.

"I want everything in your cash box."

Ivy jumped at the sound of Eric's voice. His finger poked her in the back. Someone else laughed – Gregory.

She spun around to face both of them.

"Oh, sorry," Gregory said when he saw the look on her face. "We didn't mean to really scare you."

"I meant to," Eric said with a high-pitched laugh.

"We thought you'd be finishing up soon, so we stopped by," Gregory said, touching her on the elbow, his voice soft and easy.

"To get your cash before you put it in the safe," Eric interjected. "About how much do you have?"

"Ignore him," Gregory told Ivy.

"She does. She always has," Eric remarked, and started rifling through the shop's bins.

"We're just hanging out tonight," Gregory said. "Want to hang out with us?"

Ivy forced a smile and flipped through the store receipts. "Thanks, but I've got a lot to do."

"We'll wait."

She smiled again and shook her head.

"Come on, Ivy," Gregory urged. "You've hardly been out in the last three weeks. It'll be good for you."

"Will it?" Ivy looked up, gazing directly into Gregory's eyes. "You're always looking out for me."

"And I'll continue to," he replied, smiling at her. There wasn't a hint of what he was thinking behind his gray eyes and too-handsome face.

"Teeth!" Eric exclaimed. "Look at these blood-sucking teeth. This is cool." He ripped open a plastic package and stuck the vampire teeth in his mouth, grinning at Gregory. His skinny arms dangled by his sides, and his fingers danced with nervousness. Ivy thought about the way Gregory had applauded Eric the night his friend conned them at the railroad bridges. She wondered how far Eric would go to amuse Gregory and win his approval.

"It's an improvement, Eric," Gregory said, "and some girls get turned on by vampires." He gave Ivy a sly smile. "Don't they?"

Like the last time Gregory had come late to the shop, when he had dressed up as Dracula. Ivy remembered his insistent kisses and how she had given in to them. Now her skin grew warm, and she could feel herself flushing with anger. Her fingers curled into fists, which she quickly put behind her.

I can play this game as well as he can, she thought, and tilted back her head. "Some girls do."

Gregory stared at her neck, his eyes glimmering, then focused on her mouth, as if he wanted to kiss her again.

"Ivy, what in the world are you doing?"

The question stunned her. It was Tristan's voice. She hadn't been aware of him slipping inside her mind, yet clearly neither Eric nor Gregory had heard him speak. Ivy knew her face was red, and she quickly dropped her chin.

Gregory laughed. "You're blushing."

Ivy turned and walked away from him. But she couldn't get away from Tristan.

"You think he wants to kiss you?" Tristan asked scornfully. "Strangle you, maybe! Ivy, don't be stupid. These are tricks."

Silently she told Tristan, "I know what I'm doing."

Gregory followed her over to the counter and slid his hand around her waist.

"Gregory, please," she said.

"Please what?" he asked, his mouth close to her ear.

"Eric is here," she reminded him, and glanced over her shoulder. But Eric was on the other side of a rack, lost in a world of costumes.

"My mistake," Gregory said softly, "bringing Eric along."

"Get rid of Gregory," Tristan cut in. "Get rid of both of them and lock the door."

Ivy slid away from Gregory.

"Call security," Tristan continued. "Ask them to walk you to your car."

"Besides," Ivy said to Gregory, "there's Suzanne. You know Suzanne and I have been friends forever."

"Ivy!" Tristan exclaimed. "Don't you know anything about guys? You're setting yourself up. Now he's going to use one of those old excuses."

Ivy silently retorted, "I know what I'm doing."

"Suzanne is too easy," Gregory said, moving closer to Ivy. "Too jealous and too easy. I'm bored."

"I guess it's a lot more interesting," Tristan remarked, "to get it on with the girlfriend of the guy you murdered."

Ivy jerked her head as if she had been slapped.

"What's wrong?" Gregory asked her.

"Ivy, I'm sorry," Tristan said quickly, "but you're not listening to me. You don't seem to understand—"

"I understand, Tristan," Ivy thought angrily. "Leave me alone before I mess up."

"What are you thinking?" Gregory asked. "You're mad, I can tell." He smoothed her brow, then traced her cheek, his fingers lightly touching her neck. "You used to like it when I touched you," he said.

Ivy could feel Tristan's anger surging up inside her. She felt as if she was losing control. She closed her eyes, focused her attention, and pressed him out, out as far as she could from her mind.

When she opened her eyes Gregory was staring at her. "Out?" he said. "Were you talking to me?"

"Talking to you?" Ivy echoed. Terrific. She had spoken aloud. "No," she told Gregory, "I don't remember saying anything to you."

He frowned at her.

"But you know me," she said cheerfully, "I'm just a little crazy."

He continued to stare at her. "Maybe," he said.

Ivy smiled and moved past him. For the next fifteen minutes she paid attention to Eric, helping him find parts of costumes, while keeping one eye on the shop door, waiting for security to pass by. When the guard did and pointed to his watch, signaling that it was well past nine-thirty, she called out to him. Since the mall was officially closed, she asked him if he'd show Eric and Gregory a door where they could exit.

Then she locked the shop door behind them and leaned back against it, limp with relief. "I'm sorry, Tristan," she said, but she was pretty sure he didn't hear her.

Tristan watched Ivy, her head bent over the store receipts, her curly hair a web of gold under the one light that now shone over the desk at the cash register. The rest of the shop was dimly lit, its corners receding into darkness.

He wanted to touch her hair, to materialize his fingers and feel the softness of her skin. He wanted to talk to her, just talk to her. But he remained hidden, still angry, hurt by the way she had thrust him out of her mind.

Ivy raised her head suddenly and glanced around as if she sensed his presence. "Tristan?"

If he stayed outside of her, she wouldn't hear him. But what did he have to say to her? That he loved her. That she had hurt him. That he was terrified for her.

She saw him now. "Tristan." The way she said his name could still make him tremble. "I didn't think you'd come back. After putting you out like that, I didn't think you'd come to me."

Tristan stayed where he was.

"And you're not coming to me, are you?" she asked.

He heard the tremor in her voice and couldn't decide what to do. Leave her? Let her wonder for a while. He didn't want to fight, and he had work to do that night.

If only you knew how much I love you, he thought.

"Tristan," she said silently.

He was in her mind now and knew the thought they had shared: If only you knew how much I love you.

Ivy was crying.

"Don't. Please don't," he said.

"Try to understand," she begged him silently. "I gave my heart to you, but it's still mine. You can't just come in and take over. I have my own thoughts, Tristan, and my own way of doing things."

"You've always had your own thoughts and your own way of doing things," he said. Then he laughed in spite of himself. "I remember how you were leading your guide around your very first day in our school – that's when I fell in love with you," he told her. "But you've got to understand, too. I'm afraid for you. What were you doing, Ivy, playing like that with Gregory?"

Ivy slid off the desk stool and walked toward a dark corner of the shop. Eric had left a pile of costumes on the floor. Tristan could feel their silky softness through Ivy's hands as she picked them up. "I'm playing Gregory's game," she said. "I'm playing the role he's given me – keeping him wondering and keeping him close."

"It's too dangerous, Ivy."

"No," she replied firmly. "Living in the same house with him and trying to avoid him – that would be dangerous. I can't hide from him, so the trick is never, ever to take my eyes off him." She picked up a glittering black mask and held it in front of her face.

"I have to know what he's doing and what he's saying," she continued. "I have to wait for him to slip up. As long as I'm here – and I told you, Tristan, I'm staying here – it's the only way."

"There's another way to keep track of him," Tristan said, "and to keep a person between you at the same time. Will is his friend. You could date Will."

There was a long silence, and Tristan could feel Ivy cloaking her thoughts from him. "No, that's not a good idea," she said at last.

"Why not?" His voice came out too sharply. He could feel her searching carefully for the right words.

"I don't want to get Will involved."

"But he already is," Tristan argued. "He knows about me. He took you to the train station to help you remember what happened."

"That's as far as it goes," Ivy said. "I don't want you to tell him anything else." She started sorting through the costumes, shaking them out, then folding them.

"You're protecting him," Tristan said.

"That's right."

"Why?" he asked.

"Why put someone else in danger?" she replied.

"Will would put himself in any kind of danger for you. He's in love with you." As soon as Tristan said it he wished that he hadn't.

But certainly Ivy had already figured that out. Maybe not, he thought suddenly. He felt her struggling. He was caught in a swirl of emotions that he couldn't understand. He knew she was confused.

"I don't think so," Ivy said. "Will's a friend, that's all."

Tristan didn't say anything.

"But if it is true, Tristan, then it's not fair to use him like that. It'd be leading him on."

Would it really? Tristan wondered. Maybe Ivy was afraid to admit her attraction to Will.

"What are you thinking? What are you cloaking?" Ivy asked.

"I'm wondering if you're being honest with yourself."

Ivy walked briskly across the shop, as if she could walk away from him, hanging up the costumes, tossing misplaced objects into their bins. "I don't know why you think the way you do. It's almost as if you're jealous," she said.

"I am," he replied.

"You're what?" Her voice sounded frustrated.

"Jealous." There was no point in trying to hide it, Tristan thought.

"Who said that?" Ivy demanded.

"Who said what?" Tristan asked.

"Who said what?" a female voice echoed, the same voice that had sounded frustrated a moment ago.

"Lacey!" Tristan exclaimed. He hadn't seen her come in.

"Yes, sweetie?" Lacey was projecting her voice so Ivy could hear it, too. Ivy glanced around the room.

"This is a private conversation," Tristan said.

"Well, her half was private," Lacey replied, still projecting her voice. "When your chick speaks inwardly, I can hear only your part. Talk about frustrating! This year's romantic smash, and I'm missing half the dialogue. Ask your chick to speak out loud, okay?"

"Your chick?" Ivy repeated aloud.

"That's better," said Lacey.

"Is she that purplish blob?" Ivy asked.

"*Ex-cuuuse* me?" Lacey said.

Tristan could feel a headache coming on. "Yes, that's her," he told Ivy.

"A blob?" Lacey spit out the word.

"That's how you look to Ivy," Tristan said. "You know that."

"How does she look to you?" Ivy asked Tristan. He hesitated.

"Yes, tell us both, how do I look to you?" Lacey asked.

Tristan tried to think of an objective description. "Like . . . five foot something . . . with brown eyes, I think . . . and a roundish nose, and sort of thick hair."

"Good job, Tristan," Lacey remarked. "You've just described a bear." To Ivy she said, "I'm Lacey Lovitt. Now I'm sure you can picture me."

Tristan could feel Ivy's mind searching, trying to remember who Lacey Lovitt was.

"The country-western star?"

A plastic turkey was hurled across the room.

"And to think I *bothered* to come back to warn the chick."

"Why does she keep calling me the chick?"

"I guess it's movie star talk," Tristan said wearily.

"You were a movie star?" Ivy bent down to pick

up the thrown turkey. "So you're pretty," Ivy said quietly.

"Ask Tristan," said Lacey.

"Is she?"

Tristan felt trapped. "I'm not a good judge of those things."

"Oh, I see," Ivy and Lacey said at the exact same time, both of them sounding irritated. Ivy paced one way, Lacey the other.

"How did you throw this, Lacey Lovitt?" Ivy asked, squeaking the turkey. "Can Tristan do it?"

Lacey snickered. "Not with any kind of aim," she said. "He's still learning to materialize his fingers, to make himself solid. He's got a lot to learn. Luckily he's got me as a teacher."

She moved closer to Ivy. Tristan could feel Ivy tingle when she felt Lacey's fingers resting lightly on her skin. Through Ivy's eyes he saw the long purple nails slowly appear on her arm.

"When Tristan slips back out of your mind," Lacey said, "he'll look and feel solid to me. But unless he materializes himself, like I just did, he'll be just a glow to you. It takes a lot of energy to materialize. He's getting stronger, but if he uses up too much energy, he'll fall into the darkness."

"He'll look and feel solid to you?" Ivy repeated.

"He can hold my hand, see my face," Lacey said. "He can – well, you know."

Tristan could feel Ivy prickling.

"But he hasn't," Lacey said bluntly. "He's *totally* hung up on you." She picked up a hat and spun it on a fingertip, lifting it above her head. To Ivy she looked like a lavender mist with a mysteriously spinning top hat. "You know, I could have a lot of fun haunting this place. I could get the old ladies some real publicity come Halloween."

"Don't even think about it," Tristan said.

"Forgive me if I forget that you said that," Lacey told him. "Anyway, I'm here to give you the skinny. Gregory's picked up some new drugs."

"When?" Tristan asked quickly.

"Tonight, just before he got here," Lacey replied, then said to Ivy, "Be careful what you eat. Be careful what you drink. Don't make it easy for him."

Ivy shivered.

"Thanks, Lacey," Tristan said. "I owe you – even though you did sneak in and listen to what was none of your business."

"Yeah, yeah."

"I'm the one who owes you," Ivy said.

"That's right," Lacey snapped, "and for more than just that! For the last two and a half months I've had to listen to enough heaving and sighing over you to fill three volumes of bad love poetry. And I've got to tell you—"

"Lacey's never been in love," Tristan interrupted, "so she doesn't understand—"

"Excuse me? Excuse me?" Lacey challenged him. "Do you know that for a fact?"

Tristan laughed.

"As I was saying . . ." Lacey moved closer to Ivy. "I just don't know what he sees in you."

Ivy was stung into a moment of silence. At last she replied, "Well, I know what he sees in you."

"Oh, *puh-lease*."

Ivy laughed and picked up a top hat, spinning it on her own fingertip. "Tristan's always been a sucker for girls with their own way of doing things."

37

Tristan lay quietly, listening to Eric's breathing and conserving his own energy, watching the sky outside the bedroom window beginning to lighten. The numbers on Eric's clock radio glowed: it was 4:46. As soon as Eric showed signs of stirring, Tristan planned to slip inside his mind.

He had checked on Eric on Friday night, several hours after his visit to the mall, and Saturday night as well, after Eric came home from a drinking binge. Lacey had repeatedly warned Tristan about time-traveling in a mind confused by alcohol and bent by drugs. But it had been twenty-four hours since Eric's last beer, and Tristan was willing to take a chance to learn just what kind of dirty work Eric had done for Gregory.

He had lucked out when he arrived in Eric's room early Monday, discovering on one of his shelves an old book about trains. Materializing a finger, he had paged through the book, searching for a photo of a train that looked similar to those that ran through Stonehill's station. Now he watched Eric sleep, waiting for his chance to show him that picture and slip in on a shared thought. With a little more luck, he could ride the thought into a memory, the memory of the night Ivy had been drugged and taken to the station.

He waited patiently as the digital clock flashed the passing minutes. Eric's breathing was becoming shallow, and his legs grew restless – now was the time. Tristan nudged him awake. Eric saw the book on his pillow and pulled his head up sleepily, squinting at the picture.

Train, thought Tristan. Whistling. Slow down. Looks like an accident. Wasn't an accident. Gregory. Blew it. Chick, chick, chick, who wants to play chick, chick, chick?

Tristan ran through as many thoughts as he could that were related to the picture. He didn't know which thought was his ticket in, but he suddenly saw the photograph through Eric's half-closed eyes. Eric seemed just alert enough to take a suggestion. Tristan pictured as clearly as he could a baseball cap and school jacket, the ones that Gregory had worn that night, the ones that he had insisted Eric find.

Tristan felt Eric tense. For a moment he felt

suspended in timeless darkness, then he pitched forward with him, his fist glancing off something hard. He was swiftly thrown backward, making him lose his balance, then was pushed forward once more. Every muscle strained – Eric was fighting with someone. A sharp punch to his stomach made him lurch. Eric twisted his head around – Tristan twisted his – and saw his opponent: Gregory.

Tristan saw the road, too, as he spun with Eric one way, then the other, beneath Gregory's blows. He thought he was about thirty yards from the entrance to the train station. As he struggled with Gregory his feet kept slipping on small stones at the side of the road. Something sharp bit into his hand. Tristan realized suddenly that Eric was clinging to a set of keys.

"You dumb—ss." Tristan felt Eric's words slur in his mouth. "You can't drive my machine. You'll crash us and you'll kill us both. It'll be you, me, and Tristan forever, you, me, and Tristan forever, you, me, and Tristan—"

"Shut up. Give them to me," Gregory said, ripping the keys out of his hand, leaving his palm raw and bloody. "You can't even hold your head up."

Tristan suddenly felt as if he were going to be sick. Trapped inside the body of Eric, he leaned on the Harley, holding his stomach and breathing hard. Gregory fumbled with something on the back of the bike. He was trying to tie something to it – the jacket and cap.

"We've got to get out of here," Gregory said to him.

They struggled to climb onto the motorcycle. His leg felt unbearably heavy as he lifted it over the seat. Gregory shoved him toward the back of the machine, then climbed on the front.

"Hang on."

He did. When Gregory hit the accelerator, Tristan felt his head snap back. His upper jaw crunched down on his lower, and his eyes felt as small and hard as marbles rolling inside his head. In that brief moment he saw a blur behind him. He turned just as the clothes tumbled off the bike, but he didn't say anything.

They rode toward town, then up the long hill to Gregory's house. Gregory got off and rushed inside. Now the motorcycle was in Eric's hands – Tristan's hands, though he had no control. He raced down the hill again, driving crazily. Suddenly the road snaked out from under the wheels, and Eric was on another path.

Were they in another memory? Had they somehow linked up with another part of the past? The road, with its sharp twists and turns, seemed familiar to Tristan. The Harley skidded to a stop, and Tristan felt ill all over again: they were at the spot where he had died.

Eric parked and got off the motorcycle, surveying the road for several minutes. He stooped down to examine some sparkling blue stones – bits of shattered glass among the gravel in the road. Suddenly he reached over and picked up a bouquet of roses. They looked fresh, as if someone had just left them there, and were tied with a purple ribbon. Eric touched one rose that hadn't opened. A tremor ran through him.

One rose, unopened, stood in a vase on Caroline's table. Eric's mind had jumped again, and Tristan knew he had been in this memory before. The picture window, the brewing storm outside, Eric's intense fear and growing frustration were all familiar to Tristan. Just as before, the memory ran like a piece of damaged film, frames spliced out, sound washed over by waves of emotion. Caroline was looking at him and laughing, laughing as if nothing in the world could be funnier. Suddenly he reached for her arms, grabbing her, shaking her, rocking her till her head flopped like a rag doll's.

"Listen to me," he said. "I mean it! It's not a joke! Nobody's laughing but you. It's not a joke!"

Then Eric groaned. It wasn't fear that rippled through him now. It wasn't frustration and anger burning out of his skin, but something deep and awful, despairing. He groaned again and opened his eyes. Tristan saw the book of trains in front of him.

The book looked blurry, and Eric passed his hand over his eyes. He was awake and crying. "Not again," he whispered. "Not again."

What did he mean? Tristan wondered. What didn't Eric want to happen again? What didn't he want to do again? Let Gregory kill? Let himself get out of control and do Gregory's killing for him? Maybe they had each done some of it and were tied together in a guilty knot.

Tristan struggled hard to remain conscious and stay with Eric through the rest of Monday morning. He had slipped out of Eric's mind the moment he was fully awake but accompanied him to school, guessing that the memories that haunted Eric would lead him toward some kind of confrontation with Gregory. He was caught off guard at lunchtime when Eric moved quickly through a crowded cafeteria toward the table where Ivy sat alone.

"I have to talk to you."

Ivy blinked up at him, surprised. His pale hair was matted. Over the summer, he had grown so thin that his white skin barely seemed to cover the bones of his face. The circles under his eyes looked like bruises.

When Ivy spoke, Tristan heard an unexpected gentleness in her voice. "Okay. Talk to me."

"Not here. Not with all these people."

Ivy glanced around the cafeteria. Tristan guessed that she was trying to decide how to handle this. He wanted to slip inside her and shout, "Don't do it! Don't go anywhere with him!" But he knew what would happen: She'd throw him out just as she had the last time.

"Can you tell me what this is about?" Ivy asked, her voice still soft.

"Not here," he said. His fingers played nervously on the tabletop.

"At my house, then," she suggested.

Eric shook his head. He kept glancing left and right.

Tristan saw with relief that Beth and Will were carrying their lunch trays toward Ivy's table. Eric saw them, too.

"There's an old car," he said quickly, "dumped about a half mile below the train bridges, just back from the river. I'll meet you there today, five o'clock. Come alone. I want to talk, but only if you're alone."

"But I—"

"Come alone. Don't tell anyone." He was already moving away from the table.

"Eric," she called after him. "Eric!"

He didn't turn back.

"What was that about?" Will asked as he set his tray on the table. He didn't seem aware of Tristan's presence. Neither did Beth or Ivy. Maybe none of them saw his light because of the sun flooding through the cafeteria's big windows, Tristan thought.

"Eric looks kind of crazed," Beth said, taking the seat next to Will and across from Ivy. Tristan was glad to see a pencil and notebook among Beth's clutter of dishes. Through her writing, he could communicate with all three of them at the same time. "What did he say?" she asked. "Is something wrong?"

Ivy shrugged. "He wants to talk to me later today."

"Why doesn't he talk to you now?" Will asked.

Good question, thought Tristan.

"He said he wants to see me alone." Ivy lowered her voice. "I'm not supposed to tell anyone."

Beth was watching Eric as he made his way toward the cafeteria doors. Her eyes narrowed.

I don't trust him, Tristan thought as clearly as possible. He had guessed right: Beth and he matched thoughts, and a moment later he was inside her mind. Then he felt her pull back.

"Don't be afraid, Beth," he said to her. "Don't throw me out. I need your help. Ivy needs your help."

Sighing, Beth picked up the pencil next to her notebook, and stirred her applesauce with it.

Will smiled and nudged her. "It'd be easier to eat with a spoon," he said.

Then Ivy's eyes widened a little. "Beth's glowing."

"Is it Tristan?" Will asked.

Beth dried her pencil and flipped open the notebook.

"Yes," she wrote.

Ivy frowned. "He can talk to me directly now. Why is he still communicating through you?"

Beth's fingers twitched, then she wrote quickly: "Because Beth still listens to me."

Will laughed out loud.

Beth's hand moved toward the page again. "I'm counting on Beth and Will to convince you – don't take chances with Eric!"

"Counting on me?" mumbled Will.

"It's too dangerous, Ivy," Beth scribbled. "It's a trap. Tell her, Will."

"I need to know the facts first," Will insisted.

"Eric asked me to meet him at five o'clock, by the river about a half mile below the double bridges," Ivy said.

Will nodded, tore the tip of a catsup packet, and spread its contents evenly on his hamburger. "Is that all?" he asked.

"He said to come alone and to look for him by an old car that's back a little from the river."

Will methodically opened a second catsup packet, then a mustard one. His slow and deliberate actions annoyed Tristan.

"Tell her, Will! Talk sense to her!" Beth wrote furiously.

But Will would not be hurried. "Eric could be setting a trap for you," he said to Ivy thoughtfully, "maybe a deadly one."

"Exactly," wrote Beth.

"Or," Will continued, "Eric could be telling the truth. He could be running scared and trying to give you some important information. I honestly don't know which it is."

"*Idiot!*" Beth wrote. "Don't do it, Ivy," she added out loud, her voice shaking. "That's me telling you, not Tristan."

Will turned to her. "What is it?" he asked. "What are you seeing?"

Tristan, inside her mind, was seeing it, too, and it shook him just as badly.

"It's the car," Beth said. "As soon as you mentioned it I could see it, an old car sinking slowly into the mud. Something terrible has happened there. There's a dark mist around it."

Will took Beth's trembling hand.

"The car's slipping into the ground like a coffin," she said. "Its hood is torn off. Its trunk . . . I can't see – there are lots of bushes and vines. There's a door partway open, blue, I think. Something's inside."

Beth's eyes were big and frightened, and a tear

ran down her cheek. Will wiped it away gently, but another ran over his hand.

"The front seats are gone," she continued. "But I can see the back seat, and there's something . . ." She shook her head.

"Go on," Will urged softly.

"It's covered with a blanket. And there's an angel looking down on it. The angel is crying."

"What's under the blanket?" Ivy whispered.

"I can't see," Beth whispered back. "I can't see!"

Then her hand started scribbling: "I can see only what Beth sees. The blanket can't be lifted."

"Is the angel you, Tristan?" Ivy asked.

"No," Beth wrote. Then she grabbed Ivy's hand. "Something terrible is there. Don't go! I'm begging you, Ivy."

"Listen to her, Ivy!" Tristan said, but Beth's hand was shaking too hard to write it.

Ivy looked at Will.

"Beth has been right twice before," he said.

Ivy nodded, then sighed. "But what if Eric really has something important to tell me?"

"He'll find another way," Will reasoned. "If he really wants to tell you something, he'll figure out a way."

"I guess so," Ivy said, and Tristan sank down in relief.

Soon after that, he left the three of them. He heard Ivy ask mentally, "Where are you going?" But knowing she was in safe hands, he kept on. He had recovered from the exhaustion of time-traveling but wasn't sure how long his second wind would last. He wanted time to search Gregory's room while everyone was out of the house. If he could find Gregory's latest purchase of drugs, Ivy would have evidence for at least a drug charge.

Still, what she really needed was the jacket and cap, Tristan thought as he passed through the school door. The clothes might convince the police to reconsider Philip's story. A single piece of hair could establish the important link to Gregory.

Somebody must have found the clothes after they rolled off the motorcycle. Did that person know how important they were? Philip's story hadn't been released to the public, but it could have leaked out. Was there, Tristan wondered, an unidentified player in Gregory's game?

"But Ivy," Suzanne wailed, "we had plans to find the crystal slippers – the ruby shoes – the only pair of heels in all New England that are exactly right for my birthday party. And I've got only a week left to hunt!"

"I'm sorry," Ivy replied, reaching into her locker for another book. "I know I promised." She shifted the stack in her arms, clutching a note beneath the books. Three minutes before Suzanne had arrived, Ivy had opened her locker and found Tristan's picture gone. The note she grasped had been taped in its place.

"How about Wednesday?" Ivy proposed. "I have to work after school tomorrow, but we can shop till we drop on Wednesday and find you an incredible pair of shoes."

"By that time Gregory and I will have made up and be doing something again."

"Made up?" Ivy repeated. "What do you mean?"

Suzanne smiled. "It worked, Ivy, worked like a charm." With her back against the wall of lockers, Suzanne bent her knees and slowly slid down till her bottom touched the floor – no easy feat in tight jeans, Ivy thought. A group of guys down the hall admired her flexibility.

"Since you wouldn't mention Jeff to him," Suzanne went on, "I did. I called Gregory Jeff."

"You called him Jeff? Did he notice?"

"Both times," Suzanne replied.

"Whew."

"Once when things were pretty hot and heavy."

"Suzanne!"

Suzanne threw back her head and laughed. It was a wild and infectious laugh, and people grinned as they passed her in the hall.

"So what did Gregory say? What did he do?" Ivy asked.

"He was unbelievably jealous," Suzanne said,

her eyes flashing with excitement. "It's a wonder he didn't kill us both!"

"What do you mean?"

Suzanne slid closer to Ivy and bent her head, her long, dark hair falling forward, like a curtain for telling secrets behind.

"The second time, we were in the back seat." Suzanne closed her eyes a moment, remembering. "His face went white, then the red started creeping up his neck. I swear I could feel a hundred and five degrees rushing through him. He pulled away from me and raised his hand. I thought he was going to hit me, and for a moment I was terrified."

She gazed into Ivy's eyes, her pupils large with excitement. Ivy could see that Suzanne might have been terrified then, but now found it thrilling and fun to talk about. Her friend was enjoying the memory the way someone delighted in a good scare at a spook house – but Gregory was no papier-mâché monster.

"Then he dropped his hand, called me a couple of names, got out of the back seat and into the front, and started driving like crazy. He opened all the windows and kept yelling back at me that I could get out. But of course he was driving so fast and weaving left and right, and I was trying to straighten myself up and kept slamming from one side of the car to the other. He'd watch me in the rearview mirror; sometimes he turned all the way around. It's a wonder he didn't kill us both."

Ivy stared at her friend in horror.

"Oh, come on, Ivy. In the end, when I had my right arm in the left arm of my vest and my hair flopped over my face, he slowed down, and both of us started laughing."

Ivy dropped her head in her hands.

"But when he took me home that night," Suzanne continued, "he said he didn't want to see me anymore. He said I make him lose control and do crazy things." She sounded pleased with herself, as if she had been given a huge compliment. "But he'll come around by next Saturday. He'll be at my party, you can bet on that."

"Suzanne, you're playing with fire," Ivy said.

Suzanne smiled.

"You and Gregory aren't good for each other," Ivy told her. "Look at you. You're both acting crazy."

Suzanne shrugged and laughed.

"You're acting like a fool!"

Suzanne blinked, stung by Ivy's criticism.

"Gregory has a terrible temper," Ivy went on. "Anything can happen. You don't know him the way I do."

"Oh, really?" Suzanne raised her eyebrows. "I think I know him pretty well."

"Suzanne—"

"And I can handle him – better than you can," she added, glancing sideways, her eyes gleaming. "So don't get your hopes up."

"What?"

"That's what this is all about, isn't it? Ever since you lost Tristan, you've been interested in Gregory. But he's mine, not yours, Ivy, and you're not going to get him away from me!"

Suzanne stood up quickly, brushed off the back of her jeans, and stalked down the hall.

Ivy leaned back against her locker. She knew it was pointless to call after Suzanne and thought about summoning Tristan, asking him to watch over her friend. Maybe Lacey could help them out. But that request would have to wait. Ivy had changed her plans for the afternoon, and if Tristan read her mind, he might try to stop her.

She unfolded the square of paper that had been taped in place of Tristan's picture. The note, signed with Eric's initials, was short and convincing:

"Come alone. Five o'clock. I know why you're dreaming what you're dreaming."

38

Ivy parked her car close to the train bridges. She was in the same clearing where Gregory had stopped months ago, the night Eric wanted to play chicken. She got out and walked the short distance to the double bridges. In the late-afternoon sun, the rails of the new bridge gleamed. Next to it stood the old bridge, a rusted orange fretwork reaching halfway across the river.

When Ivy saw the parallel bridges clearly in the sunlight, when she saw the seven-foot gap between them and the long fall down to the water and rocks below, she realized the kind of risk Eric had taken when he pretended to leap from the new bridge. What went on inside Eric's head? she wondered. Either he was totally insane or he just didn't care whether he lived or died.

Eric's Harley was not in sight, but there were

plenty of trees and brush to hide it in. Ivy glanced around, then picked her way carefully down the steep bank next to the bridges, sliding part of the way until she reached a narrow path that ran along the river. She walked as quietly as possible, alert to every sound around her. When the trees rustled she looked up quickly, half expecting to see Eric and Gregory ready to swoop down on their prey.

"Get a grip, Ivy," she chided herself, but she continued to tread softly. If she could surprise Eric, she might see what he was up to before she walked into a trap.

Ivy glanced at her watch several times, and at five minutes past five she wondered if she had passed the car. But after a few more feet, something flashed in her eyes – sunlight glinting off metal. Fifteen feet ahead, she saw an overgrown path that led from the river to a metal heap.

Ivy worked her way into the brush, keeping herself hidden as she crept closer. Once she thought she heard something behind her, a soft crunch of leaves beneath someone's foot. She turned quickly. Nothing. Nothing but a few leaves drifting in the breeze.

Ivy pushed aside some long branches and took two steps forward, then drew in her breath sharply. The car was just as Beth had described it, its axles sunk into the earth, its rear buried beneath vines. The car's hood was ripped off, and its vinyl roof had decayed into papery black flakes. Its scarred doors shone blue – exactly as Beth had said.

The back door was open. Was there a blanket on the seat inside? Ivy wondered. What was under the blanket?

Again she heard rustling behind her and turned quickly around, searching the trees. Her eyes ached from focusing and refocusing on every shadow and flutter of leaf, searching for the shape of a person watching her. No one.

She glanced at her watch. Ten after five. Eric wouldn't have given up on her this soon, she thought. Either he's late or he's waiting for me to make the first move. Well, two can play the waiting game, Ivy reasoned, and crouched down quietly.

A few minutes later her legs began to ache with the tension of holding still. She rubbed them and looked at her watch again: quarter after. She waited five more minutes. Maybe Eric has lost his nerve, she thought.

Ivy stood up slowly, but something kept her from moving any further. She heard Beth's warning as if her friend were standing next to her, whispering in her ear.

"Angels, help me," Ivy prayed. Part of her wanted to find out what was in the car. But part of her wanted to run away. "Angels, are you there? Tristan, I need you. I need you now!"

She walked tentatively toward the car. When she

reached the clearing she paused for just a moment, waiting to see if anyone had followed. Then she bent down and looked in the back seat.

Ivy blinked, unsure for a moment that what she saw was real – not another nightmare, not one more of Eric's jokes. Then she screamed, screamed until her throat was raw. She knew without touching him – he was too pale, too still, his blue eyes open and staring at nothing – that Eric was dead.

Ivy jumped when someone touched her from behind. She started screaming again. Arms wrapped around her, pulling her back, holding her tight. She thought she'd shriek her brains out. He didn't try to stop her, just held her till she went limp, her whole body sagging against him. His face brushed hers.

"Will," she said. She could feel his body shaking.

He turned her toward him and held her face against his chest, his hand shielding her eyes. But in her mind Ivy could still see Eric staring upward, his eyes wide, as if he were quietly amazed by what had happened.

Will shifted his weight, and Ivy knew he was looking over her shoulder at Eric. "I – I don't see any signs of trouble," he said. "No bruising. No blood."

Ivy's stomach suddenly rose up against her ribs.

She gritted her teeth and forced it back down. "Maybe drugs," she said. "An overdose."

Will nodded. His breath was short and quick against her cheek. "We have to call the police."

Then Ivy pulled away from him. She bent down and forced herself to look long and hard at Eric. She should memorize the scene, she thought. She should collect clues. What had happened to him could be a warning to her. But as she looked at Eric all she felt was the loss; all she could see was a wasted life.

Ivy reached into the car. Will caught her hand. "Don't. Don't touch him," he said. "Leave his body just as it is so that the police can examine it."

Ivy nodded, then picked up an old blanket from the car floor and gently laid it on top of Eric. "Angels—" she began, but she did not know what to ask for. "Help him," she said, and left the prayer at that. As she walked away she knew that a merciful angel of the dead was looking down on Eric, weeping – just as Beth had said.

"Despite what you say, Lacey, I'm glad I missed my own funeral," Tristan observed as the mourners gathered at Eric's graveside. Some of them stood solitary and stiff as soldiers; others leaned against each other for support and comfort.

Friday had dawned pale and drizzly. Several people raised umbrellas now, like bright nylon flowers blooming against the gray stones and misty trees. Ivy and Beth stood on either side of Will, bareheaded, letting the rain and tears run together. Suzanne stood with one arm around Gregory, staring down at the bristling grass.

Three times in five months the four of them had stood together at Riverstone Rise, and still the police asked only routine questions about the deaths.

"No luck?" Lacey called down from her perch in a tree.

Tristan grunted. "Gregory's built a wall around himself," he replied, and walked in frustrated circles around the elm. He had tried several times during the church service to get inside Gregory's head. "Sometimes I think that the moment I approach him, he senses me. I think he knows something's up as soon as I get near him."

"Could be," Lacey said. Materializing her fingers, she swung from a branch, dropping down neatly beside him. "In angel matters, you're not exactly a smooth operator."

"What do you mean?"

"Well, let's put it this way. If you were stealing TVs instead of thoughts," she told him, "you'd have been caught by a half-deaf, mostly blind, fifteen-year-old dog three robberies ago."

Tristan was stung. "Well, give me two years to procrastinate," he retorted, "excuse me, I meant two years to *practice*, and I'll be as good as you."

"Maybe," Lacey said, then added with a smile, "I tried getting inside him, too. Impossible."

Tristan studied Gregory's face. He gave away nothing, his mouth an even line, his eyes focused straight ahead.

"You know," Lacey said, materializing the palm of her hand and holding it up to catch raindrops, "Gregory doesn't have to be responsible for *everything* bad that happens. You saw the report. The police found no signs of a struggle."

The coroner had listed Eric's death as a drug overdose. Eric's parents insisted it was an accident. At school it was rumored to be suicide. Tristan believed it was murder.

"The report doesn't prove anything," he argued, pacing back and forth. "Gregory didn't have to force-feed Eric. He could have bought him a heavy dose without telling him how powerful it was. He could have waited till Eric was too high to know better, then given him more. The reason the police aren't thinking murder, Lacey, is because they have no motive for it."

"And you do."

"Eric was ready to talk. He was ready to tell Ivy something."

"Aha! Then the chick was right," Lacey needled him.

"She was right," he admitted, though he was still

angry with Ivy for trying to meet with Eric on Monday afternoon. She had called out to him at the very last minute, when it would have been too late for him to save her. Rushing to her side, Tristan had found her walking with Will away from the dangerous site. Will said he had followed Ivy that afternoon on a sudden hunch.

"Are you still feeling left out?" Lacey asked.

He didn't reply.

"Tristan, when is it going to sink in? We're *dead*," Lacey said. "And that's what happens when you're dead. People forget to invite you along."

Tristan kept his eyes on Ivy. He wanted to be next to her, holding her hand.

"We're here to give a hand when we can and then let go," Lacey told him. "We help, and then it's bye-bye." She waved both hands at him.

"Like I said before, Lacey, I hope you fall in love one day. I hope that before your mission's done, some guy teaches you how miserable it feels to love somebody and watch him reach out for someone else."

Lacey stepped back.

"I hope you learn what it's like to say goodbye to someone you love more than that person will ever guess."

She turned her face away from him. "You just might get your wish," she said.

He glanced at her, surprised by her tone of voice. He didn't usually have to worry about hurting Lacey's feelings. "Did I miss something?" he asked.

She shook her head.

"What?" he asked. "What is it?" He reached for her face.

Lacey pulled away from him.

"You're missing the final prayer," she said. "We should pray with everyone else for Eric." Lacey folded her hands and looked extremely angelic.

Tristan sighed. "You pray in my place," he said. "I don't have many good feelings toward Eric."

"All the more reason to pray," she replied. "If he doesn't rest in peace, he may be hanging out with us."

"Angels, take care of him. Let him rest in peace," Ivy prayed. "Help Eric's family," she said silently, and gazed back at Christine, Eric's older sister. She stood with her parents and brothers on the other side of the casket.

Several times during the service, Ivy had caught Christine looking at her. When their eyes met, the girl's mouth trembled a little, then became a long, soft line. Christine had Eric's pale blond hair and porcelain skin, but her eyes were a vibrant blue. She was beautiful – an uncomfortable reminder of what

Eric might have been like if drugs and alcohol had not wasted his body and mind.

"Angels, take care of him," Ivy prayed again.

The minister concluded the service, and everyone turned away at the same time. Gregory's fingers brushed Ivy's. His hand was as cold as ice. She remembered how cold it had felt the evening the police told them of Caroline's death.

"How are you doing?" she asked.

He slipped his hand through hers and held her fingers tightly. The night Caroline had died, when he had done the very same thing, she had believed that he was finally reaching out to her.

"I'm okay," he said. "How about you?"

"Glad it's over," she answered honestly.

He studied her face, every centimeter of it. She felt trapped, anchored by his hand, his eyes invading her, reading her thoughts.

"I'm sorry, Gregory. You and Eric were friends for so long," she said. "I know this is much harder for you than for any of the rest of us."

Gregory continued to gaze at her.

"You tried to help him, Gregory. You did all you could for him," Ivy said. "We both know that."

Gregory bowed his head, moving his face close to hers. Ivy's skin tingled. To someone who didn't know better, to Andrew and Maggie watching them from a distance, it would look like a moment of shared sorrow. But to Ivy it felt like the movement of an animal she didn't trust, a dog that didn't bite but intimidated by moving its teeth very close to her bare skin.

"Gregory!"

He was so focused on Ivy that he jumped when Suzanne rested her hand on the back of his neck. Ivy stepped back quickly, and Gregory let go of her.

He's as edgy as I am, Ivy thought as she watched Suzanne and Gregory make their way to the cars parked along the cemetery road. Beth and Will started off, and Ivy followed slowly behind them. Out of the corner of her eye she saw Eric's sister walking toward her with long strides.

Ivy had told the police that she and Will were on an after-school hike when they came upon Eric in the car. After Dr. and Mrs. Ghent learned of Eric's death, they had telephoned her to discuss the story she'd given to the police and probe for more details. Now she steeled herself for another round of questioning.

"You're Ivy Lyons, aren't you?" the girl asked. Her cheeks were smooth and pink, her thick hair shining in the rain. It was startling to be confronted by such a healthy version of Eric.

"Yes," Ivy replied. "I'm sorry, Christine. I'm really sorry for you and your family."

The girl acknowledged Ivy's sympathy with a nod. "You – you must have been close to Eric," she said.

"Excuse me?"

"I figured you were special to him."

Ivy looked at her, mystified.

"Because of what he left. When – when Eric and I were younger," Christine began, her voice shaking a little, "we used to leave messages for each other in a secret place in the attic. We put them in an old cardboard box. On the box we wrote 'Beware! Frogs! Do Not Open!'"

Christine laughed, then tears sprang into the corners of her eyes. Ivy waited patiently, wondering where this conversation was leading.

"When I came home for this – for his funeral, I looked in our box, just on a whim," Christine continued, "not expecting to find anything – we hadn't used it for years. But I found a note to me. And this."

She pulled a gray envelope from her purse. "The note said, 'If anything happens to me, give this to Ivy Lyons.'"

Ivy's eyes widened.

"You weren't expecting it," Christine observed. "You don't know what's in it."

"No," Ivy said, then took the sealed envelope in her hand. She could feel a small, stiff wad inside, as if a hard object had been wrapped in padding. The outside of the envelope intrigued Ivy even more. Eric's name and address had been typed neatly onto it and her own name scribbled in big letters across it. The return-address sticker bore the name and address of Caroline Baines."

"Oh, that," Christine said when Ivy fingered it. "It's probably just an old envelope Eric had lying around."

But it wasn't just an old envelope. Ivy checked the postmark: May 28, Philip's birthday. The day Caroline died.

"Maybe you didn't know," Christine continued. "Eric was very close to Caroline. She was a second mother to him."

Ivy looked up, surprised. "She was?"

"From the time he was a kid, Eric and my mother never got along," Christine explained. "I'm six years older, and I took care of him sometimes when my mother worked long days in New York. But usually he was at the Baines house, and Caroline became closer to him than any of us. Even after she divorced and Gregory didn't live with her, Eric would often go see her."

"I didn't know that," Ivy said.

"Are you going to open it?" Christine asked, looking at the envelope curiously.

Ivy tore off one corner and slit the envelope with her finger. "If it's a personal note," she warned Christine, "I might not show it to you."

Christine nodded.

But there was no note, just dry tissue wrapped around the hard object. Ivy tore at it and pulled out a key. It was about two inches long. One end was oval, with a lacy design cut into the metal. The other end, which would fit into a lock, was a simple hollow cylinder with two small teeth at the tip.

"Do you know what it's for?" Christine asked.

"No," Ivy replied. "And there isn't a note."

Christine bit her lip, then said, "Well, maybe it was an accident after all." Ivy could hear the hope in her voice. "I mean, if Eric planned to kill himself, he would have left a note explaining this – wouldn't he?"

Unless he was murdered before he got a chance, Ivy thought, but she nodded in agreement with Christine.

"Eric didn't commit suicide," Ivy said in a firm voice. Then she saw the gratitude in Christine's eyes and blushed. If Christine only knew, Ivy thought, that I might have been the cause of her brother's death.

Ivy dropped the key into the envelope, tucked the flap in, and folded the envelope in half. Slipping it in her raincoat pocket, she told Christine she'd let her know if she figured out what the key was for. Christine thanked Ivy for being a good friend to Eric, which sent more color rushing into Ivy's cheeks.

Her face was still warm when she joined Will and Beth, who had been watching her from twenty feet away, huddled together under an umbrella.

"What did she say to you?" Will asked, pulling Ivy under the umbrella with them.

"She – uh – thanked me for being Eric's good friend."

"Oh, boy," Beth said softly.

"Is that all?" Will asked.

It was a question Ivy had come to expect from Gregory when he was pumping her for information.

"You talked pretty long," Will observed. "Is that all she said?"

"Yes," Ivy lied.

Will's eyes dropped down to the pocket where she had shoved the envelope. He must have seen the exchange, and certainly he could see the edge of the envelope now, but he didn't question her further.

They had been excused from school that day, and the three of them drove quietly to Celentano's for a late lunch. As they pored over their menus Ivy wondered what Will was thinking and if he was suspicious of Gregory. At the police station on Monday, Will had let her do the talking, then echoed her story, neither of them mentioning Eric's request for a secret meeting. Now Ivy wanted to tell Will everything. If she looked too long into his eyes, she would.

"So how are you all doing?" Pat Celentano said, coming to take their order. Most of the lunchtime customers had left the pizza shop, and the owner was speaking in a quieter voice than usual. "Rough morning for you."

She took their order, then set an extra basket of pencils and crayons on the paper tablecloth.

Will, who already had several tablecloth drawings hanging on Celentano's walls, began sketching immediately. Ivy doodled. Beth made long chains of rhyming words, murmuring to herself as the lists grew. "Sorry," she said when one of her chains ran into Will's drawing.

He was writing and illustrating knock-knock jokes. Beth and Ivy leaned over to read them, and started laughing together softly. Will sketched them in their Old West photo costumes. "Virginia City Sweethearts," he titled it.

Beth pointed to the drawing. "I think you missed a few curves," she said. "Ivy's dress was a lot tighter than that. Of course, not as tight as your cowboy pants."

Ivy smiled, remembering the voice that had confused them all that day, a voice coming out of nowhere – Lacey having a little fun.

"Love those buns!" Ivy and Beth said at the same time, and this time they laughed out loud.

With the sudden laughter came tears. Ivy covered her face with one hand.

Will and Beth sat silently and let her cry it out, then Will gently placed her hand on the table and began to trace it. Over and over the pencil ran along the sides of her fingers, the smooth touch of it soothing her. Then Will positioned his hand on the paper at an angle against hers and traced it too.

When he lifted their hands, Ivy gazed down at the design. "Wings," she said, smiling a little. "A butterfly, or an angel."

He let go of her hand. Ivy longed to move close to Will and rest against him. She wanted to tell him everything she knew and ask his help. But she knew she couldn't put him in danger. Because of her, one guy she had loved with all her heart had already been murdered. She wasn't going to let it happen to the— Ivy caught herself. To the other guy she . . . loved?

39

When Ivy was dropped off later that afternoon, she never went into the house. With Eric's envelope still in her pocket, she climbed into her own car and started driving. After an hour of going nowhere, taking back roads that followed the river north, then crossing over, winding her way south, and crossing again into town, she stopped at the park at the end of Main Street.

The rain had finally ended, and the empty park was drenched with late-afternoon color, the sun slanting through blue-black clouds and turning the grass a brilliant green. Ivy sat alone in the wooden pavilion, remembering the day of the arts festival. Gregory had watched her from one side of the lawn, Will from the other. But it was Tristan's presence she had felt when she played. Was he there?

When she played the "Moonlight Sonata," did he know it was for him?

"I was there. I knew it."

Ivy gazed down at her shimmering hands and smiled. "Tristan," she said softly.

"Ivy." His voice was like light inside her. "Ivy, what were you running from?"

The question caught her off guard. "What?"

"What were you driving away from?" Tristan asked.

"I was just driving."

"You were upset," he said.

"I was trying to think, that's all. But I couldn't," she confessed.

"What couldn't you think about?"

"You." Ivy ran her hand up and down the smooth, damp wood of the railing she sat on. "You died because of me. I knew it, but I didn't face it, not until now, when I realized that Eric might have died because of me. Not until I thought about what could happen to Will if he learns what's going on."

"Will's going to find out one way or the other," Tristan told her.

"We can't let him!" Ivy said. "We can't endanger him."

"If you feel that way," Tristan observed dryly, "you shouldn't have left your coat with him at the table."

Ivy reached quickly into her pocket. The envelope was still there, folded in half, but when she pulled it out she saw that the flap was no longer tucked in.

"He looked as soon as you and Beth left him alone."

Ivy closed her eyes for a moment, feeling betrayed. "I guess – I guess I would have been curious, too," she said lamely.

"What do you think the key goes to?" Tristan asked.

Ivy flipped the envelope over in her hands. "Some kind of small box or cupboard. At Caroline's house," she added, looking at the address. "Can you get inside?"

"Easily, and I can materialize my fingers to undo the latch to let you in," he told her. "Bring the key, and we'll find what Eric wanted you to find. But not today, okay?"

Ivy heard the strain in his voice. "Is something wrong?"

"I'm tired. Real tired."

"The darkness," she whispered in a frightened voice. Tristan had said there would be a time when he wouldn't return from the darkness.

"It's okay," he assured her. "I just need rest. You're keeping me busy, you know." He laughed.

It's because of me, Ivy thought. He died because of me, and now—

"Ivy, no. You can't think that way," he said.

"But I do think that way," she argued. "I was the one who was supposed to die. If it weren't for me—"

"If it weren't for you, I would never have known how it is to love someone," he told her. "If it weren't for you, I would never have kissed a mouth so sweet."

Ivy longed to kiss him now. "Tristan," she said, trembling with the sudden idea, "if I died, I could be with you."

He was silent. She could feel the confusion of thoughts, all the emotions tossing within him, within her.

"I could be with you forever," she told him.

"No."

"Yes!"

"That's not how it's supposed to be," he said. "We both know that."

Ivy got up and walked around the pavilion. His presence within her was stronger than the autumn day outside of her. When he was with her, the smell of soaked earth, the ribbons of emerald grass, and the first scarlet leaves all paled like objects on the edge of her vision.

"I wouldn't have been sent back to help you," Tristan continued. "I wouldn't have been made an angel if it weren't important that you live. Ivy, I want you to be mine" – she could hear the pain in his voice – "but you're not."

"I am!" she cried out loud.

"We're on different sides of a river," he said, "and it's a river that neither of us can cross. You were meant for somebody else."

"I was meant for *you*," she insisted.

"Hush."

"I don't want to lose you, Tristan!"

"Shhh. Shhh," he soothed. "Listen, Ivy, I'm going to be in the darkness soon, and it may be a while before I reach you again."

Ivy paced around.

"Stay still. I'm going outside of you, so you won't be able to hear me," he told her. "Stay still."

Then all was silent. Ivy stood motionless, wondering. The air around her began to shimmer with gold. She felt hands touching her, gentle hands cradling her face, lifting her chin. He kissed her. His lips touched hers, actually touched hers with a kiss long and unbearably tender. "Ivy" – she couldn't hear him, but she felt her name whispered by him against her cheek. "Ivy." Then he was gone.

40

Ivy hung a long dangle earring on each ear, wiped away a smudge of mascara beneath one eye, then took a step back from the mirror, surveying herself.

"You look hot."

She glanced at Philip's reflection in the mirror and burst out laughing. "You didn't pick up *that* expression from Andrew. And how do you know what hot looks like, anyway?"

"I taught him."

Ivy spun around. Gregory stood in the entrance to her bedroom, leaning casually against the door frame. Since Eric's death nearly a week before, Ivy had felt Gregory's presence following her like a dark angel.

"And you do look hot," he added, his eyes moving down her slowly.

Maybe I should have chosen a skirt that's not so

short, Ivy thought, or a top that isn't scooped so low. But she was determined to show the others at Suzanne's birthday party that she wasn't a depressed girl ready to choose the suicidal path everyone thought Eric had taken. Suzanne was still having her party, though it was the day after the funeral. Ivy had encouraged her, telling Suzanne it would be good for everyone – the kids from school needed to come together now.

"It's the colors. They make you hot," Philip said to Ivy, anxious to sound as if he knew what he was talking about.

Ivy glanced at Gregory. "Good job, teach."

Gregory laughed. "I did my best," he said, then he held up his car keys and rattled them.

Ivy grabbed her own keys and purse.

"Ivy, this is silly," Gregory said. "Why are we going to the same place and taking two cars?"

They had already argued about her decision during dinner. "I told you, I'll probably leave before you do." She picked up a wrapped gift for Suzanne and turned out the lamp on her dressing table. "You're dating the hostess – everyone will probably leave before you do."

Gregory smiled slightly and shrugged. "Maybe, but if you want to leave, there will be lots of guys there glad to give you a ride home."

"Because you look hot," Philip said. "Because you—"

"Thank you, Philip."

Gregory winked at her brother. Philip jumped off her bed, using her scarf as a parachute, and scooted through the bathroom that joined his room with hers.

Gregory continued to lean against Ivy's door. "Is my driving that bad?" he asked, stretching one arm across the doorway, blocking her exit. "If I didn't know better, I'd think you were afraid to drive with me."

"I'm not," Ivy said firmly.

"Maybe you're afraid of being alone with me."

"Oh, come on," Ivy said, walking briskly toward him and pulling his arm down. She turned him around by the shoulders and gave him a push. "Let's get going or we'll be late. I hope your Beamer has gas."

Gregory reached back for her hand and pulled her close to him, too close. Ivy's heart was beating fast as they moved down the stairs – she really didn't want to ride alone with him. She wished he weren't so attentive when she got into his car. The constant small and needless touches jangled her nerves. He kept looking at her as he drove slowly down the driveway.

When they stopped at the bottom of the ridge, Gregory said, "Let's not go to Suzanne's."

"What?" Ivy exclaimed. She tried to cover her growing apprehension with a show of disbelief and amazement. "Suzanne and I have been friends since we were seven, and you think I'm skipping her seventeenth-birthday party? Drive!" she commanded. "To Lantern Road. Or I'm getting out."

Gregory rested his hand on her leg and drove to Suzanne's house. Fifteen minutes later, when Suzanne answered the door, she did not appear overly delighted to see Gregory and Ivy together.

"He insisted on driving me," Ivy said. "He'll do anything to make you jealous, Suzanne."

Gregory shot her a look, but Suzanne laughed, her face brightening.

"You look gorgeous," Ivy told her friend, and gave her a hug. Ivy felt a moment of hesitation, then Suzanne hugged her back.

"Where do I stash this present?" Ivy asked as a large group of kids who had crammed themselves into a Jeep came in behind them.

"End of the hall," Suzanne said, pointing to a table with an impressive pile of boxes. Ivy headed quickly in that direction, glad to be away from Gregory. The Goldsteins' long center hallway led to a family room that ran along the back of the house, its floor-to-ceiling windows facing a porch and the back lawn, which sloped down gently to a pond. It was a warm September night, and the party had spread out from the large room to the porch and lawn below.

Walking out on the porch, Ivy saw Beth sitting

in the swing at one end, deep in conversation with two cheerleaders. The two girls were talking excitedly at the same time, and Beth's head went back and forth as if she were watching a tennis match.

Out of the corner of her eye she caught sight of Will, sitting on the wide porch steps next to a girl with auburn hair, the girl he had been with six weeks ago when Ivy ran into him at the mall. Now, *she* was hot.

"Wish I could read minds," Gregory said, touching a cold glass to Ivy's arm.

It seemed impossible to move out from under his shadow.

"What are you doing – putting a hex on that girl?" he asked.

Ivy shook her head. "I was just thinking, thinking that when it comes to hot, that girl is *it*."

Gregory watched Will's companion for a moment, then shrugged. "Some girls look hot on the outside, but it's just a tease. Other girls, they put you off, play hard to get, act like ice queens" – he looked at her with laughing eyes – "but they're running hot." He moved closer to her. "Real hot," he whispered.

Ivy flashed him an innocent smile. "Like Philip, I can always learn something from you."

Gregory laughed. "Did you get a drink?" he asked, offering with his left hand a plastic cup.

"I'm not thirsty," Ivy said. "Thanks anyway."

"But I got this for you. I saw you standing over here, checking out Will—"

"I wasn't checking out Will," she protested.

"Okay, checking out the redhead, then – her name's Samantha – and I thought you could use something to cool off."

"Thanks." Ivy reached for the cup in his right hand.

Was it her imagination, or did Gregory move it away from her? Ivy had remembered Lacey's warning and didn't want to drink from the cup he was offering. But he insisted that she take it, and she finally did. "Thanks. I'll be seeing you around," Ivy told him airily.

"Where are you going?"

"Cruising," she replied. "I didn't wear this short skirt for nothing."

"Can I come?"

"Of course not." She laughed up at him as if he had said something he knew was silly. Inside she was so tense, her stomach hurt when she breathed. "How can I check out guys with you around?"

To her relief, Gregory didn't follow her. Ivy dumped her soda in the garden as soon as he was out of sight. Working her way around the party, she smiled and listened to any guy who looked as if he needed an audience, while always steering clear of Gregory. She circled around Will, too, and didn't see either of them again until Suzanne blew out the candles on her cake.

When everyone had gathered for the song and cake-cutting, Suzanne wanted Ivy to stand on one side of her and Gregory on the other. Mrs. Goldstein, who trusted Suzanne enough to watch the party from an upstairs window – without her glasses, she told them – made an entrance with the cake and took what seemed like a hundred pictures of Suzanne, Ivy, and Gregory.

"Now each with your arm around her," Mrs. Goldstein directed them.

Ivy slipped her arm around Suzanne's back.

"Beautiful! You're all beautiful!" *Flash*.

"Let me get another shot," Mrs. Goldstein said, then shook the camera and muttered to it. "Don't move."

They didn't, not from the front, but behind Suzanne's back, Gregory began to run a finger up and down Ivy's arm. Then he used two fingers, stroking her in a slow, caressing motion. Ivy wanted to scream. She wanted to slap him away.

"Smile," Mrs. Goldstein said. *Flash*.

"And one more. Ivy—"

She forced a smile. *Flash*.

Ivy tried not to pull away too quickly from Gregory. She remembered Philip's dream about the train – the silver snake – that wanted to swallow her up. He's always watching, Philip had said, and he smells it when you're afraid.

Suzanne began cutting the cake, and Ivy handed it out. When she gave Gregory a piece, he touched her lightly on the wrist and wouldn't take the cake till she met his gaze.

Will was next in line. "We keep missing each other," he said to Ivy.

She was about to tell him to take two plates and meet her by the pond in ten minutes, but then she saw Samantha standing right behind him.

"Big party," Ivy said.

Fifteen minutes later Ivy was sitting alone on a bench about twenty feet away from the pond, eating her cake and watching Peppermint, Suzanne's Pomeranian. The little dog, who was regularly shampooed and conditioned, and let outdoors only on a leash, had escaped that night and was happily digging holes in the muddy bank. Then she waded into the pond and began to do the doggy paddle.

Some girls and guys standing by the pond called to the dog, trying to get her to fetch sticks, but Peppermint was as headstrong as her mistress. Then Ivy called softly. Too late she realized her mistake. Peppermint knew Ivy. Peppermint liked Ivy. Peppermint loved cake. She came running on her short little legs, made a flying leap for Ivy's lap, then scrambled up the rest of the way with her muddy back feet. She put her slimy front paws on Ivy's chest so she could stand up and lick her face, then dropped down in Ivy's lap and shook out her thick coat full of water.

"Pep! Hey!" Ivy wiped her face, then shook her own mane of hair. The dog saw her chance and gulped the rest of Ivy's cake. "Pep, you muddy pig!"

Ivy heard a burst of laughter next to her. Will dropped down on the bench beside her. "I'm sorry Mrs. Goldstein wasn't here with her camera," he said.

"And I'm sorry you didn't call Peppermint first," Ivy replied.

He couldn't stop laughing. "I'll get some towels," he sputtered, "for both of you."

He was quick about it and brought back a pile of wet and dry cloths. Sitting on the bench next to her, Will cleaned the dog while Ivy tried unsuccessfully to remove the mud from her skirt and top.

"Maybe we should just dump you in the pond and make you all one color," Will said to Ivy.

"Great idea. Why don't you go see how deep it is for me?"

He grinned at her, then reached over with a clean cloth and wiped her cheek close to her ear. "It's in your hair too," he said.

She felt his fingers pulling gently on her hair, trying to get out the mud. She held still. When he let go of the strands, something inside her floated upward, wanting to be touched again.

Ivy looked down quickly at her skirt and ferociously attacked a mud stain. Then Will set Peppermint on the ground between them. The clean dog wagged its little tail at him. "I bet you wish you were a puppy like me."

Ivy and Will turned at the same time and bent down to the dog, bumping their heads together.

"Ow!"

Will started laughing again. They looked in each other's eyes, laughing at themselves, and didn't see if Peppermint's mouth moved when she "spoke" a second time.

"If you were a pup like me, Will, you could jump into Ivy's arms."

Ivy thought she recognized the voice and glanced around for a suspicious purple shimmer.

"You could put your head in Ivy's lap and be cuddled. I know that's what you'd like."

Ivy sneaked a peek at Will, embarrassed, but he didn't look at all sheepish. He was staring at the dog, his mouth drawn up in a little smile. "You can put words in a dog's mouth, angel," he said, "but not in mine."

"You're no fun! Even if you do have nice buns," Lacey added.

"I thought they were *great* buns," Will said.

Lacey laughed. Ivy spotted her then, right behind them. Apparently she could throw her voice. Now the soft purple shine moved around in front of them.

"Her name's Lacey," Ivy told Will.

"I'm disappointed in you two," Lacey said. "I keep waiting for you to get things going, but you just tippy-toe around each other. As a romance, you get two thumbs down. I'm going to hang out with the kids by the pond."

Will shrugged. "Have a good time."

"Something tells me Peppermint won't be the only one taking a swim tonight," Ivy remarked under her breath.

The purple mist drifted back to them. "It's amazing how much we think alike, chick," Lacey said. "But the fact is, Tristan is still in the darkness, so I'll probably behave myself tonight. Without him around to fuss at me, it's not as much fun."

Ivy smiled a little.

"See, I miss him, too," Lacey said. For a moment her voice sounded different to Ivy, girlish and wistful. Then the tone became theatrical again: "Whoops, here she comes. Warning, ten feet behind you – chick with a capital *C*. I'm all gone, boys and girls."

But Lacey didn't leave immediately. "Mommy, I went swimming! I had so much fun!" Peppermint "said" in a voice loud enough for Suzanne to hear.

The purple shimmer slipped away as Suzanne came around to the front of the bench.

"Pep! Oh, Pep!" She felt the dog's wet fur. "You bad girl. I'm going to put you in your kennel."

Then she saw Ivy's mud-splattered skirt and top. "Ivy!"

"You going to put me in the kennel, too?" Ivy asked.

Will laughed.

Suzanne shook her head. "I'm so sorry. Bad girl!"

Peppermint lowered her head contritely, until Suzanne turned to Ivy. Then her head popped up, and her tail wagged again.

"It's my fault," Ivy said. "I called Peppermint while she was swimming. It's no big deal – all I need is a little soap."

"I'll get it for you," Suzanne said.

"No, it's okay," Ivy replied, smiling. "I know where it is." She stood up.

"If you want to throw your clothes in the wash," Suzanne told her, "wear something of mine. You know which is the clean stuff."

"Whatever isn't on the floor," they both said at the same time, and laughed.

Ivy started toward the house and heard Suzanne ask Will how he made that dog voice. She was still smiling to herself when she entered the house. Then she hurried down the hall, glancing around for Gregory, hoping he didn't see her heading upstairs.

Ivy relaxed when she reached Suzanne's bedroom, a room she had spent countless hours in, gossiping, reading magazines, trying on makeup. The large, square room was furnished in dark polished wood and carpeted wall to wall in a pure, plush white. Suzanne and Ivy always joked that the best way to keep the carpet clean was to walk on her clothes. But that day Ivy removed her shoes. The room was picked up, with the green silk coverlet pulled smooth on the bed and just one filmy top tossed aside, one with buttons down the front. Ivy took off her stained shirt, slipped on the top without bothering to do it up, and headed for Suzanne's bathroom.

The soap worked well on her knit top. She squeezed the top out in a towel, then hung it on a hanger. She turned the hairdryer on, propping it up to dry the knit while she worked on her skirt. Ivy was standing close to the sink, pulling up her pale denim skirt and scrubbing it hard, when she felt the hot air on her back and her hair and the top blew loose. She glanced up quickly.

In the mirror she saw Gregory, aiming the hair dryer at her and laughing.

Ivy wrapped the open top around her as if it were a coat. "It's the top that needs drying, not me," she said crisply.

Gregory laughed, flicked off the dryer and dropped it, letting it dangle from its electric cord.

"I'm losing patience," he said.

Ivy stared at him wide-eyed.

"I'm getting tired of chasing you," he said.

She bit her lip. "I don't know why you keep trying."

He tilted back his head, studying her as if he were making some kind of decision. He moved close to her. She could smell the alcohol on his breath. "Liar," he whispered in her ear. "Every guy out there would be chasing you if they thought they had a chance."

Ivy's mind raced. How much had Gregory drunk? What kind of game was he playing?

His arms encircled her. Ivy fought the panic that was growing inside her. She could not get away from him, so she put her arms around him lightly, trying to draw him out of the secluded bathroom. She had left the bedroom door open, and if she made it to where they could be seen and heard—

He moved easily with her into the bedroom. Then she saw that the door to the hall had been closed. He started pushing her toward the bed.

He can't kill me, not here, she thought as she was pushed back. It'd be too easy to trace him. She stepped back again. His fingerprints are on the hair dryer and the door, she reminded herself, stepping back and back. And someone could walk in at any moment, she told herself. He moved with her, so close she couldn't see his face.

Ivy tumbled onto the bed and stared up at him. Gregory's eyes were like hot gray coals. Color crept high in his cheeks. He's too smart to pull a gun, she thought. He'll jam a capsule down my throat.

Then Gregory was on top of her. Ivy struggled against him. Gregory laughed at her efforts as she squirmed beneath him, then he groaned softly. "I love you," he said.

Ivy held still, and he lifted his head, staring down at her, his eyes burning with a strange light. "I want you. I've wanted you for a long time."

Was this some kind of terrible joke?

"You know things about me," Gregory said softly, "but you're in love with me, aren't you, Ivy? You would never do anything to hurt me."

Was his ego that big? Was he that crazy? No, she thought, he's warning me.

He laid his hand on her neck. He stroked her throat with his thumb, then pressed it against her pulse. A smile spread across his face. "What did I tell you? Running hot and fast," he said. Then he removed his hand from her throat and slowly traced the edge of her unbuttoned top. Ivy's skin crawled.

"Goose bumps." He seemed pleased. "If a month from now I can't give you goose bumps with my touch, if you don't get hot when we kiss, I'll know you don't feel the same way you do now."

He really believed it!

"And that would be too bad," he said, still tracing her shirt with his finger. "I'd have to figure out what to do with you then." He leaned on her heavily and pressed his mouth against hers.

Play along, Ivy thought. Play to stay alive. Angels, where are you? She kissed him back, though everything inside her rose up in protest. She kissed him again. Oh, angels, help me! Gregory's kisses grew more passionate, more insistent.

She pushed against him, catching him by surprise. Shoving him away, she rolled off the bed. She could not hold it back – Ivy threw up on the rug.

When she stopped retching, she turned to look at Gregory, wiping her mouth with one hand, steadying herself against a chair with the other. She saw an entirely different expression on his face. He knew now. The curtain had been lifted, and there was no more pretending. He had seen exactly what she thought of him. His eyes showed what he now thought about her.

Before either of them could say anything, the bedroom door swung open. Suzanne stood in the doorway. "I noticed both of you were missing," she began, and gazed past them at the rumpled bed. Then she looked at the mess on the floor. "Oh, God!"

Gregory was ready for her. "Ivy's had too much to drink," he said.

"I haven't. I haven't had a thing!" Ivy said quickly.

"She can't tolerate alcohol," Gregory said, walking toward Suzanne, reaching out toward her.

Ivy moved with him. "Suzanne, please, listen to me."

"I was worried about her and—"

"I just talked to you," Ivy reminded Suzanne. "I just talked to you – did I seem drunk?"

But Suzanne looked at her blankly.

"Answer me!" Ivy demanded. The faraway look in Suzanne's eyes scared her. Her friend's mind had already been poisoned by what she saw.

"Nice top," Suzanne remarked. "Couldn't find the buttons?"

Ivy pulled it closed.

"I came up to see if she was all right," Gregory continued, "and she, you know—" He paused as if he were embarrassed. "She came on to me. I guess that doesn't really surprise you."

"It doesn't," Suzanne replied in a cool, distant voice.

"Suzanne," Ivy pleaded, "listen to me. We've been friends all this time and you trusted me—"

"This time she came on strong," Gregory said. He frowned. "I guess it was the booze."

This time? Ivy thought. "I swear to you, Suzanne, he's lying!"

"Did you kiss him?" Suzanne asked, her voice shaking. "Did you?" She looked again at the rumpled bed.

"He kissed me!"

"What kind of friend are you?" Suzanne cried. "You and I both know that you've been after Gregory since Tristan died."

"But he's been after me since—" Ivy saw Gregory glance at her out of the corner of his eye, and she broke off her sentence.

She knew she had lost the battle.

Suzanne was trembling so, she could hardly get the words out. "Leave," she said in a low, husky voice. "Get out of here, Ivy. Don't ever come back."

"I'll clean up—"

"Leave! Just leave!" Suzanne shouted.

There was nothing she could do. Ivy left her friend crying and clinging to Gregory.

41

Ivy didn't think about how she was getting home. She ducked into a bathroom farther down the hall and washed her mouth out with toothpaste. After buttoning the top, she raced downstairs, snatched up her bag, and hurried out of the house.

She struggled to hold back the tears. She didn't want Gregory to hear stories later on about how upset she was. Philip's words came back to her once more. "He can smell it if you're afraid."

Now Ivy was terrified – for both herself and her friends. At any point they could stumble upon one of Gregory's secrets. And his ego was big enough, he was crazy enough to assume that he could get away with silencing not just her, but Suzanne, Will, and Beth, too.

Ivy walked briskly along the side of Lantern Road. The houses in Suzanne's neighborhood were far apart, and there were no sidewalks. It was another dark mile to the intersection and two more miles into the town itself. The only light was a soft yellow moon.

"Angels, stay with me," Ivy prayed.

She had walked about a third of a mile when the headlights of a car bore down on her. She stepped quickly off the road and ducked into some bushes. The car drove ten feet more, then screeched to a halt. Ivy scrambled to get deeper into the brush. The driver suddenly extinguished his bright lights, and she could see the shape of the car in the moonlight: a Prius. Will's car.

He climbed out and looked around. "Ivy?"

She wanted to rush out of the bushes and into his arms, but she held back.

"Ivy, if you're here, tell me. Tell me you're okay."

Her mind raced, trying to think what she could tell him without spilling the whole and dangerous truth.

"Answer me. Are you okay? Lacey said you were in trouble. Tell me if there is some way I can help."

Even in the pale light, the look of worry on his face was visible. She longed to reach out to him and tell him everything. She wanted to run to him and feel his arms wrap around her, keeping her safe for a moment. But for his sake she couldn't – she knew that. Her eyes burned. She blinked several times to clear them, then emerged onto the road.

"Ivy." He breathed her name.

"I – I was going home," she said.

His glance flicked to the bushes behind her. "Taking a shortcut?"

"Maybe you could give me a ride," she said softly.

He studied her face a moment, then silently opened the door for her. When he had locked and closed it again, Ivy leaned against the door, feeling safe. She would be safe till she got to the house on the ridge.

Will got in on the driver's side. "Do you really want to go home?" he asked.

In the end, she'd have to. She nodded, but he didn't start the car.

"Ivy, who are you afraid of?"

She shrugged and looked down at her hands. "I don't know."

Will reached over and laid his hand on top of hers. She turned it over and examined the small flecks of oil paint that the turpentine rag had missed. Ivy could picture Will's hands with her eyes closed. The way his fingers felt now entwined with hers made her feel strong.

"I want to help you," he said, "but I can't if I don't know what's going on."

Ivy turned her face away from him.

"You have to tell me what's going on," he insisted.

"I can't, Will."

"What happened that night at the train station?" he asked.

She didn't answer him.

"You must remember something now. You must have some idea about what you saw. Was someone else there? What made you try to cross the tracks?"

She shook her head and said nothing.

"All right," he said in a resigned voice. "Then I've got just one more question for you. Are you in love with Gregory?"

Ivy was caught off guard, and her head spun toward him. Will looked into her eyes. He studied her whole face. "That's what I needed to know," he said quietly.

What had she given away? Ivy wondered. What had her eyes revealed? That she hated Gregory? Or that she was falling in love with Will?

She let go of his hand. "Please take me home," she said, and he did.

"And now," said a voice quivering with emotion, "we return to today's program . . . *For Love of Ivy.*" A soap opera tune was hummed loudly – and pretty badly, Tristan thought.

Will heard it, too. He glanced around the school darkroom, where he had been working alone, and saw Lacey's purple shimmer. "You again," he muttered.

589

As always, Tristan found it remarkably easy to match thoughts with Will. He slipped quickly inside him, so he could communicate with both Will and Lacey.

Will blinked. "Tristan?" he said aloud.

"Yeah," he replied. The soap opera music continued in the background. "You're off key, Lacey," Tristan told her.

The humming stopped, and the purple shimmer moved closer to him and Will.

Will quickly put a roll of film behind him. "Could you step back a little, Lacey? You might mess up my pictures."

"Well, ex*cuse* me!" she replied. "I guess you two heroes don't need me around. I'll be on my way." She paused to give them time to protest. When neither of them did, she added, "But before I go, let me ask you lover boys a few questions. Who got Rip van Winkle here out of the darkness before the next hundred years had passed? Who directed him to this darkroom?"

"I've been calling for you, Tristan," Will explained. "I need your help."

"Who played guardian angel at Suzanne's party?" Lacey continued. "Who told you when Ivy was in big trouble?"

"Ivy was in trouble? What happened?" Tristan asked.

"Who, tell me, *who's* playing secretary to this pitiful Ivy fan club?"

"Tell me what happened," Tristan demanded. "Is Ivy okay?"

"Yes and no," Will replied, then told Tristan about the incident at the party, including Gregory's account of it. "I don't know what really happened," he said. "I caught up with Ivy afterward on the road. She was upset and wouldn't tell me anything. On Sunday she worked, then went straight to Beth's. At school today she'd talk only to Beth but wouldn't tell even her what really happened."

"Lacey, did you see anything?" Tristan asked.

"Sorry, I was, uh, socializing at the time."

"What do you think she was doing?" Tristan asked.

"Throwing the shoes of ungrateful movie fans into the pond," Will told him.

"I'm talking about Ivy!" Tristan snapped, but he was more upset with himself than Will. Twice now Will had been there for Ivy when Tristan had not.

"I've been calling you—" Will began.

"And calling and calling," Lacey said. "I told him you were in the darkness. I knew love was blind, but I guess it's deaf too. I guess—"

"You've got to tell me some things, Tristan," Will interrupted her. "You've got to tell me now. How can I help Ivy if I don't know what's going on?"

"But you know enough," Tristan challenged him. "More than you've admitted to Ivy." He began to probe Will's mind, but was swiftly pushed aside. "I know you looked in the envelope, Will," Tristan said. "I was watching when you pulled out the key."

Will didn't seem surprised or apologetic. "What does the key go to?" he asked.

"I thought you might have figured it out," Tristan baited him.

"No."

Tristan tried again to probe Will's thoughts, completely silencing his own, moving slowly and carefully. He got slammed like an ice-hockey player against the wall of Will's mind.

"Okay, okay, you two, what's going on?" Lacey asked. "I can see your face, Will. You've got the same pigheaded expression that Tristan gets."

"He's blocking me out," Tristan charged.

"Like you haven't done the same thing to me," Will replied heatedly. "First you send me racing up the ridge to save Ivy's life. I let you take over. I go along with you and do just what you say, and I find Ivy with a bag over her head. Gregory's there with a strange excuse, but you won't tell me a thing about what's going on."

Will walked up and down the narrow room, picking up and putting down filters, markers, boxes of paper. "You get me to speak for you. You get me to dance with her and warn her and tell her you love her." Will's voice trembled a little. "But you don't tell me anything to explain why this is happening."

Ivy won't let me, Tristan thought, but he knew that wasn't the only reason. He resented the fact that he needed Will, and he didn't like the way Will was calling some of the shots now.

"I don't like this mind-control stuff," Will went on angrily. "I don't like your trying to read my mind. If there's something you want to know, ask it."

"What I want to know," Tristan said, "is how I'm supposed to trust you. You're Gregory's friend—"

"Oh, grow up, you two!" Lacey interrupted. "I don't like mind control. How can I trust you?" she mimicked. "*Puh-lease* don't bore me with the rest of your excuses. You're both in love with Ivy, and you're jealous of each other, and that's why you're keeping your little secrets and squabbling like two kindergarten kids."

"*Are* you in love with her, Will?" Tristan asked quickly.

He felt Will thinking, he felt Will dodging him.

Will didn't answer straight away. "I'm trying to do what's best for her," he said at last.

"You didn't answer my question."

"I don't see why it matters," Will argued. "You were there when I danced with her. You heard what

Ivy said. We both know she'll never love anyone the way she loves you."

"We both know you hope it's not true," Tristan replied.

Will slammed his hand down on the table. "I've got work to do."

"So do I," Tristan said, and slipped out of Will before he could be thrown out.

He knew that Ivy would love someone else someday and that that person might be Will. Well, if he had to leave her in Will's hands, he was going to check him out thoroughly first.

As Tristan left the darkroom he heard Lacey's soap opera voice. "And so our two heroes part," she said, "blinded by love, neither of them listening to the wise and beautiful Lacey" – she hummed a little – "who, by the way, is getting a broken heart of her own. But who cares about Lacey?" she asked sadly. "Who cares about Lacey?"

42

Ivy sat at the kitchen table glancing over legal forms that she had just pulled out of a manila envelope – Philip's adoption papers. Across from her, her brother and his best friend Sammy dug spoons into a peanut butter jar.

Sammy was a short, funny-looking kid whose hair stood straight up from his head like bristly red grass. Ivy saw him eyeing her. He nudged Philip. "Ask her. Ask her."

"Ask me what?"

"Sammy wants to meet Tristan," Philip said. "But I can't get him to come. Do you know where he is?"

Ivy instinctively glanced over her shoulder, but Philip assured her, "It's okay. Mom's upstairs, and Gregory likes to hear about angels now."

"He does?" Ivy asked with surprise.

Philip nodded.

"I really want to see an angel," Sammy said, pulling a little camera out of his grubby school pack.

Ivy smiled. "I think Tristan's resting now," she said, then she turned to Philip. "What kind of angel things have you and Gregory been talking about?"

"He asked me about Tristan."

"What exactly did he want to know?" Ivy asked. She had suspected that the train incident haunted Gregory. After all, there was no way Philip could have gotten to the station that quickly without help from someone. Did Gregory guess that he was up against more than herself, more than just a person?

"He asked me what Tristan looked like," Philip told her. "And how I know when he's there."

"And how to get him to come," Sammy said. "Remember, he asked that."

"He wanted to know if you ever talked to Tristan," Philip added.

Ivy tapped the manila envelope against the table. "When did you talk about all this?"

"Last night," her brother replied, "when we were playing in the tree house."

Ivy frowned. She didn't like the idea of Gregory's playing with Philip up in the tree house, where one accident had already occurred during the summer.

She glanced down at the adoption forms. Andrew hadn't told Gregory that he was about to make Philip his legal son. Ivy wondered if Andrew had the same kind of fears that she did.

"When will Tristan be finished with his nap?" Sammy asked.

"I don't really know," Ivy replied.

"I have a flashlight, in case I see him at night," he told her.

"Good idea," Ivy said with a smile. She watched as the two boys licked the last bit of peanut butter off their spoons and ran outside.

Since Saturday night, she too had been trying to reach Tristan. Rumors about the party were flying at school. Gregory and she had managed to avoid each other in the halls. So had she and Suzanne, but while Gregory slipped past Ivy, Suzanne dramatically played out each snub. Her anger at Ivy was obvious to everyone.

Ivy was relieved when Beth had told her that Gregory and Suzanne were going to the football game that afternoon. Having slept little in the past two nights, she could finally rest, knowing that Gregory wouldn't walk in on her. Even though she locked her bedroom door now, she never really felt safe.

Ivy slipped the envelope and forms in her stack of schoolbooks and was about to head upstairs when she heard a car pull up behind the house. It sounded like Gregory's BMW. Her first instinct was to rush up to her room, but she didn't want Gregory to think she was afraid of him. Sitting back down, she opened the newspaper and hunched over the table, pretending to read. The kitchen door was pushed open, and instantly Ivy smelled the perfume. "Suzanne."

Suzanne responded with a sullen look.

"Hi," Gregory said. His tone of voice was neither warm nor cold, and his face was expressionless – though ready to flash into a smile if anyone else happened to walk into the kitchen. Suzanne continued to look at Ivy with pouting lips.

"This is a surprise," Ivy said. "Beth said you were going to the football game."

"Suzanne was bored, and I had to pick up something," Gregory told her. He turned his back to Ivy, reached into the cupboard, and pulled out a tall frosted glass. "Would you get her a drink?" he asked, handing Ivy the cup.

"Sure." Gregory exited the kitchen quickly.

Ivy checked the refrigerator for sodas. "Sorry, no cold ones," she told Suzanne.

Suzanne remained silent.

Except you, Ivy said to herself, then reached under the counter for a bottle. She wondered why Gregory would leave them alone to talk. Perhaps he was standing outside the kitchen door, waiting to hear what she would say. Maybe this was a test to see if she'd tell Suzanne what she knew about him.

"How are you doing?" Ivy asked.

"Fine."

A one-word answer, but it was a start. Ivy dropped some ice cubes into the soda and handed it to Suzanne. "At school a lot of kids were talking about your party. Everyone had a good time."

"Downstairs and upstairs," Suzanne replied.

Ivy remained silent.

"How bad was your hangover?" Suzanne asked.

"I didn't have one," Ivy told her.

"Oh, that's right, you got rid of all the booze in you." Ivy bit her lip.

"I couldn't sleep in my room Saturday night," Suzanne said, and walked around the kitchen, swirling the drink in her glass.

"I'm sorry about that, Suzanne. I really am. But the truth is, I didn't have anything to drink," Ivy said firmly.

"I want to believe you." Suzanne's lip trembled. "I want you and Gregory to tell me I dreamed it all."

"You know he won't. And I won't, either."

Suzanne nodded and dropped her chin. "I know everybody cries when they break up with a guy. But I never thought I'd get out the tissues because I was splitting up with you."

"You've known me longer than any of your

guys," Ivy replied quickly. "You trusted me for ten years. Then one guy says something, and you don't."

"I saw you with my own eyes!"

"What did you see?" Ivy almost shouted. "You saw what he wanted you to see, what he told you to see. How can I convince you—"

"You can stop fooling around with my boyfriend, that's how! You can keep your hot little hands where they belong!" Suzanne took a large gulp of her drink. "You're making a fool of yourself, Ivy, and you're doing it at my expense."

"Suzanne, why can't you admit that it's at least possible that Gregory was coming on to me?"

"*Liar,*" Suzanne said. "I'll never trust you again." She took another angry gulp of soda, leaving a print of her lipstick on the frosted glass. "I warned you, Ivy. But you didn't listen to me. You didn't care enough to."

"I care about you more than you realize," Ivy said, taking a step toward Suzanne.

Suzanne turned on her heel. "Tell Gregory I'm on the patio," she said as she walked out the kitchen door.

Ivy let her friend go. It's useless, she thought. He's poisoned Suzanne's mind. Fighting back the tears, Ivy rushed out of the kitchen toward the stairs. She ran headlong into Gregory and pushed past him. She didn't bother telling him where

Suzanne had gone. She was sure he had been listening to every word.

Ivy didn't pause to catch her breath until she reached her music room. She slammed the door closed behind her and leaned against it. Keep cool, keep cool, she said to herself.

But she couldn't stop shaking. She had lost all hope that she could win against Gregory. She needed help, needed someone to assure her that things would get better. She remembered the day Will had driven her back to the train station, how he had believed in her and given her the confidence to believe in herself.

"I'll find Will," she said aloud, then turned toward the door and was surprised to see the shimmering gold light. "Tristan!"

His gold light surrounded her. "Yes, *Tristan*," he said, within her now.

"Are you all right? Where have you been?" Ivy asked silently. "You were gone so long this time. A lot has happened since you fell into the darkness."

"I know," Tristan replied. "Will and Lacey filled me in."

"Did they tell you about Suzanne? She thinks — she believes whatever Gregory says, and she hates me now, she—" The flood of tears was uncontrollable.

"Shhh. Ivy, shhh. I know about Suzanne," Tristan told her. "And I'm sorry, but you have to forget about her right now. There are a lot more import—"

"Forget about her?" The tears became furious ones, and Ivy spoke out loud. "He wants to hurt me any and every way he can!"

"Ivy, speak silently," Tristan reminded her quickly. "I know this is hard for you—"

"You don't know! You don't understand how I feel," Ivy said, sitting down at the piano. She ran her finger sharply up the keyboard.

"Listen to me, Ivy. I found out something you have to know."

"I can't keep losing people," she said.

"There's something I want to tell you about," Tristan persisted.

"First I lost you, now Suzanne, and—"

"Will," he said.

"Will?" The tone of Tristan's voice, low and firm, alarmed her. "What about Will?" she asked, crossing her arms.

"You can't trust him."

"But I do trust him," Ivy replied, determined not to be persuaded otherwise.

"I just came from searching his house," Tristan told her.

"Searching?"

"And I found some pretty interesting things there," he added.

"Like what?" she demanded.

"Books about angels. A tracing of Caroline's key."

"Well, what do you expect?" Ivy asked "Of course he's read about angels. He's trying to understand exactly what you are and why you've come back. And we already knew he was curious enough to look in the envelope that contained the key. I would have done the same thing if I were him," she added defensively.

"There was also a copy of Beth's story," Tristan said. "The one about the woman who committed suicide, the one she recited for your drama club assignment the month before Caroline died. Do you remember it?"

Ivy nodded slowly. "The woman tore up photographs of her lover and his new sweetheart, leaving them like a suicide note when she shot herself."

"Just as Caroline supposedly tore up photos of Andrew and your mother," Tristan said.

Once before Ivy had thought about the similarity between Beth's story and the setup the police had found at Caroline's house. She had assumed it was another example of the uncanny way Beth anticipated events, but now she realized that Gregory could have borrowed the idea from Beth.

"And there's a clipping of the story about the girl in Ridgefield," Tristan went on. "The one who was attacked right after you were, in the exact same way. It worked, didn't it? The style of attack convinced everyone that it was part of a series of crimes by someone who didn't know you."

Ivy dropped her head in her hands, thinking about the girl.

"So what are you saying?" she asked at last. "That Will has figured out a lot more than we thought? I'm glad. I wanted to protect him, but now there's no reason to hold anything back."

"But there is a reason," Tristan replied quickly. "Will has something else. The jacket and cap."

Ivy sat up straight. How had he gotten the clothes? Did he know they were important evidence? Why hadn't he told her?

"Oh, he knows they're important," Tristan answered her thoughts. "They were wrapped carefully in plastic bags and hidden with everything else."

"But I never told him what I saw. I never told him what tempted me to cross the tracks, and that story wasn't released to the papers."

"So either he was in on it—"

"No!" said Ivy.

"—or he's somehow figured it out. Maybe Eric told him something. In any case, he knows a lot more than he's telling either of us."

Ivy remembered the day at the station when they had caught Eric searching the drainage ditch by the side of the road. Will must have already found the cap and jacket. He was faking it in front of Eric – and her.

She stood up abruptly, pushing back the piano bench.

"Ivy?"

She mentally pushed Tristan away and walked over to the window. Dropping down on her knees, Ivy rested her arms and chin on the windowsill.

"Ivy, talk to me. Don't push me away."

"He's just trying to help us," Ivy said. "I'm sure it's nothing more than that."

"How can he be helping when he's hiding things from us?"

"Because he thinks that's what's best," she replied, though she knew it didn't make sense. "I know him. I trust him."

"Suzanne trusts Gregory," Tristan pointed out.

"It's not the same!" Ivy cried, thrusting Tristan out of her mind altogether. "It's not the same!"

She had cried out loud, and for a moment she thought she heard her own voice reverberating in the room. Then she realized the shouting came from below. Suzanne was calling out. Ivy heard Gregory's voice drowning out Suzanne's. She rushed down to her bedroom and raced across the second-floor hall to the back set of steps. Suzanne was hurrying up the narrow stair, her long black hair fanning out behind her, her face pale and glistening with perspiration.

She clutched the glass in which Ivy had fixed her soda.

Gregory trailed her. "Suzanne," he said, "give Ivy a chance to explain."

Suzanne threw back her head and laughed wildly, so wildly she almost fell backward down the stair. Then she looked at Ivy, and Ivy knew something was terribly wrong.

"I can't wait," Suzanne said. "I can't wait to see how she explains this one."

Suzanne shoved the soda toward Ivy, forcing her to take the glass in her hands. Then she uncurled her left fist. In the damp palm of her friend's hand, Ivy saw a round orange pill. Ivy glanced quickly at Gregory, then back at the tablet.

"What is it?" Suzanne asked. "Tell me, what did I find in my drink?"

"It looks like a vitamin," Ivy said cautiously.

"A vitamin!" Suzanne shrieked with laughter, but Ivy saw the tears in her friend's eyes. "That's good," Suzanne sputtered. "A vitamin. What were you going to do, Ivy? Send me on a nice trip like Eric's? You're crazy. You're a screwed-up, crazy, jealous witch." She dropped the orange tablet in the soda. "Here, let's put the vitamin back. Now you drink it, drink all of it."

Ivy stared down at the glass. She knew that Gregory had set her up, and she figured it was harmless, but she couldn't take the chance.

"Swallow it," Suzanne said, tears running down her face. "Swallow the vitamin."

Ivy put her hand over the top of the cup and shook her head. She saw Suzanne's mouth jerk.

Suzanne turned, ducked under Gregory's arms, and ran down to the first floor. Gregory followed her. Ivy sank down on the steps and dropped her head to her knees. She didn't try to hide the tears, though she knew that Gregory paused to look over his shoulder, enjoying the view.

43

Tristan thought that warning Ivy about Will would have made him feel good. After all, his suspicions were right. Will was not admitting to them what he knew, and he wasn't telling them how he knew it. Now Ivy could trust only Tristan. He should have felt smart and victorious – at least satisfied. He didn't. No matter how much they needed and loved each other, he and Ivy stood on either side of an uncrossable river.

Monday evening the world seemed grayer, chillier to him. He stood outside of Caroline's dark house and felt the autumn coming on like a creature who has no home. When Tristan slipped through the walls, he felt like an intruder, a ghost who haunted, not an angel who helped those he loved. He longed to be with Ivy, but he didn't dare go to her now. He knew the information about

Will had hurt and angered her. Now that he had told her, what could Tristan say to make things better?

"Tristan?"

He looked around, surprised.

"Tristan?"

He wanted so much to hear Ivy's voice that he thought he did.

"Are you in there?" she called. "Let me in."

Tristan hurried to the door, focusing quickly in order to materialize his fingers. They kept slipping on the latch as he struggled to undo it. He wondered if it looked strange to Ivy when the door of the darkened house swung slowly in on its hinges.

She stepped inside and stopped just within the moonlit rectangle made by the gaping door. In the silver light her hair shimmered, and her skin looked as pale as an apparition's. For a moment Tristan believed something terrible and wonderful had happened, and she had come to him as a spirit like himself. But then he saw how she turned toward him, her eyes full of love but unfocused, the way eyes see a glow, but not the features of a face.

"I love you." They shared that thought, and he moved easily inside her mind.

"I'm sorry, Tristan," she said softly. "I'm sorry I pushed you out like that."

He was so glad to be with her, so glad she had come to him, he couldn't speak for a moment. "I know I hurt you when I told you about Will," he said at last.

She gave a little shrug and closed the door behind them. "You had to tell me the truth."

Tristan knew from the small shrug that the news still upset her. I should make her talk about it, he thought. I should remind her that she'll fall in love again, there will be someone else she'll love one day—

"I love you, Tristan," Ivy said. "Please, no matter what happens, promise you won't forget that."

Another time. They could talk about the future another time.

"Are you listening?" Ivy asked. "I know you're there. You're cloaking, Tristan. Are you angry?"

"I'm wondering," he said. "How did you know to come here?"

He felt the smile on her lips. "I'm not sure," she said. "I guess I just needed to see you so badly, and after this afternoon, I didn't think you'd come when I called. I figured it was up to me to find you. I got in the car and drove, and here's where I ended up."

He laughed. "Here's where you ended up. After all this is over, you and Beth are going to have to open a shop – Palms, Tea Leaves, and Telepathy."

"You could join us for séances," Ivy suggested. Her smile warmed him through.

"Lyons, Van Dyke, and Spirit. Sounds good," he said, but he knew that when his mission was over he wouldn't come back. None of the angels Lacey had known ever returned.

Ivy was still smiling as she walked around Caroline's kitchen. He saw through her eyes as they slowly adjusted to the dark. "It looks as if you've been searching the house," she said, observing the open kitchen drawers and cabinet doors that hung ajar.

"Lacey and I searched here back in August, long before you got the key, but we didn't leave the place like this," he replied. "Someone else has been here since."

He heard the thought, though she tried hard to repress it. Will.

"It could have been a lot of people," Tristan said quickly. "Gregory or Eric. Or Will," he added as softly as possible. "Or even that guy who visits Caroline's grave and leaves her red roses."

"I saw a long-stemmed rose there."

"Did you see him?" Tristan asked as Ivy peeked inside the open cupboards. Most of them were empty, but she found a flashlight in a shallow drawer.

"No. What's he look like?"

"Tall, slim, dark-haired," Tristan replied. "His name is Tom Stetson, and he works at Andrew's college. Lacey followed him around at your Labor Day party. Ever hear anyone talk about him?"

Ivy shook her head, then said suddenly, "If I

shake my head, or make a face, I guess you don't know it when you're inside me."

"I know it. I feel it. I love it when you smile."

The smile grew so that it seemed to wrap itself around him.

"So what do you think?" Ivy asked. "Was Tom Stetson Caroline's new love? Was he involved some-how?"

"I don't know," Tristan said, "but both he and Gregory must have a key to this house. I think Tom's the one who's been boxing things up."

"And searching through cupboards and drawers at the same time," Ivy said.

"Maybe."

She reached for the string around her neck and pulled out the key that was dangling beneath her shirt. Under the beam of the flashlight, its silver shaft and two jagged teeth gleamed.

"Well, I'm the one who's got the key," she said. "Now if we can just find the lock . . ."

They began to search together. In the living room they discovered a desk with a locked drawer which had been forced open. Close by, on the mantel, was a box with a brass lock whose hinges had been broken. It now lay empty. Ivy tested the key in both locks and found that it had not been made for either.

In the bedroom Tristan called Ivy's attention to a rectangular design pressed into a bureau cloth, as if a heavy box had sat there for a long time but was gone now. Caroline's closet was still full of shoes and purses, which looked as if they had been searched. Ivy pulled them out and felt behind them. They moved on to other rooms. An hour and a half later, their search had turned up nothing.

"There's a lot of junk here, but we're not getting anywhere," Tristan said, frustrated.

Ivy sank down in the corner of the hallway. He noticed that she avoided sitting in any of Caroline's chairs.

"The problem is, we don't know what's been carried out of here already or where it's been carried to," Ivy observed. "If only we had some clue about what we were looking for."

"How about Beth?" Tristan asked suddenly. "What if we got her to help? She has a sixth sense. Maybe if you show her the key, let her hold it and meditate on it, she'll be able to tell us where to look – at least give us a hint."

"Good idea." Ivy glanced at her watch. "Can you come with me?"

Tristan knew that he shouldn't. He was tired and needed to pace himself if he wanted to keep from falling into the darkness. But he couldn't give her up. Something told him there was not much time left for him to spend with Ivy.

"I'll come, but I'd better just observe," he said. He was quiet most of the way to Beth's house.

Mr. Van Dyke must have been getting used to Ivy's calling at unexpected times. Standing in the doorway, he glanced at her over his half glasses and law brief, hollered "Beth!" and left Ivy to find her way upstairs.

Tristan was startled by the sight of Beth and her room, but Ivy told him silently, "She's been writing."

Beth blinked at Ivy as if she were worlds away. A binder clip held her hair in a lopsided ponytail. An old pair of glasses sat partway down her nose; they also were lopsided, since they were missing an arm. She wore baggy gym shorts and scuzzy-looking slippers with animal heads on them and popcorn embedded in their fur.

Ivy reached toward Beth and pulled a yellow Post-it off her T-shirt. "'Lovely, lingering, delicate, devious, delicious,'" she read, then said, "I'm really sorry about barging in like this."

"That's okay," Beth replied cheerfully, and reached for the Post-it. "I was looking for this – thanks."

"It's just that we need your help."

"We? Oh." Beth closed the bedroom door quickly and cleared a spot on the bed, dumping folders and notebooks on the floor. She studied Ivy's face, then smiled. "Hello, Mr. Glow," she said to Tristan.

"Beth, do you remember the envelope Eric's sister gave me?" Ivy asked.

Tristan saw the sudden brightness in Beth's eyes. She had watched Ivy open the envelope at the cemetery and must have been dying with curiosity.

"This is what was in it." Ivy pulled out the key and placed it in Beth's hand.

"It looks as if it goes to a box," Beth said, "or a drawer. It could be an old door key, but I don't think so – it doesn't look long enough."

"The envelope it came in had Caroline's name and address on it," Ivy said. "We've been searching her house but can't find what it goes to. Can you work on it? You know, keep it for a while and think about it and see if anything comes to you?"

Tristan saw Beth draw back. "Oh, Ivy, I—"

"Please."

"She's afraid," Tristan said softly to Ivy. "You have to help her. Her own predictions have frightened her."

"I'm not asking you to predict anything," Ivy said quickly. "Just hold it and think about it and see what comes to you. No matter how strange or ordinary it seems, it may be a clue to tell us where to look."

Beth looked down at the key. "I wish you hadn't asked me, Ivy. When I do something like this, it stirs up all kinds of other things in my mind, things

615

I don't understand, things that frighten me some-times." She turned and looked longingly at the computer screen on her desk, where the cursor blinked, waiting for her to return to her story. "I wish you hadn't asked me."

"Okay, I understand," Ivy said, picking up the key.

Beth's hand closed around Ivy's. Tristan could feel how cold and clammy it was. "Leave it with me till tomorrow," she said. "I'll give it back to you at school. Maybe something will come to me."

Ivy threw her arms around her friend. "Thank you. Thank you. I wouldn't have asked you if it weren't important."

A few minutes later Ivy headed home. "You're still with me," she said as she turned up the long driveway.

The happiness in her voice warmed Tristan, but he could not throw off his weariness and a growing sense of dread that the darkness would soon over-take him. What if he was in the darkness when Ivy needed him most?

"I'll stay with you until you get to your room," he said. "Then I'll return to Beth's."

As they passed a bush Ivy suddenly bent down. "Ella? Ella, come out and say hello. Your buddy is with me."

The cat's green eyes glinted at them, but she didn't budge.

"Ella, come on, what's wrong?"

Ella mewed, and Ivy reached into the bushes to pull her out. She lifted up the cat, rubbing her in her favorite spot around her ears. The cat didn't purr.

"What's wrong with you?" Ivy said, then gasped. Tristan felt the shudder run through her as if it rippled through his own body. Ivy turned the cat over gently. Along her right flank was a stripe where fur had been roughly stripped away. Her pink skin was scraped bloody and raw.

"Ella, how did this—" But Ivy didn't finish the question. She realized the answer the same moment Tristan did. "Gregory," she said.

44

All night Ivy had dreams about Ella, long, winding dreams in which Gregory chased the cat and Ivy chased Gregory. Then just as she got close, he turned on her. Ivy's sleep did not grow peaceful until after the sky was light. Now, with eyes closed against the brightness, she counted the muted gongs from the clock in the dining room. They sounded a million miles away – five million, six million, seven million, eight million—

"Eight!" She sat up quickly in bed.

Ella, who had been snuggled close, pressed her body hard against Ivy's, burying her face in Ivy's side. As gently as possible, Ivy lifted the cat onto her lap. When she saw the wound again, tears came to her eyes. "Okay, girl, let's clean you up."

She carefully lifted Ella off the bed and carried her toward the bathroom.

"Ivy, Ivy, aren't you ready yet?" her mother called from downstairs.

Ivy turned and walked out to the hall, staying close enough to the wall to remain hidden from Maggie. "Almost," she called down.

"Everyone else is gone," Maggie shouted back at her. "I'm leaving now, too."

"See you," Ivy said with relief.

She heard the click-click of her mother's heels on the hardwood floors and the sound of the back door closing. Then she lifted Ella up to her face to look at the wound again. The cut was straight, as if made by a sharp razor.

The previous night Tristan had had to use all of his powers of persuasion to restrain her from charging into Gregory's room. This morning she knew Tristan had been right to hold her back. She'd confront Gregory, but when she was cool and calm. Gregory wanted to see her upset, and her anger would just encourage him.

"Okay, baby, everything's going to be all right," Ivy soothed Ella as she reentered her room.

The morning sun was high enough now to flood the room and stream across the top of her bureau, brightening every speck of dust and picking up flecks of gold paint in the frame around Tristan's picture. Ivy gazed at the picture for a moment, then pulled back. In front of it were shavings of black hair – Ella's fur. Ivy held Ella against her with one

619

arm and reached out to touch the soft fur. Then she picked up a lock of curling gold hair.

Her hair! Someone had cut a piece of her own hair.

Gregory, of course. Ivy sank down into a chair next to the bureau and rocked back and forth, hugging Ella. When had he done it? How?

Every night since the day Tristan had told her what he knew about Gregory, Ivy had locked the bedroom door that led to the hall. There was another entrance, however, through the bathroom that connected her room and Philip's. Ivy had rigged the latch on that door so that Philip could push it open in an emergency, but not without a lot of effort and noise. Somehow Gregory had worked it silently. Her skin prickled all over, thinking of him holding a pair of scissors, bending over her while she was asleep.

Ivy took a deep breath and stood up again. She cleaned up Ella, then wiped off the top of the bureau, her hands still trembling. Then on a sudden impulse she rushed into Gregory's room, wanting to see for herself the scissors, the razor, the proof of what he had done.

She started picking up and throwing papers and clothes and magazines. From between the pages of *Rolling Stone* a piece of art paper slipped out. It was folded in half and had dark printing inside. When Ivy opened it, her heart stopped. She recognized the handwriting instantly: the strong, slanting style was identical to that of the captions on Will's cartoons.

She read through the note quickly, then read it again very slowly, word by word, like a first grader surprised by each set of printed letters and what they meant. As she read Will's note she kept telling herself that these weren't his words – they couldn't be. But he had signed it.

"Gregory," he had written, "I want more. If you're serious about it, you'll bring twice the amount. I'm taking a chance, I'm an accomplice now – you've got to make it worth it. Bring twice the money if you want the cap and jacket."

Ivy closed her eyes and leaned against Gregory's desk. She felt as if her heart were being squeezed, transformed into a small stone. When all was done, there would be nothing soft left inside her, nothing left that could bleed . . . or cry.

She opened her eyes again. Tristan had been right all along about Gregory and Will. But Tristan hadn't guessed how Will would betray her – how he'd cover for Gregory and leave her vulnerable if paid the right price.

Ivy felt beaten, not by Gregory's hatred and dark threats, but by the pale heartlessness of Will. What was the point of trying? she thought. There was too much going against her. She slipped the letter back in the magazine. Then she saw a tattered book about Babe Ruth, one of Philip's paperbacks, on top of Gregory's pile.

She had to keep going. Philip was in this with her.

Opening the magazine again, she snatched up the letter, then hurried back across the hall to dress for school. Before leaving the house that morning, Ivy brought Ella's water bowl and dry food up to her room. She left Ella there, locking both the bathroom and hall doors.

Ivy had missed homeroom. When she entered English class with a late slip, Beth lifted her head. She looked tired and worried. Ivy winked, and Beth smiled a little.

After class they walked together, trying to get away from the crowd of kids surging through the hall. Nothing could be heard over the talk and banging locker doors unless it was shouted. Ivy linked arms with her friend and opened the palm of her hand. Immediately Beth slipped the key into it.

When they finally reached an empty room at the end of the corridor, Beth said, "Ivy, we have to talk. I had a dream last night. I don't know what it means, but I think—"

The school bell rang.

"Oh, no, I've got a test next period."

"Lunchtime," Ivy said. "Try for the table back in the corner," she added as they parted.

Two hours later Ivy got lucky. Ms. Bryce, the

school counselor, let her out early for lunch, saying how pleased she was by Ivy's progress, her fresh hope and positive attitude toward life. I guess drama club pays off, Ivy thought as she staked out the small table in the corner of the cafeteria. Beth joined her a few minutes later.

"Will's in line. Should I wave him over here?" Beth asked.

Ivy chewed her sandwich quickly and swallowed hard. Will was the last person in the world she wanted to see. But Beth still trusted him. She was already signaling to him.

"Did you mention anything to Will about the key or our search?" Ivy asked.

"No."

"Good," Ivy said. "Don't. I don't want him to know about it – not yet," she added, softening her tone when she saw the surprised look on Beth's face.

"But Will might have some good ideas," Beth said, opening her lunch bag, pulling out her usual first course – dessert. "I'm sure he'd want to help you search."

No doubt, thought Ivy. Who knows what he'd find that might be worth some money.

"You know how he feels about you," Beth added.

Ivy couldn't squelch her sarcasm. "Oh, yeah, I know, all right."

Beth blinked at her. "Ivy, he'd do anything for you."

And make some bucks while doing it, Ivy thought, but this time she spoke more carefully. "Maybe you're right, Beth, but still, don't tell him, okay?"

Beth's eyebrows drew together. She wouldn't argue further, but she clearly thought Ivy was making a mistake.

"Tell me what you dreamed last night," Ivy said.

Her friend shook her head slowly. "It was weird, Ivy, so simple but so weird. I dreamed the same thing over and over. I don't know if it had anything to do with the key, but it was about you."

"Tell me," Ivy said, leaning close to her while keeping one eye on Will's progress in the cafeteria line.

"There were these big wheels," Beth recalled, "two, three, I don't know how many. Big wheels with rough edges, notches in them, like tractor wheels or snow tires or something. They were all turning one way. Then you came. There was nothing else in the dream but you and the wheels. You put out your hand and stopped them. Then you pushed, and the wheels all started spinning the opposite way."

She fell silent. Her eyes had a faraway look, as if she were seeing the dream again.

"And?"

"That's it," Beth said. "That's all I dreamed, over and over."

Ivy sat back in her chair, puzzled. "Do you have any idea what it means?" she asked.

"I was going to ask you the same thing," Beth replied. "Ivy, here comes Will. Why don't we tell him and—"

"No," she said quickly.

Beth bit her lip. Ivy looked down at the soggy layers of her sandwich.

"Hi!" said Will, scraping back a chair and setting down his tray. "What's up?"

"Nothing much," Ivy said, avoiding his eyes.

"Beth?"

"Nothing much," she echoed lamely.

Will was silent for a moment. "How come you were late this morning?" he asked Ivy.

She glanced up sharply. "How do you know I was late?"

"Because I was, too." Will tilted his head a little, as if he was trying to read her.

Ivy looked away.

"I came in just after you," he said, then reached for her hand, touching her lightly, trying to get her to look at him again. She would not.

"What's wrong?"

She hated the innocent and concerned tone of his voice.

"Beth? Tell me what it is."

625

Ivy peeked up at her friend. Beth shrugged, and Will glanced back and forth between them. His face was calm and thoughtful, like that of a teacher patiently searching for an answer, but his hands gave him away, gripping the edge of his tray.

Now he's worried, Ivy thought, really worried, but not about me. He thinks we both know the truth about him.

Will sucked in his breath, then said quietly, "Surprise. Here comes Gregory."

Ivy looked up, hoping to see Suzanne with him. If Suzanne put in her usual effort at snubbing her, Ivy would have an excuse to walk out. But Gregory came alone, striding confidently toward them, smiling, as if they were all good buddies.

Will greeted him.

"I didn't know you were off this period," Ivy said.

"My history class is in the library," he told her. "I'm doing research, can't you tell?"

Ivy laughed lightly, determined to seem as much at ease as he. "What's your topic?"

"Famous murders of the nineteenth century," Gregory replied, pulling out a chair.

"Learning anything?"

He thought for a moment, then smiled and sat down next to her. "Nothing useful. Will, I'm sorry I missed you last night."

Ivy turned to look at Will.

"How about getting together later this afternoon?" Gregory proposed.

Will hesitated, then nodded in agreement. "Celentano's," he said.

"Can I come?" Ivy asked. She caught both of them off guard.

"Oh, I forgot," she said with a casual wave of her hand. "I'm working today."

"Too bad," Gregory said, but his and Will's surprised expressions had told her what she wanted to know. This meeting was business. Gregory was going to pay off Will. At least Will was smart enough to make the exchange in the safety of a public place.

Throughout the conversation, Beth didn't say a word. She watched with wide blue eyes, and Ivy wondered if she could read any of the thoughts behind their faces. She had left her brownie half eaten in its tinfoil.

"If you're not going to finish that, I'll have some," Ivy said, struggling to find normal things to say, working to keep up the pretense that nothing was wrong and she wasn't afraid.

Beth pushed the brownie over to her. While Gregory and Will set a time to meet, Ivy broke off a piece, then placed what was left of the dessert in front of Gregory.

"What time did you get home last night?" she asked him.

Gregory looked at her silently for a moment and rocked back on his chair. "Let's see . . . nine o'clock, I think."

"Did you hear anything strange outside?"

"Anything like what?" he replied.

"Whining or howling, a cat in pain."

"Did something happen to Ella?" Beth asked.

"Something went after her," Ivy told them.

Will frowned. His old concerned look was getting to Ivy.

"Scraped the fur off in a strip and drew some blood on her right side," Ivy continued. "But there weren't any bite marks. What kind of animal would have done something like that?" she asked, looking directly at Gregory.

"I have no idea," he said coolly.

"Do you know, Will?"

"No . . . no. Is Ella all right?" She heard the slight tremor in his voice, and it almost drew her back to him.

"Oh, sure, she's fine," Ivy said, standing up, tossing her half-finished lunch into a nearby trash barrel. "Ella's a tough little street kitten."

"Just like her mistress," Gregory said, smiling. "Just like her."

45

Ivy couldn't stop thinking about wheels. All day she drew circles with notches in them . . . in her math notebook, on a Spanish quiz, and on a handout in history. They became tractors, snowflakes, strange knobs on a door. Later, at 'Tis the Season, she noticed every item in the store that was round – Christmas wreaths, swimming tubes, and a pincushion made to look like a chocolate-frosted doughnut.

Ivy tried not to think about what was going on at Celentano's and was just as glad when Tristan didn't answer her call. She didn't have to tell him about the blackmail note, she reasoned. It wasn't Tristan who had foolishly trusted Will.

When Ivy got home from work that evening, Maggie and Andrew were out, and Philip was in the family room with Gregory watching a DVD.

"Did you finish your homework?" Ivy asked her brother.

"Yup. Gregory checked it."

Gregory, playing the role of good and helpful older brother, smiled up at her. Ivy returned the smile, though she tingled with fear at Philip's growing attachment to him. What would Gregory do, she wondered, when he found out that they'd be legally sharing a father? For Gregory, money was status. It was how he controlled the people around him. How would he react if he found out he and Philip might be sharing the Baines fortune?

"Stay awhile," Gregory said to her, gesturing casually to the seat next to him.

"Thanks, but I've got stuff to do upstairs."

She started toward the hall, but Gregory got up quickly and stood in the path Ivy meant to take. "Your mother left a pile of laundry outside your bedroom," he told her. "Maggie said she hoped you had a key. The bathroom door was locked too."

"I have a key."

He leaned close to her and lowered his voice. "She said she hopes you're not doing drugs in there." His mouth twisted up in a grin.

"I'm sure you set her straight," Ivy replied.

He laughed, and she walked past him.

At the top of the steps she pulled the key out of

her purse. When she pushed open her bedroom door, she expected the captive Ella to spring out.

"Ella?" She stepped inside the room. "Ella?"

She saw a round lump beneath the quilt on her bed. Ivy dropped her books by the side of the bed, then pulled back the cover. Ella was huddled in a tight ball.

Touching the cat gently, Ivy rubbed her with one finger in her favorite spot around her ears, then stroked her, studying the bare strip on her side. The scratches were beginning to heal.

"You look so frightened, Ella."

The cat slowly got to its feet and limped to the edge of the bed. Ivy quickly reached for her, picking up the paw Ella wouldn't use.

"Oh, my God!" The pink pads on the bottom were pricked and striped with dark blood. When she touched them, they oozed fresh red beneath their drying crust. Ivy scooped the cat up in her shaking arms and huddled over her.

"Oh, Ella, I'm sorry. I'm sorry." She laid her face on Ella's fur, hot tears rolling down. "I locked the door – both doors. I'd never have left you if I thought he could get in."

How did he get in? Ivy wondered. Her bedroom had been his once, so perhaps he had another key. Tonight she'd sleep with furniture against the doors. "Tomorrow when I'm at school, I'll keep you in the car," she promised Ella.

She got up and closed her bedroom door, wondering if Gregory had been lurking outside and enjoying the scene. After cleaning Ella's foot and side, Ivy cuddled her for a long time. The cat purred a little, slowly closing her eyes.

When Ella was sound asleep, Ivy gently laid her in bed. As soon as she put the cat down, her hands began to shake again. She picked up a sturdy chair and positioned it under the knob of the hallway door. After making certain it was secure, she undressed. Maybe a long, hot shower would calm her down.

Ivy locked the door between the bathroom and Philip's room, then turned on the water full blast. For the first ten minutes she was able to push everything out of her mind. But troubled thoughts kept circling at the edge. The wet string with the key hanging on it rubbed against her neck. Ivy squeezed her eyes shut, but she kept seeing images of wheels and handprinted words, the words of the blackmail note.

At last she shut off the shower and stood still and dripping in the tub. She wondered if Tristan missed the feel of water running over his body. She missed the touch of Tristan. She tried to recall it, but her mind kept jumping back to Will. She focused on Tristan's face, but her mind remembered how it had felt when Will held her hand the day they went back to the train station. She tried to remember how Tristan's hand looked resting on hers, but again she felt Will's touch when he had reached to get the mud out of her hair, when he had laid his hand on hers at lunch to make her look at him.

Ivy thrust aside the shower curtain and stepped out of the tub. Instantly her foot stung as if a hundred small needles had been jabbed in it. She fell back against the tub. Steadying herself, she sat on the edge and gingerly lifted her foot to examine it. Splinters of glass protruded from her foot and sparkled on the bath mat.

Ivy's mind raced, and she rocked back and forth, holding on to her ankle, squeezing it hard. Then she calmed herself and began to pick the glass out of her foot, removing all she could with her hands. After folding over the glass-covered bath mat and setting it aside, she checked the floor, then hopped to the cupboard to get a pair of tweezers.

None of the glass had gone in deeply. It was just enough to make her sore – just enough to rattle her. Ivy made herself work calmly and methodically, then she put on her robe and lifted her foot to look at it again. It was striped and dotted with droplets of blood – just like Ella's.

Suddenly Ivy sank down on the floor. She drew her knees up to her chest. "Tristan!" she cried out. "Tristan, please come! I need you."

She began to sob uncontrollably. "Tristan! Don't

leave me alone now. I need you! Where are you? Please, Tristan!"

But he did not come. At last Ivy's sobs softened, her shoulders grew still, and she cried slow, silent tears.

"Aa-hmm."

It was the sound of someone clearing her throat.

"Aa-hmm."

Ivy glanced up and saw a purple mist in front of the vanity mirror.

"I don't know where he is," Lacey said in a brisk, businesslike tone. Then the shimmering purple moved closer to Ivy.

Ivy tried to blink back the tears, but they kept coming. A tissue was plucked from the box and hung in the air in front of her, waiting to be taken.

"Thanks . . . Lacey."

"You look terrible when you cry," Lacey said, and Ivy heard the pleasure she took in that observation.

Ivy nodded, wiped her eyes, then blew her nose hard. "I guess you looked pretty good," she said. "Movie stars always do."

"But I never cried."

"Oh."

"Never sigh, never cry," Lacey boasted. "That was my rule."

"And you kept it?"

"During my life I did," Lacey replied.

Ivy heard the small catch in Lacey's voice. She reached out, accepting another tissue, then asked, "How about now?"

"None of your business," Lacey told her. "Let me see your foot."

Ivy obediently held it up. She felt the tips of fingers gently probing it.

"Does it hurt much?"

"It'll be all right." Ivy lowered her foot and stood up, putting her weight on it slowly. It hurt a lot more than she wanted to admit. "Actually, I'm more worried about Ella. Her paw has been cut up." Ivy told Lacey about the fur that had been shaved from Ella and the lock of her own hair that had been clipped. "By Gregory, I'm sure."

"What a clever guy," Lacey remarked sarcastically. "I guess you got his message: What happens to Ella will happen to you."

Ivy swallowed hard and nodded. "Did you look for Tristan?"

"At Caroline's house. At Will's. At his graveyard condo. He's nowhere – maybe in the darkness again."

Lacey sighed, then caught herself doing that and tried to pretend she was clearing her throat again.

"You're worried," Ivy said, opening the door and leading the way into her bedroom.

"About Tristan? Never." The purple mist passed

Ivy and stretched out on the pillows across the top of her bed.

"You're worried. I can hear it in your voice," Ivy insisted.

"I'm worried he'll fly off somewhere and I'll get stuck with his job," Lacey retorted.

Ivy sat down on the bed, and Ella raised her head. "It was nice of you to come when you knew I needed help."

"I didn't come for you."

"I know," Ivy said.

"You *know*," Lacey mocked. The purple shimmer sprang from the pillow like the glimmering ghost of a cat. "And just *what* do you think you know?"

"That you care a lot about Tristan," Ivy said aloud. That you're in love with him, she thought. "That you care so much, you'd help someone you absolutely can't stand and wish would disappear, just to make it better for him."

For once Lacey didn't say anything.

"As soon as I see Tristan again, I'll tell him you came when I called," Ivy added.

"Oh, I don't need anybody scoring points for me," Lacey said quickly.

Ivy shrugged. "Okay, I won't tell him."

Lacey came closer to the bed. Ivy saw Ella's injured paw being lifted up.

"Nasty."

"Lacey" – Ivy's voice shook a little – "can you talk to cats? Can you explain to Ella that I didn't know Gregory had a way of getting in? Could you tell her I would never have left her if I'd known, and that tomorrow I'll—"

"Who do you think I am," Lacey interrupted, "Dr. Doolittle? Snow White? Do you see little *birdies* landing on my hands?"

"I can't even see your hands," Ivy reminded her.

"I'm an angel, and I can no more talk cat than you can."

Ella began to purr.

"But I'll tell you what I can do," Lacey said in a softer voice. "What I'm gonna do. If it works," she added. "It's kind of an experiment."

Ivy waited patiently.

"First, lie down," Lacey commanded. "Relax. Relax! No, wait. Get a candle."

Ivy rose and searched through her desk drawers, at last holding up an old Christmas candle that Philip had given her. "Where do you want it?"

"Somewhere where you can see it," replied Lacey.

Ivy set it on her bedside table and lit it. At the same time she saw Ella get up as if being prodded. The cat limped down to the other end of the bed.

"Now lie down with your feet at this end, next to Ella," Lacey said.

Ivy stretched out on her bed as directed, and the bedroom light clicked off.

"Look at the candle. Relax!" Lacey barked.

Ivy laughed a little. Lacey wasn't exactly a pro at making someone else feel comfortable. But after several minutes of staring at the warm and flickering flame, Ivy did begin to relax.

"Good. Don't fight me now," Lacey said in a quieter voice. "Keep your eyes on that candle. Let your thoughts, your mind, your spirit float toward it, leaving your body behind. Leave it with me so I can do my work."

Ivy watched the flame, watched how it shaped and reshaped itself. She imagined herself like a moth, flying toward the fire, circling it. Then she felt the sole of her foot growing hot. She felt as if a burning hand were wrapped around her foot, and she fought the reflex to pull away. Watch the candle, watch the candle, she told herself as the heat became more and more intense. Just when she thought she couldn't take any more, the burning lessened. There was a cool touch, then a tingling feeling.

"Done."

Lacey's voice was so weak that Ivy had to strain to hear it. Even in the darkness, Ivy could barely see Lacey's shimmer now. She sat up quickly. "Are you all right?"

Lacey didn't answer the question. "Turn on the light," she said, her voice as thin as thread.

Ivy got up to do so and, without thinking, stepped down hard on her injured foot. There was no pain, not even a tingling. She switched on the light, then sat down quickly and lifted up her foot. Her sole was smoother than the palm of her hand, smoother than the sole of her other foot, and without a trace of the cuts. Ella's paw was also healed.

"Yes! Oh, yes!" Lacey congratulated herself. "Lacey, you are good!" she said, but her voice still rasped like an old woman's, and her purple shimmer lay low to the floor.

"Lacey, what's happened to you?" Ivy asked. "Are you okay?"

There was no answer.

"Talk to me," Ivy demanded.

"Tired."

"Tristan," Ivy called softly on the outside, but loudly on the inside. "Please come. Something's happened to Lacey. You have to help her, Tristan. Angels, help Lacey!"

"Just tired," murmured Lacey.

"You shouldn't have tried that. You did too much," Ivy said, frightened. "I don't know how to help you. Tell me what to do."

"Go. Gregory's in Philip's room now. Go."

Ivy didn't move.

639

"Take Ella," Lacey said weakly. "Let him see. It'll be fun."

"No. I'm not leaving you like this."

"I said *go!* Make it worth my time."

"Stubborn angel," Ivy muttered. She picked up Ella and reluctantly started toward the door. As she passed through it she heard Lacey say softly, "You're all right, Ivy, you're all right."

"What did you say?" Ivy called back.

But Lacey wouldn't repeat it.

Carrying Ella like a baby over her shoulder, Ivy walked into Philip's room. When Gregory saw her standing in the doorway, his eyes brightened. He's hoping I'll scream like I'm crazy and accuse him, Ivy thought. She smiled at him and saw him glance down. His smile flattened when she padded in comfortably barefoot and without pain.

"Ella wants to say goodnight," she said. Ella was squirming wildly in her arms, wanting to get as far away as possible from Gregory.

Though Ivy felt bad about restraining Ella, she knew that she could score some points against Gregory, psychological points that might keep her and Ella safe for a while. She purposely kept Ella's shaved flank next to her. The wounds were healed, but the skin was still bare. Sitting on Philip's bed, Ivy drew her feet up next to her so Gregory could see her smooth, bare soles.

She saw the flicker, the momentary puzzlement

in his eyes, and then the mask was back in place – the nice-big-brother mask he wore while putting Philip to bed. Of course, he could think of an explanation for her unscarred feet: she had known something was up, she had looked before she stepped out of the shower and avoided the glass.

"I want to give Ella a hug," Philip said.

He reached for her, but Ivy held on tightly to the wriggling cat.

"What's wrong with kitty?" Gregory asked.

"I don't know. I think she wants to play."

Gregory smirked.

"Is that it, Ella?" Ivy asked. "Feeling your oats, girl?" She flipped the cat on her back as if she were going to scratch her tummy.

That's when Gregory saw it, the small foot with its tender pads as pink and smooth as a kitten's. His eyes flicked to Ella's other feet, as if he thought he had forgotten which one he had hurt. Ivy kept the cat on her back, giving Gregory plenty of time to look at her paws. His breathing became shallow. The color drained from his face.

"I want to give her a hug," Philip said again.

"Her, and not me?" Ivy teased, then set Ella in his lap. The cat was off like a shot, running back to Ivy's bedroom, too fast for an animal with an injured paw, too fast for anyone to notice the bare strip of skin on her side.

"Oh, well," Ivy said, leaning over to kiss Philip.

"Goodnight, sleep tight." She brushed past Gregory. "Don't forget to pray to your angels."

The next day Ivy put a box of litter and a pile of blankets in her car and took Ella to school with her. It was clear that whether or not her bedroom doors were locked, Gregory had a way of getting in. Maybe he had a key, or maybe he was good at picking locks. Perhaps there was another way into the attic, she thought, a trapdoor he could climb through that would let him come down again by way of her music room. In any case, she couldn't leave Ella home alone.

Ivy parked at the far end of the school lot, beneath a cluster of weeping willows. The trees would shield the car from both sun and rain, she reasoned, glancing at the clouds rising in the west. She lowered the windows to give Ella some air, but not far enough to allow someone to unlock the car.

"That's the best I can do, cat," she said, and hurried off to homeroom.

Ivy caught up with Beth first period, as they were going into English class. "Any more dreams?" Ivy asked her.

"The same one, over and over. If you don't figure it out soon, I'm going to go crazy."

They both stepped back as people pushed by them to get in the classroom.

"I wish I could talk to Tristan," Ivy said. "I can't reach him."

"Maybe he's working with Will," Beth suggested.

Ivy shook her head, certain that Tristan would not have asked Will for help, but Beth went on. "Will wasn't in homeroom this morning."

"He wasn't?" Ivy tried to stifle a new fear that awakened in her. Why should she worry about Will? He knew what kind of person Gregory was, and he thought he could handle him. He thought he could betray her with no consequences.

"He called me from work late last night," Beth went on. "He was supposed to help me with my computer today, but he said he was caught up in something and couldn't meet me."

Oh, angels, watch over him, Ivy prayed silently. Had Will gotten himself in deeper? Was he working for Gregory now, the way Eric once had? Angels, protect him, she prayed in spite of herself.

"Ladies," Mr. McDivitt called out to them, "the rest of us are doing English. How about you?"

Ivy spent English class, and every class that followed, drawing wheels with notches. And she continually tried to reach Tristan. Each hour of the day seemed to stretch, then collapse like an accordion: minute by minute, the hour dragged itself out, then suddenly was gone, moving them all one hour closer to whatever Gregory was planning

643

next. Ivy longed to climb up on a desk and move the clock's hands ahead, set the wheels in motion.

Wheels . . . clocks, she thought. Clocks had gears – notched wheels – and old clocks, like the one that sat on the dining room mantel at home, had keys to open their casing. Why hadn't she thought of it before? In Beth's dream the wheels were spinning one way, then Ivy reached out and pushed them in the other direction – sending time backward, she thought, sending them into the past. In the past Caroline had lived in the house on the ridge. She could have hidden something in the mantel clock long ago.

Ivy glanced again at the clock on the classroom wall. There were twenty-five minutes left in the last period of the day. She knew her mother would be leaving to pick up Philip from school, and Gregory should still be in class. This was her chance. As soon as written work was assigned, she carried her books to the front of the room. "Mrs. Carson," she said weakly.

Ivy was excused immediately and didn't make the required stop at the nurse's office. Fifty feet from the school door, she made a dash for her car.

A cool autumn rain had moved in and was misting the town. Ivy drove two blocks before thinking to put on her windshield wipers. Her foot was fast and jerky on the clutch, and she started and stopped, impatient with the traffic in the narrow streets. Ella kept trying to climb onto her lap. "Hang on, cat!"

When she finally got to the driveway to the house, she raced to the top, yanked on the parking brake, and got out of the car, leaving the door open. No one was home – at least no one else's car was there. Her hands shook with excitement as she unlocked the house door and turned off the alarm system.

Ivy ran through the kitchen and into the dining room. On the mantel sat the two-foot-high mahogany clock with its beautiful moonlike face and gold pendulum swinging steadily behind painted glass. She had remembered right: there was a keyhole in its casing.

Ivy lifted the string necklace over her head, then reached up with the key and inserted it in the lock. She turned it gently to the left, then the right. The lock clicked, and she opened the clock's door.

She expected to see something immediately. There was nothing, and for a moment she couldn't breathe. Don't be stupid, she told herself. Someone has to wind the clock, someone else has a key – probably Andrew – so nothing's going to be left in plain view. She cautiously reached out and caught the pendulum in midswing, then slipped her other hand in and felt around.

She'd need a stool to reach all the way up into the clock's works. Standing on tiptoe, Ivy moved her fingers slowly up one side of the wood case. She felt an edge, a paper edge. She pulled it gently at first, afraid she'd tear it and leave part of it up in the clock. It was a thick folded edge, like that of an envelope. She tugged on it harder, and it came free.

Ivy stared at the old brown envelope she held in her hands. Then she swiped a dinner knife from the silverware drawer and quickly slit it open.

46

Inside the envelope Ivy found three pages. The first was a handwritten note that was barely decipherable, but Ivy recognized the signature at the end: Caroline's. Beneath it was a letter from the office of Edward Ghent, M.D. – Eric's father, Ivy realized with a sudden jolt. The third page looked like a photocopy of a technical report from a company called MediLabs.

Ivy skipped to the short letter from Eric's father. There were odd spaces between the words and several corrections.

Dear Caroline,
The enclosed report indicates the situation is as you suspected. As I explained in the office, this type of DNA test proves, in

instances where there is no match, that a man is not the father. Clearly Andrew is not.

Not Gregory's father? Ivy wondered, then went on.

The tests show that Tom S is the father, but I take it that that was not a question for you.

"Tom S., Tom S.," Ivy murmured. Tom Stetson, she thought, the man at the party, tall and lean and dark-haired like Gregory, the one Tristan said was a teacher at Andrew's college – the man who left roses on Caroline's grave. She finished the letter.

If I can be of any further assistance, let me know. Of course, this will remain confidential.

Meaning, Ivy thought, that no one else would know who Gregory's father was. No one else, including Andrew? The answer to that question might be buried in the scrawl of Caroline's letter. Ivy read it all the way through.

Andrew,
   I'm leaving this here for when the right time comes. In the divorce your son sided with you, lied for you, convinced the judge to let him live with you – or was it your

money he wanted to live with? And is he really your son?

Sorry about that.

Caroline

So Andrew didn't know, Ivy thought. And if Gregory knew, he wouldn't want anyone else to. He was counting on the Baines money. Ivy wondered what would happen if Andrew found out that Gregory wasn't really his son. And what would happen now that Andrew had another son, one he was growing very fond of?

Maybe Caroline had guessed what was coming. Maybe she'd realized that this was her chance to get back at both Andrew and Gregory. Ivy could imagine her taunting Gregory. She remembered the day that he'd come from his mother's house extremely upset – Ivy could imagine Caroline threatening to tell all.

Would Gregory have silenced her, killed her for an inheritance?

These letters were enough to take to the police, enough for them to start a serious investigation. Eric had left her what she needed. Angels, she prayed, let Eric rest in peace now.

Then she glanced up at the clock. It showed twenty-seven minutes before three, but she had stopped it with her hand, and at least five minutes had passed. Gregory would be home soon. Ivy moved quickly, starting the swing of the pendulum, closing and locking the clock door. She slipped the key string around her neck and refolded the three sheets of paper, putting them carefully in the envelope. Then she dashed toward the back door.

Outside the mist had become a light drizzle. Ivy stuck the envelope under her shirt and ran for her car. She drove to the police station, her damp arms covered with goose bumps. At a red light in town, Ivy fumbled through her purse, then dumped everything in her lap, trying to find the card with the name of the detective who had investigated her assault. "Lieutenant Patrick Donnelly," she read from the card, then tossed a lapful of tissues and hair ribbons into the back seat with the cat stuff. That was when Ivy remembered.

"Ella," she called, hoping the cat was under the blankets. "Ella!" At the next light Ivy reached back and felt the old quilt. There was no warm lump. Ivy figured the cat had escaped when she left the car door open. "Stay outdoors, Ella," Ivy whispered. "He can't corner you there."

When she arrived at the station, the desk sergeant took Ivy's name, then informed her that the lieutenant was out. "He'll be back any time now. Anytime now," he repeated, his mild blue eyes watching her as she tore at the edges of the detective's card. "Is there something I can do for you?"

"No." She tore at the card.

"I'll find you someone else to talk to," he offered.

"No, I'll wait," Ivy insisted. The story was too strange and too complicated to tell someone else.

She sat down on a hard bench and stared at the room's olive-colored walls and dreary tile. Directly across from her was a large clock. Ivy watched the minute hand jump from one black dot to the next as she tried to think what she'd say to the detective. Better leave the angels out, she thought. It would be tough enough to make him take her seriously.

The door of the station swung open, and Ivy looked up hopefully. Two young officers reported to their desk sergeant, turning their backs to her. Ivy got up to ask if someone could telephone Lieutenant Donnelly.

"Expected Pat back by now," the sergeant was saying softly to the other officers as she approached. "He's talking to the O'Leary kid."

The O'Leary kid? Will?

The officers turned around suddenly, and the sergeant's eyes met hers. "Are you sure there's nothing we can help you with in the meantime?"

"You can give this to Lieutenant Donnelly," Ivy said, pulling out Caroline's envelope. She asked for a bigger envelope, then scribbled on it: "I have to talk to you as soon as possible." She wrote down her name, address, and phone number, then sealed Caroline's envelope within. She handed it silently to the desk sergeant and hurried outside. As she sped home Ivy couldn't stop worrying about both Ella and Philip.

When she pulled up in front of the house, she saw only her mother's car in the garage. Good, she thought, Philip was safe, and she'd have a chance to find Ella before Gregory arrived. Ivy took a round-about route upstairs, passing through the dining room to make sure that she hadn't left behind any signs of her search. The clock was ticking steadily, though it was several minutes slow.

Ivy ran up the center stair two steps at a time. Hearing her mother on her bedroom phone, Ivy stuck her head in the door and gave a half wave, then continued on to her bedroom. The door was wide open, and Ella was not in sight. There were no round lumps in the bed, so Ivy checked under-neath, thinking that after all that had happened, Ella might be hiding there. She wasn't, but Ivy noticed that the shoes and boxes under her bed had been pushed to one side, forming a wall.

She studied the wall, then gripped the quilt on her bed. Maybe Gregory had done this to corner Ella the day he cut her paw. Maybe it had helped him trap Ella when he shaved her flank. But there, as part of the wall, were the slippers Ivy had kicked off this morning. She straightened up slowly and saw that the door to her third-floor music room was open. She always kept it closed.

"Ella," she mouthed, the feeling of dread so strong in her she could not speak aloud. She couldn't even walk. She crawled over to the door and saw that the light was on upstairs. Gripping the door frame, Ivy pulled herself up, then slowly climbed the stairs. What had he done to her now? Cut up another foot? Sliced a piece of her ear?

When Ivy got to the top of the stairs, she looked immediately under the piano, then beneath the chairs in the room. Finally her eyes went up to the window, the shadow in it.

"Ella! Oh, no! Ella!"

The cat swung from a rope, dangling from a nail in the low ceiling. Ivy yanked at the rope, then lifted up Ella, but her body was limp. Her head hung down, her small neck broken. Ivy shrieked and shrieked, pressing her face against the dead body of Ella, still soft, still warm. Her fingers moved around Ella's ears, touching her gently as if Ella were just sleeping.

"Ella," she moaned, then started screaming again. "He killed her! He killed her!"

"Ivy! What's wrong?" her mother called.

Ivy struggled to get control of herself. Her whole body was shaking. She clung to Ella, rubbing her face against the cat's soft fur. She couldn't bear to let her go. "He killed her. He killed her!"

Her mother was coming up the steps.

"Gregory killed her, Mom!"

"Ivy, calm down. What did you say?" Maggie asked when she reached the top of the stairway.

"He killed Ella!" Ivy let go of the cat and stood between her and her mother.

"What are you talking about?" her mother asked.

Ivy stepped aside.

"Oh, my—" Her mother's hand went up to her mouth. "Ivy, what have you done?"

"What have *I* done? You're blaming *me?* You still think I'm crazy, Mom? It's Gregory. He's the one behind all this."

Her mother stared at her as if she were speaking another language. "I'll call the counselor."

"Mom, listen to me."

But Ivy could see that her mother was too frightened of what she saw, too afraid of Ivy and what she thought Ivy had done, to listen or understand. Maggie picked up a folded piece of paper that had been left on the piano bench and turned it over and over without looking at it.

Ivy tore it out of her mother's hands, unfolded the note, and read: "I can hurt those you love."

She thrust the paper at her mother. "Look! Don't you understand? Gregory is after me! Gregory killed her just to get to me."

Ivy's mother backed away from her. "But Gregory is out with Philip," she said, "and—"

"With Philip? Where?"

"I'll call Ms. Bryce. She'll know what to do."

"Where?" Ivy demanded, shaking her mother by the shoulders. "Tell me where he took Philip."

Her mother pulled away from her and cowered in the corner. "There's no reason to get so upset, Ivy."

"He'll hurt him!"

"Gregory loves Philip," her mother argued from the corner of the room. She was moving sideways, edging toward the stairs. "You must have noticed how much he's played with him lately."

"I've noticed," Ivy snapped.

"He promised Philip they'd go hunting for old railroad spikes today," her mother went on, "and kept his promise even in this damp weather. Gregory is good to Philip. That's why I told him – though Andrew didn't want me to – I told him yesterday that he and Philip would soon be full brothers."

"Oh, no," Ivy said, sinking back against her stereo.

"I can hurt those you love" – she heard the words as clearly as if Gregory were standing next to her, whispering in her ear. She looked up at her mother and said, "Do you know where they've gone to look for the spikes?"

Her mother was backing slowly down the steps. "By the railroad bridges. Gregory said he could climb up on the old one and get a lot of spikes for

Philip." Maggie looked relieved to have reached the bottom of the stair. "You come down now, Ivy. Leave Ella alone. I'll call the counselor. Come down now, Ivy."

Ivy started down the steps, and her mother fled from the bedroom. Ivy waited till Maggie was in her own room calling Ms. Bryce, then she rushed through the bathroom and Philip's bedroom and down the back stairs.

"Tristan, where are you?" she cried, running out to the car. She jammed her key into the ignition.

"Tristan, where are you?"

Ivy took off, her wheels slipping, her door rattling. She opened and slammed it again while she was speeding downhill. As fast as she drove, as dangerously fast as she took the curves on the wet asphalt, she felt as if she would never get there.

"Angels," she prayed, tears running down her face, "don't let him . . . don't let him."

47

As soon as he arrived at the top of the ridge, Tristan knew that Ivy wasn't there. Her car was gone. Maggie was standing at the edge of the driveway, clutching a cordless phone, looking distraught. "I don't care what meeting he's in, I have to speak to him."

What happened? Tristan wondered. Where was Ivy? He was still extremely groggy, like a person who had slept too long and too heavily. When he had fallen into this last darkness, it felt as if a force much greater than he, one more powerful than any he had ever experienced, had forced him over the brink and into the dreamless black.

"It's an emergency!" Maggie was shouting into the phone.

Tell me, Maggie, tell me what happened, Tristan thought.

"Andrew. Oh, Andrew." Maggie closed her eyes with relief. "It's Ivy – she's gone crazy. She's run off."

Run off where?

"I don't know what started it. She went upstairs and all of a sudden I heard her screaming. I went up after her, up to her music room. She – she killed Ella."

What?

"I said she killed Ella . . . Yes, I'm sure of it."

Gregory killed Ella, Tristan thought.

"I don't know," Maggie moaned. "I told her Gregory had taken Philip to the bridges to collect railroad spikes."

Now Tristan's mind started clicking. Just before Tristan had fallen into the darkness, Gregory had shaved Ella's flank. Tristan had thought Gregory was just trying to rattle Ivy, but now he recognized it as a warning. Gregory was striking closer and closer.

"I thought I'd calmed her down, Andrew," Maggie said. "I told her how good Gregory was being to Philip. I thought I was handling her right. Then I went to call the counselor, and she ran out. She drove out of here like she was crazy. What should I do?"

Tristan didn't wait to hear anything more. He rushed off toward the bridges, taking the route Ivy would have taken by car. He was fully awake now and felt stronger than he ever had. His mind was moving fast. Did Gregory plan to kill Philip? Was he crazy enough to think he could get away with one murder after another?

Crazy like a fox, Tristan thought. What if this was a trap? What if it was just a way to con Ivy out to the railroad bridges?

Tristan caught up with her on the winding route that followed the river. He rode beside her in the car, but she was so focused on where she was going that she didn't notice his golden light. A sudden bump from a pothole broke through her concentration.

Pothole! More of them. Watch out. Got to get to the bridges. Find Philip, Tristan thought, until he matched a thought with her and slipped inside.

"It's me."

"Tristan! Where have you been?"

"The darkness," he said quickly. "Ivy, slow down. Listen to me. It could be a trap."

"That's what you said about Eric," she reminded him, and drove faster. "Maybe if I had gotten to Eric a little earlier—"

"That's not how it was," he interrupted her, "and you know it. You couldn't have saved Eric."

"I'm going to save Philip," she said. "Gregory's not taking anyone else away from me."

"What are you going to save him with? A gun? A knife? What do you have with you?"

He felt the doubts growing in her mind, fresh fear icing her veins.

"Turn back. Go to the police," he urged.

"I went to the stupid police!"

"Then try Will," Tristan said. "We'll go get Will."

"Will can't be trusted," she replied quickly. "You said so yourself."

"I was jealous, Ivy, and mad about the way he was keeping secrets. But we need him now, and he'd do anything for you," Tristan argued.

He felt Ivy draw back. She was keeping something from him. "What? What is it?"

Ivy shook her head and said nothing.

"He can help us," Tristan persisted.

"I don't need his help. I have you, Tristan — at least I thought I did," she challenged him.

"You know you do, but I can't stop bullets."

"And Gregory can't risk them," Ivy said with confidence. "That's been his problem all along. He's got to do it better than that, sneakier than that. There've been too many deaths now. Too many people close to him have died. He can't get away with a murder that has any evidence attached."

Her certain tone told Tristan that this was a losing battle. She had made up her mind.

"I'll be back for you," he said.

"Tristan?" she called out.

But he raced ahead of her now and came to the bridges almost instantly. The weather had worsened, the light drizzle becoming a cold, slicing rain that swept both sides of the river. A mist rose from the warmer water rushing beneath the bridges. Tristan saw the fog, and yet somehow he could clearly see the parallel bridges it blanketed. Gregory and Philip were not in view. Then Tristan heard voices upriver. They were moving north, in the opposite direction from where Eric had died, where there were no easy paths to walk. He felt like an eagle, targeting the two of them exactly, then dropping down beside them. Something had changed in him since the last deep darkness. His own abilities surprised him.

Gregory was standing with Philip in front of a tiny shack that was well camouflaged by bushes and vines. He pushed open the wooden door, and Philip walked into the ramshackle building without hesitation.

"We'll be like real hunters," Gregory was saying to Philip. "I know where there's a pile of wood. I can pull out some dry pieces and build a fire."

Tristan listened, trying to figure out Gregory's plan. Would he set the building on fire and trap Philip inside? No, Ivy was right: it was too obvious, and Gregory had to be very careful now. Besides, Maggie knew that Philip was out with him.

Philip set down his iron spikes. "I'll help. The spikes will be safe here."

Gregory shook his head. "No, you'd better stay and guard our treasure. I'll go get the wood and be back in a few minutes."

"Wait," Philip said. "I can put a magic spell on our treasure. Then no one will be able to take them and—"

"No," Gregory cut him off.

"But I want to help."

"I'll tell you how you can help me," Gregory said too quickly. "Lend me your jacket."

The little boy frowned.

"Come on, give it to me!" Gregory demanded, unable to hide his impatience.

In response Philip's jaw got that stiff, stubborn look. His eyes narrowed suspiciously.

"I need it to carry the wood in," Gregory explained in a gentler voice. "Then we'll build a good fire and get warm and dry."

Reluctantly Philip took off his red jacket. Then his eyes suddenly widened. Tristan knew that he had been spotted.

"What? What are you looking at?" Gregory asked, whirling around.

Tristan quickly ducked out the door so the boy couldn't see his shimmering light, hoping that Philip understood this silent message.

Philip did. "Nothing," he said.

There was a long silence, then Gregory went to the doorway and glanced outside, but he didn't perceive Tristan.

"I thought I saw a big spider," Tristan heard Philip say.

"A spider won't hurt you," Gregory told him.

"A tarantula would," Philip replied stubbornly.

"Okay, okay," Gregory said, his voice hoarse with irritation. "But there isn't one. Stay and guard our treasure. I'll be back."

As soon as he stepped out of the shack, Gregory closed the door and scanned the surrounding bushes and trees. Satisfied that he was not being observed, he pulled a padlock out of his pocket, slipped it over the rusted latch, and silently locked Philip inside.

"Lacey, Lacey, I need your help. Philip needs your help," Tristan called to her, then passed through the walls of the shack.

Philip greeted him with a bright smile. "How come you're here? How come you were hiding?"

Tristan remained where he was and waited for the little boy to move close to him, then he walked over to the door. Just as he had hoped, Philip followed him. Tristan put his hand on the latch, knowing the boy would see the latch glow. Philip immediately reached out and jiggled the handle.

"I can't open it," Philip said.

Matching that thought, Tristan slipped inside

him. "You can't because there's a padlock on the outside of the door. Gregory put it on."

Philip reached for the latch again. As if he couldn't believe it, he kept jiggling and pulling on it.

"Stop. It's locked. Philip, stop and listen to me."

But the little boy started banging on the door with his fists.

"Philip—"

He began to kick the door. Growing desperate, he threw his body against it over and over again.

"Stop! It won't work. And you may need your strength for other things."

"What's going on?" Philip demanded. He was breathing fast, his mouth open, his eyes darting around the room. "Why'd he lock me in?"

"I'm not sure," Tristan said honestly. "But here's what I want you to do. I'm going to have to leave you, Philip, just for a while. If Gregory comes back before I do and lets you out, run toward the road. Get to the road as fast as you can and try to get the attention of someone driving by. Don't get back in the car with him, okay? Don't go anywhere with him."

"I'm scared, Tristan."

"You'll be all right," Tristan assured him, glad that Philip couldn't probe his mind and know how much he himself feared. "I've called Lacey."

"I've called Lacey," a voice mocked. "And lucky for you she didn't have something better to do."

Philip's face brightened when he saw Lacey's purple mist.

"What kind of mess have you two gotten yourselves into?" she asked.

Tristan ignored the question. "I've got to leave. You'll be all right now, Philip," he said, slipping outside of him.

"Not so fast." Lacey spoke silently to Tristan so Philip couldn't hear. "What's going on?"

"I'm not sure. I think it's a trap. I have to find Will," he replied quickly, moving toward the shack walls. "Ivy needs help."

"So when hasn't she?" Lacey called to him, but Tristan was already on his way.

48

Ivy drove toward the double bridges, gripping the steering wheel, leaning forward, straining to see. She flicked on her lights, but the mist absorbed them like pale ghosts. The rain and early fallen leaves made the pavement slick, and at a curve in the road the tires suddenly lost their grip on the road. Skidding sideways, her car slid all the way over to the oncoming lane. Without blinking an eye, she pulled it back in line.

The river, woods, and road went for miles and miles. If Philip and Gregory weren't at the bridges, it would be difficult to search for them alone. Ivy wanted to call Tristan back, but he wouldn't come, he just didn't understand. The weather was getting worse, and there was no time to get the police.

Tristan was right, of course. She didn't have a weapon, unless she could count the rusty nail that rattled around in her cup holder. But she did have a threat: she had left the information with the police. And if Gregory hurt Philip, he'd have a lot more explaining to do.

Ivy suddenly jammed on the brakes and wrenched the steering wheel around, almost missing the turn into the clearing. Her headlights made an arc of light against the trees. Her heart started thumping in her chest. Straight ahead was Gregory's car. They couldn't have gotten far on foot, she told herself.

Ivy parked her car facing the road and left the front door gaping open, but this time for a reason. If she and Philip were chased back, she'd push him in the open door, get in behind him, and lock Gregory out. Now she hurriedly searched the ground for a rock. Finding one, she bent down by the rear tire of Gregory's car and used the rock to drive her rusty nail into the rubber.

Ivy ran through the trees, scrambling up on the railroad track. On either side of her the tunnel of trees closed in, heavy and dripping. She raced along the rails, and suddenly the green tunnel opened out and the parallel bridges hung before her as if suspended in midair.

The fog rising from the river hid their long-legged supports, and only the sound of rushing water proved the river ran fast beneath them. Sections of the bridges continually disappeared and reappeared as wisps of clouds caught on their skeletons like filmy scarves, then floated past. In the rain and mist, it was impossible to see where the old bridge abruptly broke off.

The weather was making it easy for Gregory, Ivy thought. All he'd have to do is lure Philip onto the track with him, then give him an unexpected push. In Gregory's twisted mind, what was one more "accident"?

Ivy focused on the old track, where Gregory was supposed to have collected spikes for Philip. She squinted until her eyes stung, then glanced over at the new bridge. The shifting fog swirled up, and she saw a flash of red. Just as quickly, the clouds covered it again. Then the red waved at her once more from the new bridge – the bright red of Philip's jacket.

"Philip!" she screamed. "Philip!"

She started running down the track of the new bridge. "Stay where you are," she called to him, afraid that if he ran to her he'd trip and fall. But as she got closer she realized it was just his jacket lying on the track. Ivy's heart sank, but she kept going, fearing the worst yet needing to find any clue she could about her brother.

The jacket was soaked by the rain, but there were no rips and only a splatter of mud on the cuffs – no sign of a struggle. For a moment she was hopeful. Of course, there didn't have to be a struggle, Ivy thought. Philip could have been conned into taking off his jacket as part of a game, then quickly pushed. She picked up the jacket and held it in her arms close to her, as she had held Ella.

"Find something?"

She whirled around, nearly losing her balance.

"Hello, Ivy," Gregory said. In the mist he looked like a gray shadow, a dark angel perched on the bridge ten feet away from her. "Hunting for spikes?"

"I'm hunting for my brother."

"Not here," he said.

"What have you done with him?" Ivy demanded.

He grinned and took several steps toward her. Ivy took several steps back, still clutching the jacket.

"Chick, chick, chick," Gregory chanted softly. "Who wants to play chick, chick, chick?"

Ivy glanced toward the far bank, expecting to see a train loom up, as in Philip's nightmare, eager to swallow her.

She turned back to Gregory. "What have you done with him?" she asked again, keeping her voice low, struggling to keep down the hysterical fear that was rising within her.

Gregory laughed softly. "Chick, chick, chick," he said, then took a few steps backward.

Ivy moved with him, her anger overcoming her

fear. "You killed Eric, didn't you?" she said. "You were afraid of what he'd tell me. It wasn't an accidental overdose."

Gregory stepped back again. She matched him step for step.

"You killed your best friend," she said. "And the girl in Ridgefield – after you attacked me at home, you killed her as a cover-up. And Caroline. That's how it all started. You murdered your own mother."

Step for step she moved with him, wondering what kind of game he was playing. Was a train coming? Was that what she heard in the distance?

Gregory suddenly reversed his direction, moving toward her. Ivy backed up. They were two dancers on a tightrope.

"Tristan too," Ivy shouted at him. "You killed Tristan!"

"And all because of you," he said. His voice was as soft and eerie as the twisting shapes of fog. "You were supposed to die, not Tristan. You were supposed to die, not the girl in Ridgefield—"

A train whistle sounded, and Ivy spun around.

Gregory exploded with laughter. "Better say your prayers, Ivy. I've heard tales about Tristan becoming an angel, but no one has seen a shimmering Eric. I hope you've been a good girl."

The train whistle sounded again, higher in pitch, closer. Ivy wondered if she could make it to the other bank in time. She could hear the train itself, rumbling through the trees now, close, already too close to the river.

Gregory was walking steadily backward, and Ivy guessed his plan. He'd keep her on the bridge between him and the train. The girl thought to be crazy enough to throw herself in front of a train once would seem to have tried it again.

As Gregory moved backward Ivy stayed with him. "You've got things wrong," she said. "It was all because of *you*, Gregory. You were terrified of being found out. You were terrified of being left out. Your true father could never give you the kind of money Andrew has."

Gregory's mouth opened a little, and he stared at her. She'd taken him by surprise. They weren't far from the bank now, and he stepped back uncertainly. Ivy inched toward him. If he stumbled, she'd have a chance.

"You didn't think I knew the whole story, did you, Gregory? The funny thing is, the day you killed your mother I never saw you. I never saw past the reflections on the glass. If you'd left me alone, I would never have guessed it was you."

She saw his face darken. He clenched his fists.

"Go ahead," Ivy challenged him. "Come get me. Push me off the tracks, but it's one more murder on your head."

She glanced down. Ten feet more – ten feet more and she'd have a chance, even if she fell.

"Caroline gave Eric a key," Ivy continued, "and Eric left it to me. I found some papers in Andrew's clock."

Nine feet more.

"Some pretty interesting letters from your mother," she told him.

Eight feet.

"And a medical report as well."

Seven.

"I turned them in to the police an hour ago," Ivy said.

Six feet. Gregory stopped. He stood absolutely still. So did Ivy. Then, without warning, he lunged for her.

Tristan arrived at Will's just as a dark car pulled away from the house. With his sharpened vision, he saw the man inside: he wondered why the detective who had investigated Ivy's assault was visiting Will.

Will stood alone on his front porch, so deep in thought that Tristan couldn't find an easy way to slip in. He saw a pencil in Will's pocket and pulled it out, but Will didn't notice. Tristan tapped the pencil against a wooden post and wrote his own name with materialized fingertips, underlining it twice, amazing himself with the new strength he felt in his hands.

"Tristan!" Will said, and Tristan slipped inside. He didn't waste any time. "Ivy needs help. She's gone to the bridges, thinks Gregory took Philip there. It's a trap."

"Have to get my keys," Will replied mentally, and hurried inside.

"No!"

Will stopped and looked around, confused.

"Just run. Run!" Tristan urged.

"All the way to the bridges?" Will argued. "We'll never get there in time."

"I'll get you there," Tristan said. "We can do it faster off the road, out of the traffic." He knew how crazy it sounded, just as he knew somehow it was true. The last darkness had given him more strength than he had ever had, powers that he hadn't yet tested.

"Trust me," Tristan said. "For Ivy's sake, trust me," he pleaded, though he had never completely trusted Will.

Will took off, and they moved together as one. Tristan could feel Will's bewilderment and fear. What was happening to Ivy? What was happening to his own body, taken over by Tristan? What did people see?

"I don't think they see us at all," Tristan said. "But I don't know much more than you."

They were on the winding road now. As they traveled strange voices rose up all around them. Were the voices inside his own head? Tristan wondered. Or was it Will's mind rebelling? Maybe they were human voices pressed together the way space seemed to be compressed as they raced across the landscape.

The voices murmured at first and seemed indistinct, but now they grew louder and clearer – noisy jabbering and clear singing, dark voices threatening and high voices arching over all the others.

"What is it?" Will cried, covering his ears with his hands. "What am I hearing?"

"I don't know."

"What is it? I can't stand it!" Will said, shaking his head as if he could shake the voices out of him.

Tristan was experiencing more than the voices. He was seeing things he had never seen before – scared animals hiding behind trees; jagged rocks, though they were covered completely by leaves; roots buried deep in the ground.

They were at the clearing now, and he saw the tracks behind the wet screen of trees. As they rushed toward the bridges the high voices grew higher and more intense, the low grew deep and furious.

"Demons," Will said, trembling, as they came upon the bridges. "It's demons we hear."

As soon as Gregory lunged for her, Ivy turned and ran. There was no way around him on the narrow bridge. As she started running she saw the headlight of the train, like a small sun brightening the fog, rushing through the trees close to the bridge. She couldn't make it to the other side in time – she couldn't beat out the train. But there was no turning back. She had Philip's bright red jacket. If she waved it, the engineer might see her.

Gregory was gaining on her. The whistle sounded again, and Gregory laughed. He was only a few feet behind her, laughing and laughing, as if they were playing tag in the park. He was insane! He didn't care; he'd die with her as long as he could kill her. With each stride he moved closer – she could see him out of the corner of her eye. In desperation, Ivy threw Philip's jacket on the track behind her. It blew and tangled around Gregory's legs. Gregory stumbled. She glanced back and saw him go down on his knees.

Ivy kept going. She could hear the long rumble of the train and ran as hard as she could toward it. If she put enough distance between herself and Gregory, she could try to find a place to cling to, some fingerhold beneath the track to dangle from.

"Angels, help me!" she prayed. "Oh, angels, are you there for me? Tristan! Where are you?"

"Here, Ivy! Ivy, here!"

There were voices all around her, calling her name. She slowed down. Were they just echoes in her head, the sound of the wind being twisted by her frightened mind? Then she saw that Gregory had stopped, too, listening for a moment, his face shining with sweat, his eyes wide, their gray centers ringed with white.

Then Ivy heard one voice clearly. "Ivy."

She recognized it. "Will!" she exclaimed.

He was running along the opposite track, calling to her. The other voices rose behind it, and a dark fear rushed over her. It's some trick, thought Ivy. It's all part of Gregory's plan.

Gregory started after her again, and Ivy rushed on.

Will was running with incredible speed along the parallel bridge. He had caught up to her and was three steps ahead of her when he reached the end of the old bridge.

"Ivy!" he yelled. "Ivy, over here! Leap!"

She stared at him across the seven-foot gap. All around her voices called and chattered, the high voices ringing in her ears and making her head feel light, the low voices drawing her down in despair.

"Leap!" he shouted, stretching his hands out toward her.

Even if he caught her, there was nothing to keep him from tumbling over the side with her. She'd kill them both.

"Ivy, leap!" It sounded like Tristan's voice.

"Ivy, leap. Ivy, leap," Gregory taunted. He had stopped running. He was walking backward on the track now, watching her, watching the clearing where the train would appear any second, his face flushed and a trickle of blood coming out of his nose. His eyes shone – brilliant, triumphant, insane.

"Tristan!" Ivy called out.

"He's here," Will said. "He'll help us."

But she didn't feel Tristan within her and she didn't see him glowing inside Will.

"Where?" she cried out. "Where?"

"Where, where?" the deep voices mocked. The train thundered onto the bridge.

"Tristan, where are you?" Ivy screamed.

"Reach for her, Will. *Reach for her!*"

Will reached out, and Ivy leaped. For a moment a golden arc shimmered between the two bridges, holding up Ivy and Will. Then they fell onto the old track, clinging desperately to the edge so they wouldn't roll off.

The train rushed along the new bridge, and Gregory started running for the opposite bank. Ivy and Will pulled themselves up and screamed at the train till their throats burned. Their voices were drowned out by a growing wave of dark jabbering, an ominous rumbling of voices so deep they seemed to come from beneath everything that lived.

Ivy and Will watched helplessly as the train bore down on Gregory. He'd never make it. He'd have to try to leap to the old bridge. The voices began to shriek. Ivy held her hands over her ears, and Will gripped her tightly. He tried to turn her head away, but she kept looking.

Gregory leaped, reaching up, his arms flung forward, his fingers reaching out. For a moment he stretched like an angel, then he plunged into the mist below.

The train rushed past him, never slowing. Ivy pressed her face against Will. They held on to each other, barely breathing. The tumult of voices murmured and ceased.

"Chick, chick, chick," one sad voice sang out. "Who's a chick, chick, chick?"

Then all was silent.

49

"One box of tissues," Suzanne said Saturday night. "Help yourself, girls. One large pan of brownies."

"Why are you putting the tissues by us and the brownies by you?" Ivy asked. She, Suzanne, and Beth were sprawled on the floor in the middle of her bedroom.

Beth quickly pulled the brownies closer to her sleeping bag. "Don't worry," she said to Ivy, "I've got the knife."

"Suzanne will use her fingernails," Ivy replied. "Keep the pan between us."

"Now, just a minute," Suzanne said, pursing her lips. They were paler than their usual flame red. "For the last four days I have been thoughtful, caring, polite—"

"And it's really getting to me," Ivy said. "I miss

the old Suzanne . . . I've missed her for more than the last four days," she added softly.

Suzanne's pouty face changed, and Ivy quickly reached out to touch her friend's hand.

"Uh-oh, tissue time," Beth said.

Each of them reached for one.

"I've cried off more mascara in the last four days," Suzanne complained.

"Let's hit the brownies," Ivy suggested, snatching the knife from Beth and cutting three large ones.

Beth trailed a finger along the inside of the pan, picking up big crumbs as well as her brownie, then grinned at Suzanne. "It's been ages since I've been to a sleepover."

"Me too," Ivy said.

"How long has it been since you've had a good night's sleep?" Suzanne asked Ivy, her eyes still watery.

Ivy moved closer to her friend and put her arm around her. "I told you, I slept all the way through last night."

The other nights had been more difficult for Ivy, but she hadn't had any nightmares. At odd times during the night she would awaken and glance around the room, as if her body, having been on alert for so long, was still conditioned to check that all was well. But the fear she had lived with day and night was gone now, and with it the dreams.

The police had arrived at the bridges almost immediately on Tuesday, Lieutenant Donnelly responding to Ivy's note and to an emergency call for help by Andrew. They found Gregory on the rocks in the river below and pronounced him dead at the scene. A little while later, Philip was released from the shack.

"How's Philip doing?" Beth asked.

"He looks okay," Suzanne observed.

"Philip sees the world the way a nine-year-old does," Ivy told them. "If he can explain things with a story, he's all right. He's made Gregory into a bad angel, and he believes good angels will always protect him from the bad, so he's okay – for now."

But Ivy knew that sooner or later her brother would be asking a lot of hard questions about how someone could act nice to him and still want to hurt him. He'd ask again for all the details.

By the time Ivy and Andrew left the police station Tuesday night, the facts of the case had been sketched out. The lieutenant said the police would inform the family of the girl in Ridgefield, as well as Eric's and Tristan's parents, regarding the further investigation of the case.

Later that evening the Reverend Mr. Carruthers, Tristan's father, came to the house. He stayed with Ivy and her family for several hours, and remained close by until the memorial service three days later, which he presided over. Now that it was over, both

Andrew and Maggie looked fragile and worn, Ivy thought – haunted.

"Of course they do," Beth said, as if she had read Ivy's mind. "They've seen a side of Gregory that they never knew about, and it's horrifying. They're just starting to understand what you've been through. It's going to take them a long time."

"It's going to take us all a long time," Suzanne said, blinking back tears. Then she reached for the kitchen knife. "Do you think there are enough tissues and brownies?"

There's something different about her tonight, Tristan thought as he stared down at Lacey on Saturday evening. He found her where he had first met her, lounging on his grave, one knee up, the other leg stretched straight out in front of her. Her spiked purple hair caught the moonlight, and her skin looked as pale as the marble she leaned against. Her long nails gleamed dark purple. But there was something different about her.

In Lacey's face Tristan saw a wistfulness that made him hesitate before speaking to her, some touch of sadness that was new to her or that she usually kept well hidden.

"Lacey."

She looked up at Tristan and blinked twice.

"What's up?" he said, sitting down next to her.

She stared at him and said nothing.

"What were you just thinking about?" he asked gently.

Lacey quickly looked down at her hands, touching fingertip to fingertip, frowning. When she glanced up again, she looked as if she were staring straight through him.

He felt uneasy. "Is something on your mind?"

"Have you been to Gregory's plot?" she asked.

"I just came from—"

"*Puh-lease* don't tell me he's winging around here," she interrupted, waving her hands dramatically. "I mean, I know Number One Director chooses the least likely, but that's pushing it just a *little* too far."

Tristan laughed, glad she was acting like herself again. "I haven't seen a sign of Gregory," he said. "Everything's quiet by his grave and up on the ridge, too."

She dropped her hands. "You've been with Ivy."

"I've been there, but I can't reach her," he said. "Neither she nor Philip sees me, and I can't get inside either of their minds. I need your help, Lacey. I guess you're tired of hearing that, but I need you now more than ever."

She held up her hand, silencing him. "There's something I should tell you, Tristan."

"What?" he asked.

"I can't see you, either."

"What!"

"All I can see is a gold shimmer," Lacey explained, rising to her feet, "the same thing everyone else has been seeing when they look at you." She sighed. "Which means either I'm a living person again . . . *brrrt!* She made her obnoxious TV game show buzzer sound, only it was a halfhearted effort. "Or you're something angelic far beyond me."

"But I don't want to be!" he protested. "All I want to do is tell Ivy—"

"I love you," Lacey said quickly. "I love you."

Tristan nodded. "Exactly. And that I love her so much I want her to find the love she was meant for."

Lacey turned away from Tristan.

"What can I do?" he asked.

"I dunno," she mumbled.

He reached for her to stop her from pacing, but his hand went right through her arm.

Lacey touched her arm where he had tried to grasp it. "You're way beyond me now," she said. "I can't even guess what's happening to you. Do you have any of your old powers?"

"When I came out of the darkness the last time, I had more powers than ever," Tristan replied. "I could project my voice like you. I could write by myself. I was strong enough to hold up Ivy and Will. Now I don't have the strength to do even simple things. How can I reach her?"

"Pray. Ask for another chance," Lacey said, "though reaching her one last time may take everything you have left."

"Is that how it's supposed to end?" Tristan asked.

"I don't know any more than you do!" Lacey snapped. "And you know how I hate to admit that," she added in a softer voice. "All you can do is pray and try. If – if you don't get through, I'll let her know you wanted to. I'll deliver your message. And I'll check on her now and then – you know, give her some angelic advice."

When Tristan didn't say anything, Lacey said, "All right, so you don't want me giving your chick advice. I won't!"

"Please check on her," he said, "and give her all the advice you want. I trust you."

"You trust me – even if I advise her on love?" Lacey said, testing him.

"Even on love," he said, smiling.

"Not that I know anything about . . . love," she said.

Tristan eyed her curiously. Then he stood up to get a closer look.

"What?" Lacey said. "What?" She backed away from his probing light.

"That's it, isn't it?" he said with quiet wonder. "That's what you were thinking about when I found you. You've fallen in love! Don't deny it.

Angels shouldn't lie to each other, and neither should friends. You're in love, Lacey."

"Better dead than never, huh?" she replied. "And now you've got your wish, so you can go on."

"Who is it?" Tristan asked curiously.

She didn't answer him.

"Who is it?" he persisted. "Tell me. Maybe I can help. I know you're hurting, Lacey. I can see it. Let me help."

"Oh, *my!* Lacey walked a circle around the grave. "Look who's orbiting in the upper realm now."

He ignored the remark. "Who is it? Does he know you're here for him?"

She laughed, then dropped her chin and silently shook her head.

"Look at me," he said gently. "I can't see your face."

"Then we're even," she said quietly.

"I wish I could touch you again," Tristan told her. "I wish I could put my arms around you. I don't want to leave you hurting like this."

Lacey grimaced. "That's about the only way you can leave me," she replied softly, then looked at him with a full and steady gaze, her dark eyes shimmering with his own golden light. "Unless . . .," she said, "unless *I* leave you first. Good idea, Lacey. No sighing, no crying," she said resolutely.

Then she turned and started walking down the cemetery road.

"Lacey?" Tristan called after her.

She kept on walking.

"Lacey? Where are you going?" Tristan shouted. "Hey, Lacey, aren't you even going to say good-bye?"

Without turning around, she raised her hand and wiggled her fingers in a bright purple wave. Then she disappeared behind the trees.

Like the windows of the sleepy town Tristan had passed through on his way back from the cemetery, like the windows of his parents' house that he had looked through one last time, every window in the big house on top of the ridge was dark. Tristan found the three girls asleep on the floor of Ivy's bedroom: Beth with her round, gentle face bathed in moonlight, Suzanne, her mass of black hair flung like shiny ribbons over her pillow, and Ivy in between her friends, safe at last.

What the girls didn't know – or at least had pretended not to notice – was that Philip had crept into Ivy's bedroom and was asleep now in her bed, his head at the lower end where he could listen to their secrets. Tristan touched him with his golden light. Only Ella was missing from the quiet scene, he thought.

He sat for a long time, letting the peace of the room seep into him, reluctant to disturb Ivy's sleep, reluctant to bring the time left between them to an end. But it would end, he knew that, and when the sky began to lighten, he prayed.

"Give me one last time with her," he begged, then he knelt beside Ivy. Focusing on the tip of his finger, he ran it along her cheek.

He felt her soft skin. He could touch her again! He could sense her warmth! Ivy's eyes fluttered open. She looked around the room, wondering. He brushed her hand.

"Tristan?"

She sat up, and he pushed back a tumble of golden hair.

Her lips parted in a smile, and she reached to touch her hair where he had touched it. "Tristan, is it you?"

He matched that thought and slipped inside. "Ivy."

She rose quickly and walked to the window, wrapping her arms around herself. "I thought I'd never hear your voice again," she said silently. "I thought you were gone forever. After that moment on the bridge, I didn't see your light anymore. I can't see it now," she told him, frowning and gazing down at her hand.

"I know. I don't understand what's happening, Ivy. I just know that I'm changing. And that I won't be back."

She nodded, accepting what he said with a calm that surprised him. Then he saw her mouth quiver.

She trembled and looked as if she would cry out loud, but she said nothing.

"I love you, Ivy. I'll never stop loving you."

She leaned against the window, looking out on a pale and glittering night. She looked through tears.

"I prayed for one more chance to reach you," he said, "to tell you how much I love you and to tell you to keep on loving. Someone else was meant for you, Ivy, and you were meant for someone else."

She stood up straight. "No."

"Yes, love," he said, softly but firmly.

"No!"

"Promise me, Ivy—"

"I'll promise you nothing but that I love you," she cried.

"Listen to me," Tristan pleaded. "You know I can't stay any longer."

The pale, glittering night was raining now, and fresh tears gleamed on her cheeks, but he had to leave.

"I love you," he said. "I love you. Love him."

Then Tristan slipped out and saw her standing at the window in the early-morning light. He stepped back and watched her as she knelt down and rested her arms and face on the sill. He stepped back again and saw her tears dry and her eyes close. When he stepped back a third time, Tristan thought the sun had risen behind him, shattering the pale night into a thousand silver fragments.

He turned suddenly to the east, but the brilliant circle of light was not the sun. There was no knowing what it was, except that it was a light meant for him, and Tristan walked swiftly toward it.

50

Ivy awoke with the sun in her eyes. Before she remembered Tristan's visit, and before Beth said drowsily, "I had a dream last night that Tristan came," Ivy knew that he was gone. It wasn't a feeling she could explain, just a clear sense that he was no longer with her and wouldn't be back. The struggle to hold on to what they had, the longing to reach back in time for Tristan, and the dream of living in another world with him had ceased within her. She felt a new kind of peace.

Maggie, Andrew, and Philip were up and out of the house early that Sunday. The girls had a leisurely brunch, then Suzanne and Beth gathered their belongings and carried them out to Beth's car. Suzanne waited till then to ask the question Ivy had expected several times the previous night.

"I've been good," Suzanne began. "All last night

and this morning I haven't said one thing I shouldn't have."

"You ate two brownies you shouldn't have," Ivy reminded her. She watched with amusement as Beth caught Suzanne's eye and made quick cutting signs across her throat. But Suzanne would not be silenced.

"Beth told me that if I brought this up, she'd stuff a purseful of paper in my mouth."

Beth threw her hands up in the air.

"But I've got to ask. What's going on with you and Will? I mean, he saved your life. Am I right?"

"Will saved my life," Ivy agreed.

"Then what—"

"I told Suzanne that you just needed some time to sort things out," Beth intervened.

Ivy nodded.

"But he's totally hooked on you!" Suzanne said, exasperated. "He's head over heels in love – he has been for months."

Ivy didn't say anything.

"I hate it when she gets that stubborn look on her face," Suzanne complained to Beth. "She looks just like her brother."

Ivy laughed then – she guessed she and Philip did share a mulish streak – but she refused to say anything more about Will.

After her friends left, Ivy walked toward Philip's tree house, pausing on the way at the patch of golden chrysanthemums where Ella was buried. She brushed the flowers with her fingers, then moved on. Beth was right, there was a lot to sort out. Tuesday night she had told the police everything she knew about the case against Gregory – everything but Will's attempt at blackmail. Against her better judgment, Ivy had kept quiet about the note she had found in Gregory's room.

Tuesday night she had succeeded in convincing herself that the police already knew about Will. She had reasoned that they traced the blackmail money when Will deposited it. That's why Donnelly went to Will's house, she told herself now as she climbed the rope ladder of the tree house. But Ivy knew that in the end she had to tell the police about the note. The danger of keeping big secrets had been made all too clear by Caroline's life and death.

She reached the top of the ladder and walked the narrow bridge to the other tree. Brushing aside some leaves, she sat down on the wooden floor. Far to the north, she could see a small strip of the river, a peaceful snippet of blue ribbon. Lying back, she stared up at the tiny patches of sky – not much more than blue stars now – but soon, with the falling leaves, it would be the only roof the tree house would have. That's all right, she thought. The sky was the angels' roof, too.

Angels, take care of Will, she prayed. It was the best she could do for him now. She couldn't trust him. And she could never love someone who had betrayed her as he had. Still, her heart went out to him. Angels, help him, please.

"Hey, is there a doorbell to this house?"

Ivy jumped at the sound of Will's voice, then quickly rolled over on her stomach to look down at him through the slits between the boards. "No."

He was silent for a moment. "Is there a knocker?"

"No." Her mind raced – or was it her heart? She wished she could think of a clever line to turn him away. She wished he didn't make her ache inside.

"Maybe there are some magic words?" he said.

Ivy didn't reply. Will backed up in the grass, trying to see into the tree house. She lifted her head and looked down over the edge at him.

"If there are magic words, Ivy, I sure wish you'd tell me what they are, because I've been wondering for a long time, and I'm just about ready to give up."

Ivy bit her lip.

"You know," Will continued, "when two people narrowly escape falling to their deaths, they usually have something to talk about. Even if they hadn't met before that moment, they usually have some-thing to say to each other afterward. But you haven't said anything to me. I've been trying to give you some time. I've been trying to give you some space. All I want is—"

"Thank you," Ivy said. "Thank you for risking your life. Thank you for saving me."

"That's not what I wanted!" Will replied angrily. "Gratitude is the last thing I—"

"Well, let me tell you what *I* want," Ivy shouted down at him. "Honesty."

Will looked up with a bewildered expression. "When haven't I been honest?" he asked. It was as if he had totally forgotten about the blackmail. "When?"

"I found your note, Will. I know you black-mailed Gregory. I didn't tell the police yet, but I will."

He frowned. "So tell them," he said, his voice rising with frustration. "Go ahead! It's old news to them, but if you've got the note, it's one more piece for the police files. I just don't get—" He started walking away from the tree house, then stopped. "Wait a minute. Do you think— You couldn't really think I did that to make money, could you?"

"That's usually why people blackmail."

"You think I'd betray you like that?" he asked incredulously. "Ivy, I set up that blackmail – I got the Celentanos to help me out, and I recorded it – so that I had something to take to the police."

Ivy sat up and moved closer to the edge of the platform.

"Back in August," Will said, "when you were in the hospital, Gregory called and told me you had tried to commit suicide. I couldn't believe it. I knew how much you missed Tristan, but I knew you were a fighter, too. I went to the train station that morning to look around and try to figure out what had gone through your head. As I was leaving I found the jacket and hat. I picked them up, but for weeks I didn't know how or even if they were connected to what had happened."

Will paced around, bending over and picking up small sticks, breaking them in his hands.

"When school started," he said, "I ran across some file photos of Tristan in the newspaper office. Suddenly I figured it out. I knew it wasn't like you to jump in front of a train, but it was just like Eric and Gregory to con you across the track. I remembered how Eric had played chicken with us, and I blamed him at first. Later I realized that there was a lot more than a game going on."

"Why didn't you tell me this before?" Ivy asked. "You should have told me this before."

"You weren't telling me things, either," he reminded her.

"I was trying to protect you," she explained.

"What the heck do you think I was doing?" He threw down the sticks. "I figured that Eric died because he was going to spill the beans. I didn't know why Gregory wanted to kill you, but I figured if he'd murder his best friend, he'd go after you no matter what the risk. I had to distract him, give him another target, and try to get something on him at the same time. It almost worked. I gave the tape to Lieutenant Donnelly on Tuesday afternoon, but Gregory had already laid his trap."

He paused, and Ivy moved to the very edge of the platform, dropping her legs over the side, hanging on tightly to the rope that dangled next to her.

"You thought I'd betray you," Will said, his voice sounding hollow and incredulous.

"Will, I'm sorry." She knew from his tone that she had hurt him deeply. "I was wrong. I really am sorry," she said, but he was walking away from her.

"I made a mistake. A big one," she called after him. "Try to understand. I was so mixed up and afraid. I thought I had betrayed myself when I trusted you — and betrayed Tristan when I fell in love with you. Will!"

Grasping the rope, she dropped over the side, then swung free of the tree house. But Will had turned back a moment before. She landed on top of him, and they rolled together to the ground.

They lay there for a moment in a heap, Ivy on top of Will, neither of them moving.

"Nice catch," Ivy said. She was trying to laugh, but all she could do was tremble. She was so afraid he'd get up, dust himself off, and walk away. Why shouldn't he?

"You fell in love with me?" Will asked.

She looked into his deep brown eyes, eyes that

shimmered with hidden light, then she saw a smile spreading across his face. His arms encircled her, and she relaxed against him, her face close to his. "Love you, Will," she said softly.

"Love you, Ivy." He held her close and rocked her a little. "You know," he said, "it's a good thing this didn't happen before. If I had known how heavy you were, I would never have reached for you."

"What?"

"Without an angel around, I'd have been a goner," he said.

Ivy pulled herself up abruptly.

Will laughed. "Okay, okay, that was a lie. But this is the truth. The angels will swear to it," he said, then pulled her down for a kiss.